MYSTERY
WITH A
SPLASH OF
BOURBON

MYSTERY AND HORROR, LLC
CLEARWATER, FL

MYSTERY WITH A SPLASH OF BOURBON
COPYRIGHT© 2020
MYSTERY AND HORROR, LLC
CLEARWATER, FL
EDITED BY
Susan Bell
Elaine Munsch
Sarah E Glenn

ISBN: 978-1-949281-12-5

Acknowledgements

It might take a village to raise a child, but it takes even more people to compile and polish an anthology.

We raise a glass to salute those who offered their time and energy to a project they barely heard of a year ago. So, thanks to Beth Henderson, Carol Preflatish, Natalie Reichenbach, Lynn Slaughter and Pam Turner.

And, of course, the authors who contributed to this enterprise deserve at least one glass, if not a whole bottle: Deborah Alvord, Edmund August, Susan Bell, Barbara Blackburn, Karen Quinn Block, Mike Bradford, Virginia 'Din' Dulworth, Mary Gaskins, Sarah E. Glenn, Debi Huff, Shirley Jump, Sandra Cerow Leonard, Gwen Mayo, Elaine Munsch, Lorena Peter, Debby Schenk, Tamera Shaw, Sheila Shumate, Milton Toby, Jo Tucker, and Heidi Walker.

Finally, a special toast to Sandra Cerow Leonard for her leadership in corralling this project from its inception, and to Susan Bell and Elaine Munsch for pushing it over the finish line.

TABLE OF CONTENTS

WHAT IS BOURBON?
BY SANDRA CEROW LEONARD

Bourbon smells like Grandma's kitchen when sweet buttery sauce smothers warm bread pudding. The clear amber color reflects sunlight on a golden summer day. Its rich silky smoothness slides down your throat with no final sting. If you were raised in Kentucky, your Great Grandpappy or PawPaw operated his own still out under the barn or back in the woods.

Almost 200 years ago, bourbon was an American creation and fans developed throughout the world as it evolved and was refined. In time, aggressive overseas distilleries started to label their various spirits "Bourbon" and some even had the audacity to market them in Kentucky. A resolution was introduced in the United States Senate by Thurston Morton and in the House by John C. Watts. Each represented the state of Kentucky in Congress.

The declaration said bourbon whiskey was a distinctive product of the United States and directed federal agencies to prohibit importing whiskey labeled "Bourbon" unless the label clearly showed the country of origin as an integral part of the name.

Two nice old ladies, the Dowling sisters of New York, each owned distilleries in Mexico and exported their bourbon to the United States. Their tactics helped hold up passage of the resolution for a year. It finally passed May 4, 1964.

The Federal Standards of Identity for Bourbon were promulgated to legally define bourbon. Title 27, Part 5, Subpart 5.22 of the Federal Regulations contains the following requirements for a whiskey to be branded "Bourbon". It must be:

- Not less than 51 percent corn with lesser amounts of other grains, usually malted barley, wheat and rye. Most Bourbons contain 60 to 80 percent corn.
- Produced from a fermented mash not exceeding 160 proof.

- Aged in new, white oak containers at not more than 125 proof that are charred inside to produce a caramelized layer of wood. As the Bourbon ages, the char creates the characteristic amber color and mellows the flavor, often adding vanilla notes.
- Bottled at 80 proof or more like all whiskey which is 40% alcohol by volume.
- To be labeled *straight* bourbon whiskey, it must be aged at least two years. Most bourbons sold by Kentucky distilleries are aged four to eight years. Premium bourbons may be aged many more years.

And, no, the spirit does not have to be made in the Bluegrass State to be labeled *Bourbon*. But Kentuckians know that the 75 to 95 percent of the world's bourbon production made in their state is definitely the finest. The combination of minerals in the unique limestone spring water found in Kentucky makes the smoothest bourbon.

Sip the amber liquid from a crystal glass with a just an ice cube or two. Mix it with mint and sugar to toast the Kentucky Derby. Add it to cake or candy for an extra kick in the flavor buds. Bourbon is the versatile beverage enjoyed by many today, and many long ago.

THE PROOF IS IN THE KILLING
BY MILTON C. TOBY JD

Winston Craig's dream lasted two decades.
His nightmare came in a single night.

Craig pushes open the heavy, wooden door of Warehouse No. 1, taking in the intoxicating aroma of bourbon and smiling as he watches a steady procession of automobiles turn into the distillery's parking lot. *Good turnout*, he thinks, but that isn't a surprise. The evening's festivities have been anticipated for months and the guest list includes everyone on the small community's "A" list, along with a good number of out-of-towners.

The occasion is a birth of sorts: "Kentucky's Finest Single Barrel Bourbon", aged a full 17 years, will be unveiled at a formal sampling staged in a pristine white tent erected adjacent to the warehouse. "Tonight is the culmination of a dream, *my* dream," Craig rehearses as he reads from a sheet of paper. "But it's more than that. It's a dream that traces back several generations of my family, back to Elijah Craig, a true visionary who brought bourbon to Kentucky."

It's also a scam, Craig thinks, his mind wandering off script. He conveniently shares a surname with a famous Kentucky family, but nothing else. The Craigs—*his* Craigs—might have rubbed shoulders with Elijah Craig or one of his relatives back in the day, but if that occurred, and that was a very big "if," it was happenstance and nothing else. The blood relationship that Winston Craig sought for so long simply didn't exist. High-priced genealogists had established that fact with absolute certainty.

Hardly anyone knows about the fraud, of course, and Craig intends to keep things that way if he can. When a relationship with the "real" Craigs, the bourbon-tinged ones, comes up in conversation, Winston makes no effort to correct the misunderstanding.

Craig looks up from his notes as a distant bolt of lightning arcs across the sky. *Beautiful*, he thinks, *but dangerous*. A lightning strike destroyed a nearby bourbon warehouse a few years earlier, and Craig knows that a fire fueled by thousands of barrels of highly flammable bourbon is an inferno impossible to control.

He counts the seconds between the lightning and the subsequent rumble of thunder and does the math: nine seconds, not quite two miles away. *Time to get the show on the road.* He crumples the sheet of paper with his notes, straightens his tie, and strides out to greet his guests before the rain starts.

A dusty oak barrel waits for him. Full at the start of the aging process, the barrel now is less than three-quarters full after years of evaporation. The "angel's share" of the bourbon, they call it. A distillery worker tacks a brass plate engraved with the day's date onto one end of the barrel, works the bung free, and then steps aside. It's Craig's show now. With a flourish worthy of a master magician, he inserts a glass siphon into the barrel, draws off a sample of the amber liquid, and decants the whiskey into a half-dozen heavy crystal glasses.

Craig lifts one of the glasses to his nose, swirls the liquid, inhales deeply, and smiles. He then holds the glass up to a bare light bulb and nods with satisfaction at the rich amber color. Finally, with a quick glance out at his friends, investors, and even a competitor or two, Craig takes a sip. He pauses a couple of beats for dramatic effect, an affectation that in another life always gets a jury's attention, and then gives a dramatic thumbs up to cheers and applause.

Life is good, he thinks, *couldn't be better.*

The dream is alive and well.

A waiter wanders among the crowd, looking for Craig. He finds the distillery owner and hands over a letter, the tan envelope spotted with rain.

"This was just delivered," the waiter says. Craig takes the envelope and turns back to his friends, looks of puzzlement and amusement on his face.

"A letter," he says to no one in particular. "Who writes letters anymore?"

It must be another note of congratulations, one of many Craig thinks, and he stuffs the envelope into a pocket without looking at the contents. Such messages might have come by telegram in the past, but no longer. Anachronisms in an era ruled by the Internet, email, and cell phones, telegrams had gone extinct when Western Union terminated the service earlier in the year. Craig missed them, and the urgency implied by the flimsy yellow sheets.

Two hours later the guests have left, the caterers have finished their work, and Craig sits alone in the tent. An empty glass dangles from his hand. Rain pelts the canvas. He remembers the letter, pulls it from his pocket, and for the first time examines the envelope. It's addressed simply to "Winston Craig," with no address. Curious. He tears open the sealed flap. Inside, Craig finds two sheets of lined paper, apparently torn from a notebook and folded into thirds. The handwritten lines, done in an elegant script, seem at odds with the cheap paper.

Mr. Craig,

You have been poisoned. Or, if you're lucky, maybe not yet. I apologize that I don't know with certainty your fate, but I cannot be sure which barrel of whiskey you selected for your extravaganza this evening. Let me explain. Some months ago, I injected a particularly nasty poison into several barrels. I won't tell you how many barrels are affected, or which ones, because such certainly would make your decision too easy.

The poison was derived from the skin toxin of golden poison dart frogs. Perhaps you have heard of them. The scientific name of the little creatures is Phyllobates terribilis *if you're so inclined to do some research, but I caution you against dawdling. They live in Western Colombia and indigenous tribes in the area use the toxin on their blowgun darts for hunting. As you might surmise, this is why they are called "poison dart" frogs.*

The poison is a steroid alkaloid called batrachotoxin and it is very, very effective. The symptoms are convulsions, paralysis, and my personal favorite, a gruesome and painful death. One milligram of the poison, not much at all, can kill ten people. I am told that chemical tests for the toxin are unreliable and that there is no truly effective antidote.

How are you feeling, Mr. Craig? A little shaky, perhaps? A better question is this: how will you feel when your customers start falling ill and dying from drinking your whiskey?

I have a list of all the barrels that were poisoned, identified by the serial numbers stamped on the barrels. There is only one copy of the list, and it is for sale. The asking price is a non-negotiable $1,000,000, delivered within six hours of receipt of this letter. Lock the money in the *trunk of your car and leave the car at mile marker 70 on Interstate 64 West. Walk away. I have a key.*

It would not be prudent to notify the authorities. I will know if you are foolish enough to do so. Wait by a telephone. I know the number. I will call you if everything is in order.

Tick Tock, Mr. Craig. Tick Tock.

Craig reads the letter a second time. His hands are shaking. This has got to be a joke, he thinks, but what if it isn't? He looks down at his watch. The waiter had delivered the letter around nine in the evening, a few minutes after the sampling as best he could recall, but Craig had not taken time to read it immediately. Now it was almost midnight, and he's wasted three hours. Just three more hours left. Craig flips open the cover of his cell phone and punches a familiar speed dial button.

"What time is it?" Craig hears the irritation in the sleepy voice coming from the phone.

"It's midnight, Jack, but that's not important," Craig says. "I need a million dollars and I need it now."

"You need what?" the banker says, suddenly alert. Large sums of money have that effect on bankers.

"A million," Craig replies. "In hundreds, with non-sequential serial numbers, I guess. It's an emergency."

"You're joking, right?" Jackson Burns finally says. Craig keeps the phone at his ear but doesn't say anything.

"Okay, you're not joking. Can't it wait until tomorrow?"

"No, it can't wait," Craig says. "I told you, it's an emergency. I've got the money, you know that. I'll meet you at the bank in an hour."

"I know you've got the money, Win. That's not the point. But listen to reason."

"I don't have time for this," Craig interrupts. He takes a few deep breaths, trying without much success to stave off the rising panic. "Just meet me at the bank, and I'll explain everything."

Craig drives directly to the bank and waits, staring at his watch, pacing and fuming, until Burns pulls into an adjacent parking space. It's past midnight, almost exactly a half hour since the two had spoken. Craig steps around the silver Halliburton suitcase he's taken from his trunk and walks to the banker's battleship gray Lexus. He snatches the driver's side door open and pulls the banker roughly from the car. Burns wears an expensive navy suit over a pale-yellow pajama top and running shoes.

"Where the hell have you been?" Craig demands. "There can't be any traffic at this hour." His voice rises to a near shout.

"Calm down," Burns answers as he jerks his arm free from Craig's grip. "I got here as quick as I could. Now tell me what this is all about." Craig rests his right hand on Burns's shoulder and shoves the man toward the bank building.

"When we get inside," he says, hefting the Halliburton case in his left.

Burns unlocks the heavy glass doors and they walk into the bank. Craig places the case on a table, takes the folded pages from his pocket, and hands them to the banker. "This was delivered to me a few hours ago, at the tasting."

Burns reads through the letter, frowns, looks up at Craig, then reads it again, more carefully this time. "You've got to call the police," the banker finally says. "Right now."

"I'm going to call the authorities," Craig says, "but not now. I made some friends in the FBI when I worked in D.C. We keep in touch. They'll help. But before that I'm going to follow these instructions exactly.

"You read what this lunatic said. I've got to know which barrels of whiskey he poisoned. Hell, I've got to know whether *I've* been poisoned. Not that I can do anything about it if I have, apparently."

"How do you even know this is for real?" Burns asks. "Whoever wrote this letter is a Grade A nut, and maybe the whole thing is some kind of sick joke. Have you even thought about that? Not everyone is pleased that you've got the old distillery up and running again, you know."

Burns is right about that, Craig thinks. Trademark litigation over his appropriation of the Elijah Craig name has been moving at glacial speed through the courts for years.

"Besides, look at yourself."

"What are you talking about?" Craig asks.

"You're standing here having a conversation with me," Burns explains. "You're not writhing on the floor in the throes of agony because you've been poisoned with voodoo frog sweat. You're just fine. If this poison is used to kill animals, it must be quick.

7

"Think about it. Hunters aren't going to shoot a poison dart into an animal's butt and then follow it around for hours waiting for it to die.

"You obviously haven't been poisoned, and odds are that none of the whiskey has been poisoned, either. You've got 24/7 security at those warehouses, remember?"

Craig thinks about that for a minute. Physically, he feels fine. Maybe his friend has a point.

"You might be right," Craig says finally, "but I'm not going to take a chance. Read the letter again. He said the poison was a derivative. Maybe it was altered to have a delayed effect. He wouldn't want me to die before I could gather the money.

"Besides, it doesn't matter. I couldn't live with myself if a single person got sick from drinking my whiskey." He snaps the latches on the case, opens it, and motions toward Burns. "Now get my money. I haven't got a lot of time."

It takes 10,000 hundred-dollar bills to make a million dollars. Two hundred paper-wrapped bundles, $5,000 each, pack the Halliburton case almost to capacity. Craig closes the case, hoists it off the table, and starts for the door. Burns falls in step beside him, his running shoes squeaking on the polished marble floor.

"Where are you going?" Craig asks the banker.

"I'm going to follow you," Burns replies. "Somebody's got to take you home after you abandon the car. Jesus, Win, you think you can just call a cab from the Interstate in the middle of the night? Besides, whoever wrote this letter might be waiting for you out there. For all we know, he really wants you as a hostage. If he's as crazy as we think, he might believe someone would hand over a decent ransom to save your hide." Craig hadn't considered that possibility.

"I know better," Burns adds, "but why take the chance?" Craig looks at his friend, who returns the look with a grim smile.

The streets are deserted in the middle of the night and the drive from the bank to the appointed spot on the road to Louisville takes a quarter hour. Craig drives onto the shoulder, and Burns pulls in behind him. They get out of their cars and look around. The thunderstorm has moved on and the clouds are breaking up. Rising in the eastern sky, in tight formation, are Venus and Jupiter.

"Look at that," Craig says, pointing to the celestial display. "It's called a conjunction, supposed to bring good luck." A friend of a friend who claimed to be an astrologer had suggested the date for the tasting because of the conjunction and Craig had gone along with the idea as a joke. *So much for good luck*, he thought.

"Why here?" Burns asks as he scans the highway again.

"Why not?" Craig responds. "There's an exit a mile away, and there are a half-dozen places where whoever this is could watch from without being seen." He angles his wrist to look at the luminous dial on his Rolex, then glances over Burns' shoulder into the darkness. "He's probably watching us right now." Both men involuntarily step closer to each other.

"Let's get out of here," Burns says. "Then we're calling the police."

"No!" Craig says. "Drop me off at the distillery, then you go home. Try and get some sleep. I'll call the FBI, I promise, but not until I've got the list of poisoned barrels in my hand."

"I hope you know what you're doing," the banker says as he slides into the driver's seat of the Lexus.

Craig climbs into the passenger seat. *So do I*, he thinks. *God help me, so do I.*

The distillery warehouses always have been among Craig's favorite places, ever since he swapped one Georgetown in the District of Columbia for another Georgetown in Central Kentucky, and he often visits the cavernous buildings late at night. Some evenings he'd wander by himself for hours, walking among the stacked rows of barrels and anticipating the day when the aging process would finally run its course.

Now, though, Warehouse No.1 is a forbidding place, dark and alien and threatening. Craig steps inside the building, pulls the heavy door closed behind him, and latches it shut. He drops onto a battered wooden chair and looks at his watch: 3:20 in the morning. *It's time*, Craig thinks to himself, *past time*. He takes his cell phone from a pocket and waits for the call.

Craig still remembers the exact day he decided to buy an old distillery. He'd just argued a high-profile money laundering case before the federal court of appeals in Washington, going toe-to-toe against an overworked government lawyer with scuffed shoes and a cheap suit. Like most, it was a case Craig expected to win and did, but during the cab ride back to his Georgetown office he suddenly realized that winning or losing in a courtroom no longer mattered to him. B. B. King got it right, he'd thought at the time, the thrill was definitely gone.

9

Kentucky's Finest, the idea at least, was conceived on that fine spring day. The delivery took a little while longer, almost 20 years. Good years, until tonight.

Money hadn't been an issue for Craig's new venture. One of his first-year law professors told him that the best client to have was a very rich man in very big trouble, and the young attorney took the advice to heart. He learned quickly that spending time with run-of-the-mill criminals, especially the unsuccessful ones, the ones who got arrested and called in the middle of the night looking frantically for a lawyer, were a poor investment of his time and energy.

Drug dealers, who often paid with garbage bags of cash, no questions asked, scared him, so Craig specialized in white collar crime, which brought in a decidedly better class of clients. They frequented the classiest restaurants, drank the best wine, and wrote checks with rows of zeroes that didn't bounce. Craig started winning his cases, a lot of them, and the clients started lining up outside his door, checkbooks in hand.

Exactly one month after the fateful cab ride, on a Saturday in May when 130,000 people pushed through the turnstiles at Churchill Downs to watch Alysheba win the 113th Kentucky Derby, Craig stood alone on a weedy patch of ground 80 miles away, surveying what remained of the old Lebanon Town Distillery. The red brick building housing the massive wooden fermentation vats and the tarnished brass still was standing, but looked as if it had been hit by a bomb. The aging warehouses, their gray, sheet metal walls streaked with green mold, their dark windows heavily barred, looked to Craig like relics from a World War II concentration camp.

It was love at first sight.

The lawyer, who'd spent his entire life on the East Coast, saw neither the neglect nor the ruin. Instead, he envisioned a small, high-end operation, much like his successful boutique law firm, everything first class. It took six months to locate a suitable master distiller and hire him away from a rival whiskey maker and almost two years to get the physical plant up and running to Craig's satisfaction. The first barrels rolled into Warehouse No. 1 on June 17, 1989, where they sat, he'd thought undisturbed, for 17 years.

Dreams or nightmares?

If you think about the question, and Craig had done a lot of thinking over the last six hours, there is at most a very fine line separating the two. In the end, he'd come to realize that the answer usually turns on your point of view, and on timing. Always timing.

The cell phone finally chimes softly at 5:28 a.m. Craig lets it ring three times while he takes a few deep breaths, and then puts it to his ear.

"Yes," he says. His voice is raspy, barely above a whisper.

"Is this Winston Craig?" the voice asks. Who else would it be, for God's sake? Craig thinks, "Yes, that's me. Who's this?"

"This is Officer Roy Simpkins, with the Kentucky State Police," the voice says. "Do you own a new Jaguar convertible, dark green? Tag number . . . let's see . . ." Craig hears pages on a notebook being flipped. "ELIJAH1?"

"That's my car," Craig says. What was this all about?

"When did you see it last?" Simpkins asks.

"A few hours ago," Craig answers. "Why?"

"I'm afraid I've got some bad news for you," the officer says. "There's been an accident, a bad one."

"What kind of accident?" Craig interrupts.

"There's a bad curve on US 62," the officer says. "The pavement was wet. Your car went off the road and hit a tree sometime during the night. There was a fire. The driver . . ." Simkins hesitates, reluctant to be the bearer of bad news. "The driver, I'm sorry, but your driver was killed. He was burned very badly, beyond recognition I'm afraid. And he wasn't carrying any identification, no driver's license, nothing. Can you identify who was driving your car? Was he a friend of yours, an employee, maybe?"

A friend of mine, Craig thinks. He's pacing now, his footsteps echoing through the deserted warehouse.

"Did you find any papers in the car?" Craig asks.

"Papers?" the officer replies. He sounds confused. "Can't that wait until we identify the driver?"

"Papers," Craig insists. "A list of some kind, with numbers?"

"We found what was left of a canvas briefcase," Simpkins says. "It looked like there had been some papers inside, but there was nothing but wet shreds by the time the fire department got the blaze put out. Nearly everything in the car was destroyed."

"Everything?" Craig asks. His heart sinks with the news.

"Well, almost everything. There was only one item that survived the fire and I have to tell you, it caught our attention. We hope you can

11

explain why there was a metal suitcase full of money in the trunk. We haven't counted it yet, but there looks to be several hundred thousand dollars there."

Craig hesitates. The full import of the wreck hits him hard in the gut. One copy of the list, the letter said. Only one copy.

"It was a million," he whispers, "an even million dollars." Craig hears a quick intake of breath, then snaps the cell phone cover closed before Simpkins can reply. He sinks back onto the rickety chair. *The police will be here soon*, he thinks. *There's only one thing left to do, and not much time.*

The barrels of whiskey, thousands of them, are held in place in their rows by wooden chocks that months or years earlier were hammered into place by the warehouse workers. Craig stands up and walks to a large wooden toolbox, where he finds a sledgehammer, an eight-pounder he guesses. A little unsteady on his feet, he hefts the hammer, decides the weight is enough for the task he has in mind, and carries the tool to the middle of the warehouse.

He looks at the stacked rows of barrels disappearing upward into the darkness of the cavernous warehouse and thinks again of his dream. He feels sick and his hands are shaking, but is it from the poison? He wonders again if the threat was a hoax, like Burns had suggested. Craig knows he can't take that chance.

He turns, grabs the hammer in both hands, and slams it hard into the end of the barrel closest to where he stands. The oak boards fracture with a loud crack that resounds through the warehouse and whiskey gushes out onto the wooden floor. Craig walks a few feet, and crashes the hammer into another barrel, then a third, a fourth, a fifth. Spent by the effort, he drops the tool and falls to his knees, splashing down into a river of whiskey.

Craig pulls the letter from an inside pocket of his jacket, along with a silver cigarette lighter. The lighter is engraved with the date and the distillery logo, one of a hundred he'd commissioned from Tiffany & Co. as keepsakes to hand out at the tasting.

He flicks the lighter into life on the first try—*you get the quality you pay for*, he thinks—and touches the flame to a corner of the letter. The paper ignites and the flame flares up toward Craig's hand. There is a moment of hesitation, but only a moment, before he tosses the burning paper into a pool of whiskey. The volatile alcohol fumes ignite with a soft whoosh and ribbons of fierce, almost colorless flame shoot off in every direction.

The blaze engulfs Craig's body and he collapses onto his right side. He barely hears the muffled rumble as barrel after barrel of whiskey burn and explode, spreading a raging river of fire throughout the warehouse. *It sounds like thunder, he thinks.* Another storm must be coming.

Dreams fade away when the dreamer wakes, or when the dreamer dies.

PROHIBITION IN AMERICA
BY KAREN QUINN BLOCK

The history of man is also the history of alcohol. Many archaeologists believe that early man began making intoxicating beverages, such as wine, beer, and mead drinks, more than 10,000 years ago. Alcohol, that "gift of the gods," has emerged from the mists of time as man's consistent companion. Liquor has been used to celebrate or mourn, instill courage or fear, seal a deal or break a contract, and befuddle or seduce. As civilization advanced, so did the production and consumption of liquor. However, for a small blink in the continuum of time, sincere although arguably misguided Americans sought to eliminate alcohol consumption in the United States by prohibiting access to a ready supply.

Prohibition was instituted on January 16, 1920, by enactment of the Eighteenth Amendment to the Constitution of the United States of America. Contrary to what many people believe, Prohibition did not ban drinking. It instead prohibited "the manufacture, sale, or transportation of intoxicating liquors within, the importation thereof into, or the exportation thereof from the United States ..." Congress passed the Volstead Act on October 28, 1919, which set down the rules for enforcing the Eighteenth Amendment, including exceptions for religious and medicinal purposes.

For more than 100 years, the "dries" had championed a cause they believed would end alcoholism, family violence, and destitution in the United States. Proponents included many prominent political and religious leaders and social activists, including William Jennings Bryan who promised to "carry to the world the new doctrine that has found such favor here." This "Noble Experiment" was opposed by the "wets" who believed that Prohibition was an attempt to force a standard of morality on all citizens, a decidedly un-American course of action.

Although banning the manufacture and sale of alcohol in the U.S. seemed like a good idea to its supporters, Prohibition had horrifying and long-ranging consequences for the nation. Prohibition led to widespread contempt for the law, a rise in violent and organized crime, widespread alcohol smuggling from Canada, Mexico, and Caribbean nations, devastating unemployment that crippled the American economy during the 20s and 30s, destruction of private businesses, and expansion of the Federal income tax system.

For those who had the foresight to stockpile a substantial supply or enough cash to purchase their favorite beverage from a local bootlegger, a stiff drink was readily available throughout the nearly fourteen years the Eighteenth Amendment was in effect. Supplies of all types of liquor on store shelves and in restaurants or saloons were, in many places, sold out days before enactment. In New York City during the final hours leading up to Prohibition, citizens anticipating a long dry spell filled wheelbarrows, shopping baskets, and coat pockets with their drink of choice. Outgoing U.S. president Woodrow Wilson moved his supply of liquor from the White House to his home and incoming president Warren Harding moved his supply from his private home to the White House.

As Prohibition dragged on, local entrepreneurs (i.e., bootleggers) set up illegal stills that produced sometimes dangerous concoctions for those desperate enough to risk their lives for a drink of the "devil's broth." Speakeasies (illegal stores or nightclubs selling alcohol) sprang up everywhere. Intricate smuggling rings run primarily by mob bosses operated a brisk trade by car and small watercraft from border cities in Canada and Mexico. Owners of larger water vessels who chose to smuggle liquor from Caribbean port cities found it profitable enough to run the risk of property confiscation and imprisonment.

Foreign nations typically did not support Prohibition and often did not cooperate with the U.S. government in its efforts to shut down smuggling rings. For example, the British Colonial Office refused to prosecute smugglers operating out of the Bahamas, and Winston Churchill called Prohibition "an affront to the whole history of mankind."

By 1930, the citizenry was heartily fed up with Prohibition. The cost of enforcing the Volstead Act, the rise in violent crime, the loss of respect for the law, and out-of-control unemployment all led to the repeal movement. Whereas pre-Prohibition politicians had been eager to jump on the "dry" bandwagon, by the early 30s, they found it more politically expedient to embrace the "wet." Franklin Roosevelt ran for president in 1932 on a repeal platform. His victory ensured a fast track to the end of Prohibition.

Political clout passed the 18th Amendment; national discontent forced its repeal. On December 5, 1933, President Franklin Roosevelt signed the Twenty-First Amendment, officially ending what the "dries" had hoped was a movement to achieve worldwide sobriety. Roosevelt said, as he laid down his pen, "I think this is a good time for a beer." The majority of Americans agreed with him.

BACKDOOR BOURBON
BY HEIDI WALKER

"Saddle up, Abigail," Midwife Simmons ordered. "Miz Purcell's got a feverous child up Dixon Creek."

"Yes, ma'am." Abigail Worthington hid her delight at being chosen to deliver medical care to the mountain family. She'd spent two grueling weeks training as a volunteer courier for the Frontier Nursing Service, and she loved the daily horseback trips with Nurse Constance to isolated ridgetop homesteads. Already, she'd helped set a child's broken arm and wrapped a knife wound.

The midwife continued, "No one can go with you. I've a baby due anytime, and Nurse Constance is down at the clinic tending a sheriff's deputy with a gunshot wound."

Abigail bit her lower lip. She hadn't expected to be allowed to go out on her own this soon. "A lawman's been shot?" she asked.

"Not unusual hereabouts. Some moonshiner's no doubt got a matching bullet hole."

Abigail shuddered. She clearly wasn't in Beacon Hill any more.

"Show Miz Purcell how to mix aspirin powder into her boy's drink," Midwife Simmons said. "Check on the child and come right back. You know the way?"

"Nurse Constance and I rode by the Purcell place three days ago. I remember the route."

"Miz Purcell lost her husband to the law and is leery of strangers, so when you get there, be sure to identify yourself before getting off your horse. Last night's rain'll make slippery going. Don't dawdle."

Abigail shoved the paper packet of medicine into her knapsack and slipped a cap over her recently shortened curls. Her parents would be horrified that she'd cut her hair, but caring for long hair took time away from her responsibilities. The wool hat matched the uniform of jodhpurs and shirt that all Frontier Nursing Service couriers wore. Being free of constricting skirts and learning about nursing and eastern

Kentucky—its family pride, stills, and traditions—thrilled her. Even saddling and bridling Buckshot, the quarter horse assigned to her, was a welcome challenge. She'd honed her skills as an equestrian in Boston, where stable hands readied the mounts. Now she could tack up Buck herself in record time.

The early morning sun hadn't yet reached the valley floor where the stable stood, and the air held a chill. As she tightened the girth, the bay gelding stamped one black-socked hoof.

"Settle down, Buck." Abigail spoke gently to the young horse. "You don't want me falling off, do you? You're as eager as I am to get on the trail."

Half an hour later, all traces of civilization disappeared as she turned up a steep, rock-strewn path toward the Purcell place. She'd made good time, letting the gelding have his head on the dirt road that ran along the middle branch of the Kentucky River. Frequent flash flooding forced homes to be built high up the hillsides, and the Purcell cabin was no exception. The trail climbed beside a narrow creek gully, its water running fast and full after the recent downpour. Buck's hooves slipped on the muddy track. Abigail held on and prayed he'd keep his footing.

Compared to the pretentious tea parties she'd endured while being looked over as a marriage prospect back home, she treasured her days on horseback tending to children of the poor families living in these hills. Her parents had sent charitable donations to the Frontier Nursing Service for the past five years, ever since the organization began in 1925, but took some convincing to let their only daughter travel alone to volunteer for a year. Fortunately, the daughter of their family friends, the Cabots, had spent the previous summer there and returned safely. She'd told Abigail all about it during one of those interminable society balls, explaining that couriers delivered medicine on horseback and helped the nurses, nothing dangerous or improper. Abigail had begged to go, craving the adventure and escape from the strictures of Boston high society. Until she arrived, helping mountain folk had been such a vague notion that she hadn't given it much thought. Now she finally understood the critical need the Frontier Nursing Service provided.

Buck stumbled, and she pitched forward, the reins flapping loosely around his neck. She sat up straight and chuckled, thinking what her mother would say about such clumsiness. Well, she was out of sight of all those matrons now. She suspected that the real reason her parents had agreed to send her here was so her status as an old maid wouldn't be so obvious to their friends and neighbors. Abigail herself felt that eighteen was far too young to be married.

A shaft of sunlight shone on a flat limestone rock jutting into the path. Buck whinnied and reared. The saddle slipped sideways on his heaving flanks and Abigail tumbled to the ground, landing flat on her stomach. The horse backed away, his hooves inches from her nose. She raised her head and froze. A snake faced her, its triangular head swaying above a thick brown-black body. She'd been warned about copperheads, plentiful in these hills. Its bite could kill. The creature must have emerged from its winter rest recently, been drawn to the warmth of the stone. For long minutes she stayed immobile, her racing heartbeat hammering in her ears, unable to take her eyes off the reptile. At last it relaxed its coils and slithered under the rock.

Abigail slowly pushed herself away from the snake's hiding place before standing. Her neck ached from the strain of holding it upright. Mud covered the front of her uniform. Best to let the muck dry, then brush it off. Where was Buckshot? She looked down the trail and was relieved to see him peering up at her. Talking soft words of reassurance, for herself as well as her mount, she descended the path to the skittish animal. That had been close. She'd need to pay more attention to what lay ahead of her.

Abigail adjusted the saddle, swung up and guided Buck in a broad half circle through the woods, circling around the rock.

A half hour later, she managed to scrape most of the dried mud off her wool clothes. Flecks of white sweat covered Buck's chest as they crested the rise and entered the clearing where a one-room log cabin stood, wisps of smoke emerging from its chimney. Good that they were keeping the sick child warm.

Abigail halted Buck at the edge of the yard and called out that she was from the Frontier Nursing Service. The front door opened and Mrs. Purcell hustled out, clutching a shawl around her broad shoulders. Right after Prohibition began, Nurse Constance had explained, a federal lawman had killed the woman's husband over an illegal still, leaving her to raise her family of four sons alone. Three boys of various ages and heights clustered in the open doorway.

"Stay inside, young-uns," Mrs. Purcell ordered. Her face settled into a grim expression as she approached. A short, stocky woman, she peered around the horse.

Abigail began to dismount, but the woman held up a hand to stop her.

"You alone?" Mrs. Purcell demanded.

"Yes, ma'am. Nurse Constance is—"

"Good. I'd heard the midwife and nurse had other business to mind. Don't bother gittin' down. You've a ways to go yet."

"I don't understand. I was asked to—"

"My oldest boy, Marcus, is injured, but I couldn't tell anyone that. I wouldn't have you here except he's doing poorly." She suddenly stepped forward and roughly grasped Buck's bridle, causing the gelding to quiver in fear. Her face contorted into a frown. "You've got to swear you won't tell neither."

"Mrs. Purcell, I–"

"Swear, or by god, I'll send this animal back down faster than you can say jack rabbit."

Abigail flinched at the fierceness in the woman's eyes, then unclenched her tight grip on the reins. *She's only protecting her son. He must be up to something illegal and gotten hurt.* Not her concern. Her job was to heal, not to alert the authorities about untoward behavior. If the nursing service got a reputation for snitching to the law, it would have precious few patients.

"I swear," Abigail said. "How can I help?"

The woman's shoulders relaxed, and she released Buck. "Follow me." She strode toward the woods surrounding the cabin. Abigail urged the horse after her. At the edge of the clearing, Mrs. Purcell pointed to a barely discernible track. "About an hour's ride." She turned back. "Thank ye."

Had she not been so nervous about what lay at the end of the trail, Abigail would have enjoyed the ride. The bright green foliage of early spring lined the ridgeline path. Glimpses of the valley below flickered through the dense branches. Melodious mating calls of pewees and vireos cascaded from tree to tree. She passed no one. An hour later, a sweet fragrance filled the air, vanilla and charcoal mixed together. Like the smell of the bourbon flask—legally bottled for medicinal use, she'd been assured—in the health clinic.

Her stomach tightened. An illegal still. Nurse Constance had explained that holding the location of their stills secret was a matter of survival in these hills, where barter took the place of cash, and lawmen prowled the area.

She came to a small opening in the forest and stopped. A limestone overhang, angled like a lean-to, provided some shelter from the elements. Several wooden barrels and a collection of glass jars and earthenware jugs were stacked under the rock roof. One barrel was strapped on its side into a contraption with a handle on it so that it could be rotated. Next to this apparatus lay someone tangled in a blanket on the ground. Dark tousled hair spilled out from under the coverlet. Intermittent moans confirmed that this was her injured patient.

Abigail slipped off her horse and looped the reins around a sapling. She pulled off her riding gloves, released the leather ties holding her knapsack to the saddle, and took it over to where Mrs. Purcell's son lay. Dark lashes feathered pale cheeks; a stubble of emerging beard shadowing his lower face. This was no boy. He had to be twenty at least.

"Excuse me? Marcus?" Abigail whispered.

The man started, opened blue eyes, and focused intently on her face. The sun streamed through the branches behind her and she knelt so he wouldn't have to look into it. "Your mother sent me. I'm Abigail, from the Frontier Nursing Service."

"Abby," he breathed with an effort, his voice silky with the local southern accent.

"Can you tell me what's wrong with you?"

"I'm shot." He paused, his breathing shallow. "Ma says it's infected."

"A gunshot? You'll need Nurse Constance, then. I'm not trained to—"

"No." His hand shot out from under the blanket and griped her arm. "You've got to help me."

His grip loosened and he passed out before Abigail had a chance to reply. Alarmed, she shook him gently. How could she figure out what was wrong with him now? His moaning, and passing out, signaled that he was badly hurt. She desperately wanted to go get help, but she'd promised his mother not to tell. And she feared that if she didn't help him now, he could die. She was his only hope. She'd watched Nurse Constance tend to wounds before, but if the bullet were still inside him …

23

She'd have to examine him. Best to do it while he was unconscious. She tugged the blanket off. He lay motionless on his left arm, so it must be his right side that was injured. Retrieving scissors from her knapsack, she gingerly cut off his blood-soaked shirt. She froze, then forced herself to continue. Lifting the garment from his muscled shoulder as gently as she could, she saw a bloody hole in his upper arm. A bullet wound. The edges around the hole splayed outwards, as if the bullet had exited his body there. She shifted to examine the back of the arm. Another hole. Dear God, he'd been shot from behind. But the bullet had gone right through him. She wouldn't have to try to remove it. Angry red spokes where the slug ripped through his flesh told her it was infected.

She glanced around. A trickle of water from a spring pooled in a nearby rock basin. A dented metal cup lay on its side next to the man. She washed her hands and the cup and used a cotton rag from her knapsack to clean the wound thoroughly. She still needed something to kill the infection. Alcohol would have to do.

Abigail rose and strode to the contraption holding the wooden barrel on its side. Liquid swished inside as she jiggled the turning handle. She removed the cork and amber fluid sloshed into the cup, its aroma pungent. As she doused both sides of the wound with the brew, her patient jerked and opened his eyes.

"Don't waste good bourbon on me," he moaned.

"Nonsense." She removed her cap and shook her head to loosen her sweat-dampened curls.

He stared up at her. "Are you an angel?"

Abigail laughed. "Hardly. I've cleaned the wound. Now I need to put a dressing on. I'll be as gentle as I can."

He kept his eyes on her face as she wrapped a length of cotton around his arm and tied it in place.

"You're lucky," Abigail said. "The bullet went straight through the fleshy part of your upper arm. Didn't hit any bones. It should heal just fine if you don't use it."

"I've got to turn the barrel," he protested.

"Use your other arm."

"You're God sent, Miss Abby. Thank you."

Abigail wanted to ask him what had happened, who shot him, but knew she shouldn't. He needed to drink some water and rest now. To reduce the inflammation and dull the pain, she mixed aspirin powder into a cup of water then added a few drops of bourbon to make it more palatable.

As she held the cup to Marcus' lips, Buck whinnied. She looked up to see a bearded man in grimy overalls ride into the clearing. He caught sight of Abigail and leaped off his horse with an oath.

"Who in blazes are you?" He advanced toward her, his face tight with fury.

Struggling to conceal her fear, Abigail stood and stepped away from Marcus. "Mrs. Purcell sent me. I'm with the Frontier Nursing Service."

"Marcus? She telling the truth?"

"Leave off, Osey. She fixed me up." Marcus glared at the newcomer until he turned away from Abigail and knelt by the injured man.

As they spoke, Abigail went to calm Buck. The bearded man's horse, ears pricked, edged closer to touch his muzzle to the gelding. Strapped to the other horse were a shotgun and two whiskey barrels. Osey could have another gun on him. Would he use it to keep her from leaving? What was going on here? Running her hand down Buck's muzzle helped quiet her fear. She glanced at the sky. Almost noon. Time to head down, or Midwife Simmons would send a search party for her.

She faced the two men. "I've got to get back," she said, then bit her bottom lip to keep it from trembling.

Osey rose and started toward her. Marcus gripped the bearded man's ankle with his good hand to stop him. "Let her go. Ma wouldn't have sent her here if she hadn't promised to keep quiet."

Osey pointed his finger at her. "Keep your mouth shut, woman. Don't tell anyone where we are, or what we've got going up here. If you do …" He slashed a finger across his throat.

Abigail tried to keep her voice steady. "I understand. Marcus, I'll try to get back here tomorrow to put on a new dressing. You rest."

"Yes, Miss Abby."

Abigail mounted and trotted into the woods on the same track she'd taken before, eager to escape. Had that man who arrived on horseback been the one who shot Marcus? He seemed violent enough to have done it. Surely not. They appeared to be partners.

Her thoughts turned to her patient and she smiled. No one had called her Abby in years. Or mistaken her for an angel.

She'd just turned off the track from the Purcells' onto the road along the river when she saw someone on horseback approaching. Her heart beat faster. Did Osey take another route down the mountain and lie in wait for her? As the horse drew closer, she made out a five-pointed star pinned to the man's wool coat and realized he was a lawman.

With a two-fingered touch to his broad-brimmed hat, he stopped his horse in front of her. She had no choice but to stop, too. Thick salt and pepper sideburns framed a weathered face.

"Sheriff Knowles, ma'am. May I have a word with you?" His eyes swept over the brown smudges on her uniform and her flushed face.

"Why, good day, Sheriff." She removed her riding gloves and wiped her sweaty palms on her pants.

"What brings you out this fine afternoon?" the sheriff said, his lips thin beneath a gray mustache. "Riding alone, no less."

"I'm a courier with the nursing service."

"I could tell that from your outfit." His gaze traveled from her chest to her thighs, and she cursed herself for being unsettled by his insolence. "You heard my deputy's been shot?"

Her throat went dry. "Midwife Simmons mentioned it this morning."

"A bootlegger shot him. The scoundrel got away, but we're sure he was working with someone. My deputy was investigating barrel thefts from a distillery. One man stole the barrels, and someone had to stay behind to turn them."

Abigail felt lightheaded. The sheriff was after Marcus. She gripped the pommel of the saddle and willed her back straight. Trying to avoid giving anything away, she purposefully widened her eyes as if the thought had never occurred to her.

"You notice anything unusual on your rounds, ma'am?"

Abigail slowly shook her head. "I just deliver medications. The nurses talk to the patients," she said. It was near the truth.

Sheriff Knowles let the silence hang for a moment. "I'll be sure to ask the nurses about it, then. Good day."

He flapped the reins against his horse's neck and rode past her. Abigail clucked to Buck and rode on at a controlled walk, though inside she felt like galloping. She'd withheld information from a lawman. Could she go to jail for that? She'd always been law abiding, but then she'd never had any reason not to be. Her shoulders sagged under the weight of the secret she carried. As Marcus's nurse, wasn't she obligated to do whatever it took to make him healthy, even if it meant breaking the law? Someone had shot the deputy. Surely that person should be caught and punished. Could Marcus have done such a thing? Her hands went clammy at the realization that she might be harboring the shooter.

The next day, Abigail crammed beaten biscuits, ham, and dried apple slices into her knapsack and left before breakfast. After a restless night, she'd decided to keep the Purcells' secret to herself. If the midwife learned about Marcus' gunshot wound, she'd send the nurse to tend to it and tell the sheriff. She'd told Midwife Simmons she needed to make sure that Mrs. Purcell was administering the aspirin powder correctly, and had been permitted the morning to ride back up.

Before turning up the Purcells' track, Abigail scanned the road in both directions to be sure no one was watching. When she finally reached the cabin, detouring around the snake's stone, she knocked on the door to let Mrs. Purcell know she was going back to see Marcus. She'd stopped on her way down the day before, so the woman was expecting her.

"I'll come with you," Mrs. Purcell said gruffly. She turned to shout some orders at her children and gather her shawl. Abigail offered to let her ride, but she refused. They reached the clearing mid-morning. Marcus was sitting up. He'd changed into a clean shirt and appeared freshly shaven. A razor nick in his chin indicated he'd heeded her advice and not used his right arm. Abigail was glad to see no sign of Osey.

"How you be, son?" Mrs. Purcell asked, kneeling by him.

"Miss Abby cured me." His alert eyes sought Abigail's. "The bullet passed clear through my arm. No harm done."

Abigail caught a quick smile flash across the woman's face. An odd reaction, as if she were pleased, or proud. Mrs. Purcell untied and removed the bandage, examined the wound, then stood. "I've got to get back to the little ones. Marcus, you come home when you're able."

"I'll bring him back with me after I've treated his wound," Abigail said.

As she passed Abigail, Mrs. Purcell uttered a brief, "Thanks."

Abigail hobbled Buck's front legs so he could nibble on nearby grass while she checked on Marcus.

"I've brought some breakfast for after I change your dressing. You seem to be better today."

"You saved me, Abby."

27

"Don't be silly." She liked it, his gratitude and gentleness, and the unabashed way he said what he was feeling. Not like the men she'd suffered back home. They'd been after her money and status, no more.

She'd brought a square of gingham fabric for a tablecloth and laid the food on it after she'd attended to his wound. His eyes brightened at the ham.

"Have you had any food since you were injured?" Abigail asked.

"Ma brought some corn pone. Nothing near as good as this."

They ate in silence for a while. Then Marcus spoke. "You must be wondering how I came to be shot."

She shook her head. "That's your business, Marcus."

"You deserve to hear, for tending to me. The truth of it is, I don't know who did it. I was turning the barrel when Osey rode in, yelling that some sheriff's deputy was on to us."

Abigail tried to stop him. "Marcus, please. Don't say anything more."

"I want to. I've been cooped up here for days with no one to talk to. I trust you."

She'd already broken the law to protect him. No reason for her to repeat anything he told her. She'd honor his trust. Abigail nodded for him to continue.

"Osey wanted me to go with him after the deputy. I ... I didn't want to, but he insisted. I started to jump up behind him and someone shot me. From behind. Neither of us saw who it was. Osey's horse tore off and I fell. Must've passed out."

Abigail guessed that Osey must have ridden away, found the deputy, and shot him. "Marcus, I ran into the sheriff on my way back yesterday."

He went white, his voice came out a croak. "What … what'd you tell him?"

"I didn't say anything about you. He knows whoever shot the deputy is a bootlegger. And that he has a partner."

Marcus dropped his chin. "We've been making our own bourbon up here using barrels from a distillery up the Kentucky River."

"I thought with prohibition all the distilleries were closed."

"It's shut down all right, but a bunch of barrels that hadn't been rinsed yet are stored there. Osey swipes them and packs them up here. I add a gallon of spring water and turn the barrel to pull out the alcohol from the oak staves. Only takes a couple of days to get a right tasty drink. He trades it all around and we split the proceeds."

He glanced up. As if sensing Abigail's censure, he mumbled, "I do it to help Ma and my brothers. Better'n working down them coal mines."

At only a gallon per barrel, it was a small-scale operation, but the income Marcus received as his share would go a long way in these hills. Abigail had seen men who'd come home after being in the mines: broken, hardly able to breathe. She was glad Marcus tried to avoid that job.

"But if the sheriff is on to what you're doing?" she said.

"I know. We're going to have to quit." He gazed sadly at the barrel in the rotation contraption.

"I think you'd better." She considered the mystery of who shot Marcus. "What happened after you were shot?"

"Don't know. Next thing I knew, I was wrapped in that blanket and you were bending over me."

"Which direction did the shot come from?"

Marcus pointed toward the trail leading back to the Purcells' cabin. If Osey shot the lawman, who shot Marcus? Someone who cared enough to wrap him in a blanket.

Abigail remembered the flash of pride on Mrs. Purcell's face when Marcus confirmed that only the fleshy part of his arm was injured. How far would a mother go to stop her son from getting in trouble with the law? Enough to shoot him herself? Abigail plucked aimlessly at the hem of her wool jacket, keeping her lashes lowered so Marcus wouldn't read her thoughts.

Mrs. Purcell had lost a husband to the law, and wouldn't risk losing her son the same way. She must have heard that a deputy was looking for them and gone to warn Marcus. She was probably a crack shot, like most mountain wives. Knew just where to place that bullet without serious harm to her boy.

Beside her, Marcus finished the last of the food and began folding the napkins, humming under his breath. Abigail noticed a smile on his lips. Best if Marcus never knew it was his own mother who shot him to keep him from going after that deputy.

"What will you do now?" she asked.

"Help families get their spring crops planted. Tend livestock. Split wood. There's always work come warm weather."

"And Osey?"

"He hightailed it out of the county. Claims the deputy didn't see who shot him. He'll hole up awhile 'til the distillery forgets about the thefts."

The sheriff had no idea who shot the deputy. Abigail could mention to him that she'd seen Osey leaving the area. Knowing he was a suspect would keep Osey from coming back and implicating Marcus.

Marcus nodded toward the barrel-turning contraption. "Soon's I'm able, I'll dismantle this thing and burn the evidence."

Marcus seemed confident that he'd be under no suspicion for the distillery's losses. Perhaps he deserved a second chance. There were always chores needing doing at the nursing service. She could try to find him a paying job.

"Miss Abby?" Marcus lightly touched the back of her hand to get her attention. "Would you care for a sample before we head back?"

A bird trilled, and a breeze shook the young leaves above her. Marcus looked so eager, Abigail was loath to deny him. Besides, her patient would need something to fortify him for the ride back to the Purcells' place. Surely it would be rude to refuse a single drink. She wanted to linger, savor a job well done, and listen to his sweet voice.

"Do you have another cup?" she asked.

"We can share," he said softly.

ALLTECH LEXINGTON BREWING & DISTILLING
BY KAREN QUINN BLOCK

The history of the Lexington Brewing Company is long, varied, and sometimes a little checkered. Founded in the mid-1790s by Thomas Carneal, the brewery operated under several owners until 1830. Picking up again in 1856 under a new name, the malt house was blown up by the Confederates during the American Civil War in 1862. After the war, production resumed until Prohibition, when beer production ceased by law. The owners attempted to keep the business afloat by bottling a variety of alcohol-free drinks, including one called Bourbonola, a name that piqued the interest of Federal agents. One day, the Feds raided the brewery, seized 5,000 bottles of "high proof" beer, and closed the business. It wasn't until 1994 when the Second Lexington Brewing Company began producing a variety of craft beers that the brewery once again came into its own. In September 1999, Pearse Lyons, PhD, president and founder of AllTech, Inc., purchased the business.

Dr. Lyons, a biochemist by trade, came to Kentucky in 1976 to solve a problem for some ethanol producers. He fell in love with the state's rolling green hills, which reminded him of his home country, Ireland. He stayed, and over the next twenty years founded and built an international corporation. However, his first love was distilling, so when presented with the opportunity to jump into the brewery business, Dr. Lyons seized the initiative. Since brewing and distilling share some of the same tasks, it was just a short step to add distilling spirits to the original brewery. Today, the Alltech Lexington Brewing & Distilling Company is one of the few brewery/distillery combinations in the world.

Located at the corner of Cross and Pine Streets, this little gem is nestled close to the center of downtown Lexington, Kentucky. The campus includes a gift shop and tour center housed in the old Lexington icehouse, a brewery where several varieties of beer and spirits begin life, and a glass front distillery opposite the brewery on Cross Street. Mash, once fermentation is complete, is pumped through outdoor stainless steel pipes to the distilling room. The distillery produces not only its signature bourbon, Town Branch, but also an *après-dinner* drink consisting of bourbon infused with coffee called Bluegrass Sundown, in addition to Kentucky's first malt whiskey since 1919, rye whiskey, and rum.

This enterprise is small craft all the way. The distillery only fills about eight barrels of spirits per day, which is transported in 80-keg batches to a nearby distillery warehouse for aging. At any one time, there are only 2400 barrels in storage. Once aged to perfection (for Town Branch this means four to five years), the barrels are returned to the distillery's bottling room. The 124-proof liquor is dumped in a metal trough, then pumped to a huge closed-top tank where it is infused with Kentucky's famous limestone water from Lexington's Town Branch (the underground stream that runs beneath Lexington and for which the company's bourbon brand is named) to reduce the brew to eighty proof. From there, the liquid is pumped to the chill stabilization tank where any impurities are filtered out, then onto the bottling tank, which is connected by hoses to the dispenser.

Bottling is accomplished by hand. A crew of five bottle the beverage in elegant glass containers. For example, Town Branch is dispensed into gorgeous rectangular bottles with thick walls that are imported from France. Bluegrass Sundown is dispensed into a long-necked black bottle with a gold label. Once the liquid passes into the bottling tank, the first person on the line swishes sanitizer in an empty bottle, empties the contents, and passes on the bottle. The filler takes the bottle, attaches it to the dispenser, which fills the containers by gravity in about thirty seconds, pulls the filled bottle off the dispenser, corks it, and passes it on. The next technician affixes the seal label over the cork and the neck label, which seals the top label, then slides the bottle to the next person on the line, who places the body label. Finally, the packer places the finished product in boxes for distribution.

Once the bourbon barrels are emptied, they are filled with Kentucky Ale, one of the company's signature beers, and allowed to marinate for six weeks. What results is a unique sipping beer with the distinctive aroma and taste of Kentucky bourbon—and about 8.2 percent alcohol. A similar product, Kentucky Bourbon Barrel Stout, is a beer brewed with coffee and aged in Kentucky bourbon barrels. The company plans to add to their Barrel-Aged Seasonal Series line to capitalize on the growing demand for unique flavors.

Two new brew houses were completed in 2016, which expanded storage capacity to 140,000 barrels of product. This expansion was planned to not only increase production potential, but also to allow passersby to view brewing operations through glass outer walls on two sides of the building. With this attention to not only the mechanics of brewing/distilling, but also to the aesthetics of the campus, the company is poised to build a dedicated fan base and ensure success for many years to come.

TAKE THE FALL
BY SHIRLEY JUMP

"It's all that freakin' tightwad's fault," Kline muttered. He reached out with the garbage grabber and picked up a ball of newspaper. Beside him, traffic rumbled down I-64 so close the breeze lifted his hair and flattened his jeans against his legs. People in fancy SUVs and soccer mom minivans flicked disgusted gazes at the line of orange vests marked Kentucky Department of Corrections. Kline wanted to tell those nosy, judgmental biddies a little community service trash collection didn't make him no criminal.

Herbert Kline—no one called him by his first name and kept their teeth—knew one thing. Life was about taking what you could when you could. Trouble was, not a thing in the little pissant town of Horizon Valley was worth a frickin' damn.

Well, that wasn't quite true. Kline knew where the money was in Horizon Valley. The problem was getting to it. Without getting caught.

Kline snagged an empty Coke can, then dropped it into the bright orange trash bag attached to his waist. God, the bag stunk. Filled with all kinds of crap, from rotting apples to train-tracked boxers. Nastiness all around him, the kind you never saw when you were hauling butt down the highway in a Toyota Corolla, knocking back a few Buds with your buds.

That's where he oughta be right now. And would be, if not for Martin Bishop. Vindictive bastard. Couldn't share one dime, not one damned dime. A tightwad, through and through.

"That frickin' judge was an idiot," Dennis Wilkins said, sidling up to Kline. "Picking up trash ain't 'character forming'."

"Character building," Kline corrected. He speared a wadded tissue, but it had something on it that made it stick to the rubber grips coating the ends of the tongs. The long metal grabber gadget probably had some fancy name, but the masochist running the orange line hadn't told them. He'd just shoved the tool into Kline's hands and said, "Make yourself useful, punk."

Kline dug a pair of latex gloves out of his pocket, another gift from Punk-man, and picked off the tissue before shoving it into the bag. "This shit's disgusting."

"Yeah."

Dennis's trash bag held only a tenth of Kline's. Clearly, one of them had been building more character than the other. Hadn't it been that way forever with him and Dennis? One always did the heavy lifting, and the other took the light end. That was Dennis, the lightweight. Dennis thought he was smart, because he'd done a couple years at some artsy-fartsy community college, and was always talking about crap like light and composition, as if he ran a freakin' museum. But then he'd gone and quit college, to work in the distillery. That proved he was stupid. Hell, he'd almost been out of this no-good town, and then he'd come back like a ricocheting bullet.

Dennis was the kind of guy who never wanted to get his hands dirty, never had a plan, never knew what the hell was going down. But he had a decent car, and that was more than most of them had in this God-forgotten Kentucky town. Plus, Dennis was dumb enough to let everyone tell him where to go and not ask for gas money.

Kline glanced at the sun, already beating down on them. Soon, the heat would be an oven, cooking them and the trash smells. "And this is only the first hour."

"Only ninety-nine to go." Dennis grinned at his joke, then his face fell flat. "One hundred freaking hours of this crap." This time his voice was quiet, lower than the soft roar of the passing traffic.

Kline didn't have anything to say to that. It sucked, but it was better than jail.

He slipped the tongs under a shrub and collided with something hard. He heard a soft ping. He almost walked away—why go to extra trouble?—then noticed Punk-man watching him. Half the time the guy was busy flirting with the two blondes at the end of the line, a couple of girls Kline had known in high school. Cheerleaders, probably here because they had convinced some judge a little trash collection was a good way to work off a DUI.

Their keeper was still staring, his mouth in a straight, pissed-off line, so Kline bent down and fished a bottle out from under the thorny bush. The sun glinted off the clear glass, danced sparkles of gold in front of Kline's eyes. Not because of the glass, but what was inside the bottle.

Bourbon.

Kline turned the long rectangular shaped bottle over, the few dregs of liquid inside sloshing. He already knew what he'd find. He could have drawn the label in his sleep. He'd seen it often enough. Clutched in his father's hands, every night after work, like it was glued to his palm. The old man would wake up the next day still holding that damned bottle. He'd take a welcome-to-the-day swig, pull on whatever clothes he found on the floor and head back to the distillery, where he spent his day shoving those same bottles into crates.

Bishop's Bourbon. The name as simple as the design on the label—a guy who looked like a monk, sitting down with a glass of the liquor, as if having a nip or two was a religious experience. The closest Kline's father had come to a religious experience was taking the Lord's name in vain while he beat the crap out of his son.

Kline was about to shove the bottle into his trash bag and be done with it, forget it, put it from his mind, when he spotted a second one a few feet into the woods. Then a third, a little further back. Sort of a trail. "Hey, Dennis."

"What?"

"Where we at?"

"In hell."

"No, dude. I mean, where we at in Kentucky?"

Dennis squinted into the sun, peering down the long stretch of highway, chewing on the inside of his cheek while he thought. He was dumb in a lot of ways, but he knew roads. Knew directions. "Mile marker 36."

"*Habla ingles,* you moron."

"About twenty miles east of Louisville."

Kline considered that a second. "Ain't that where the boss man lives?"

"Yeah, it is. Right next to his factory," Dennis added, as if Kline and the whole damned town didn't know that.

Kline tapped the bottle against his palm. "I thought so."

Dennis's gaze fell on the label. His eyes widened. "Yo, that's one of his."

"I know that, idiot. There's another one over there. One more further down. The whole place is filled with empties." Kline ran his thumb over the bottle's smooth neck. The glass slid beneath his touch, silky, tempting. He thought of the day Martin Bishop had called him into his office and fired him, leaving the door open so the whole damned factory floor could hear Kline's dressing down. Said Kline had stolen a case of bourbon, bit off the hand that fed him. Bishop was always thinking someone was taking what was his, when far as Kline knew, no one had stolen a thing. Except maybe Bishop's crazy mind.

Kline had wanted to lunge across that too-wide cherry desk and beat Bishop within an inch of his life for yelling at him. Only one other man had ever yelled at Kline that way, and that man shared Kline's blood.

But Kline didn't do nothing in Bishop's office. He took it like a man and waited. After hours him and Dennis had come back and smashed in a few windows. Scrawled words his momma didn't like all over Bishop's desk, and left without what he'd come looking for. Bishop's money.

Bishop had called the cops, and Kline and Dennis had ended up here, under the hot sun, picking up other people's shit. "I bet the workers come out here at the end of the day, with a few they've snagged off the line."

Dennis nodded. Smiled. "Maybe we'll get lucky. Find a half-filled one."

Kline's thumb circled the neck again and again. "I'm thinking we've gotten a hell of a lot luckier than that."

The two-story Victorian house sat on a hill, at the end of a shaded lane running behind the small distillery and bottling plant. Rumor had it the old cheapskate had built up the hill until his house was the highest thing in Horizon Valley, because he wanted to let people know he was bigger than them. Richer. Safer.

Kline believed it. A man like him, a man who'd fire you as soon as look at you, he'd think that kind of thing. Just because he'd made millions off what he called a "boutique bourbon," which was a bunch of bull. All Bishop had done was charge five times the cost and get lucky when some rapper sang about slugging Bishop's Bourbon while he tapped some chick in an Escalade.

"I bet he sleeps on his money," he said to Dennis.

"Probably uses it to start the fireplace."

The two of them had a laugh about that, but it didn't last long. They exchanged a long look, the kind that said some of that money should be theirs. They'd worked hard for Martin Bishop, harder than they'd worked for anyone. And in the end, he'd stiffed them. Fired Kline over something he hadn't even done, then fired Dennis because he could, and screwed them both out of unemployment by getting them arrested.

When Kline had seen the bottles and realized where he was, he'd known there was only one option—sneak back after they were done trash collecting and get what they were due. The day wore on, hours passing until they took the Department of Corrections bus back to the courthouse, then got into Dennis's car and backtracked to Bishop's place. Now Kline was hungry and hot and pissed.

"We gotta get our money. No unemployment, no pay. Bishop owes us, big-time," Kline said. His fingers danced against the side of his pants, jonesing for a Camel, but it'd have to wait. No way he wanted to warn the old man he was coming.

Martin Bishop didn't deserve that. Hell, he didn't deserve much of anything, except what was coming his way today.

"How we gonna do that?" Dennis asked.

That was Dennis, always relying on Kline to be the brains. He gave Dennis a don't-ask-questions look, then pointed at Dennis's right hand. "Why the hell are you still carrying that thing around? They're gonna notice it's gone."

Dennis held up the garbage grabber. "I dunno. I like it. Besides, the warden didn't count 'em. He only said to load them up. I didn't load." Dennis grinned. "Freebie for me."

"Idiot," Kline said, but kept the word under his breath. Dennis got ticked when people called him stupid, went all postal. Kline didn't need that crap right now. Dennis had to be alert. Cooperative. Kline motioned to Dennis to take the left side of the house, while Kline took the right.

It took twenty minutes of sneaking along the house, poking between shrubs and thorny flower things, before Kline found an unlocked door. He raised his hand, signaling Dennis. Kline lifted the latch on the basement door—slow, slow, slow—then slid in, followed by Dennis. He paused, steeling himself for the siren scream of an alarm, but there was … nothing.

He smiled to himself. Bishop had gotten comfortable, forgotten about the hungry wolves waiting to nip at his heels. That was about to change.

Kline gestured to Dennis to start searching. He wasn't sure what he wanted was in the basement, or hell, even in the house, but it was as good a place to start looking as any. Bishop, a man who trusted no one but himself, was bound to keep his secrets close to home.

His secrets, and most of all, his money.

Ten minutes passed, fifteen. The full moon cast enough light through the floor-to-ceiling windows to help them search. The basement smelled sweet, like too many roses. It didn't hold any of that musty smell his basement, and most of the others he'd been in, had. No, this one had a special *eau de cellar*. Too fresh, too clean. Too rich.

Kline lifted the lid on a box and cursed under his breath. Nothing but stupid statues still packed in crates, fake straw cushioning them in their temporary home. A bunch of vases on one shelf, a stack of paintings against another wall. Dust collectors, one and all.

Still, maybe they were valuable if Bishop had bought them. Kline had heard rumors Bishop liked to collect crap. And they weren't talking about a bunch of porcelain pigs he'd bought on eBay. No, Bishop went all over the world picking up junk. Whatever it was, Kline would make Dennis carry it out of here. He'd have to pawn it out of state, probably, but if he took enough, Kline wouldn't have to worry about working. Ever again.

"Kline! Check this out! You won't believe what I found!" Dennis's strained whisper cut across the room. Kline's fist clenched at his side. Hadn't he told him a hundred times, no words, no names, and most of all, no noise?

He made his way across the room, then smacked Dennis on the back of the head. A reminder he better stay in line, or he'd end up empty-handed.

Dennis shot him a glare, rubbed his head with one hand and pointed with the other into the shadowy corner.

Case after case of Bishop's Bourbon lined two sides of the corner. Probably the personal stash, considering one of the cases was open, and a couple of used glasses sat on top of a second case. Not the jackpot Kline was hoping for, but a damned fine end to a damned sucky day. Kline nodded toward the glasses, then hoisted one of the bottles out of the box. Wouldn't that frost Bishop's socks, to know Kline, of all

40

people, was sucking down *his* bourbon in *his* basement, using *his* glasses?

He poured two double shots, handed one to Dennis, then tipped the glass. The liquor slid down smooth, hot. Bishop might have been a sadist in a suit, but he made a damned fine bourbon.

Kline started to pour another, then changed his mind. If he got drunk, he'd make mistakes.

He flicked out his lighter, thumbed a flame to life, then saw what Dennis had missed. Idiot had gotten too excited about the bourbon to see the real prize. The safe. One of those wall jobbies, with the big-ass door and combination lock built into the handle. The kind you could hide a football team inside, and still have room for valuables. Wasn't that just like Bishop, to overdo something as simple as a safe?

The problem was getting inside it. Kline tried the handle twice. Fiddled with the lock. No go. He tried to think up what combination Bishop could have used, but he didn't know the man well enough to figure out any three numbers he'd care about.

A creak sounded above them. Dennis's eyebrows shot up, and he tapped Kline on the shoulder, rat-a-tat, rat-a-tat. Kline shoved Dennis's nervous fingers away. Jesus H. It wasn't as if Kline were deaf. Bishop—or one of his minions—was in the house.

Kline was about to grab a few of those paintings and make a run for it when he got an idea. He always got his best ideas under pressure. That was him, the one who thought of what to do when they were between a rock and the crappy place while Dennis, well, Dennis panicked.

Kline crossed the room, still holding the bottle of bourbon, and tipped one of the vases onto the floor. It hit the tile surface with a crash as loud as a sonic boom in the dark silence of the basement. A rainbow of porcelain shrapnel burst outward, showering them with tiny fragments.

Dennis's jaw stood open, his mouth in a horrified O. "What'd you do that for?"

"Shut. Up." Kline waved toward the door leading from the basement to the first floor. He held up three fingers. Three. Lowered one. Two. Lowered another. One. Lowered the last one, and pointed it at the stairs. *Go.*

But Dennis stayed glued to the floor, probably pissing his pants. He kept mouthing to Kline that they had to get out of here. Kline ignored him.

The door above them opened.

"Who's down there?" Bishop called, in the loud, demanding, don't-mess-with-me voice he used on the factory floor. He took a step. Another. A third.

Kline waited.

"The police are on their way. You try and take anything, and they'll get you on the way out." Step. Step. Step.

Kline waited. His heart hammered in his chest, loud enough he was sure Bishop could hear it.

"If I don't shoot you first, you thieving bastards."

Kline waited. No sound for a long time, and then Bishop's pride, or his curiosity, got to him, and he started moving again. Step. Step. Step.

Kline raised his right arm. In his high school days, he'd been a hell of a batter. Had a shot at something once—a college recruiter in the stands to see him and everything—then his father had showed up at the game, drunk, and screaming obscenities at the ump. Kline had lost his concentration, lost the game, and lost the recruiter.

He'd gone home that night and taken care of his father once and for all. Done in by his own empty bottle and a tumble down the stairs. There'd been no more screaming after that.

Bishop's foot hesitated over the next step, as if he sensed Kline down there in the dark, waiting. "I'll shoot." His voice was still cold, but it shook a little, and Kline knew he had him. Martin Bishop was nothing but a scared old man.

In one swift move, Kline grabbed the railing, swung his body onto the edge of the staircase, raised his right arm, and brought the bottle down square against Bishop's head. The old man let out an oomph. He teetered, then pitched forward, tumbling head over ass down the last few stairs. He sprawled at the bottom, legs underneath him, twisted like pretzels, arms splayed in some last-ditch effort to save himself. The gun skittered across the floor and spun to a stop.

"Are you insane?" Dennis whispered, his voice high and soft at the same time. He ran to Bishop's body, standing over it, that damned garbage grabber still in his hands. "You killed him."

"Nah. I think he's still breathing. And as long as he's breathing, he's giving us that combination." Kline toed at Bishop's body.

Bishop didn't move. Didn't grunt. Didn't do anything.

Kline bent down, curling his lip in distaste as he felt around Bishop's neck. Where the hell was that pulse place? He felt a big vein, pressed his fingers against it.

Nothing.

"Oh my God, oh my God." Dennis paced in a little circle, the garbage grabber slapping at his thighs. "You killed him, Kline."

"He fell down the stairs. Happens to old men all the time. People will think it's an accident." Kline headed across the room, snagging a box as he went. "Now come on, help me get some of this stuff. Oh, and get the gun. Maybe I can shoot the lock off that safe."

But Dennis was still circling in the shadows, muttering to himself about the dead man. "We can't take anything. We can't. They'll know it wasn't an accident. You really screwed up this time, Kline."

Kline turned back, charged over to Dennis and snatched him by the shirt, jerking him until his eyeballs focused. "Now you listen to me, you idiot. No one is going to think this was anything but an accident. Bishop had no friends. No family. Who the hell was he going to tell about his stupid vases and crappy little paintings?"

"I don't think those are crappy, Kline, they're actually—"

"Who gives a shit what you think? God, your momma didn't give you enough brains to function. Now shut up so I can think." Kline wanted to shake Dennis again, but figured the last thing he needed was two dead bodies. He threw off Dennis, and Dennis stumbled back a couple paces. "God, I'm sick of dealing with you. Do you know how to spell moron? D-E-N-N-I-S. I don't give a shit what Bishop's got down here. We're taking everything we can carry and pawning it in Lex."

Dennis's eyes narrowed. His face darkened. "I don't like it when you call me stupid."

"Yeah, well, there are days when the lack of brain cells fit." Kline shoved the box against Dennis's chest. "Now get packing."

Dennis's eyes glittered in the darkness. For a second, it seemed as if he was going to say something. Instead, he dropped his garbage tool to the floor by Bishop, then took the box and turned away. He put the smaller paintings inside, stacking them slow, like he was afraid of hurting them.

Kline glanced back at Bishop. Still dead. He looked at Dennis. Still pissed.

Then he looked down at the bottle in his hands. For the first time saw the blood spatter on the glass and the sheen of spattered bourbon on his fingers. Damn. Dennis might be stupid, but he was right about one thing. No one would believe Bishop's death was an accident, what with the impression of one of his own bourbon bottles in his damned cranium.

Kline slipped his finger around the neck of the bottle, through the stickiness of blood and alcohol. He toyed with the bottle for a minute. The glass caught the moonlight and reflected it in shimmering slivers.

"Hey, Dennis."

He looked up at Kline, a slim white face in the dark shadows. "Yeah?"

Kline ambled over, easy as you please. "Let's have another swig. A celebration. What do you say?"

"Kline, I don't know. We should—"

"Here, take this. I'll get the glasses." He held the bottle out to Dennis and before he could say *get a clue, moron,* Dennis had taken the bottle with Bishop's blood into his own hands.

"That was a terrible thing you did, Dennis." Kline shook his head. "Killing a defenseless old man like that."

"What? I didn't … how could you …" He glanced down at the bottle. "No. I am not taking the rap."

Kline crossed to the glasses and tucked them into his pockets. He tried to think if he'd touched anything else. The patio door. The safe's lock. The railing. He circled the room, wiping away traces of his presence. Dennis followed him, still sputtering. "I don't know what you had against the old man. Must have been him firing you." Kline tugged his sleeve over his hand, then rubbed at the spot on the railing where he had swung up and held on. "You let that stew and stew, and then saw his house, and wham, couldn't take it one more second."

Dennis threw the bottle onto the floor and backed away from the spreading puddle of bourbon. It leaked into Bishop's hair, onto his fancy carpet with the curlicue design. "No, no, it ain't like that. I didn't do this. You did!"

Kline looked around the room. From far away, the high-pitched whine of sirens cut through the air. Bishop hadn't been lying about calling the cops. They had maybe three, four minutes. Time to go. "No,

44

Dennis, that's where you're wrong. All I did was come up with the plan. You were the idiot—"

"Don't call me that! I'm warning you."

Kline laughed. "You were the *idiot*," he said again, "who went along with it. Now you're the idiot who'll go to jail." Then he grinned at Dennis, flipped him the bird, and headed for the door.

Dennis let out a roar and whipped around in front of him. There was a whoosh, then Kline couldn't breathe. He opened his mouth, tried to pull air into his lungs, but nothing came. Nothing happened. His mind went blank for one long second, then he drew himself up and focused, focused.

What the hell? It took a second for his mind to put the images together.

Dennis's garbage grabber stuck out from Kline's chest like a giant pair of tweezers reaching for his lungs. He tried to pull it out, but the tongs were wedged tight. The world kept going black, gray, color, black, gray—

"You think I'm so stupid," Dennis whispered in his ear, spitting the last word against Kline's neck. "But I'm the one who pried off those rubber caps and spent my lunch hour sharpening the edges on a rock. I've been dealing with garbage all day. Most of it from you. And I'm sick of it."

Kline waved his arms, trying to grab Dennis. Not getting anything. His brain pounded louder than his heart, demanding oxygen. The sirens were ringing in his head, over and over, whoop-whoop-whoop. "You … you…"

"Yeah, me. And guess what? I was smart enough to wear these, too." Dennis held up his hands, waved them in front of Klein's face until he noticed the one detail that had been hidden by the shadows.

Gloves. The same sheer latex ones they'd been given out on the line.

"No prints, Kline. Except yours. Police will think Bishop stabbed you, then you hit him." Dennis picked up another bourbon bottle and shoved it into one of Kline's bare hands.

"No, no," Kline said, the words a gasp.

"I warned you. Told you not to call me that. One more time, I kept telling myself, one more time, and I was going to make sure you never called me idiot again." Dennis laughed, a sound that chilled Kline.

45

The whoop-whoops were closer now, maybe a minute away. "Sounds like it's time for me to go. Bye, old friend."

Dennis clapped him on the back. Kline stumbled, but his balance was gone, his vision blurred. The world rushed toward him as he fell, fell, fell, landing with a crash in the puddle of Bishop's Bourbon. The last thing he saw was Dennis wrapping Bishop's fingers around the handle of the tongs. The dead man's eyes stared into Kline's as if saying *look what you did, you idiot.*

Some would have called it retribution. Dennis Wilkins called it karma. You get what you give, he always said, and Kline had given two men the wrong end of the bottle. Seemed apropos to leave his body here, in the basement of the man who'd created the very thing Kline had hated.

For years, Dennis had waited for an opportunity such as this to come along. The minute he'd seen the Picasso in the crate, he knew this was the chance he'd wanted. The way out of this town, and away from stupid people like Herbert Kline.

As the sirens grew in volume, closer now, but not quite here yet, he hoisted the painting under his arm and disappeared into the deep, dark night. A smarter man than anyone had ever suspected.

MEDICINAL ALCOHOL
BY SARAH E. GLENN

From ancient times, alcohol's potency has been revered and yet feared. It was celebrated as the wine of Dionysus, the sacred barley-drink of the Eleusinian Mysteries, and the reason John Barleycorn had to die. Even so, the classical Greeks warned against drinking unwatered wine, and the Bible advises its readers to only drink in moderation.

Alcohol's use in medicine is equally ancient. Wine enhanced the potency of herbal medicines and extended their shelf life. The invention of distillation improved this even further. Certain essences from plants are more easily extracted by alcohol than water, and tinctures formed a large part of the pharmacopeia before modern chemistry took over. Many nostrums sold in the nineteenth century counted alcohol as a major ingredient, their effect sometime heightened with narcotics. Homemade cold remedies like hot toddies and buttered rum were popular.

During the 1830s, however, the Temperance movement swelled in the United States and public pressure to ban alcohol sales mounted. Alcohol was seen as the source of many evils, no matter the method or reason for its administration, and even medical authority seemed to bend under the political winds. In 1917, shortly before Prohibition began, the American Medical Association proclaimed that alcohol was "detrimental to the human economy" and had "no scientific value". The organization passed a resolution that it was opposed to the use of alcohol as a beverage or "as a therapeutic agent".

The AMA may have echoed the public sentiments of the time, but a medical loophole was created in the Volstead Act for the therapeutic prescribing of alcohol. As a result, medicinal alcohol, also known as *Spiritus frumenti*, was prescribed throughout American Prohibition.

Under the provisions of this loophole, only a physician with a proper permit could write a prescription for medicinal liquor.

Furthermore, the dose of this medical dispensation was limited to one pint every ten days, or ten to sixteen shots depending on the generosity of the patient's pouring hand. The government issued books of specially designed forms for this purpose. The designs were changed often to outstrip counterfeiters.

Economist Clark Warburton stated that the consumption of medicinal alcohol increased by 400 percent during the 1920s. By 1929, there were 116,756 physicians working in the twenty-six states that permitted the use of medicinal alcohol. According to the Journal of the American Medical Association, about half of those physicians prescribed it for their patients.

Which ailments, you might ask, required a prescription for alcohol? In 1922, the AMA—the same body that declared alcohol without value—took a referendum of its members. According to prescribing physicians of the time, medicinal alcohol was useful in the treatment of asthma, cancer, typhoid, pneumonia, snakebite, general debility, and old age. They also recommended it for diabetics, strongly counter-indicated by modern medicine.

Physicians also expressed preferences for certain types of therapeutic libation over others. Wine was preferred by some big-city doctors, while beer was preferred in Jersey City and Scranton, Pennsylvania. The overwhelming winner, however, was whiskey. Perhaps this snub of Dionysus was due to ignorance of wine's flavonoids, since these would not be discovered for several more decades.

Kentucky was a major source for medicinal alcohol. One of the more famous locations to take your prescription for *S. frumenti* was Krause's Drug Store in Covington, Kentucky. Its unofficial name was the 'Bootleg Drug Store', due to its no-questions-asked prescription policy and the still that Old Man Krause kept in the basement. Other area pharmacists, particularly ones in Cincinnati, often refused to refill prescriptions for alcohol and sent those customers to Krause's establishment. Mr. Krause, always the obliging health provider, kept his store open during Thanksgiving, Christmas, New Year's Eve, and New Year's Day so no customer would suffer without his medication during the holidays.

Mr. Krause had his own supply of alcohol, but most pharmacies acquired their goods from other sources. Most distilleries closed operations during Prohibition, dwindling from 965 distillers in 1899 to around 30 during Prohibition. Only six survived.

One major distributor was the American Medicinal Spirits Company, formed in 1920 in Louisville, Kentucky. Its founders, Otho and Richard Walthen, who owned the R.E. Walthen Distillery and the Old Grand-Dad brand, saw the opportunity to continue their business under a new name. They acquired casks of aging liquor from former distilleries and stored them in 'concentration warehouses' under governmental supervision. The American Medicinal Spirits Company then distributed the stores to pharmacists, often in brand-name bottles created before Prohibition. Why spend money on new glass?

Only a small number of distilleries received permits to produce liquor for medicinal purposes, several in Kentucky. The Stitzel Distillery and Brown-Forman were located in Louisville; another, Glenmore Distilleries, was located in Owensboro. The longest-lived, the George T. Stagg Distillery, operated along the Kentucky River in Frankfort. In 1925, it bottled 1 million pints of 'medicinal whiskey'. Today known as Buffalo Trace, it is one of the few American distilleries that can claim to have been in continuous operation since the 1700s, due to its medical connections.

Two Old Crows
By Sarah E. Glenn & Gwen Mayo

Cornelia steered the nearly new 1925 Dodge Brothers car to the curb in front of Burgess' Drugstore. It was so early that the only other car visible in downtown Fisher's Mill was a Ford Runabout parked in the driveway beside the church. Teddy straightened her hat and descended via the running board, turning to take the cane that Cornelia offered.

"Maybe today he'll give me my whiskey," Teddy said. "Now that it's day eleven."

"Medicinal spirits, and it's day ten."

"Eleven," she repeated, stamping the cane on the cobblestones for emphasis. "I ran out on Tuesday. Remember? My coughing kept you up all night." The day before, Teddy had given the pharmacist her prescription for one pint of *spiritus frumenti*, usually dispensed as bourbon in the state of Kentucky. Mr. Burgess had informed her that the legally required ten days had not passed since her last prescription, and Teddy had been fit to be tied.

"Coughing? No. Snoring? Yes." Cornelia pushed open the door to the drugstore. The shelves inside contained inviting displays of nostrums, but no other customers were present. "I see we are his first visitors of the day," she said, looking around.

Teddy walked in and stopped near the empty lunch counter. She peered toward the rear of the store, where the pharmacy was. "I don't see Mr. Burgess."

"He may be compounding a prescription. I hear music from the back."

Teddy was already heading towards the pharmacy, moving very sprightly for someone with lung problems. Cornelia wondered if perhaps she was a little too fond of her evening toddies. She would hate for dear Teddy to become known as a tippler to her new neighbors.

"Yoo hoo!" Teddy rapped the rear counter with the brass head of her walking stick. "Mr. Burgess, it's Theodora Lawless. I'm here to pick up my prescription."

Cornelia joined her, and the two women waited for a response.

After a minute, Cornelia rang the bell. "Mr. Burgess? You have customers."

"He wouldn't leave the store empty, would he?" Teddy asked.

"No, but he might be in a storeroom." Cornelia leaned over the counter for a better look into the back. In an instant, her demeanor changed to that of the seasoned battlefield nurse she was, and she hoisted herself over the polished oak surface.

"Teddy, call the authorities."

"What is it?" Teddy adjusted her spectacles and stretched her head of silver curls across the counter.

"Mr. Burgess," Cornelia knelt over the pharmacist's sprawled form. "He's dead."

Blood had congealed under the pharmacist's head and along the side of the nearby desk. In the corner was a Radiola, switched on at full volume. On cue, it began to blare Louis Armstrong's "Heebie Jeebies".

The deputy tugged at his collar, a little tight for his plump neck, and tapped his notepad with his pencil. "Your names, please?"

"Cornelia Pettijohn. This is my companion, Theodora Lawless."

"Which one of you disturbed the body?"

Cornelia gave him a scathing look. "I did nothing of the kind, young man. As a registered nurse, I have a duty to render aid to the wounded."

"When she found out he was dead," Teddy quickly added, "we called you."

"Did you touch anything other than the body?" They moved aside so Burgess' corpse could be carried out to the Packard hearse, which also doubled as the community ambulance. Dr. Wells tipped his hat to the ladies before leaving the store.

"I touched nothing besides the counter. I had to climb across it to reach Mr. Burgess," Cornelia said curtly. "Once I determined that he was beyond help, I thought it best to leave everything as I found it."

"Was anyone else in the store when you entered? Someone leaving, perhaps?"

"It was deserted," Teddy said. "At first, we thought that Mr. Burgess had stepped out, but then we heard the music. 'Black Bottom', I believe."

The deputy stopped writing. "What?"

"'Black Bottom'. The dance where the young girls leap." She looked at her own feet and sighed. "I wish I didn't lose my breath so quickly when I dance."

"No one else was there," Cornelia said, eyeing the clenched muscle in the young man's jaw. "We looked around the store for assistance when we entered."

Teddy, who had been tapping the toe of her shoe on the sidewalk, dissolved into a coughing fit and Adkins glanced her way, concerned. "Consumption?"

"No. She was exposed to poison gas near Verdun."

"You were in The Great War?" He eyed Cornelia's tin-colored bun and Teddy's silver hair more closely.

"We were with the Army Nurse Corps. We supervised the younger ladies, which required traveling to the front often. Miss Lawless was in the trenches when the Germans attacked."

The memory of Teddy in the hospital bed, bandages over her eyes and gasping for breath, was a familiar and recurring pain for Cornelia, even after eight years. She shook her head, dismissing the image. "Whom should we contact about Miss Lawless' prescription?"

"I guess you should ask Dr. Wells when he gets back. He might be able to get you the medicine you need today, but you may need to travel to Midway or even Frankfort if the pharmacy doesn't reopen."

The news from Dr. Wells was not good. Mr. Burgess' entire supply from the Stagg Distillery was missing, making his death very likely a murder. Furthermore, the doctor was now besieged by patients demanding replacements for unfilled prescriptions, claims he suspected to be mostly false. He refused to write anyone a new prescription for medicinal whiskey until ten more days had passed. Cornelia doubted that Deputy Adkins would be of any help. He seemed convinced that the theft of bourbon could only mean bootleggers were responsible for the crime, and the goods were already being resold to the community at a higher price.

She hung up the receiver to the candlestick phone and returned to the drawing room, where Teddy rested in an armchair from her latest coughing fit. Perhaps it had been a mistake to keep the farm she had inherited from her mother and ask Teddy to move from Colorado to the damp climate of Kentucky.

"The deputy thinks the liquor was taken for black market sales. Some person or persons waited for Mr. Burgess to come downstairs to open the store, then killed him during the robbery."

Teddy set the Willa Cather book down in her lap and scowled. "That makes no sense. Why would criminals wait until he opened the doors for them, when they could simply smash the door or the glass?"

"Exactly my thinking, but he argued that breaking in would attract a lot of attention."

"And a robbery in broad daylight wouldn't?" Her snort turned into a cough. "It would be smarter to take the liquor and leave the pharmacist alive, so he could order more. Then they could rob him again."

Cornelia frowned. "Not having alcohol is giving you a strange turn of the mind, Teddy."

"Temperance makes me intemperate. Don't worry. When Dr. Wells writes me a new prescription, we can go to Midway."

"That won't be for ten days. It's a major inconvenience to wait for that long and then have to drive to another town."

Teddy smiled and shrugged. "Midway is not nearly as far as Mexico."

"Mexico? How intrepid. When did you go?"

"When I was convalescing in Arizona. I went with a pair of young ladies who were seeking cheap tequila. My job was to handle the guards on the American border in case they had questions about the contents of the trunk. I can look rather responsible when I need to."

"They didn't know you the way I do. We're going to find some bootleggers, dear, and see if we can get you a substitute medication."

Locating a bootlegger wasn't as easy as Cornelia thought it would be. Despite the rumors she had heard overseas about speakeasies and underground bars in every Kentucky town, no one seemed to know where alcoholic refreshment could be purchased. Fisher's Mill was no longer a booming stop for flatboats, and Cole's Bad Tavern was closed.

Finally, she decided to see if old Mrs. Taggart were still alive. Her mother had always said that Mrs. Taggart was the biggest gossip in town. If anyone knew where the bootleggers were, or at least their customers, she would.

Taggart longevity was on Cornelia's side. Edwina Taggart was still alive, and her tongue was still wagging. She was pleased to receive a visit from Dovie Pettijohn's surviving child and invited her inside for coffee. Since she was a world traveler, though, Cornelia was forced to surrender accounts of the customs in France, Germany, and the Philippines, the more scandalous the better. The widow Taggart also assumed that, being retired Army, Cornelia had personal knowledge of every soldier that had ever come out of Fisher's Mill.

Rather than admit her ignorance and disinterest, she diverted the discussion to the peccadilloes of male officers stationed in Paris during the Great War. These delighted Edwina, and made her ill-fitting dentures click with each cackle.

When the time came for *quid pro quo*, Edwina allowed as how young Lester Scroggins, not his father (bless his departed soul), sold moonshine out of his house. Young Scroggins resided in a cabin near the end of Pea Ridge Road.

After promising to use her nurse's eye on one Suzy Jenkins, suspected of carrying an illegitimate child, Cornelia escaped from the Taggart house.

At home, she found Teddy waiting in the drawing room with a smug smile on her face.

"I have a name …" Cornelia began.

"Lester Scroggins?"

Her mouth dropped open. Teddy had only been in town for a month. No one knew her yet. "How did you learn that?"

"While you were gone, I sat in the hallway and listened to the party line. I put the mouthpiece in the desk drawer and coughed into a pillow so they wouldn't hear me. Did you know that I am a suspected blackmailer?"

"What?"

"They're all very curious about the woman you brought home from Colorado. Mrs. Withrow opined that I had some goods on you from the War. Later, Mrs. Taggart came on the line and added some logs to the fire. They think you became a drinker during your time in the Army and my lung ailment is merely a cover story. I have no visible means of support, and they think I'm too lively to be sick." She stretched her legs out on the love seat. "I am a woman of mystery, it seems."

"You had the goods on me the first time we met." Cornelia patted one of Teddy's knees. "Move over."

They prepared for their trip to Pea Ridge. Teddy wanted to drive, but Cornelia quickly argued that she was more familiar with the back roads. Teddy's driving was dreadful, especially when she was sober.

"Then give me your field glasses. I'll watch for armed miscreants lurking in the trees."

"You're overdramatizing. But bring the glasses anyway. You'll need to help look for this cabin. As I recall, the Scroggins place is set back from the road."

Cornelia donned her great coat and the broad-brimmed hat she had worn in the fields of France. She also put on the belt that held her service revolver, given to her by a lieutenant who felt that she needed extra protection. Despite her pooh-poohing of Teddy's imagination, it always paid to be prepared.

The drive wasn't a long one, but it was largely through deep ruts and around hairpin turns. She began to wonder how badly Teddy needed this alcohol.

Almost as if she'd read her mind, Teddy broke into a fit of coughing that left her brow damp with perspiration and her face drained of color. Cornelia leaned over to ask if she were all right, but Teddy was lifting one shaky arm.

"Is that di ..." she stopped to gasp, "dilapidated shack the Scroggins homestead?" The pale arm dropped into her lap, and she leaned back against the seat.

Cornelia examined the frame house up the hill, grayed by the elements and half-hidden behind leafless trees. *Too poor to paint, too vain to whitewash.* "Rustic cabin, dear," she corrected. "It's not polite to say that the neighbors live in a shack."

"I'll call it a palace if it'll help things along," Teddy replied, as they pulled into a dirt driveway covered with fallen leaves.

"Do you want to wait in the car?"

Teddy straightened up immediately. "No, I want to see if his still is any better than the one in the Officers' Club."

"He probably has it hidden in the hills or down by the creek somewhere. It's expensive to have the revenuers bust it up."

She murmured her disappointment but climbed out of the car anyway.

Lester Scroggins was a skinny man with long legs. At least two days' worth of stubble spread across his chin. Mrs. Taggart's description of him as 'young' must have been based on her own perspective, since the stubble was sprinkled with gray.

Cornelia introduced herself as Dovie Pettijohn's daughter and Scroggins offered his condolences. "She was a fine woman. I done a few odd jobs for her over the years. Are you going to take over the farm, or are you plannin' to sell?"

"I haven't decided yet."

Teddy coughed behind her, and Lester's dark eyes shifted focus.

"Your friend ain't got consumption, does she?"

Cornelia had to remind herself of the number of tuberculosis hospitals in nearby Lexington before replying. "No, when we were stationed in France, she was caught in a gas attack. She's lucky she didn't lose her eyesight."

Lester rubbed his bristly chin. "Well, then … are them French people as rude as I've heard?"

The two women began to laugh. "Not when you get to know them. At least, not all of them," Cornelia said.

The conversation went more fluidly after that. Normally, Mr. Scroggins charged five dollars for a quart of product, but news of the Burgess murder had brought a number of his customers looking for another source of medication.

"I'm sorry, ma'am, but I'm plumb out at the moment. If the weather holds, I should have more in a couple of days. Another cold spell, and it might be next week. Slows down the working of the mash."

"I'm sure you're doing the best you can. One can't really plan on the weather in Kentucky. Tell me, have you heard anything about the stolen whiskey?"

"No ma'am, and I think that deputy's on the wrong track. If a bootlegger had took it, I'da heard about it. The bootleggers around here are a sight more honest than Old Man Burgess."

"You don't say," Cornelia replied. "Was he watering the whiskey?"

Lester Scroggins snorted. "Everybody does that. 'Ceptin' me, of course. The way I hear it, he was spending a lot more money than he was making. More than his pa ever did, anyway. Kinda peculiar, since the town's getting smaller."

Rain was sprinkling the dried leaves on the ground when they left Scroggins' cabin. Teddy wheezed all the way back to the house. A cup of tea and honey eased her congestion for a while, but the cough returned. Cornelia knew intellectually that she had done everything possible, but it didn't stop her from feeling as if she'd failed.

When the hacking from the mound of pillows woke her for the third time that night, Cornelia sat up and lit the lamp.

"I'm sorry," Teddy sniffled. "I can go sleep in the lounge chair. It's more elevated, and I might cough less there."

"That won't solve the problem," said Cornelia wearily, as she stepped into her slippers and began hunting for her clothes.

"What are you doing?"

"I'm going to go to Burgess' place and find your prescription. He didn't fill it, so he didn't stamp it cancelled. When the pharmacy in Midway opens, we're going to be there at the door to get your medicine."

Her companion blinked bleary eyes. "But it's two in the morning. The police probably have it locked up tight."

"If I have to, I'll chain the door to the car and pull it off."

Teddy insisted on going with Cornelia. After all, she explained, she wasn't getting any sleep anyway. They bundled up in dark clothing—blue serge in Cornelia's case—and headed for the car. The autumn night was made even colder by the drizzle.

The Dodge's motor started with a loud roar, and Teddy pulled her cloche hat further down over her curls. "Maybe we should park the car somewhere on the side of the road and walk up the hill to the store."

"Your cough will be louder than the engine if you climb that hill. Besides, the side of the road is the ditch. I'm going to park the car behind the store."

"Won't people hear us?"

"The person most likely to hear us is dead."

"You should cut the lights and the engine when we get up the hill. We can coast the rest of the way."

Since they were nearly up the hill in question, Cornelia decided it wasn't worth arguing further. She shut off the engine and steered the rolling metal frame behind Burgess' store. They came to a stop near two other cars in the gravel lot, presumably Burgess'.

"Ooh, a new Franklin Sedan *and* a Ford Runabout," Teddy whispered. "Very impressive."

"Mr. Scroggins may be on to something." Cornelia set the brake and opened her door.

Teddy climbed out the other side with her cane. "We'd best leave the car doors ajar, since we're being quiet."

"Yes, dear." The gravel was broken up with mud-filled ruts. She was glad they'd worn their army boots.

Burgess had lived above his store, and the door to his rooms was up a set of wooden stairs. Cornelia took Teddy's elbow and steered her towards them.

The slightly built woman eyed the steps with trepidation. "Shouldn't we go around to the pharmacy entrance?"

"The pharmacy has thicker doors and better locks. No one wants to break into his house. It'll be easier to get in this way."

Teddy took a deep breath and gripped the railing. "Don't expect speed."

By the time Teddy reached the top landing, Cornelia was puzzling over the door. "This lock has been forced."

"Maybe someone else—needed their prescription," Teddy puffed. "Go on—I'm right behind you."

They switched on their flashlights and swept them across the room before they entered. The thin beams picked out overturned mahogany tables and thick velvet cushions pulled from a couch.

Cornelia switched hands and drew her gun. She motioned for Teddy to get behind her. They crept further into the apartment, listening for sounds of movement.

After advancing crablike down the hallway, they found an office. Nearby, stairs led downward. The office had been as haphazardly searched as the living room. Desk drawers and their contents were strewn across the hardwood floor. Books had been pulled from the shelves.

The ladies glanced at one another. Cornelia indicated the stairs with a jerk of the head. Teddy yanked her hat off and pressed it over her mouth to muffle a cough.

"Why don't you wait in the car?" Cornelia whispered.

"Don't worry about me." Teddy jammed the hat back over her curls and brandished her cane. "I'm ready." She looked as fierce as an offended kitten.

Cornelia sighed and began creeping down the stairs. She hoped they didn't squeak, since the intruder could still be there. When she reached the door at the bottom, she slowly turned the knob and eased it open.

The sound of a screwdriver slipping, followed by cursing, greeted them as they entered the store. Light from the streetlamp cast in shadows the opened door to the pharmacy and a figure within.

The women shut off their torches and moved closer, shielding themselves with store shelves in case they were spotted. Their efforts to be quiet hardly mattered. The burglar was so intent on prying open Burgess' desk that a company could have marched through and he wouldn't have noticed it. He was young enough to still have a little blond in his hair, and certainly no professional.

Cornelia stepped into the doorway of the pharmacy and raised her weapon. "Young man!" she barked.

The burglar yelped and dropped his instrument. He drew himself up and faced the women. His eyes were focused on the gun.

"Put your hands on the counter and keep them there. Move them, and I'll shoot."

"This isn't what it looks like," the burglar said.

Now that he was facing her, Cornelia estimated his age as somewhere in the late twenties. "What are you looking for?"

"A—a prescription." His eyes cut to the nearby window where customers were served. He stepped back, though, when Teddy's face popped up on the other side.

"Nonsense," Teddy said. "Everybody knows Mr. Burgess keeps—kept—prescriptions in the box under the counter." She tapped the wood. "You trashed the entire upstairs."

"What are you ladies doing here?" the burglar blurted.

"We're apprehending a burglar," the curly-haired woman chirped in response. "Dear, you ought to call the sheriff."

Cornelia took a stride towards the phone. "Stealing from a dead man's family is shameful. I should call the Sheriff's Department and have them come down."

"Wait!"

60

"Why should she?" Teddy said. "Are you going to tell us the truth?"

"I truly am looking for a prescription. It's just not a new one. Mr. Burgess was a crook. He's been blackmailing my family."

Cornelia sighed again. "Why don't you sit down in that chair and explain?"

"You won't call the police?"

"I can't promise that. Did you kill Mr. Burgess?"

The young man crossed the room to the desk and sat down. "No," he said miserably. "Father did. But it's my fault."

Cornelia relaxed slightly but kept her gun hand leveled. "Go on."

"When I returned from the War, I was ill. Dr. Wells took over my treatment, but I have … problems that require special prescriptions. He ordered those through Mr. Burgess."

"What course of treatment?"

The young man flushed deeply and stared at his shoes. "Injections of silver-salvarsan."

"Oh." Salvarsan was the most effective treatment available for syphilis. No wonder he was blushing. It was regrettable and embarrassing, but surely not something the man's father would kill over.

Teddy, sitting on the counter now and rooting through the prescription box, asked the question for her. "Mr. Burgess found out you had syphilis and put the squeeze on you." At his opened mouth, she added, "We're Army nurses, dear. We've heard worse. But why would your father allow himself to be blackmailed over your youthful indiscretion?"

Cornelia and the young man clenched their teeth simultaneously.

Their prisoner shook his fair-haired head. "My father is the Reverend Anthony Newsome."

"Tony Newsome became a preacher?" Now Cornelia stared. "My, things have changed in my absence. His own youthful indiscretions could fill a book."

"*My* father? He's never set a foot wrong in his life."

"I would think killing Mr. Burgess counts," Teddy said. "Even if he was a dirty blackmailer."

"He didn't mean to kill him," young Newsome said. "Burgess had bled us dry and wanted Father to dip into the church building fund. Father wouldn't do that, even for me. He went early, before the store properly opened, to tell him that he wouldn't pay. They got into a

61

shoving match, and Mr. Burgess' head hit the corner of the desk. Father panicked and fled."

"What about the whiskey?" Teddy demanded. "A man that panics isn't going to think about grabbing a couple of cases."

"No," he said, "I came back and did that to make it look like someone was after the liquor. I didn't want my father to go to prison."

"Of course you didn't, silly me." She pulled a slip out of the box with a crow of triumph. "Why did you come back tonight, Mr. Newsome? The blackmailer is dead, after all."

"I wanted to get my old prescriptions back. The store was about to open, and I didn't have time to hunt for them. Junior Burgess is going to be here tomorrow from pharmacy school, and he's as sleazy as his old man."

"It's time to call the police and make a clean breast of this," Cornelia said. "You can't be Burgess' only victim. A preacher doesn't make enough to pay for that fancy sedan behind the store. Besides, no matter how sleazy Junior Burgess is, he can't blackmail you if you have nothing to hide."

"He might view it as a cautionary lesson about blackmailing," Teddy added. She pulled out her hatpin and approached the desk. "I used to relieve Captain Peterson of his Scotch this way. There should be a little latch way back" —the drawer popped open— "there."

The open drawer contained a ledger and a bundle of cancelled prescriptions.

Cornelia gave the young man a final cursory look. "Why don't we leave these with you? Tell your father that Cornelia Pettijohn said he had twenty-four hours to clean up after himself, or I'll do the same thing I did when I caught him stealing chickens from my mother's henhouse."

"My father was a chicken thief?"

"Not in the end. It was his first attempt—and last. Perhaps I helped him on his path to God."

En route to Midway later that morning, they passed the Reverend Newsome's house. A Sheriff's Department car was parked in the driveway.

"It looks like the good preacher took your words to heart," Teddy said. "What exactly did you do to him?"

Cornelia smiled smugly. "That's between the good preacher and me."

Teddy *hmphed* and returned her eyes to the road. "I think we might want to give Midway all our business in the future. Junior Burgess sounds like a perfect rotter."

"I doubt he'll reopen the store here when he graduates. That was a thick ledger."

Teddy looked at the road again. After a moment, she said, "Sleeping sickness."

"What?"

"He should have said his son had sleeping sickness. That's the other use for salvarsan."

"Maybe you could be a blackmailer after all."

"Hah! I know who did the real blackmail job today."

They both laughed as they made the turn leading into Midway.

HEAVEN HILL DISTILLERY
BY ELAINE MUNSCH

The repeal of Prohibition on December 5, 1933 opened the door for many opportunities in the field of liquid libation of the 'proof' variety.

In 1935, nine men, including the five Shapira brothers, pooled their resources to build a modern distillery on a site located south of Bardstown, Kentucky. This land was the home of the Heavenhills, one of the first families to settle in the wilderness known then as *Kaintuck*. William Heavenhill was purportedly the first white child born to the settlers of this territory. As an adult, he was primarily a maker of fine spirits. He and his father ran the business for many years, supplying Talbott Tavern, the oldest western stagecoach stop, with whiskey in the early 1800s.

This group of investors not only built a new distillery on the old site, but also planned to name it after the spring once used by the Heavenhill family. However, the story is told that a secretary typing out the permit application accidentally put a space between 'Heaven' and 'Hill'. A correction meant filing again for the distilling permit and that would have been expensive, so the space remained. Folklore also suggests that the descendants of William Heavenhill, having now forsaken strong drink, were not happy to have the family name connected to bourbon whiskey. The space between the words Heaven and Hill seemed to fix that. And the Old Heaven Hill Springs Distillery was formed. In 1946, the company name was changed to Heaven Hill Distillery.

The investors hired a master distiller by the name of Joseph L. Beam to oversee the distilling. He was a brother to Jim Beam, also a distiller, and a descendant of Jacob Beam, an early distiller of whiskey in Kentucky. Today, a sixth and seventh generation Beam work as co-master distillers at Heaven Hill.

On Friday, December 13, 1935, one year after opening, the company produced eighteen barrels. By 1949, that figure was a quarter of a million barrels; eighty years after the first barrel was produced, seven million barrels have been filled. Heaven Hill warehouses hold the second largest amount of aging Kentucky Bourbon in the world.

As the company grew, so did its needs. By 1949, there were a total of eleven warehouses. Production continued to expand. In 1999, Heaven Hill purchased Bernheim Distillery in Louisville to replace the still house and bottling facility lost in a fire in 1996 at the Bardstown facility.

The colorful history of Kentucky bourbon is celebrated by Heaven Hill Distillery. Initially, the brands being bottled were called Bourbon Falls and Old Heaven Hill. Today, many of its brands commemorate the various personages connected to the inception and improvement of Kentucky's premier liquid, including:

- *Evan Williams*: Kentucky's first distiller (1783). During the Christmas season, an Evan Williams Holiday Egg Nog is available to add to the celebrations.
- *Elijah Craig*: the man who first charred barrels, resulting in the amber color of bourbon.
- *Henry McKenna*: an Irishman who brought the family recipe from the Auld Sod and settled in Fairfield, Kentucky, seventeen miles north of Bardstown.
- *Old Fitzgerald*: originally bottled by John E. Fitzgerald, who sold it exclusively to private clubs, rail and steamship lines.

During the last thirty years, Heaven Hill Distillery has expanded by acquiring foreign whiskey from Scotland and Ireland. Distributorships of other types of liqueur, such as brandy, gin, cognac and rum, round out their selections for customers.

The Evan Williams Bourbon Experience was opened in 2013 on Whiskey Row in downtown Louisville. Here, the visitor can take a trip through the history of bourbon and taste-test several brands. Both sites are stops on the Kentucky Bourbon Trail.

Through the years, several investors sold their shares to the Shapira brothers. By 1972, they had acquired all the shares, effectively making Heaven Hill a family-owned and operated business.

George Shapira, the last of the founding brothers, passed away in 1996. Since then, a second, and now a third generation of Shapiras has joined the business. Heaven Hill continues to be the longest running family-owned distillery in the country.

Capitalizing on increasing tourist interest in all things bourbon, Heaven Hill constructed a bourbon heritage center on its grounds in Nelson County, Kentucky, in 2004. The barrel-shaped center houses a gift shop filled with many bourbon-related products.

Both the bourbon heritage center and The Evan Williams Experience are stops on the Kentucky Bourbon Trail.

ALL BUNGED UP
BY MIKE BRADFORD

With bourbon on their mind, the crowd, seventeen in all, milled about in the Visitor Center at the Old Frankfort Distillery, waiting for the afternoon tour. Docent Will Stephenson, who would be their tour guide, slipped on his uniform jacket, and stuffed a couple of well-chewed bungs into his pocket. "October 13, 2005, another show time," he muttered.

The curious came day after day from all over the globe to settle their itch to learn how the famous concoction was made—bourbon, hallmark of Kentucky—the devil's brew—Jim Barleycorn. They came to learn the truth, and to enjoy that complimentary tasting at the end of tour. This bunch today was pretty much like the many before—except for one, and that one makes this story worth telling.

Will Stephenson stepped from the storeroom into the display area. "Gather close, folks. My name is Will, and I will take you through today. Stay close. Listen close. Don't hesitate to ask questions. We'll go to the barrelhouse first."

Will walked through the door into a crisp October afternoon, took about fifteen steps, and waited for the group to gather.

A dog, Jack Russell Terrier by breed, pranced beside him, barking and spinning in eager circles. Driven by his own enthusiasm, the dog could barely wait for the action to start.

"What's with the dog?" one asked.

"That's Bung. Watch this!" Will Stephenson removed a wooden disk from his pocket and tossed it off toward the barrelhouse.

Bung pursued the flying chunk with a furious display of growls and blurred fur. He caught the thing in mid-air and pranced happily back.

The crowd laughed, cheered, and called for more.

"One more time," said Will Stephenson. He flung the disk hard across the pavement, with Bung in hot pursuit.

The little dog's energy loosened up the members of the tour group, preparing them to hear the rest of the story. "Bung is an official member of our staff. He adopted us; showed up one day and just stayed. One of the guys dropped a bag of bungs, and the dog went wild chasing them down. We named him Bung, and he's been entertaining the tours ever since."

"What's that bung thing?"

"Come on to the Barrelhouse. I'll show you."

Once inside the building, Will Stephenson pointed out the use of the bung. "There are about three thousand barrels of bourbon in this building. Each contained fifty-three gallons when first stored. The barrels lose about five percent of their volume each year. They are tracked for age and sampled from time to time to determine which blend the bourbon is best suited for. The bung is the stopper in the side of each barrel. It's where they are filled and emptied. Look down one of the rows of barrels. We store them on their sides, and you will notice a round plug on the up side of each barrel. That's the bung. The barrels are made of white oak. The bungs are yellow poplar. The poplar expands more than the oak. That keeps the bung in place."

"How do you get all the bungs on top?"

"It's part of the art. The barrel handlers can count the number in the rack, eyeball each barrel as it's loaded, and, if properly turned, the barrel will roll into place and stop with the bung side up."

"So," asked a tour member, "Is that were the term all bunged up comes from?"

"That, I don't know," said Will Stephenson. "I'm asked that several times each week. If you ever find out, let me know."

The crowd laughed, listened to the rest of the barrelhouse spiel, and followed Will Stephenson through the remainder of the one-hour tour.

Bung followed happily along, listening to the strange grunts made by the humans. He felt sure these sounds were attempts to communicate. Occasionally one would make a familiar mouth sound or call his name. Other than that, the whole process was one more round of idle human grunting.

As they approached the Visitor Center, Will Stephenson stopped the group again, "People, if you will look to the far end of the area, you will see something that is one of a kind in the world. That small building at the end is the only barrelhouse in the world government certified and licensed to contain only one barrel of whiskey. We put our one-millionth barrel in there for display, and then our second millionth barrel. At the turn of the century, someone had a big idea. At the end of the production day on December 31, 1999, they drew off a barrel of whiskey and stored it in that warehouse. That barrel down there is the last barrel of whiskey in the world made in the last century, and the last millennium. We're going to age it for seven years. Then we'll bottle it and sell the bottles at auction."

"How much will the bottles be worth?"

"You tell me. What would you give for a bottle of the last whiskey made in the Twentieth Century?"

"Fifty bucks!" someone shouted.

"Make it seventy!" said another.

"I suspect you had better add some zeros to that," replied Will Stephenson. "Let's wait a couple of years. Then we can find out. Should make the news."

Bung caught the excitement of the moment, but the human grunting left him baffled.

The tour ended, and the tourists made their way inside to line up for a taste of quality Kentucky Bourbon—except for one.

Bung followed the lone young man to the single barrel warehouse that contained the last whiskey of a century—of a millennium. As the man gazed at the special barrel, Bung huffed a half-bark to get the man to acknowledge his presence.

"Yeah, little guy, I know you're there. What do you think of this?" Justin Settles studied the sign over the display window: *Internal Revenue Bonded Warehouse No. 43, "V"*. He studied the markings on the end of the barrel and noticed that it was truly stored bung up. He looked at the heavy padlock on the door, then shook the steel bars covering the plate glass window. Something on the floor in the back corner of the small room caught his eye. There, he saw a small foil packet with a logo on the top. "Hmmm," he said. That could be the key—rat bait in the corner of a whisky barn. He made a mental note and walked away.

Bung remained behind. There was something strange about that last grunt the young human had made. The hair on Bung's back stood up—and he didn't know why.

Back in his room at the frat house, Justin Settles thumbed through the Yellow Pages. His slid his finger down a page to the name he looked for—*Able Pest Control, insured, bonded, certified.* A plan cooked in Justin Settles' mind. Before he graduated, he wanted to pull off a stunt that outdid all stunts. He dreamed of a party that would make his name legend at the house for decades to come. He punched a button on his cell phone and waited. "Dude, we got to talk. What? Well yeah, now." He put the phone away. A small smile came to his lips as wheels turned in his mind.

Moments later best friend and compliant sidekick, Barry Archer, flung open Justin's door. "Talk, dude, wha'sup?"

"I toured the distillery today."

"So?"

"Always wanted to. You had that test. I got bored. Want to know what I saw?"

Barry nodded and Justin spun the tale of the Old Frankfort Distillery and the whiskey barrel of the ages in Warehouse 43.

"Now that is way cool. That is going to be one smooth batch of hooch. Wonder what it would take to get a shot?"

"I got a plan, dude."

"No way—what you got?"

"You and me—we going to steal that barrel and throw a house party that will echo in these halls forever."

Barry Archer's jaw dropped as he stared at is friend. "What?" he said.

Wasting no time, Justin Settles laid out his plan.

"This ain't going to work, dude."

"Sure it'll work. Here's what you do. Go over to Able Pest Control and take pictures of their trucks. Be sure to get a sharp picture of the side of one of the trucks. Then go to the Media Lab, doctor the prints, and make a file of the logo that we can take to the graphics department. Pay somebody a few bucks to make stick-on signs to go on a truck. While you work on that, I'm going to make some phone calls."

Barry Archer cast a wary eye at his friend as he lumbered out the door to do as commanded.

Justin Settles found an off-campus payphone and placed a call to Able Pest Control. "Hey—I'm over at Old Frankfort Distillery. We're making some changes in our security routine. What's the next time for your regular visit? Yeah, not a problem." He waited. "Right—OK—got that. Appreciate the help." He smiled. *This plan is a piece of art*, he thought. *And, if something goes wrong, we cut and run—no trail—no clues. If we get caught, we're just a couple of misdirected college kids who got stupid. They'll slap our wrists and turn us lose. Old Man may have to pay a fine.*

Later that evening, Barry Archer came back to Justin's room. "Got pictures. Made logo files, got a frat brother in the graphics shop to cut signs. They look like the ones on the trucks. What's next?"

"Now we wait. Able Pest Control is due at the distillery Wednesday night. Tuesday afternoon, we rent a truck similar to the ones that Able uses. Tuesday night late, maybe after midnight, we drive up to the gate at Old Frankfort, and tell the guard that the regular crew is on vacation, and we had to come a night early to make our schedule work. He waves us through. We go in and steal the thing."

"That's it?"

"There's more. I'm going to buy a small hydraulic jack that we can use to force the doorframe apart. I'll swipe the furniture dolly the janitor keeps in the basement and pick up some steel rebar to use as levers to move the barrel."

Barry said, "Justin, you're all cool with this thing. Got it all figured out."

"There has to be more. What are we leaving out?"

"Uniforms?"

"Damn right! Barry, you go hang around outside Able Pest Control. Check out what their guys wear. We'll have to find something that looks similar. Oh, yeah! On Tuesday we'll have to get some hamburger. They have a little dog that's sort of a mascot. We're gonna have to keep the mutt quiet. Wait! This is real classy booze we're stealing. Let's buy that dog a steak!"

"One more question," Barry said.

"Which is?"

"How much does that barrel weigh?"

"Well hell—I don't know. Wait! I do know. The old guy at the distillery said that the barrels contain fifty-three gallons of whiskey and that they lose about five percent per year to evaporation."

"That's why bourbon barns smell so good!" Barry said.

"Shut-up a minute! Let me think!" Justin tapped out a few strokes on his computer keyboard, gazing intently at the screen. "Here it is! Water weighs 8.345 pounds per gallon, and the barrel's been in there almost six years. Five percent per year is about twenty pounds. Hell, hand me that calculator."

"Three hundred and twenty pounds," Barry said.

"What?"

"Three hundred and twenty pounds. Did it in my head."

"That's just the hooch. What's the barrel weigh?"

"I used to move those half-barrels when I worked for a landscaper—fifty pounds, maybe sixty."

"Then a whole barrel is about a hundred or so, maybe. Barry, we're looking at moving four-hundred and twenty pounds!"

Silence dominated the next several seconds.

Then Barry Archer spoke, "What did Archimedes say?"

"Give me a place to stand," Justin Settles replied.

"And a lever long enough!"

Together they chorused, "And I will move the world!"

The two exuberant young men leaped to their feet, exchanged high-fives, and went out to drink beer while planning the party of the ages.

Tuesday evening a security guard put Bung into the Dry House for the night. Bung was weary from the romp of the day and climbed slowly to the second floor where he would wiggle into a warm nest in one of the piles of distiller's dry feed. The dry feed was what was left after fermentation and distilling. This residue could be sold for feed for hogs and cattle, but Bung didn't know that. He knew that this was a warm place to sleep, and that when an occasional rat came snooping around—he would give that pest the business.

Bung enjoyed sleep that was deep and renewing as the night wore on, then his head popped up. Bung had heard one sound— distant—strange—what? He stood to stretch, yawn, and listen. There! Another sound—softer this time. It was a human sound—maybe a shout. Bung wasted no time. He raced down the stairs and bolted toward his secret escape hole. He bounded across the main yard, growling with every breath. Something was not right, and Bung the Bourbon Dog was hot to do his job.

Bung came to a sudden stop, holding up one front paw in a moment of cautious indecision. A strong scent was in the air—bourbon, raw and acrid—unusual, from Bung's perspective. He had seldom smelled the raw stuff, and there was more. The smell of blood tainted the air. Bourbon and blood—mingling together—this odor triggered instincts new to the little terrier. Hair on his spine stood high. A deep growl rumbled in his chest. Slowly Bung moved forward. He could hear human sounds now, soft and sizzling, full of anger and fear. Bung put a paw on the sidewalk, drawing it back quickly. He had stepped into a rivulet of the aged whiskey, running over the curb and into the nearby storm drain. Bung stepped into the doorway of the little warehouse marked *43-V* He sounded with one sharp, "Yap!" He heard human sounds, angry and ugly. Suddenly Bung flew through the air with pain driving through his ribs. First, he saw white, and then the darkness.

"Damn that dog!" Justin Settles snarled.

"You didn't have to kick him so hard!" Barry Archer replied.

"Hell I didn't. That barking would have brought trouble!"

"Yeah, like we don't have enough trouble, thanks to you and your big plan!"

"Shut up and think! What do we do now, Barry?"

"Justin, let's get in the truck and go—now. The barrel is busted, and I think this guy is dead."

"No, he can't be dead. The barrel didn't hit him that hard."

"He's bleeding, fool! His eyes are wide open, and he ain't moving. Get in the truck."

"You're the fool! You let your lever slip."

"You're the one that shouted when the guy walked in. How did I know the barrel was going to roll and smash him against the wall?"

"Damn dog!"

"Forget the dog. Justin, let's go!"

Bung whimpered as consciousness drove its way into his brain, and he winced from the fire in his side. He was hung in the branches of the hedge near 43-V. Yelping as he twisted himself free, Bung rolled onto his feet and struggled to move against the pain in his right ribs. The night was quiet now. He heard normal noises from the city, and the gentle trickle of bourbon, still flowing from the little warehouse. Cautiously he peered inside, repulsed by the mix of bourbon and blood. There he found a friend—a nice human whom the others called Jack. Motionless he was, this human. Bung nudged his hose against a still hand, sniffing cautiously at the familiar, musty, human smell on his friend's clothes. Bung had never smelled death before—not in a human, but he knew. Rage coursed through him as he howled loud and long. Fighting the pain, Bung began the long run to the guard shack. He yelped with every long stride, a primal growl rumbling deep in his tortured frame. Once at the shack, Bung barked endlessly. The humans had to act, and Bung was prepared to bark forever.

"What's with that dog?" muttered the guard in the shack. He pulled out his walkie-talkie. "Larry, report."
"All clear here. I'm in the east parking area."
"Bung's up here going berserk. You seen anything?"
"That's a negative. I'm coming to your twenty."
"10-4 that. Jack, report."
The silence told the tale. The guard chilled as he waited for an answer, Bung barking furiously. "Jack, I say again, report!"
The guard named Larry lumbered to a breathless halt. "What is it?"
"Jack Peterson didn't report."
"I heard. What you figure?"
They both looked at the insistent Bung.
"Bung," Larry commanded. "Go! Go find Jack!"
Bung turned and ran with all his might, his pain forgotten now. Away they raced—the dog and two frightened guards. Away they raced toward the little, single-barrel warehouse 43-V.

As the light of day spread across The Old Frankfort Distillery, the scene danced under the flashing blue strobes of four city police units, two sheriff's units, and one ominous gray cruiser from the Kentucky Sate Police. The red lights of a single EMS unit flashed next to the warehouse as the coroner pondered his determinations.
"The State Technical Services Division will have a forensics team on the scene shortly," the state trooper said. "In the meantime, keep the two guards out of the way, and do not allow first shift workers through the gate. Find out who's in charge of this operation, and get them on the scene!"

The relentless Bung had been locked up in the guard shack to keep him from being underfoot. He had leaped onto the supervisor's desk, and now raced from window to window, continuing to bark his persistent commands. No one listened. No one seemed to care. Whining, he peered at the frightening array of flashing lights, and strained to hear some familiar words in all the shouted commands. Frustrated, Bung continued has tirade.

The Security Supervisor shouted, "Larry, call the day guys. Tell them to remain on standby until called in."

"Roger that," guard Larry replied.

Now Bung had his chance. Larry opened the guard shack door to use the phone, and Bung was out like a shot. Furiously he raced toward the place where he had found his friend. Halfway across the parking area he came to an abrupt stop. The van that he had seen backed up to the little warehouse was gone, but the scent of the bourbon and blood was in the air, and beneath his feet. Bung put his nose to the ground. Abruptly, he raised his head and sniffed the wind. The tires of the van had rested in the evil mix after the accident in the warehouse. Now Bung found the scent left by the two rear tires as the tainted spot rolled round and round. Bung the Bourbon Dog had the trail and he was off—out past the guard shack, and toward Wilkinson Boulevard at the foot of the hill.

"Somebody get that dog!" a policeman shouted.

"Let him go," another said. "I'm tired of the yapping."

Bung stopped before he reached the busy boulevard. He stared back at the milling humans, wondering why they had so little sense. Could none of them understand what they had to do? He jogged back a few yards, barking loudly.

"What's his name?" a policeman said.

"Bung."

"Here Bung. Come here, boy!" The officer put two fingers to his lips and whistled loudly. "Come on, Bung."

Bung trotted to within ten feet of the calling human and barked one time. The human took a step toward the dog, and Bung scampered away, barking loudly.

Several humans joined in the task, each seeking to show his superior ability at calling dogs. The most frustrated was a K-9 officer who pronounced that the dog was a jughead and had no sense.

Finally, Larry the guard said, "I think that dog's trying to tell you boys something."

An officer shouted, "Belkins, you get in your unit and follow that dog."

"Sergeant!"

"Do it! Son, You're K-9, you got dog patrol!"

Bung watched anxiously as one of the cruisers pulled away from the group and came his way. The officer hung his arm and head out the door and said, "Bung, go boy, go!"

Finally! Human sounds he could understand! Bung put his nose to the ground and darted into the traffic on Wilkinson Boulevard, ignoring blaring horns and screeching tires.

Blue lights flashing, Officer Belkins pulled his cruiser into the flow to protect the scampering dog. Off they went—the speeding dog and the slow-moving K-9 unit.

"Damn," Belkins said to the German shepherd in the back seat. "How am going to explain this to the boys at Central?"

Eventually, Bung slowed, hopping onto a sidewalk on a side street. He was fatigued now, the pain in his side pounded with every heartbeat, and he had a desperate need to pee.

Officer Belkins keyed his mike, "K-unit 6 to Lincoln 12. Sergeant, this dog has stopped to cock his leg. Wait—now he's sniffing in the bushes. Please advise."

"Belkins, you carry a pooper scooper. Take care of it."

"Roger that, K-6 out."

Officer Belkins got out of the car and stepped toward Bung. Now Bung crouched low and waited for the human to pick him up. He yelped as he was lifted. He tried to get comfortable in the human's arms and enjoy his soft sounds and gentle scratching. An instinct nagged at Bung. The strange scents he had found near the bushes called to him. Something wasn't right here. Then it came back—the boot. He had found the scent of the boot that kicked him. That and other strange smells stirred his canine brain. He twisted from the human's grasp, and, landing with a yelp, went bounding into the bushes.

Officer Belkins watched with curiosity, and then followed into the brush-covered area. In moments, he had the squirming Bung back in his arms, and ran back to his unit with eager excitement. "Lincoln 12, Lincoln 12, this is K-6. The dog has found something. You need to get some of the forensic guys over here."

"Say again, K-6. What have you found?"

"Plastic, magnetic signs and coveralls, Sergeant. Both have the logo of Able Pest Control. Isn't that the outfit the guard said came and went last night?"

"Roger that, K-6. Stay at the scene. The TSD people will send someone over there."

"Affirmative, Lincoln 12. Tell them to get a move on. This dog is about to eat me alive. He wants to get back on the trail!"

Bung went berserk when the human tossed him onto the front seat of the car and shut the door. He had understood none of the human sounds and was fed up with the barking German shepherd in the back seat. He leaped onto the top of the seatback and snarled through the steel barrier at the offending dog. The two went at it with unbridled ferocity. Their disagreement was intense, and the cruiser rocked from the action thereof.

"Good grief," said Officer Belkins.

The TSD Unit arrived, strung crime scene tape, and began their exploration of the area. Officer Belkins removed the agitated Bung from his front seat, quieted his own animal, and, releasing the terrier, watched him bound down the street with his nose to the ground.

Belkins followed and Bung did not stop until he came to the parking lot at Enterprise Rent-a-Car. Belkins screeched to a halt, leaving his blue lights flashing. Bung was carefully examining the rear tires of a white Ford Panel-van.

"Problem, officer?" asked the pretty African-American woman who came out of the Enterprise office.

"Don't know, ma'am. What's the story on this white van?"

"Two young men returned it a couple of hours ago. They seemed agitated." She dropped her eyes for a moment, looking up she said, "I put off sending it to clean-up. These guys just took their receipt and ran. I thought it was best to wait."

"Ma'am, I need a copy of that receipt. Don't touch that van. Bung, no!"

Too late—Bung had already expressed his opinion against the side of a tire.

Justin Settles sat on the side of the bed while Barry Archer paced the floor. "You said this would be a breeze, man. Best party this house has ever seen. Man, we blew it! Justin—we got trouble!"

"Cool it, Barry. Calm down. We ditched the signs and jumpsuits. We'll go back and get them tonight, take them to Lexington, and toss them in a dumpster. No problem. I put the moving dolly and rebar in the back of my PT Cruiser. We can put that stuff back where we got it."

"We should have hidden that van for a day or two, and taken more time to wipe it down. Justin, there's fingerprints all over it!"

"We're covered—I wiped it down myself while you put the signs in the bushes. I tell you—we're OK."

"Oh, man—I don't know. We got to wipe down those signs before we toss them. They got prints on them, too."

"You didn't wipe the signs?"

"Well, no, but who's going to find them? You said we can move them tonight."

"Right. Yeah, right. We're okay."

"Justin, we killed a man. You know the law won't let up on that."

"What can I say? His luck ran out. Besides, it was an accident. He did it to himself. I ain't going to lose no sleep."

"I can't get it out of my mind, Justin. I mean, the way he stared wide-eyed with that barrel pinning him against the wall. It was like he was looking right through me. We're gonna get caught. I know it!"

"The guard hardly looked at us at the gate. I used a fake driver's license at the rent-a-car place. The license says my name is Freeman, and that I live in Tennessee. The truck's clean. Tonight, we pick up the signs and uniforms. We can still have the party. We'll just have to buy our own booze."

A loud knock at the dorm door froze both men in place. Then the words came:

"Police! Open up."

Barry Archer opened the door.

"You Barry Archer?" The uniformed Sergeant was tall and swarthy-skinned, with eyes as black as coal.

"Yes. I'm Barry Archer."

The sergeant stepped into the room. "And you are Justin Settles?"

Justin Settles did not rise from the bed. "That's right. What's up?"

"Mr. Settles, Mr. Archer, I have a warrant for your arrest for the murder of Jack Peterson on the morning of Wednesday, 18 October. You have the right …"

"Say, wait a minute!" Justin Settles leaped to his feet. "You got nothing on us!"

"Two signs, son, Able Pest Control. Your prints are all over them. One truck with residue of bourbon and blood on the tires. The blood matches that of Jack Peterson. Underneath the driver's seat of the van, we found a cellophane-wrapped package of sirloin steak. Your prints are also on that package, Mr. Settles. You forgot to put it out for the dog. Oh, and there's this," The sergeant stepped back into the hall. "Belkins, let him go."

A tan and white Jack Russell terrier pranced into the room. He sniffed the shoes of Barry Archer, and then turned to the boots of Justin Settles. The terrier took one step back, sat down, lifted one paw, and said, "Yap."

The sergeant said, "This is Officer Bung. He says you're busted."

Author's note: *This short story is a work of fiction, and the characters portrayed herein do not represent any actual persons living or dead. All place names are used fictionally. However, Internal Revenue Bonded Warehouse No. 43 "V" does exist, and the final barrel of whiskey made in the previous millennium was allowed to age a full twelve years. In June of 2011 the barrel produced 174 bottles of fine bourbon which were each labeled with handwritten, signed, and numbered labels. The Millennium Bourbon bottles were each encased in a specially made individual hardwood showcase box that included a piece of the historic barrel's charred oak stave. Buffalo Trace Distillery gave these bottles to charitable institutions for fundraising purposes. In the final accounting, $152,557.00 was raised for good causes through the auctioning of these special issue bottles of bourbon. Average price per bottle—about eight-hundred and seventy-five bucks.*

Oh, by the way, on April 11, 2018, the iconic Warehouse V next became the aging place for barrel number seven million produced by Buffalo Trace Distillery.

That barrel is still there for the observing—or for the taking.

Bourbon Bread Pudding

Yield: About 12 – 15 servings

Ingredients:

Pudding
3 Tbls. good quality Kentucky bourbon
1 cup raisins
12 country sized biscuits
4 cups milk
6 eggs
2 cups white sugar
2 Tbls. vanilla
2 Tbls. butter
Whipped cream

Bourbon Sauce
½ cup butter
1 cup white sugar
¼ cup water
1 egg
1/3 cup Kentucky Bourbon

Pudding Preparation:

Overnight: Soak 1 cup raisins in 3 Tbls. good quality Kentucky bourbon.
Next day:
Preheat oven to 350º.
Break up 12 country sized biscuits (baked first) into a large bowl.
Soak biscuits in 4 cups milk for 5 minutes.

Beat together:

6 eggs

2 cups white sugar

2 Tbls. vanilla

Add raisins to egg mixture.

Add egg mixture to biscuit mixture.

Melt 2 Tbls. butter and pour in bottom of 9x13 baking dish. Swish around so bottom is coated in butter.

Pour biscuit mixture in baking dish.

Bake on middle rack for about 1 hour in preheated oven until set.

Serve warm liberally slathered with bourbon sauce and maybe a dollop of whip cream, if desired.

Bourbon Sauce Preparation:

Prepare shortly before serving.

In saucepan, melt ½ cup butter.

Add 1 cup white sugar.

Add ¼ cup water.

Stir until well mixed.

Cook over medium heat for 5 minutes, stirring occasionally. Remove from heat to cool slightly.

In a separate bowl, beat one egg.

Whisk egg into warm (*not* hot or egg will curdle) mixture, stirring constantly.

Add 1/3 cup (or a little more, if so inclined) Kentucky Bourbon.

Return to heat to reheat. Serve warm over bourbonized bread pudding.

Recipe courtesy of Kurtz Restaurant, Bardstown, Kentucky

Just Desserts
By Karen Quinn Block

Mavis Hawkins mechanically dropped another peeled potato into the maw of her cast iron vegetable grinder and gave the handle a half dozen sharp cranks. Streams of fresh white potato noodles oozed through the holes of the grinder plate. She curled her nose in distaste at the pile of ground raw potatoes that half filled her enamel turkey roaster. If she had to make another potato and cheese casserole in this lifetime, she would stuff herself in the grinder. It fried her bacon that she was associated with such a mundane dish, while that witch of a first cousin, Clarice Johnson, lorded her prize-winning bourbon bread pudding over the whole community of Buttermilk Falls, Kentucky.

Their grandmother, Ida Snipes, had been famous for that recipe. Family lore said their granddaddy had succumbed to cirrhosis of the liver from tasting her early attempts at perfecting the technique. Mamaw had persevered, though, and the result was a fluffy pudding with the melt-in-your-mouth consistency of heavy whipping cream. Straight from the oven, the finished product was light golden brown in appearance and liberally laced with plump juicy raisins that were subtly flavored with bourbon. Mamaw's pudding was delicious eaten alone, but drizzled with a sauce creamy with eggs and butter and slightly sweetened and tangy with bourbon—well, that was nothing short of heaven on a spoon. A heaven that Mavis couldn't bestow, but Clarice, as sole proprietor of the recipe, could.

Mavis glanced out the kitchen window and watched her husband push shut the barn door and begin the slog through the spring mud towards the house. Raising the window a crack, she hollered, "Don't bring that dirt in my house, Stanley Joe! I just scrubbed the floor." She lost sight of him as he rounded the corner of their home, but heard him turn on the hose outside to sluice the mud off his boots and rinse his hands. When they first married forty years ago, it had taken her a day or two to instill some gentility into him, but her efforts had eventually paid off. As far as she was concerned, even though Stanley Joe was a pig farmer didn't mean he had to look and smell like one.

Mavis heard the screen door slam and the thunk of Stanley Joe's footwear hitting the back wall of the mud room, signaling he had kicked off his boots. He padded into the kitchen in sock feet and kissed her on the cheek. "Whatcha makin'?"

"Potato and cheese casserole for Clarice's new grandson's christening party tomorrow. Clarice, of course, is providing bourbonized bread pudding for dessert."

Stanley Joe rolled his eyes. "For crying out loud, Mavis, give it a rest. If I hear one more time about that dang puddin', I'll drown myself in Clarice's bourbon sauce." He poured himself a cup a coffee from the percolator simmering on the stove and eased into a kitchen chair.

"Well, it's not fair that Clarice can trot out Mamaw's pudding to every family dinner and community function, while I'm forced to slap down potato and cheese casserole." Mavis bit her bottom lip hard to dam the tears welling in the corners of her eyes. "Why can't I share in the glory? I'm sick of always being the goat."

"There ain't a dang thing wrong with your tater 'n' cheese casserole, Mavis. You get as many rave reviews as Clarice does for her puddin'. I, for one would rather eat your casserole over that unholy creation any day." Stanley Joe pulled her down in his lap and nuzzled her neck. "A man can't live by puddin' alone, you know. Once in awhile, he needs honest to goodness, stick-to-your-ribs food."

"I thank you for your loyalty, Stanley Joe Hawkins." Mavis straightened up and brushed back a strand of steel gray hair that had escaped from the tight bun cinched low on her neck. "A woman couldn't ask for a better husband. But when I see how people positively drool over that pudding, I get so ding-dong mad. Just 'taint fair. I've as much right to that recipe as Clarice does." She dabbed at her eyes with the corner of her apron. "If someone could tell me why Mamaw gave that recipe to Clarice's mother and not mine, I'd stop fretting."

"What I don't understand is why you can't figure out the recipe. You're the best cook in the county. You know how it tastes. You could cook up a batch."

She slid off her husband's lap and picked up another potato. "Goodness knows I've tried. I just can't get it right. There must be a secret ingredient or something."

"Well, then, let it go, Mavis. Life is too short to chaw the same bone twice't." Stanley Joe got up to rinse his empty cup. "Hows about you and me takin' in a movie tonight? We could eat at Sally Mae's Café beforehand." His big hands circled her waist and he waltzed her around the kitchen. "Saturday's the meat loaf special."

"I suppose we could, if I get this mess cleared away in time." Mavis flapped her apron at him. "Go on now and get washed up. I'll be done shortly."

Mavis watched her husband climb the stairs. He was a hard-working man and as good looking as the day she'd married him, not like that wimpy Lester who Clarice had married. That man looked like an apple dumpling, no matter that he was a retired banker. Stanley Joe had made a decent husband to her and father to their children too, despite Mamaw and Aunt Sadie's prediction that she'd end up trailer trash for marrying a Hawkins. She'd made sure her family hadn't, if only to prove them wrong. She'd kept them dressed decent, ensured they all went to church each Sunday, and planted red geraniums in the front flowerbeds every summer. She also nagged Stanley Joe into whitewashing the outbuildings every couple of years and keeping the house in good repair. They were now respected members of Buttermilk Falls, and this year Stanley had been elected sergeant-at-arms down at the VFW. But somehow, at least as far as Mavis' extended family was concerned, they were as common as two-penny nails. And to Mavis's mind that was the sole reason she was told to bring potato and cheese casserole to every function while Clarice prepared the glamor dish. Mavis might be nothing but a plain country gal and everything they owned might be second-hand, but she knew disrespect when it smacked her in the face.

Well, one day soon that would all change. She had a plan to get that recipe, and get it she would. When she did, she'd bake up the lightest, most golden batch of bourbon bread pudding ever made. And on that day, she would sashay into Clarice's kitchen, whip the cover off the pudding pan, and make sure everyone knew it was she, Mavis Hawkins, who had made the dessert this time, and not that selfish, nose-in-the-air Clarice Johnson.

Stanley Joe wheeled Mavis' rusting '89 Chevy Impala into a parking space next to Clarice's brand new, UK blue Ford Mustang. Stanley Joe turned to look at his wife. "There's no one else here yet, Mavis. Did you get the time right?"

"I told Clarice we'd come a little early to help set things up, what with all the extra people that'll be here. She said Lester could use a second pair of hands with the picnic tables." Mavis flushed a little. It wasn't her nature to stretch the truth with Stanley Joe, but if her timing was right, Clarice would still be mixing up the pudding. Granmaw's recipe might be lying out on the kitchen counter. All Mavis needed was a quick peek, and Clarice could no longer claim to exclusively own the recipe.

Stanley Joe opened the driver's-side door, slid out of the car, walked around to the back of the vehicle, and unlocked the trunk. He lifted a foil casserole pan out of the brown cardboard beer carton that had kept it from sliding about and set the pan on the hood. "You go on and take this one into the kitchen. I'll bring the other two inside in a minute." He flashed a warning look at her. "And for the love of Mike, don't get all riled up at Clarice over that damn pudding. There's a reason why th'all ask you to bring three pans of taters 'n' cheese and Clarice only makes one pudding, you know. Why you can't see she is yanking your chain is beyond me. Clarice is the one who should be jealous of you."

"There's no reason to come all sweet on me, Stanley Joe." Mavis looked straight into her husband's eyes. "Don't think I haven't got Clarice's number. I know exactly what she's up to."

Mavis pushed the handles of her purse over her left forearm and lifted the casserole using the new potholders she had picked up at the Dollar Store earlier in the week. Keeping potholders stain free was a task unto itself. She had dozens of them, but bought a new pair every month or so. There was no way she was walking into Clarice's home with anything that wasn't completely spotless or perfect.

Clarice tapped the bottom of the wooden screen door with the toe of her shoe. "Yoo hoo! Clarice! We're here. Could you open the door, please? My hands are all tied up."

Clarice unlatched the hook and pushed open the door. "You and Stanley are the first ones here, Mavis. I'm still making Mamaw's pudding. Why so early?"

Mavis stepped over the threshold and into the entry hall. "Well, what with all the extra people for the christening, I thought Lester could use a hand with the picnic tables. Figured you might need help getting supper on the table, too."

"I do appreciate the offer, Mavis, but you know how I feel about strangers in my kitchen when I'm cooking." Clarice dried her hands on her apron. "Here, let me take that pan. I'll put it in the warming oven. You go on into the living room and set. I won't be but a few more minutes."

"I'd hardly call me a stranger, Clarice. We are family after all." Mavis handed the foil pan to Clarice and followed her into the kitchen. The pudding ingredients were spread out on the counter. A gray tin box with a faded rooster decal on its front side and its top flipped wide open sat beside an open bottle of bourbon. Mavis stood on her tiptoes to see over Clarice's shoulder. The box was stuffed with old letters, newspaper clippings, and loose recipe cards. *Bingo!* That must be where Clarice kept Mamaw's recipe. Her eyes quickly scanned the countertop for the yellowed slip of paper on which their grandmother had written the recipe seventy years ago.

Clarice suddenly stopped dead in her tracks. Whirling around, she shoved the pan back into Mavis' midsection, knocking her back on her heels. "I know what you're up to, Mavis Hawkins," she hissed through clenched teeth. "You thought by pushing your way into my kitchen you could steal my recipe. Well, I'm on to you. Mamaw gave that recipe to my mother, not yours. The recipe is mine and nobody else's."

Mavis' hands automatically closed on the sides of the pan. Her voice was tight with anger. "I do believe, Clarice Johnson, you are the most selfish woman the good Lord ever put legs on. Why you will not share our grandmother's recipe with me, your own first cousin, chaps my bloomers. When Mamaw gave that recipe to Aunt Sadie, she did not intend for your side of the family to hog the recipe from now to kingdom come."

Clarice sucked in an audible breath and thrust out her jaw. "The day you get Granmaw's recipe is the day you pry it from my cold, dead hand. It's mine and I'm not sharing."

"Well, we'll see about that." Mavis pulled her lips into a tight line and looked down her nose at her sworn enemy. "One day I'll have that recipe and I'll make double-dawg sure to share it with everyone in town just to spite you. You'll need to find another specialty to cook up, since the rest of us will be enjoying bourbonized bread pudding whenever we want to." Mavis dropped the casserole on the kitchen table with a loud thud. "And now, if you will excuse me, Mrs. Johnson, I'll go on out and see if the men need help, since you don't want any."

Mavis sat at her kitchen table nursing a cup of cold coffee. Every day since the christening party, she'd worked on her plan to get back into Clarice's kitchen. She knew where Clarice kept the recipe now and that cheap tin box would be easy to open, even if she had to jimmy the lock. After that scene last Sunday though, there was no way she was going to get anywhere near Clarice's kitchen any time soon. In fact, chances were good she'd never be invited to Clarice's home again. And if that happened, there went her chance to possess the recipe. There had to be some way to get inside Clarice's house without her knowing. Of course, that meant she would have to copy the recipe instead of having the original, but so what? A recipe was a recipe regardless of whose handwriting it was in.

Mavis jumped as the phone rang shrilly. She'd been concentrating so hard that it took a moment to realize where the noise was coming from. She picked up the receiver.

"Oh, hello, Lester. No, Stanley Joe's not here. He ran into town for some chicken feed. Do you want him to call you back?"

Lester was whispering. Mavis strained her ears to hear what he was saying.

"No, it's okay. I won't be home. But you can give him a message for me, if you don't mind."

"Sure. What's up?"

"Well, I'm in kind of a bind. Clarice and I need to be at the Optimists' luncheon around eleven this morning. We're going to be tied up there until at least four o'clock. Don't know whether Clarice told you, but our sump pump's been acting up. Keeps blowing the circuit breaker." Lester's voice dropped even lower. "Do you think Stanley could come by around two o'clock and make sure the basement's not flooding? Would sure appreciate it."

"I know he'd be glad to," Mavis said. "I'll tell him when he gets home to go on over to your place." The hand holding the telephone receiver began to shake with excitement. She forced herself to keep her voice normal. "But how will he get in the house?"

"I'll hang a key to the back door out in my workshop just inside the door. But don't tell Clarice. My life won't be worth a plugged nickel if she thinks someone's been in the house when we're not home. Tell

Stanley to park in the back so the neighbors won't see his truck from the street. Clarice has the whole street on the look-out for her."

"Don't worry about a thing. Mum's the word." Mavis' heart gave a little skip. "'Bye now. Have fun."

Mavis replaced the receiver and collapsed in her chair. The opportunity to get into Clarice's house had fallen into her lap. Finally, Mamaw's recipe was within reach. All she had to do was run over to Clarice's house around 11:30. It would only take a minute to find Clarice's recipe box—why, she could visualize the shelf it sat on. She'd copy the recipe and be back busy in her own kitchen before Stanley Joe unloaded the feed. She'd pass on Lester's message, and Stanley Joe would go over to check for water. No one would know she'd been there. A sweet sensation of victory flowed through her.

At precisely 11:30, Mavis pulled the Impala into Clarice's driveway. Clarice's Mustang was gone. Swinging her car around the back corner of the house, she pulled onto the parking pad next to Lester's camper. She picked her purse off the passenger seat, slid out of her car, and quietly clicked the door closed. Even as excited as she was, she'd remembered Lester's warning about alerting Clarice's nosy neighbors. She trotted back to Lester's work shed and opened the door. A house key hung on a nail pounded into the door frame. Mavis stared at it. She couldn't believe breaking into Clarice's house was going to be this easy.

Returning to the house, Mavis inserted the key into the deadbolt, turned it, and pushed open the door. She stepped over the threshold. She was in Clarice's kitchen. Alone. She realized she had been holding her breath and let it go with a huge whoosh. She did a quick survey so she would remember how things looked when she got here. With the kitchen curtains pulled closed, the interior of the kitchen was dim and cool, but she could see that nothing was out-of-place. The door to the basement was open and an oval hand-braided rag rug stretched across its doorway. She could hear the sump pump working.

Mavis opened her purse and pulled out the notebook and pen she'd brought from home and placed them on the kitchen table. She then walked over to the shelf next to the oven. The grey tin box was there, as she had seen it countless times before. She lifted it down, carried it to the table and set it next to her writing materials. She depressed the lock. The hinged lid flipped up. Staring her straight in the eye was her grandmother's recipe. She lifted it with reverent slowness and laid it next to her purse. She closed the box and set it in the center of the table. Pulling out a kitchen chair, she sat down and opened her notebook.

She wrote 'Ida Lou Snipes' Bourbanized Bread Pudding' at the top of a fresh page. She laid down her pen, picked up the recipe again, and squinted her eyes at the faded blue ink. *Drat!* The recipe was not written traditionally with the ingredients listed at the top. Instead, the directions and ingredients were written as a procedure. She couldn't simply scan the recipe for the secret ingredient. She would need to record the entire recipe, as written.

She picked up her pen and wrote: *Soak one cup Sultana raisins overnight in three tablespoons of good quality Kentucky bourbon. In a large mixing bowl, break twelve country-style biscuits into small pieces. Soak biscuits for five minutes in one quart of whole sweet milk. Beat the following ingredients together and add to…*

"What are you doing in my kitchen?"

Mavis' head snapped up. *Clarice!* What was she doing home? And how had she got through the front door without being heard?

Mavis dropped her pen and leapt to her feet. "I thought you were at the Optimists' luncheon?"

"I was. I forgot my Jell-O salad." Clarice flicked on the kitchen light and advanced towards the table. The skinny heels of her open-back silver sandals made a sharp clicking noise on the hardwood floor. "I've already asked you once what you're doing in my house. You tell me right now or I'm calling the police."

Mavis grasped the back of the chair and tried to look innocent. "Lester asked me to check the sump pump downstairs. It's fine. I was just leaving."

"I don't believe you. I think you broke into my home to get your nasty hands on Mamaw's recipe." Clarice saw the grey tin box on the table and beside it, the ancient sepia-toned paper covered in her grandmother's spidery handwriting. She snatched up the recipe and waved it in the air in front of Mavis' nose.

"You *are* copying Mamaw's recipe. How dare you!"

"How dare I? How dare *you* keep that recipe to yourself all these years!" Mavis shouted back. "I have as much right to it as you do."

Mavis made a grab for the recipe. Clarice lurched backwards to evade Mavis' swinging hand.

"Right! You have no rights. Possession is nine tenths of the law, and I have possession. Your mother might have been dumb enough to lend the recipe to mine after Mamaw died, but I won't make that same mistake with you."

"What! Mamaw gave that recipe to *my* mother and not yours? Why you conniving ... no good ... low down ... spiteful ..."

Mavis launched herself at Clarice again and again. Each time she narrowly missed snatching the paper from her cousin's hand. Panting hard, Mavis pressed her attack. With each leap Clarice took a step backward, inching ever closer toward the open basement door. Her foot met the floor mat in the doorway. The heel of her sandal tangled in the loose fabric. Her ankle turned and she stumbled. Her arms flailed the air as she struggled to maintain her balance. With a piercing scream, she tumbled down the basement stairs. Her body landed with a dull thud on the concrete floor thirteen steps below the kitchen.

"Oh, my goodness." Mavis clattered down the stairs and knelt at her cousin's side. "Clarice! Clarice! Are you all right?" Clarice's head was cocked at a weird angle. She didn't seem to be breathing. It took only a few seconds for Mavis to realize her cousin was dead, the recipe still clutched in her hand.

Leaning back on her heels, Mavis assessed the situation. No two ways about it, Clarice was now deceased. And there was nothing Mavis herself could do to bring the dead back to life. Even calling 911 wouldn't change anything. And it wouldn't be like her arch enemy would lie decomposing for weeks at the bottom of the steps. When Clarice didn't return to the luncheon, Lester would come looking for her. He'd discover her body at the bottom of the stairs and assume she had accidentally tripped on the mat and fallen to her death. And that, if anyone who witnessed her fall besides Mavis could testify, was actually—sort of—what had happened. They'd all be sad for awhile, but life would go on.

However, if the police found Mavis at the scene, she would be implicated in Clarice's death. She hadn't pushed Clarice down the stairs, but if the authorities suspected she'd been in the house at that exact moment, they would think the worst. The good news was only Clarice knew she'd been there. Therefore, if she merely collected her stuff and quietly left the house, no one would ever know how Clarice had really died.

But first, she would get her grandmother's recipe. It belonged to her anyway. Clarice had admitted her mother had stolen it from Mavis'. Fair was fair, and obviously, Clarice wouldn't need the recipe again.

Mavis gently pried Clarice's cooling dead fingers from the paper. It was a little crumpled, but she smoothed the creases before folding the recipe in half and sliding it into the front pocket of her jeans. She placed Clarice's hand back in its original place beside her body and slowly climbed the stairs to the kitchen.

Methodically, Mavis returned the room to its original state. She picked up the grey tin box and replaced it in its customary spot on the shelf, pushed in the chair, and straightened the tablecloth. She pulled the recipe from her pocket and stuffed it and the writing tablet and pen in her purse and closed the back door behind her. She pulled the key from the deadbolt and rehung it on the nail in Lester's shed. Then, getting into her car, Mavis pulled out onto the narrow, twisting county road that would take her undetected, far out into the country, back to the farm.

Mavis gripped the steering wheel and willed herself to pay attention to her driving, but her mind whirled with possibilities. With Clarice gone and the recipe nowhere to be found, she'd have to pretend to work on replicating Mamaw's recipe. After a couple of almost-got-it right attempts, she would unveil the real thing. The town would hail her as a hero. All the glory Clarice had reveled in for years would now be hers.

She wouldn't let fame change her though. She'd be the same humble Mavis Hawkins, even if the Buttermilk Falls Gazette featured an article about her cooking skills. Mavis' breath caught in her throat. *Holy hopping toads!* This could be her big break. Maybe some big New York publisher would ask her to do a cookbook. Good heavens, she might end up being famous.

She pictured herself in a New York high rise, evaluating her best recipes with a food editor. For sure there would be a place for her potato and cheese casserole in the section on plain family cooking. And to prove she was willing to let bygones be bygones, she'd include a couple of Clarice's specialties as well—like that cherry Jell-O mold Clarice was so proud of, or that nice jalapeno corn pudding she served at Thanksgiving. Better yet, she'd dedicate her cookbook in memory of Clarice. Everyone would say how magnanimous Mavis was. To tell the truth though, sprinkling sugar on Clarice wouldn't be painful at all, now that that low-down dog had finally got her just desserts.

Mavis momentarily shifted her eyes from the road to look at her purse sitting on the passenger seat. The recipe inside seemed to call her with a siren's song. The impulse to discover the secret ingredient was overpowering. She absolutely, positively could not wait until she got home.

Removing her right hand from the steering wheel, Mavis dug in her pocketbook fishing for the thin paper. All she could feel was the notebook. She grabbed the bottom corner of her purse and dumped its contents onto the passenger seat. The recipe fluttered to the floor. Mavis clicked her tongue. Would nothing go right this day? She glanced down, gauging whether she could reach the paper.

She quickly checked the road to make sure there were no oncoming cars. Nothing was visible and the road was straight for about another hundred feet. Keeping her left hand steady on the wheel, she dropped her right shoulder and leaned sideways. Her eyes barely cleared the dash. She felt around on the floorboard but felt nothing except the rubber mud mat. She stretched as far as she comfortably could. Her fingers scrabbled at the pliable ridges hoping to snag the recipe. With an extra effort she lurched to the right and touched the edge of the paper.

With a sudden jerk, her left hand slipped from the steering wheel. The car careened toward the incline on the right. Mavis grabbed the wheel with both hands and cranked it hard left in a panicked effort to straighten the wheels. The tires screeched, and the vehicle slid into a wild fishtail. Mavis screamed as the Impala clipped a pin oak, bounced off the guardrail, flipped, and slid over the edge of the pavement and down the rocky embankment. Its tires spinning in the air, the vehicle came to rest upside down in the dry creek bed that paralleled the road. Mavis' head slammed against the driver's-side door frame. Everything went black.

Moments later, Mavis moaned and shook her head to clear her vision. Her body was plastered tight against the seat back upside down, her seatbelt holding her securely in place. A bright light flickered in front of her eyes. Mavis gasped as flames licked out from around the crumpled hood.

Her fingers fumbled for the catch on the seat belt. She depressed the latch and fell free from the restraint, landing in a heap on the roof's headliner. She lay on her back a moment to orient herself before rolling onto her belly. The broken side window was her only avenue of escape.

Gravel and broken glass dug into the palms of her hands and knees as she dragged herself through the opening and scrambled up the hillside towards the highway. She yelped when, with a whoosh, her car exploded into flames, sending a wave of heat cascading over her back.

Mavis sat panting on the side of the road, her back against the guardrail, watching her car burn and her most cherished dream go up in smoke. Mamaw's bread pudding recipe was no more. The only remnant was ash floating in the still air.

In the distance she could hear the faint wail of an emergency vehicle. Lester must have found Clarice. She dropped her head between her bent knees and pressed her hands to her temples in an agony of concentration. "Dear Lord, help me, please," she prayed. "Was it *three* tablespoons of raisins in *one* cup of bourbon, or *one* cup of raisins in *three* tablespoons of bourbon? And did Mamaw use buttermilk or regular milk?"

1792 BARTON DISTILLERY
BY DEBORAH ALVORD

The 1792 Barton Distillery is a tale of three dreams, all culminating in excellent bourbon.

Thomas S. Moore was a Kentucky distiller working in Bardstown, Kentucky, in the late 1890s. He dreamed of having his own distillery. He had his sights on a parcel of land that lay adjacent to the Mattingly & Moore distillery of which he was part owner with his wife and brother-in-law. This 116-acre parcel was especially desirable for its two springs, which would provide the essential limestone-filtered water (low in iron and high in magnesium and calcium) required to give bourbon its unique flavor. In 1899, Moore finally had the financial resources and purchased the land. He named the distillery Tom Moore, and produced Tom Moore, Dan'l Boone, and Silas Jones whiskey until Prohibition closed its doors. Today, the Barton distillery still produces Tom Moore bourbon, and Moore's contributions to the industry are enshrined in the Kentucky Bourbon Hall of Fame.

In 1944, the Tom Moore distillery evoked a second dream in Oscar Getz. A Chicago businessman rather than a distiller, Getz had formed Barton Brands with a partner some years earlier. When he came to Kentucky in search of property, he discovered the old Tom Moore distillery and fell in love with the land and its bourbon traditions. He purchased the property from Tom Moore's son, renamed it the Barton Distillery, and began a decades-long collection of bourbon memorabilia, which were housed in a museum on the distillery premises. Today, you can visit the Oscar Getz Museum of Whiskey History near the distillery in Bardstown.

Fast forward to the twenty-first century. The Sazerac Company, an alcoholic beverage company out of Metairie, Louisiana, had a business dilemma: not enough bottling capacity. Their dream was to find a solution to this dilemma, and they found it in Barton's Brands distillery. Though it had a vast bottling capacity, the distillery's bottling equipment sat idle, gathering dust, not earning profits, during Kentucky's hot, sticky summer months, because of the required summer siesta during the bourbon aging process. Sazerac was already producing varied alcoholic beverages, from tequila to liqueurs. Why not bring the varied beverages to Kentucky and, while the bourbon sleeps, use the bottling equipment for its other products? Add a nearby distribution center and an effective business plan was developed. The Sazerac Company acquired the distillery in 2009. Today, tours of the 1792 Barton Distillery treat guests to a year-round sight of trucks pulling in and out of the facility, while still providing an informative afternoon centered on its beloved bourbon. The distillery itself has grown through the years, now consisting of 28 warehouses, 22 other buildings and its famed two springs, Morton and Moore.

There are several other bourbons distilled at the Barton Distillery, including Very Old Barton and the newest variety, 1792, its premium brand. The name honors the year the Commonwealth of Kentucky was admitted to the Union as the 15th state.

MOSCOW BLUE
BY TAMERA SHAW

Macy's heart thumped so hard against her ribs that it stole her breath. Her badge trembled like a new recruit facing the cold barrel of a gun for the first time. She rolled down the window of her Crown Vic. A blast of cool autumn air stung her eyes, which she closed. Each breath—short, labored—she expelled from her lungs as she willed her body to inhale. Seconds stretched into long intervals between breaths until Macy's chest rose and fell normally.

One look in the mirror betrayed her newfound calm. She was ready. Wasn't she? The docs had cleared her for duty. Well, light duty. And this assignment bordered on overkill—thirty officers to babysit the formal handoff of a fancy, recovered diamond. She dabbed sweat from her brow, steadied her pulse, and opened her eyes to the October dusk slipping into night.

On the short brick walk from City Hall's parking lot to Spalding Hall, a former Catholic school, she remembered the nuns who had been so kind after her father died. Macy slapped away the memory as she would a fly. *Concentrate*, she told herself. Macy breathed in the smells of turning leaves and beer wafting from a nearby cart. The columned building had been converted to house both the Oscar Getz Museum of Whiskey History and the Bardstown Historical Museum. A quick glance reassured her that the front perimeter and exits were secure. She climbed the steps. Pain radiated up her leg, but she refused to limp.

A familiar itch crept up her back. She shook it off and glanced at the radio on her waistband. A green light blinked. Satisfied, she checked her weapon, then tugged her jacket closed.

She nodded to the deputies at the entrance.

"We'll all go for a beer after this is over," she said.

"That'd be great, Lieutenant," one of the men said before he checked her credentials. They'd never met.

"Good job," she told him before she walked inside. One thing was sure. The sheriff and his staff were professional, thorough. One of Louisville's finest, imported for this occasion, stood on the hardwood and blocked the stairway leading to the second floor.

"Evening, Lieutenant," he said.

"How's your mom?"

"Better. Thanks. We appreciated the card and, you know."

Macy nodded.

"You'll want to turn right, go to the end, then zig zag left."

Macy smiled. She did her homework, knew the layout. No need to snipe at a good man.

She walked down the hallway lined with whiskey paraphernalia, mostly bottles and labels. The downhill ramp bothered her leg as she negotiated the final turn into the chapel. Stained glass lined two sides. An altar stood at the front on a little platform. To each side were closets that held sound equipment. Along the walls were Bardstown historical dioramas encased in glass—relics from Jesse James to Native Americans who had left their marks in the area.

Her hand-picked security team of off-duty officers supplemented by the Nelson County Sheriff's men were positioned at every possible egress. Cops not making enough to send their kids to college were ready to guard a blue diamond worth, conservatively, a cool million.

She'd never understood the need for ceremony. Especially a public spectacle that risked so much. And for what? For show. But she smiled when she thought of the man who had unselfishly returned the diamond. The world needed more like him.

The clipboard listed the names of invitees and *guests*. A list too long, too vague, for her taste. She shivered as a cold blast of air drifted through the floor register and up her pant leg. The room would fill with warm bodies and tepid conversation soon enough. She imagined all that hot air sucking up the chill that now traveled up her thigh.

"This is his idea of a low profile?" Macy asked Sheriff Wilkerson, who walked toward her. His boots clicked on the hardwood floor as he closed the distance from across the room.

"Henderson was very specific. He asked for you and wanted you to supervise the security team. Heard you had experience with some big-time jewel thief in Louisville."

She nodded, remembering the aborted theft of several well-known baubles during a swanky Derby party several years earlier. Macy had foiled Tiffany DeLor's attempt to snatch the platinum and diamond necklace right off Mrs. Gibson-Wright's neck.

"Your men have the photos?" she asked.

Wilkerson nodded. "Every jewel thief in these United States and Europe as well. There'll be more money in this room than this town has seen in a long while. And that's sayin' something."

He took an unhurried look, a little too long in her opinion, at the hard, muscular physique she had worked to get back after the shooting six months earlier. Absently, she moved her hand to the hip where the bullet had entered. His eyes followed.

He said, "Don't worry, I'm not looking for a date. Just wonderin' if you're a hundred percent."

She nodded. No one's business if she still woke up, the sheets soaked, with a scream buried in her throat as she tore away from a nightmare. "I'm back to normal. Thanks for the concern."

"If we mess this thing up, it's both our butts on the line."

Macy smiled. "If that diamond gets out of here with anyone other than Henderson, I'll turn in my badge."

"Well, let's get goin'. It's your show."

"Update?"

"We have a couple of plainclothes on the door to verify invitations. Your uniforms are scattered throughout the hall, each responsible for a sector."

"I ran the guests, waiters, the caterer, musicians, support staff myself."

He nodded and said, "Yep. I got your email. But the 'and guest' is plain stupid. Off-duties from Lexington and your division in Louisville are on every exit, even the ones no one's supposed to know about. All these old places hold secrets, but we found 'em all. Five deputies patrol outside. We have cameras." He pointed to the four corners of the room. "And someone watching the console. No one's getting out of here with that diamond. Well, no one 'cept the rightful owner. One Norman Henderson. Bourbon baron."

"Is he as arrogant as I've heard?"

The sheriff nodded. "More. Big wig. Not from 'round here. New York City." He pronounced the municipality's name with the disgust of someone who'd never visited the place but was certain he hated everything about it.

"His public relations folks wanted this big spectacle," he continued, with even more spit in his eye. "More like public foolishness, you ask me. Wanted a big show to have the fella who found the diamond officially return it to Henderson."

Macy flipped through her file and stopped at a photo of the Moscow Blue. The image all but jumped from the page. Flawless and vivid, the royal stone reminded Macy of a crushed velvet dress she'd worn twenty years earlier, on her tenth birthday. The year her father died in the line of duty.

Wilkerson whistled at the image, pulling Macy back into the moment.

"This circus is happening smack in the middle of the Bourbon Festival, no less. The busiest week of the year. Most of my guys are on street patrol and crowd control. This week is one big party 'round here."

Macy nodded understanding. "How on earth do you leave something worth millions in a cab? Would it just slip your mind? I feel naked without my gun. You think I'd leave it in a taxi?"

Wilkerson shrugged. "Beats me, but Henderson's forking over a hefty reward to the cabbie."

"I've seen a lot in my years on the force, but I think, given half a chance, people are basically honest."

The two discussed further strategy then split up. Macy checked in with each officer and supervised Wilkerson's assignments of his deputies. Before long, the catering staff and the musicians trickled in. Macy distanced herself from her men and took a position by the main entrance to peruse the incoming guests.

Within the hour, excited conversation merged with soft jazz as the black-tie crowd mingled in the center of the room and at white linen-draped tables that lined the perimeter. Pint-sized bottles of Henderson's premium small-batch bourbon, Old Lexington, stood at attention among the gleaming silver and china service. White-coated waiters and waitresses served tumblers of Old Lex with canapés as they shifted through scores of revelers.

Entourages that included the mayors of Louisville, Lexington, and Bardstown filed in minutes later followed by the newly elected governor. Macy had never seen so many guests excited about something with which they had absolutely no connection.

Alerted by a short beep from her radio, Macy moved to the front landing as Norman Henderson stepped from the insulated cocoon of a long, black limo and into the moon-bathed early fall evening. The scent of freshly mown grass lingered in the air, blended with chrysanthemums.

"Nature," he complained to the driver who held the car door and his tongue. Henderson covered his nose with a handkerchief then his gaze moved to Macy, registering recognition before he moved away. He glided past her without a word and moved inside.

Macy spoke into the radio, "Send in the cabbie."

The police cruiser that had waited for the signal ducked out of a side street and pulled to the base of the stairs. A small man in an ill-fitting suit climbed out. Macy greeted him with a handshake.

"Mr. Spencer. I'm Macy Greer. You have the diamond?"

"Soon as I see the badge," he said, puffing up his chest.

She nodded and pointed to the LMPD identification on her jacket. Spencer planted his nose an inch from the shield and studied. After a long moment, he straightened and patted his breast pocket.

"It's right here."

A deputy rounded the car.

"This officer will take you inside," she said.

"Gotta tell ya, ma'am, this thing has made me a nervous wreck. 'Specially when I found out how much the sucker was worth. I'll be glad to get rid of it. Who knew that somepin' the size of a pea could be worth so much?"

Macy smiled and watched Spencer enter the hall.

"Show time," she called into the radio. "Chicken's in the coop."

Inside, Henderson hurried to Spencer. The men shared an enthusiastic handshake. Henderson cupped his guest's elbow, nudged him to the head table, and lowered Spencer into a chair.

Macy stood at attention next to their table with a good view of the duo as a waitress sporting severe bangs approached. She awkwardly balanced a tray of tumblers, each containing two fingers of bourbon. With a flick of his wrist, Spencer waved off the libation, but Henderson nodded.

"Let's celebrate, shall we?" Henderson begged Spencer. He lifted two glasses from the tray. It tilted forward. Glasses bounced off Henderson, then crashed to the floor as bourbon soaked into his jacket.

"You idiot!" Henderson screamed, dabbing his jacket with a handkerchief. The waitress shrank back. The entire wait staff descended on the bourbon-soaked man, offering napkins and apologies.

Macy fought her way through the crowd that had pulsed forward.

"Check your pocket, Mr. Spencer," she demanded.

"Excuse me?"

Henderson stopped fretting over his jacket and urged Spencer to comply.

"It's gone! The diamond's gone," Spencer said. "How can that be? It was right here."

Macy spotted the clumsy waitress fighting through the back of the crowd, which included most of the security detail lured by the commotion. The woman dodged bodies with the agility of a cat. A familiar cat. That gait, the tilt of her head. Macy hadn't caught her back in Louisville, but she believed wholeheartedly in second chances.

Not so clumsy after all, Macy thought. She shouted into the radio, alerting the guards on the exits to remain at their posts.

"The diamond is gone. Has anyone left?" she called into device.

Each sentry reported in the negative.

"No one in or out. We're looking for a woman in a waitress uniform. Short, dark hair with bangs."

She repeated the description to the rest of the security contingent as Sheriff Wilkerson joined her.

"I want every member of the wait staff searched and then brought to the front of the room," she said to the sheriff, then climbed onto the stage and grabbed a microphone.

The band stopped playing.

"Ladies and gentlemen. I'm Macy Greer from the Louisville Metro Police Department. The Blue Moscow has been stolen."

A collective gasp filtered through the hall.

"We need your cooperation. Please take a seat at one of the tables."

When no one moved, the sheriff's deputies directed partygoers to seats.

Macy stepped off the stage, spotted Henderson and Spencer sitting alone at the table. Henderson's hands shook.

104

"The Moscow Blue. It's gone. Again." He spread his empty hands in front of his face.

Macy spoke quietly, firmly, "If you want me to find the diamond, I need information." She paused. "Gentlemen. Close your eyes and describe the waitress," she said.

"Short, white. Black hair," Spencer said.

"She was average height," Henderson added. He measured Macy's frame with his eyes. "A few inches shorter than you." The other man nodded in agreement.

Macy barked into the radio, "Repeat, suspect is a woman. Black hair, but that could change. New information. Approximately five-five. Stiller, check the ladies' room."

Moments later, Stiller arrived at Macy's side with a wig and discarded waitress uniform.

"She's still in the building. The jewel's most likely on her person," Macy said. She turned to Henderson and Spencer. "With your permission, I need to search you."

Henderson started to object, but bit his lip and nodded. Spencer agreed. Macy gestured to one of the officers, who frisked the pair.

"Nothing," he reported.

"Take them to the men's room. Search everything."

Henderson gaped while Spencer shuddered.

"There are one hundred and seven guests, twenty wait staff, five musicians, and the caterer. Henderson, when you get back, I need to take you around the room. Tell me if any of the guests don't belong here."

Before long, they returned. "Gents are clean."

"Now, about the guests," Macy said.

"All of them are friends, politicians, and business associates."

"And their guests?"

"I asked each to invite someone I knew, their spouses or distillery employees or community leaders. This is a small town, officer. I can spot an out-of-towner like me from a mile."

Henderson approached three tables in turn, shaking his head after each. At the fourth round, Henderson nodded toward a mousy woman in a black dress a size too big. A rock the size of a hazelnut, which didn't fit her inexpensive dress and shoes, adorned her hand.

"Your name?" Macy asked.

"Hey there. It's a grand party, isn't it? Janet O'Connor," she said with a decidedly Texas twang. She stuck out her hand, which Macy shook.

"I'm Macy Greer, a lieutenant with the Louisville Metro Police."

"Why, this is the most excitement I've had all year. I sure hope you find who did it."

"Count on it. Are you here alone?" Macy's eyes were cold steel.

"I'm here with my Ben. Ben Rodgers. My date."

Macy checked the guest list. Ben Rodgers was listed, and his name checked. She turned to Henderson.

"Do you know them?"

"I know Rodgers. He's in public relations at the distillery. He planned the party. I've never met Miss O'Connor."

Macy turned back to her.

"The list doesn't mention a guest."

"Well, it was a last-minute thing," she said. "And since he made the guest list, they let me in."

"Where's Ben?"

"I'm afraid he had a little too much to drink." She lowered her gaze. "Ben said he was going to the men's room. To throw up," she whispered.

Macy flicked her head and a deputy turned in that direction.

"Ma'am, I'd like your permission to search your bag," she said.

"Oh my, does this have to do with that missing diamond? Everyone's talkin' about it." She smiled. "Well, sure, take a look." She handed Macy the bag. "How exciting. Am I a suspect?" Her face beamed.

Macy rifled through the purse. Lipstick, a small mirror. She felt the lining, no lumps. Two small bourbon bottles, about seven inches tall, the seals intact. Macy held out one of the bottles, and O'Connor's smile struck her as sheepish.

"Oh my gosh. The bottles were on the table at each place setting. Ben had told me that the bottles would be party favors. He planned everything to the tee. Should I put them back?"

"No need," Macy said, holding out the purse.

When the woman reached for it, Macy retracted the bag.

"On second thought, mind if I borrow the bottles?" Macy asked.

There it was. Only a flicker on her face, then O'Connor returned to all smiles.

"Why, sure. I didn't need all that liquor anyway."

As Macy strode toward the kitchen, Stiller reported.

"We found Ben Rodgers. He was out cold in a utility closet across from the men's room. Must'a thought it was the john," she said.

"Drunk?" Macy asked.

"He reeked of bourbon. There was an empty bottle by his head."

"Do everything you can to rouse him," Macy said.

Stiller moved away as Macy reached the empty kitchen off the same hallway as the restrooms. She pulled down a pan from the hooks above, broke the seals on the small bottles, poured out the contents, and dipped her fingers into the alcohol. She searched the drawers, found a fine-screened strainer, pulled down another pan, and ran the liquor through the sieve and into the second pot.

No diamond.

Macy squinted inside the bottles and shook them for good measure. Nothing rattled. She tossed both in the trash and returned to O'Connor's table.

"You'll be happy to know that we found Ben."

O'Connor scanned the room. "Where is he? Where's that rascal?"

"He's indisposed."

"You mean drunk." She shook her head.

"I'm wondering if you'd agree to a search?"

"But you already searched—" Her eyes rounded. "Me? You want to search me? Well for heaven's sake."

"Your date works for Henderson. Surely you'd want to help out."

"I don't see how that could possibly help," she said, leaning close to Macy. "Besides, I'm awful shy. And don't you need a warrant for that kind of thing? I'm not under arrest, am I?" she asked, batting those eyes and churning up fat tears.

"You're not under arrest." *Yet*, Macy thought. "But you can't leave until we finish our interviews." Macy walked off.

Macy checked in with each sentry. No movement, no one trying to leave. Her gut told her that O'Connor was Tiffany. She just had to prove it. The wait staff and the building had been searched. She couldn't keep everyone much longer, and the governor was squawking about his civil rights.

Macy jumped when she felt a tap on her shoulder. She turned to find O'Connor.

"I was wondering if I could see Ben, and maybe one of your officers could help me load him into the car. I'd very much like to leave."

"Take your seat and I'll see what I can do."

Macy and Stiller watched O'Connor walk out of view.

"She's the one, Stiller. Don't let her out of your sight."

The officer nodded and took off after O'Connor.

"Wait!"

Stiller turned.

"Did anyone search Rodgers?"

"The one passed out?" Stiller smiled and nodded. "Nothing but a wallet and car keys."

Macy shook her head and Stiller continued toward O'Connor's table.

"What am I missing?" Macy muttered.

In mid stride, Macy felt her pupils enlarge and her cheek muscles stretch as she remembered the hidden camera covering the hallway. She clicked on her radio.

"Sheriff, check with your man monitoring the cameras. I need to know when a waitress entered the restroom, then who came out afterward."

Macy returned to O'Connor's table.

"We found car keys in Ben's pocket. We're bringing around his ride. I apologize for all the hassle."

"I sure wish you luck," O'Connor said.

"Oh, we'll find it. Don't worry."

Sheriff Wilkerson took Macy aside, whispered something in her ear. The news lightened her mood.

O'Connor rose and said, "All this excitement. I need the ladies' room. Excuse me." Her smile offered an apology.

Stiller started to follow, but Macy stopped her with a look. O'Connor, headed toward the hallway that led to the restroom and the kitchen, glanced over her shoulder.

Macy counted to ten before she followed O'Connor into the kitchen, not the ladies' room.

O'Connor closed the snap on her purse as Macy entered.

"You caught me," she said, smiling widely. "I wanted the bottles as souvenirs. I assumed that you came in here to pour out the bourbon, so what could it hurt to keep the empties?" Her eyes pleaded the case.

"I'll take them now." Macy held out her hand.

"Well, if it's so important."

O'Connor reached into her bag. A knife glinted in the moonlight that streamed from a high window. She lunged. The blade lanced the fabric above Macy's bad hip. Pain screeched inside her head as she slumped to the floor.

O'Connor reared her foot back, ready to kick the wound. Macy caught her ankle and she fell hard. Macy plowed her fist into O'Connor's face, then pinned her to the floor with a boot to the throat.

"Caught you after all," Macy said with a smile in her voice.

Seconds later, officers spilled into the room.

"Cuff her," she called out. Two deputies rushed forward.

Her hip screamed as she opened O'Connor's purse and extracted the bourbon bottles. Without warning the others, she grabbed a rolling pin, covered her face, and smashed the bottles in the sink. But the bottom of one failed to break.

Grabbing a potholder from a drawer, Macy picked through the glass. The vibrant Blue Moscow peeked out from a specially made false bottom with a seamless tongue-and-groove mechanism that connected it to the glass. The rock glinted from layers of rich amber silk.

"Oh my, how did that get there?" O'Connor frowned. "Ben must have put it there."

"Run her prints. I think you'll find that Janet O'Connor isn't her real name." She walked to the woman. "Try Tiffany DeLor. Diamond thief. Hails from London, by way of Louisville. You changed your hair, Tiff, gained some weight, changed the nose. But I'll bet my pension it's you."

Macy watched DeLor's horrified expression change to pride.

"You're under arrest for grand theft, diamond."

"Well, I'll have to ring my solic—my lawyer."

"Solicitor?" Macy smiled. "That's posh talk for lawyer, right?" Macy asked in an exaggerated British accent.

The cuffed woman practically spat, "You have nothing."

"Oh, and get Ben Rodgers to a hospital," she said to Stiller. "I think you'll find she used something stronger than bourbon to knock him cold."

Macy turned back to DeLor.

"I'll find your fingerprints on this bottle. We have you going into the ladies' room in a waiter's outfit and coming out dressed like this. And we have you on camera outside the men's room, pressing something to Ben's neck, then pushing him into a closet. Missed those two during your surveillance, didn't you, Tiff? We installed both cameras this morning."

Tiffany shrugged. "Had to take the chance, didn't I? Something that valuable in a small town. Easy pickings. I didn't count on such a worthy opponent."

Macy let out a contented sigh.

When Macy returned to the ballroom, she walked over to Spencer and Henderson. The diamond winked in her palm. Henderson simply stared for a long moment then let out a squeal.

"Looks like we're having a ceremony after all," he said, beaming as bright as the diamond he held onto for dear life. "This time, we'll recognize two heroes."

EVAN WILLIAMS BOURBON EXPERIENCE
BY KAREN QUINN BLOCK

Named for Kentucky's first official commercial whiskey distiller, Evan Williams is Heaven Hill's flagship bourbon brand and is personified in the Evan Williams Bourbon Experience, Heaven Hill's artisanal micro distillery located near the intersection of 6th and Main streets in Louisville, Kentucky. From the time visitors enter through the front door of the narrow storefront and pass the five-story tall glass sculpture depicting an Evan Williams Black Label bottle pouring well-aged bourbon into a highball glass, they know they are in for an uncommon distillery tour

To start, Evan Williams Bourbon Experience is located across the street from the Ohio River-front site of Williams' late-18th century distillery. Early in the history of Louisville, at a time when whiskey was as valuable as money, there were so many whisky distilleries in the area that this section of Main Street was known as Whiskey Row, a name it retains to this day. The circa 1903 building itself is also a historical treasure. The celebrated Louisvillian architect D. X. Murphy designed the structure, and Frank Lloyd Wright designed the windows. The first two floors are dedicated to the bourbon experience and gift shop. The third floor is available for private parties, the fourth is reserved for employees, and the fifth floor is used for offices. A Prohibition-style speakeasy is located in the basement. Patrons enter through a secret door just as they would have from 1919 to 1933 when the sale and public consumption of liquor was against the law.

Upon entering Evan Williams Bourbon Experience, visitors step over the threshold immediately into a mini-museum with displays illustrating the history of Evan Williams the businessman and of commercial whisky making in Louisville. The timeline morphs into the developments and hiccups (including Prohibition) along the road that led to modern bourbon distilling.

The actual tour starts with a theatrical recreation of Evan Williams hard at work. We meet a driven entrepreneur obsessed with pleasing his customers and ensuring the integrity of his product. Moving out of the past, a high-definition presentation introduces the facts, figures, and images of modern bourbon distilling, such as the mind-boggling quantities of grain needed to produce a single batch of bourbon, the different combinations of ingredients to produce different flavors, the amount of time it takes to age the product to perfection, and finally the distilling process itself.

Then the screens retract to reveal the centerpiece of the enterprise—a two-story tall, two-pot, micro distillery complete with gleaming copper piping, gigantic vats, fermenting mash, and a heady aroma. The tour guide describes the function of the various pieces of equipment, answers questions, and gives the history of the strain of yeast dating from 1790 that is used in distilling Evan Williams bourbon. Visitors learn the distillery produces only one barrel of bourbon per day and that all bourbon distilled onsite is transported in tanker trucks to the Heaven Hill distillery in Bardstown, where it is barreled in Evan Williams branded, #3-charred kegs, and stored to age in its own section of the warehouse.

Next on the tour, visitors sample Evan Williams signature bourbons in one of two themed tasting rooms, either a beautiful vintage saloon or a circa 1950s-60s *Mad Men* style bar. Which products are sampled depends on a number of factors, but at the time of this writing, visitors are first introduced to the taste of the moderately-priced Evan Williams Black Label, which is made from a blend of bourbon with similar flavor profiles that have been aged four to six years. Next up is a sample of Evan Williams 101-proof, twelve-year-old Red Label bourbon. Hand selected for that "sweet spot", Evan Williams Red Label was only available in Japan until recently, but now can be purchased in the United States. And last, the *pièce de résistance* of the tour, visitors experience a *warm Kentucky hug*—a deep coppery-colored bourbon aged for twenty-three years. *Yum!*

The tour ends in the retail gift shop where visitors can purchase a variety of Evan Williams signature items, including bar ware and Evan Williams Red Label bourbon. Other items for sale include cookbooks, bourbon jams, jellies, and sauces, and the ultimate dessert treat—bourbon balls—made with Evan Williams bourbon.

Offering a one-of-a-kind perspective of the history, production methodology, and social side of the bourbon industry, Evan Williams Bourbon Experience is definitely a welcome addition to the Kentucky Bourbon Trail.

Make Mine Bourbon
By Jo Tucker

"If it has anything to do with bourbon, Lila's all over it," Henry Hochstrasser morosely complained to anyone within earshot. "Bourbon candy, bourbon highballs, candles that stink of bourbon. I knew when she got to be part owner of a racehorse it would end up with bourbon in its name. Sure enough, Bourbon Lad."

Henry allowed his head to sink farther toward the bar on which his folded arms rested. He cast a malevolent eye on his gin and tonic and snorted through his ample nose. "Probably why she divorced me for that dog John Redmon – he drinks her brand and I can't go near it."

The burly bartender leisurely worked along the old knotty pine bar, flipping his rag at imaginary particles of dust. There wasn't much else to do. Henry and a handful of early drinkers were the only occupants of Tweet's Grill; the lunch crowd was gone, the happy hour crowds were still at work, the four o'clock influx two hours away. A baseball game plodded along on the widescreen television in the corner, the sound turned too low to hear. No one in the bar seemed to care.

The bartender stopped in front of Henry, and asked idly, "How's that colt coming along, anyway?"

"Aw, he's doing pretty well over at Fair Oaks, I guess," said Henry. "Pete, I think he's gonna have a real good three-year-old season."

"Cheer up," said the bartender. "You still own part of the animal, don't you?"

"Yeah," Henry said quietly. "I own a quarter of it. That's a far cry from being half owner in a possible Derby horse, which is exactly what I was a year ago when Lila and I were still married."

"Lila," pronounced Pete, with an appreciative glint in his eye, "is something, isn't she? But I sure never thought she'd divorce you and marry Redmon, all within a few months. Right after that horse started winning races, too."

"Yeah," Henry intoned wryly. "Who'd have thought?"

Ambling out of the bar half an hour later, Henry shivered in the cold October air. Blue skies promised warmth they didn't deliver in Kentucky this time of year. The last remnants of autumn's gold and yellow clung to the trees, trembling in the chilly breeze. Glancing at his watch, Henry squared his shoulders, a small, secretive smile creasing the florid skin into tiny wrinkles at the corners of his mouth and eyes. He hoisted himself into the leather driver's seat of his large and well-appointed Toyota pickup and wheeled out of the parking lot.

Squinting again at his watch, Henry picked up speed, wasting no time on sightseeing along the Woodford County back roads. Black board fences flowed gracefully into the distance toward neat, luxurious barns. The fences framed perfect fields where bluegrass clung to hints of summer's lush color. Henry paid no attention, although most days he would be delighted to meander, watching for herds of broodmares and their high-spirited fillies and colts.

Fifteen minutes later, Henry turned the truck down a long, wide driveway lined with majestic oaks. He waved a key card over the security sensor beside the entrance to Fair Oaks Farm and the stout, wrought iron gate swung smoothly open. At a fork in the driveway, Henry nosed the truck to the right toward the barns and pulled up in front of a green and white stable. Sliding out of the truck, he stretched and yawned, breathed deeply of the crisp air, and strolled toward the stable.

"Hey, Laddy," he called softly. There was an immediate nicker from within. He grinned fondly – the horse had known him since it was a foal, and was always ready for a rub and a treat.

"Helloooo, Henry." This hearty, drawled greeting preceded a tall, lanky man in jeans, flannel shirt and ball cap. Although Kurt Minton didn't much look the part of a millionaire trainer and could easily have been mistaken for a stable hand, his reputation for training racehorses was the best in the business. He ran his small operation himself, turning away horses rather than delegating his owners' Thoroughbreds to assistant trainers. He extended his hand and gave Henry's a strong shake.

Henry motioned expansively toward the stalls in the well-swept interior of the stable. "Hey, Kurt, I know it's three o'clock nap time at the stables, but I had a hankering to see Bourbon Lad."

"No problem, Henry," said the trainer. "You know you're always welcome. You missed your co-owners by about an hour, in fact. John and Lila were here talking about racing schedules until Lila hustled him off to play tennis or work out or something. Why don't you come over to the office after you've fed Bourbon Lad a carrot or two, and we'll talk?"

Kurt's office put his achievements in proper perspective— pictures with owners, both famous and unknown—gold and silver trophies—awards and plaques from charitable organizations. Testaments to a long and distinguished career lined the walls and shelves.

As usual, a particular picture drew Henry's eye. Bourbon Lad, jockey, trainer, and three excited owners stood in the winner's circle. Lila, blond and svelte, tight dress smooth over plentiful curves. One arm was entwined with Henry's, while John Redmon stood slightly apart. Three successful, middle-aged people celebrating the young horse's victory. Kurt cleared his throat and Henry cast him a glance, catching a sympathetic look from the trainer.

Henry sat down on a heavy leather chair and stretched his legs to the ottoman. He contemplated the round mahogany coffee table, on which rested a beautiful Waterford crystal decanter full of bourbon for Kurt's guests. The amber liquid smoldered with a deep, warm glow, as though sunlight was magically captured within it.

"Henry, I know you don't approve of what John and Lila want to do with Bourbon Lad," began Kurt "They're pushing me hard to run him next month in the Breeder's Cup Juvenile and together they own three-quarters of the horse. Now, I've told them I think the colt has shown himself a little green for what's going to be a real tough race, and I would prefer to wait a couple months before putting him to such a test. But you know John! Lila used to see it your way, but now she seems to be going along with John."

Henry's eyes narrowed and the corners of his mouth curled down in the beginning of a scowl, but then he sighed and shook his head. "I know, I know," he said. "When Lila and I owned fifty percent and John owned fifty percent, it was easier. I don't know why John always wanted to push the colt so hard. We had lots of debates about it, but we had him outvoted. Since Lila divorced me and got half of our half in the settlement, my views don't matter much."

Kurt considered for a minute. "If I tell owners they have a possible Derby contender, most of 'em are tickled to death to take my advice on bringing the horse along carefully. Not John—he can't wait for the next race! You'd think he needed the money or something."

"Nah," Henry said. "None of us need the money. It's the thrill—seeing that horse run is like a high for him. Lila used to say he shouldn't own a horse—it robbed him of his common sense."

Kurt leaned back in his chair and spoke thoughtfully, arms folded over his chest. "I'm surprised to hear you say that. It makes me wonder why she married him."

Henry grinned. "I'm sure she thought she could handle him. Apparently, it's not as easy as she thought. She'll keep working at it. Lila usually gets what she wants." In his experience, Lila didn't let anyone push her around. She wanted what she wanted and could be crafty as a fox getting it.

Their conversation meandered from one racing topic to another, until finally Henry glanced at his watch and said, "Oh man, Kurt, it's almost four-thirty. I'd better head for the house and let you get back to your work."

The next morning also dawned clear and crisp. Henry had just finished his twenty-fifth hard-fought sit-up, and was patting his potbelly to see if it seemed less paunchy, when his doorbell rang. Kurt Minton stood on the porch, a worried frown on his face. He stepped in at Henry's invitation, but declined coffee.

Carefully choosing his words, Kurt said, "Henry, I've got some news you may not have heard yet. Yesterday afternoon John Redmon died of a heart attack."

Henry took a step backward, his jaw dropping slightly. "Are you serious? Where? When? I can't believe this!"

"Well, I don't have many details," Kurt continued, "But it seems it happened at home a while after they left the stable. Lila was with him. I thought you'd want to know."

"You mean while I was over there at the stable with you, talking about them, he was having a heart attack? Oh, man, I feel lousy."

Henry showered and sat down with coffee at his kitchen table, wondering what to do next. The decision was soon out of his hands. The phone rang, jangling and insistent. As he rose to answer it, there was an equally demanding rapping at the front door. He chose the phone first.

"Henry," shrilled Lila, in her *I've got a big problem* tone of voice—the one he knew very well, "John's dead—did you know?"

"Yeah, Kurt came by and told me. I'm sorry, hon."

The knocking at the door continued. "Hold on a minute," he hollered.

"Henry, they've taken all his pills and they won't release his body, and they're acting like I'm to blame somehow!"

"Listen, Lila, you calm down. Everything'll be okay. I'm gonna call you back in a bit. Someone's at the front door and I need to go answer it."

Lila's voice rose half an octave. "It's probably the police! They asked for your address."

"I'll call you back, Lila—maybe not today, but soon. Remember, keep calm and everything will work out fine."

A pair of Versailles Police Department detectives stood at the door, one dapper and trim, the other looking much like a balloon bifurcated by a belt. The questions focused on whether he was aware John Redmon had health problems, whether John and Lila had any financial difficulties, and who would inherit John's share of Bourbon Lad. Every now and then, though, they slipped in a question like "Were you on good terms with the Redmons?" or "How did you feel about the Redmons having controlling interest in the horse you used to own?" or "Have you spoken to your ex-wife yesterday or today?"

Although the interview was brief, Henry was irritated with himself for talking too much. He knew perfectly well he should say less rather than more, but for some reason he kept volunteering information. Not that he had anything to worry about—his whereabouts the previous afternoon were easily verified.

Henry knew they were fishing because the marital re-alignment earlier in the year among Bourbon Lad's owners had been widely covered in gossip columns, but he didn't want to be on a list of suspects if they thought there was something odd about John's death. Thinking back on the interview, he felt he rambled a little too long on John's heart condition, which he did know about, and sounded a bit gushy about the amiable relationship between the three of them after Lila ended up married to his friend and partner. They left him alone soon, though, so he breathed a sigh of relief, tossed his cold coffee down the sink, and turned on the computer to check the financial news.

Over the next difficult days, Henry spent a decorous amount of time paying his respects. Dressed in his best suit, he attended visitation at the funeral home, mingled solemnly with friends and family, and sat a few rows behind Lila at the funeral.

Lila was not doing well, in his view. She was distraught, twitchy, and nervous. He gently told people she was overwhelmed by the calamity.

Sitting at the bar in Tweet's a week after the funeral, Henry traded information with the bartender. "I guess the law came asking about me, didn't they, Pete?" he said in a frank, friendly manner.

"Yeah—boy, they were in here not twenty-four hours after John Redmon died," agreed the bartender, mixing Henry a gin and tonic. "What have you heard about the autopsy?"

Henry lowered his voice and spoke in a conspiratorial tone. Pete leaned toward him over the bar to hear. "It's crazy. John died of cardiac arrest. He took medicine for his heart, and his medicine killed him."

Pete cocked his head to one side, tugged thoughtfully on his beard, and looked skeptical. "How is that possible?"

"Okay, here's what Lila told me about the autopsy, between you and me. He took a daily dose of this stuff that's supposed to regulate the heart rhythms. Actually, it's the same stuff that comes from that plant we try to keep out of the hay because it poisons horses—fox blood or glove box, or something like that. He had a pretty normal amount of it in his system. But he had low potassium levels, and apparently if someone's potassium level drops too low, even a normal amount of the other stuff can be poisonous. He took water pills, and Lila thinks maybe he was taking too many because he wanted to lose some weight."

"Geez, that's nothin' but bad luck. You never know about things, do you?" mused Pete.

"Yeah, it's too bad. I mean, he was a pretty good guy, even if he did sort of steal my wife."

"So, what happens now?" Pete asked. "I mean, how is Lila doing and all?"

"Aw, she's taking it real hard. There were a lot of questions and she felt like everyone was blaming her somehow. Now that the autopsy results are in and his death was declared accidental, she's settling in with the grief and sorrow. You know, it's a good thing she has Bourbon Lad to think about. It's kind of taking her mind off John's death."

"You're helping her some, I guess," said Pete, with a small grin.

"Well, I don't know about that. I try, and we've spent some time working out the schedule for racing the horse, but it'll be a while before she gets over this." Henry draped his coat over his shoulders and strolled out of the bar, whistling softly.

By the time the spring racing season rolled around, Bourbon Lad was in fine form, and Kurt Minton had selected the right races for him. The colt was Derby-bound, and his owners couldn't be prouder.

One gorgeous March afternoon, Henry and Lila returned to Henry's house from the stable in the late afternoon and Lila, as usual, went straight to the bar to mix their drinks—bourbon for her, gin and tonic for him. She hummed a soft unrecognizable melody and worked slowly, getting things just right.

"Okay, my darling," Henry said as he propped his booted legs on the coffee table, "You've been telling me for months you'd spill the beans about how you did it. Now's the time."

Lila took a break from her bartending mission, and leaned coyly against the bar, looking over at Henry. "It was simple, hon. John had to take the heart drug every day. It comes in capsules, so toward the end of one month, I emptied out some of them and put in sugar. He took those. Then at the end of the next month when there weren't many left in the bottle, I put extra in them and in some gingko capsules he takes pretty regular. In the meantime, I took his water pills and did the same with them. That's why his potassium levels were low, and it's a fact that a little extra of the heart drug in combination with those water pills killed him."

"Well, I salute you on your know-how about those kinds of things," said Henry. "And, your plan has worked so well that come Derby Day we'll stand in the winner's circle as the sole owners of the best three-year-old colt in the country."

Lila finished mixing the drinks and walked over, bussing Henry's cheek with her bright red lips as she handed him his drink.

"To us," toasted Lila.

"To us," repeated Henry.

Their glasses clinked merrily, and Henry took a deep swig of his gin and tonic. It left a slightly bitter taste.

Bourbon Balls
By Edmund August & Karen Quinn Block

Bourbon Balls have continued to grow in popularity even after the passings of Rebecca Gooch and Ruth Hanly, the creators of this confection of confections, regarded by many as the iconic treat of the South. In 1919, Rebecca and Ruth decided that they would leave their jobs as teachers and start a business of their own. For many years they had given chocolates to friends and family members as Christmas presents and interpreted the praises they received for these gifts as endorsements of their plan to open a candy company. However, the male-dominated business world didn't quite see it that way.

They were ridiculed because they were women trying to do business without a man. In their beginning year they could not vote and, as unmarried women, had no property rights. But they refused to be daunted, and were rewarded by an unlikely supporter. When the Volstead Act (aka Prohibition) became law on January 16, 1920, J. J. King, owner of the Frankfort Hotel, could no longer sell alcoholic beverages. Being a man who put his business interests above any qualms or prejudices he might have had toward these two women, he allowed Ruth and Rebecca to rent the hotel's barroom. Rebecca Ruth Candies became an overnight success, due in large part to their aggressive form of advertising—hawking their candies on street corners and offering to mail orders to people's homes or businesses.

It wasn't until the late 1930s that Ruth invented Bourbon Balls. Rumor has it that she got the idea at a sesquicentennial celebration when she heard Ruby Laffoon, Kentucky's 43rd governor, declare that the finest taste treat in the world was Rebecca Ruth candy followed by Kentucky Bourbon. It took Ruth another couple of years to perfect the recipe and introduce Bourbon Balls to the world in 1938.

The recipe itself is still a closely guarded secret of the Rebecca Ruth Candy Company, but people all over the country have developed their own variations. The recipe on the next page is one such variation provided by Karen Quinn Block.

Bourbon Balls

Yield: About 3 dozen
Tip: Prepare in cool environment on low humidity day. Mixture will be difficult to work with if inside temperature is too high.

Ingredients:

1 cup walnuts or pecans
5 Tbls. good quality Kentucky bourbon
½ cup softened butter
16 oz package of white confectioners' sugar
18 oz package Toll House semi-sweet chocolate chips
½ tsp shortening
Toothpicks
Paper cupcake liners

First Day:

Mince 1 cup walnuts or pecans in food chopper. For creamiest texture, nuts should contain no solid pieces.
Place nuts in container and add 4 Tbls. Kentucky bourbon. Stir well.
Seal container and place in refrigerator overnight.

Second Day:

Cream softened butter and 2 cups white confectioners' sugar.
Fold in nut mixture.
Place in refrigerator for several hours or overnight to cool.

Third Day:

Line cookie sheet(s) with waxed paper.
Remove mixture from refrigerator.
Roll mixture into small balls and place on cookie sheets. Place toothpick in center of each ball.
Place balls in freezer for at least one hour.
Melt Toll House chocolate chips in double boiler or small crock pot.
Add ½ tsp of shortening to chocolate for easier dipping. Alternately, use meltable dipping chocolate.
Cover another cookie sheet with cupcake liners.
Remove a few balls at a time from freezer.

Holding by toothpick, quickly swirl balls in melted chocolate to cover. Gently tap off excess chocolate. Place each ball in a cupcake liner. Proceed in this manner until all liners are full. Remove toothpicks once chocolate is set. Drizzle small amount of chocolate over toothpick holes.

Store in freezer in covered container until needed.

HORNSWOGGLED
BY SARAH E. GLENN

The holidays are hard on the families of the dying. As a hospice caseworker, I spend them with bereft mothers who find the image of the infant Jesus painful, grown children reliving bittersweet memories, and people who simply feel at odds with the enforced gaiety of the season. I also answer practical but embarrassing questions: "Mr. Aleron, should we buy presents for Timmy, even if he is, um, gone by then?"

The holidays are also hard on my psychic sensitivities. They make me a better counselor, but the emotions of the grieving batter me as much as their owners. I look forward to New Year's more than any overburdened postman.

Christmas was now only six days away, though, and I planned to spend the weekend making bourbon balls. They were popular with the volunteers, and I had friends who demanded a disbursement every year. Doris, our director, had dropped hints all week.

I kept very little liquor on hand, so I borrowed a cup of bourbon every year from my neighbor across the street, Doug Clancy. He always parted gladly with it, since it meant I'd return with a Chinese take-out box full of candy. This year, the thought was painful; this would be Clancy's last Christmas.

The morning drizzle had given way to a warm afternoon, not unusual for Kentucky in December. I think maybe I'd seen a handful of white Christmases since moving to Frogtown. This promised to be another brown one. I didn't bother with a jacket. I simply crossed the street and knocked on his door.

While I waited for Clancy to answer, I saw he'd put a Santa hat on the garden gnome again. This was his only concession to the holiday besides a gold banner with an angel blowing its horn. A retired brass player should have a horn somewhere in his decorations.

The wind began cutting through my sweater. I knocked again. Clancy's car was sitting in the driveway, so he should have been home.

After a third try, I pulled my keys out and found the one he'd given me for emergencies.

The mechanical hum of his oxygen pump greeted me as I slipped inside. "Clancy?" I followed the sound to the den, where my neighbor sat quietly in a chair, empty tumbler resting near one limp hand. His eyes were closed, and if experience hadn't taught me better, I would have assumed he'd fallen asleep while enjoying his music. The gentle tick from the antique phonograph was testimony to the way he'd lived and died. I moved the needle, bouncing along the center of the vinyl record, back to its resting place. Clancy was trading riffs with Gabriel now.

Nothing remained of Clancy's spirit, of that I was sure, but I still needed to physically verify that he was gone. I shut off the pump and listened for his breath. Nothing. Then, I bent over the body and examined the eyes. The face seemed almost waxen and the corneas had already begun to cloud. Yes, it was time to call the authorities.

"Hello. This is John Aleron of Frogtown Hospice. I need to report a death." Simple words I'd said at least a dozen times. Why did they seem difficult today?

I sat in my usual spot on the sofa, but my eyes kept turning to the form at my side. My friend's empty shell, sitting and staring. No, I couldn't stay here. I needed to do something.

The bourbon was in the front of the liquor cabinet. I took the bottle back to my kitchen, mechanically doused the ground pecans with a cup of the liquor, and covered the bowl with plastic wrap. The butter went back into the refrigerator. I wouldn't be making candy today.

Officer Danny Yates met me at Clancy's door. We weren't strangers to one another; I'd reported home deaths before. When Doris, Clancy's assigned case worker, arrived, she gave the young patrolman a printout listing Clancy's doctors, the medications he was taking, and the dates they were prescribed. The police and hospice officials would want a count of the pills remaining, as much to rule out theft as suicide.

Doris followed me home to ensure that I was handling Clancy's death well. I sent her away after lunch and spent the rest of the day trying to sleep. There was one more service I could render to my friend. When night approached, I moved my ancient Packard across the street into Clancy's driveway, behind his old Caddy. It would send the message that someone was inside the house. After gathering provisions, I set up camp in his living room. My food went into his refrigerator and my blankets went under one of the end tables. The flashlight and gun, however, stayed within arm's reach.

The days immediately after a death and during the funeral always held a high risk of burglary. There were those sad specimens of humanity that scanned the papers looking for recent deaths, of course, but over the years I had spotted many a face through a window that would appear later, tear-lined, at the funeral.

The silence seemed foreign. In all my visits, the house had never been quiet. I started up Clancy's old phonograph, and soon Ella Fitzgerald's sweet voice filled the air. It reminded me of Clancy's final birthday. I'd brought a cake over, and we spent hours listening to the old songs. I plucked along with "The Nearness of You" on my double bass, accompanied by Clancy on the cornet. He'd never performed with Ella, but you wouldn't have known it from the way his horn replied to every sweet line of lyric.

That was the evening he gave me the news. I wasn't surprised. During August, he'd begun having coughing fits of an unpleasantly familiar type. I'd advised him to see someone immediately, but he insisted that it was just the blossoming goldenrod. When the autumn rains came and the goldenrod died back, he blamed the damp weather. I persisted, though, and he finally listened. Listened too late.

It was unfair, he said. He'd never smoked; it would have cut his wind and dirtied his horn. All those years of playing in smoke-filled bars caught up with him.

Despite the years he'd spent on the road with various swing bands—including a Rat Pack tour—Clancy had few visitors. He was a loner, but I don't think it was voluntary. No wife, no children, no relatives calling. He was estranged from his family. I didn't know the specific circumstances, but I was familiar with the feeling. We both felt compelled to play music; it filled the silence of missing voices. I couldn't help but glance over at his empty chair.

I'd become positively maudlin. Time to switch to Lena Horne.

Shortly thereafter, I was singing along with "I Love Paris" when I heard a noise that wasn't part of the recording. I shut up immediately. Yes, there was another sound under the drums—the barely discernable but distinct brush of shrubbery. No winter wind was that subtle. I reached for the gun, now lying under my crossword, and got up. I boldly strode to the French doors that led to the back yard and yanked one open. "Who's there?"

A scuffle and thump by the fence, followed by running footsteps, told me that my visitor wasn't interested in talk. I closed the door, but stood alert by the dark glass until the bare forsythia branches stopped scratching the siding.

My next visitor arrived at the door after the late news, when people who weren't asleep would be watching comedians' monologues. His height and build were imposing, but he had the expression of an overgrown child.

"Hi," he said. "I'm Chuck. Who are you?"

"John Aleron," I shook his hand. "I'm Clancy's neighbor."

"Oh. Were you the one that found him?"

"Yes. Would you like to come in?"

The boy shambled forward, then stopped. "Is that a gun?"

"Sorry," I said, pointing it downward. "It's for protection. Some burglars specialize in homes of the recently deceased."

"Ugh." He resumed his shamble to the couch and plopped down. "Did you know Uncle Doug real well?" His hair was short on the sides, but sported a gold-brown front crest that I hoped, for his sake, was fashionable.

I sat in Clancy's armchair and laid the gun down on the side table farthest from my visitor. "Fairly well. We were friends."

"I didn't even know he was sick. None of us did." The boy seemed genuinely hurt.

"He may not have known how to break it to the family."

"Did he tell you?"

"Yes, but I work for the Frogtown Hospice. I'm a professional."

"Huh." He tilted his head much like a curious bear. "I guess that's a good thing."

"Did you know your uncle at all? I'm sure he'd retired by the time you came along."

Chuck nodded. "Yeah. He used to visit us in Lexington, but he stopped after Aunt Margaret died. He and Uncle Allen had a big argument at the funeral."

"That's sad."

"Now they're both gone. Didn't he talk about us?"

"No," I said. "We mostly shared our mutual love of music."

"You like music, too? He showed me how to play horn a little bit. I mean, I play drums now, but I was in the school band for a while. He let me use his tuba."

"His ... tuba?"

"Yeah. That's what he played in high school. He was the only kid big enough to carry it."

I couldn't help but smile at the idea of Clancy as a pudgy teen, forced to play what must have seemed the least dashing of the brasses.

"Does he still have it?" The boy stood. "Would you mind if I went back and looked?"

I suppressed a sigh. "It wouldn't be a good idea. If it's not there any more, someone might accuse you of stealing it. After a death, families sometimes fight over the oddest pieces of property. Even a tuba."

He stared at me for a long moment, probably trying to decide if he were being insulted. I assumed a benign expression. Finally, he nodded. "You're right. I'll look for it when the family's here."

Shortly after that, he left. I watched while he squeezed his large frame into an old Honda, and I had a bad feeling as it chugged away.

My final visitor arrived around two in the morning. At least that's what my watch said when the banging woke me. It took me a moment to remember where I was and why. I rolled off the couch and fumbled for my weapon.

The door's peephole was cold against my eye. The round face of a middle-aged woman appeared in it, pale hair a halo in the entry light.

"Who's there?" I called from my side of the door.

"I'm family. Who are you?"

"John, one of Clancy's neighbors."

"This is Terri Deaver. What the hell are you doing in my uncle's house?"

I shifted the gun to my other hand and undid the locks. "Sorry. Won't you come in?" I kept the weapon behind the door as I opened it.

She bustled inside, eyes never leaving me. "You didn't answer my question. What are you doing here? You're not family."

"I'm house sitting till after the funeral."

Her gaze fell to my hand, froze. "That's a gun!" she shrieked.

131

What was I supposed to do? Stick it in the back of my pants like they do on television? "Yes, ma'am. Sometimes, people break into a house after someone dies. They hear the news and picture an empty house full of goods."

She seemed mollified by this explanation. Well, I'm here now. So, you can run along."

"No, ma'am."

She blinked. "What?"

"No. I'm here to protect the house."

"And who died and—who put you in charge? You're not family. How did you get inside?"

"I have a set of keys. Clancy always asked me to watch his house when he was out of town."

"You're crazy. I'll call the police. They'll throw you out!"

Ah, that ploy. "Please do, Mrs. Deaver. Of course, I'll insist that they take a full inventory of the house's contents. I want there to be a record of what was here before I departed."

She glared at me, and I gazed back calmly, noting the family resemblance to Clancy.

Our stare down was broken off by shouts and thrashing shrubbery outside the house. The flurry of sound ended with a thud that made me wince involuntarily. I knew immediately why I'd had the bad feeling.

Mrs. Deaver beat me to the door. I heard her scream, "Chuckie!"

The young bear lay sprawled across the bushes under a side window. His face was hidden from the entry light, but I saw that one side of his head was dark with blood. I moved closer, to see if he were still alive, and my foot struck something hard. The garden gnome lay on its side, Santa hat bloody.

The sky was deep turquoise by the time the coroner took Chuck's body away. I left the house to the crime scene technicians and returned to my kitchen, where I'd been before the trouble started. Going to bed was pointless. The image of young Chuck was embedded in my brain. He probably hadn't been at the side window for honorable reasons, but it didn't make him less likable. For a moment, I'd been able to picture him as a young Clancy. Mrs. Deaver was taking the death very badly: Chuck was her son. I didn't think their being at the house at the same time was coincidence.

I reassembled the ingredients for bourbon balls on my kitchen counter: powdered sugar, vanilla, and the bowl of ground pecans, now soaked thorough with the bourbon. I set the butter out so it could reach room temperature and located my measuring cup.

Creaming the sugar and butter together was a repetitive and soothing task. The rush of vapor when I uncovered the pecans brought back memories of happier holidays. My doorbell chimed about the time I finished rolling the mixture into little balls. I slid one of the trays into the refrigerator and went to see who was there. Detective Bethany Howard stood on my front step.

"Detective Howard. What can I do for you?"

She studied my apron. "John Aleron. I thought I saw that dinosaur car of yours across the street."

"It's a classic."

"Right. Well, I have a murder to investigate, and you're a witness. Are you going to invite me in, or would you rather talk at the station?"

"Here is fine. Preferable, in fact. I'm in the middle of making candy."

"How domestic." She followed me back to the kitchen. I offered her a seat at the table, but she waved me off.

"I've been going since midnight. Sitting now would be very bad."

"Sorry. I hope you identify the killer."

"You're the psychic." She smiled sardonically. "Didn't the dead guy tell you who bashed his head in?"

Ah, this was the Bethany Howard I remembered. "My talents don't work that way. Besides, it would be hearsay."

"I guess it's up to the evidence guys, then. Was that Santa hat on the gnome before last night?"

"Yes, Clancy liked dressing it up. You should have seen the bunny ears at Easter."

"It's screwed the fingerprinting." The detective moved closer to me and eyed the second tray of balls. "What are those?"

"Fondant for bourbon balls."

"What?"

"Filling. Would you like a taste?"

"Sure."

I got a toothpick out of the drawer and speared one for her. She nibbled at the mixture, then slid the rest into her mouth. "Mmm. That's tasty."

"Wait till I've coated them in chocolate."

"I've never met a man who made his own candy. I guess you have some redeeming qualities after all."

"Thanks, I think."

"It's bourbon I've come to talk to you about, actually. Did Mr. Clancy say anything about a bottle of bourbon?"

I blinked. "He *drank* bourbon ..."

"This would be a special bottle. Maybe he kept it in a place of honor." Bethany wandered to the table and examined the pomanders I'd made for the office party. She lifted one of the clove-studded oranges to sniff, and her thick-haired profile reminded me of Rosetti's portrait of Proserpine. "Did Mr. Clancy have a special bottle, one older than the rest?"

Suddenly, the reason for the late-night visits became clear. "Oh, that one."

"Yes, 'that one.' What's the story?"

"Clancy toured with Frank Sinatra for a couple of years. They were playing Detroit in December, and the liquor provided in the Green Room included a bottle of Old Crow bourbon. Sinatra preferred Jack Daniels, so Clancy asked if he could have the bourbon. Sinatra autographed it and told him it to consider it a Christmas present."

Bethany brushed a loose wisp of dark hair back from her face. "Your story matches the family's. Do you know where he kept it?"

This wasn't a casual question. "No. He showed it to me once, but he went to the back to get it. Is there a problem?"

"We can't find it."

"It's probably hidden."

"Or somebody stole it already. All the TV programs set in Vegas have revived people's interest in the Rat Pack. I looked up autographed items online this morning, and his bottle's probably worth several thousand dollars." She snitched another ball off the wax paper and popped it into her mouth. "These are absolutely delicious."

I chuckled and began sliding the tray into the refrigerator next to its mate. I nearly dropped it when she gasped.

"Where did you get that?" She was eyeing the bottle on the counter, half-hidden by canisters.

134

"From Clancy's. I borrow bourbon from him, rum from Mr. Baptiste down the street."

The detective shoved me aside. The bottle's amber contents sloshed as she snatched it up. "You took it, didn't you? That's why we couldn't find it." She turned the bottle around, examining the label.

"It's not *the* bottle. It was already open."

"There's writing here. I definitely see an F. And an S." She licked her lips, then frowned. "I bet you loved watching me eat that, jerk."

Her outrage slapped me hard, leaving me stinging inside. "Detective Howard." I gripped the edge of the nearby counter. "If I had stolen something so valuable, I would certainly not squander it in bourbon balls."

"But you could stretch the profits that way. Package them with Sinatra music and sell them online."

I continued to protest, but she pulled out the handcuffs anyway. "It's a good thing you were at a stopping point, Mr. Aleron. You're going to be gone for a while."

It wasn't my first stay in Frogtown's jail. Bethany was responsible that time too. I'd interfered in her homicide investigation. She didn't understand that ministering to the dying sometimes calls for continued service after death.

Doing her duty wasn't what angered me. What I found insulting was her belief that I would seek profit from the dead. I felt ashamed of taking that cup of bourbon. And stupid. Very stupid, taking the bottle because it hurt to be alone with a dead friend.

The possibility that Clancy had decided to open the bourbon on his own also worried me. It would be an excellent way to enjoy his last days, drinking his most prized possession and listening to the music he loved. I'd only seen the bottle once. What if my memory was flawed?

There was only one avenue left to find an answer. I stretched out on my cot and closed my eyes. Incense and candles are nice, but I don't need them to meditate. I pried loose the disrupting thoughts and shifted my internal focus to Clancy. Was his spirit aware of the situation? What would he have wanted? The only image that surfaced was a mental picture of Chuck/Clancy as a chubby blond teenager playing the tuba. The chortling notes from the big bell followed me back into waking consciousness.

I was bracing my digestive system for institutional food when the guard opened my cell door.

My accuser was with him. "Good news, Mr. Aleron. We've cleared up the problem."

"I hope that means I get out."

"Yes. I found other bottles in the liquor cabinet with similar scrawls. It seems that Mr. Clancy bought them all from a bar going out of business. The scrawl supposedly says, "For Sale." It wasn't exactly a level surface."

I gladly exited the cell. "Thank you for giving me the benefit of the doubt."

She gave me a smirk. "I figured that you wouldn't want to piss the deceased off. He knows where you live."

"I hope you find the real bottle. There's already been one murder over it."

"The rest of the family has arrived in town," she said. "I'm going to meet them tomorrow and see if we can put this issue to rest."

Sunday afternoon, I met Clancy's sister, sister-in-law, and their descendants. Within minutes, I began to understand why estrangement might be desirable. They were an argumentative clan.

"Let's hold it down to a dull roar," Bethany said. We had gathered in Clancy's living room. She'd surprised me by giving permission to attend the meeting.

"Okay, folks, here's what we know. Douglas Clancy had a bottle of bourbon that was autographed by Frank Sinatra. This item is valuable, and we strongly suspect that Charles Deaver's death was connected to it. I need to know everyone's whereabouts for Friday night through the wee hours of Saturday morning."

Jeanne Deaver, Clancy's sister, spoke first. "I was playing bridge with my friends. Myrtle drove me home around midnight. That was in Frankfort."

Olive Clancy, the late Allen Clancy's second wife, was next. "I was at home in Lexington until last night."

Karl Clancy, the nephew, said, "Mark and I live in Versailles. Friday ... I watched television and turned in when the news started." Karl was heavy-set and had the sort of irregular tan that came from working outside.

"And Mark?"

Mark Clancy, a thinner version of his father, shrugged. "I drove into Lexington to hit the bars. I don't know if anyone will remember me."

Terri Deaver was battling fresh tears, so I spoke for both for us. "At the time of the ... incident, Mrs. Deaver and I were engaged in conversation. I guess we can vouch for each other."

"I just wanted to find out who this ... *stranger* was." She waved in my direction.

Karl said, "Bull. You were there to distract this guy so Chuckie could break in."

Terri's mouth twisted in outrage. "My son was there for my protection."

"Then what was he doing beside the house?" Karl sniped. "I saw the crime scene tape."

"Maybe his attacker dragged him there," Terri said. "The murderer had to be pretty strong to use that lawn ornament as a weapon. Aren't you and Mark still in construction?"

Olive Clancy jumped to her stepson's defense. "You two wanted to steal Allen's heritage. Douglas would have left it to his brother, to his family."

Jeanne Deaver cut in. Her face had more lines than sheet music, but her eyes were as clear as Bethany's. "Doug would never have left it to Allen, dear. Allen stole Margaret from him. Doug never forgave him."

Now I knew the source of the estrangement.

"He loved Chuckie," Terri said. "They were close, both musicians, and Uncle Doug knew Chuckie was supporting a child now."

"An heirloom bottle of bourbon," the detective muttered. "Only in Kentucky."

"Chuckie should have looked for a real job," Olive Clancy hissed. "Bumming around clubs when he had a child to think about."

Terri flushed all the way to the part in her bleach job. "Chuckie couldn't give up music any more than Uncle Doug could."

"He should have thought about that before he got someone pregnant."

Terri wept afresh, and Jeanne spoke again. "Ollie, that's enough. My grandson is dead, and if you need to pass judgment, do so from the comfort of your hotel room. We don't need any more pain."

Bethany waved to bring everyone's attention back to her. "I'm sure you'll all learn who gets what when the will is read. Meanwhile, I think this bottle needs to be located. Does anyone know where Mr. Clancy kept important things?"

"Chuckie would have been the most likely to know," Jeanne Deaver said. "He was the closest to Doug."

Mark Clancy squinted at me. "How do we know *you* didn't take it? Are we supposed to believe that all you did in Uncle Doug's house was sing along with his old records?"

I confess I blushed.

"And we're accusing each other," Karl said. "Have you searched *his* place yet, detective?"

"Yes, we did." She sounded slightly embarrassed. "He had bourbon, but it wasn't the bottle we've been looking for."

As explanation, I added, "I was making bourbon balls. Finished them this morning."

"That sounds delicious," elderly Jeanne said.

"I share."

"Later." Bethany paced around the room. "Did Chuck say anything to you, Mr. Aleron, that would help us find the bottle? Did he want to see something, explore one of the other rooms?"

I thought back to my encounter with the ursine young man. "He wanted to know if Clancy still had an old tuba he'd borrowed in high school."

Terri smiled. "I remember. He thought it was lame, but Uncle Doug told him if he could handle that, he could handle any horn."

"Anything else?" Bethany pressed.

I searched my memories of that evening and remembered something else. "Mark, I'm curious. When you impugned my honesty, you mentioned my enjoyment of your late uncle's music."

"So?"

"I don't recall your coming to the door."

Mark shifted from one foot to the other. He knew he'd made a mistake. "There's a record on the turntable."

"Clancy listened to music all the time. You specified that I was singing along with it. I turned the music off after an intruder got my attention, at least an hour before Chuck made his first visit."

"Very interesting." Bethany said. "How did you know about that, sir?"

Terri seized upon this. "Mark was the intruder, and he came back later when my son and I were there. Chuckie must have heard him and investigated. Mark killed him!"

Another argument ensued, and Bethany shouted them down. "Everyone, stop. The police will investigate this fully."

"I demand that Mark's shoes be examined," Terri said. "He might have left prints in the mud."

Mark's response was a venomous glare.

"We'll check everyone's shoes before we're done," Bethany said. "But I don't think this bottle is with the tuba. I searched a room full of old instruments in the back when we were securing the house."

"Maybe we should look again," Jeanne said.

The family followed Bethany down the hall, peering through open doors as they passed them. I brought up the rear.

The instrument room was stuffed with cases in varying sizes and states of decrepitude. I recognized Clancy's cornet case, and the dark blue one for his trumpet. In the corner were several music stands and two boxes of sheet music.

"Stay here," the detective commanded. "I'll do the searching." She slipped on a pair of forensic gloves. The relatives muttered while she located the tuba case. "I searched this once. Did he have another tuba?"

"Isn't one enough?" Karl asked.

Bethany pointed her flashlight down into the bell. "No bourbon here."

Suddenly, I heard the music from my vision again – deep, laughing notes. "Try looking further down. Please."

Bethany peered deeper, and her eyes widened. "There's something white down there." She slid her arm in and pulled out an envelope. "To my heirs," she read.

"Pass that over." Karl stretched out his hand.

"Don't let him have it!" Terri shouted.

"No one gets it," Bethany said. "I'm taking it, still sealed, to our evidence room." She paused as everyone in the room groaned. "Or, I could examine it here first."

With everyone's assent, she opened the envelope and pulled out a sheet of paper. After a moment, she laughed. "Dear Presumptive Heirs: If you've come this far, you must be looking for the bourbon," she read aloud. "It is my pleasure to inform you that, once I learned of my impending death, I moved it to a safety deposit box at the bank. My attorney has the key. If you really want a drink that badly, you can buy it at the auction. The proceeds will benefit the Frogtown Children's Music Workshop."

Her words hung in the air for a moment before being dispersed by a collective sigh.

"Well," said Karl, "That's that."

"It isn't right, leaving it to strangers," Olive Clancy snapped. "Something like that should have gone to family."

I should have kept silent, but that whine of frustrated entitlement made me forget courtesy. "A family that never bothered to visit, until he had a house to plunder?"

Jeanne put a hand on my arm. "Don't."

Clancy's family didn't linger long after that. Mark wasn't arrested, but Bethany informed me that he was the new focus of her investigation.

"Lying to me about his whereabouts will help me get a search warrant for his clothes," she said as we exited the house. "I'm especially interested in his shoes. You can never get blood entirely out of leather."

"I know you'll find something. Don't leave quite yet. I have a gift."

I went back to my house and returned with a Chinese take-out carton. "These bourbon balls would have been Clancy's. He'd be very insulted if they were wasted."

She smiled. "Well, we mustn't dishonor the dead."

INDEPENDENT STAVE COMPANY
BY LORENA R. PETER

In 1912, T. W. Boswell founded the Independent Stave Company to manufacture smooth curved wood slats for use as the components of barrels. Company headquarters was in the heart of the Missouri Ozarks near the forests from which choice wood was harvested for the staves. Later, the business expanded operations into the assembly of finished barrels and opened a factory in Lebanon, Kentucky, to be closer to its largest customers. In more recent developments, the company has expanded into producing various forms of flavoring ingredients from the remainders of wood considered waste from the stave-manufacturing processes. During its long history, the company has been run by four generations of the Boswell family who oversee every aspect from the choice of wood to the delivery of the finished products. Currently, the plants ship staves to the best cooperages and barrels and flavorings to the best distilleries and vineyards in the world.

Fine bourbon is aged in fine barrels and, according to Independent Stave Company literature, "the best barrels are made right here." In support of this claim, the walls are lined with barrel tops imprinted with the names of premier distillers in the bourbon industry.

Construction of great barrels starts with the choice of the best wood: white oak with tight, straight grain. Clear wood yields a better-sealed final product with less waste during manufacturing. The first step is to cut trees into stave lengths and then into quarters, called *bolts*. Staves are cut from the bolts in an alternating pattern resulting in planks of wood with the same length, but different widths. These rough staves are stacked to season in the lumberyard. When dry, they are milled into smooth lengths tapered at the ends. Thick straight pieces are reserved for assembly into barrel ends.

At the barrel assembly plant, the job that was originally performed by skilled coopers is now reduced to component tasks accomplished by workers in the different areas of the facility. In the first, the staves of different widths are assembled (the term is *raised*) into a round barrel pulled together with a cable (called a *ring cable*) adjusted manually. The pieces are held together with temporary *head trusses* and *catch rings* until loose metal bands are placed. This loose construction is placed on a conveyor belt and run through the steam tunnel, where steam and heat soften the wood fibers. Once flexible, another machine tightly squeezes the staves together to form the curved barrel. The next machine sets the curves into the wood with dry heat.

The entire assemblage is held together with permanent metal bands called *belly bands*. Skilled coopers hammer these metal bands into perfect position with only a few well-placed mallet strikes.

The barrel is removed from the conveyor and placed on an incline to be rolled into position in an open furnace. A gas jet darkens the inside of the barrel according to customer specifications. Note that although all barrels are made of oak, each distiller specifies the degree of *toasting*. This toasting produces *char,* a darkened surface of caramelized wood sugar, that adds amber color and smoky flavor to the bourbon as it ages.

To assemble the ends of the barrel, broad pieces of wood are milled and grooved and fit together into a flat square by high degrees of pressure. Next, the squares are machined into a beveled round and branded with the name of the distiller. Finally, rounds are placed into grooves which have been cut into the ends of the barrel. Ends are held in place by metal bands. A hole is drilled into the side of the barrel and sealed with a *bung*, a wooden plug.

Quality control involves inspecting the outside for obvious flaws and, finally, testing for leaks by filling the barrel with air to a high internal pressure. Leaky barrels are sent for repair by a cooper who replaces defective staves. Sometimes these repairs require a complete reconstruction of the barrel by hand. The finished products are now ready to be shipped to distilleries and vineyards.

Note: The Independent Stave Company is one of at least seven cooperages operating in Kentucky, including Brown-Forman, who is the only major distiller in the world that owns and manufactures its own barrels. Other Kentucky cooperages include Kelvin Cooperage (Louisville), Speyside Cooperage Kentucky (Shepherdsville), ZAK Cooperage (Hodgenville), East Bernstadt Cooperage (East Bernstadt), and Canton Wood Products (Lebanon). Some of these cooperages offer tours. Check their web sites for more information.

THE BOURBON BROTHERHOOD
BY SHEILA SHUMATE

Charlotte Brandenburg threw the sponge into the sink full of vinegar water, which splashed all over the kitchen window. No amount of scrubbing would remove the spots on her grandmother's crystal glasses.

"I've told him over and over again not to use my crystal, and then not only does he use it, he puts it into the dishwasher of all things," she muttered under her breath.

The sound of clinking bottles sliding across the top of the antique buffet stopped her in mid rant. She threw off her yellow rubber gloves and stomped into the living room. She saw bourbon bottles on top of the buffet, but her jaw dropped at the sight of her husband, Parker, as he yanked on the arm of her mother's wing back chair.

"Stop moving my furniture. You know some of these are irreplaceable antiques. You can't shove it around like lawn furniture," Charlotte said.

"This is my house too, and if I want to move the furniture, damn it, I'll move it. We don't live in a museum," said Parker.

"This house has been in my family for generations. I'm just glad my mother isn't alive to see what you're doing to it."

Parker's eyes narrowed. He glared at the portrait of Charlotte's mother. "That's one thing we can agree on. She was the dictator of the manor. She told us how to live, and even who we could invite into our home."

"How dare you. My mother defended my family's honor."

"Who did she need to protect it from? Me?"

"You know she believed that a home reflects your family's standing in society, especially for the woman of the house," she shouted back. She grabbed one side of her mother's chair, and tried to move it back.

Parker grabbed the other side of the chair and held his ground. "I turned my life upside down to move you back here to Kentucky, to be with your family, but that wasn't enough for you, and especially not for your mother. I had to live my life up to her fanatical standards, like a trained animal. And now you're picking up where your mother left off." He tightened his grip on the chair.

The antique wood groaned as they both pulled in opposite directions. Charlotte finally gave in when she heard the wood begin to splinter. Her hands flew to her hips as she surrendered the battle, but not the war.

"Why do you have to have your men's night here anyway?"

"It's not a men's night! The members of the Bourbon Brotherhood are connoisseurs of fine bourbon and good cigars. Tonight, we're opening the first bottle of the small batch bourbon that I had bottled under my own label."

Charlotte's eyes started to glaze over and she thought she would lose it if she heard one more thing about bourbon. She retreated to the kitchen. The Bourbon Brotherhood had started out as an interest Parker used to network and to move up the corporate ladder, like other men used golf. It soon turned into a passion, a passion she didn't understand or share. They used to travel exclusively to high society vacation spots and go antiquing, but now Parker wanted to visit his bourbon forum friends and tour distilleries. They missed some of the biggest social events of the year because of these excursions, and their social standing was starting to suffer.

When Parker came home at night, he would wolf his dinner down. As she tried to engage him in conversation about the next social affair she wanted to host, he hurried off to his computer to start chatting online with others on the bourbon forums. Charlotte didn't want to share Parker with bourbon, and she certainly didn't want to share her home with the Bourbon Brotherhood.

They had grown apart and as far as Charlotte was concerned, her marriage was over. She could do without Parker, but her biggest fear was she would lose her family's home. She had promised her mother she would always keep the house in the family, and she had to find a way to keep that promise.

She opened her recipe box, a wedding present from her grandmother filled with all her secret recipes. It was still there, the money she had saved a little at a time, so Parker wouldn't miss it. It was her secret recipe for freedom.

Charlotte jumped when the phone rang, "I'll get it," she called out.

"Of course you will. It's not my house. It's not even my phone," said Parker.

"It's probably one of your bourbon buddies," she shot back.

Charlotte snarled into the phone, "What do you want?"

"Have I called at a bad time?" the caller asked.

"Oh … uh yes, my husband is here," she said in a low voice.

"I'll do most of the talking then. I'm calling to make sure you want to go through with this. Once it's done, it's done. I've had plenty of clients have a change of heart; you wouldn't be the first."

The sound of antique wood straining to almost the breaking point could be heard from the living room as Parker moved more furniture.

"Am I sure I want to end this nightmare of a marriage?" she whispered as loud as she dared. "Yes."

"You know what I charge my clients?"

"Yes, I have the money," she answered, and watched the doorway to make sure that Parker didn't overhear her.

"Then all that's left for you to do is start planning your new life as a single woman. I'll do the rest."

Charlotte quietly hung up the phone and walked back into the living room. Parker had lined up all his bourbon bottles on her antique buffet. "Was that one of the guys?" Parker asked, as he turned to face her, cradling a bottle of bourbon as if he was holding a baby. They had become two different people. *Yes*, she thought to herself, *I've made the right decision.*

"No, it was Vivian," she lied. "She wanted to make sure I remembered what time to meet her and the other wives for the wine tasting." She pretended to sulk. Vivian's husband Harvey was a member of the Bourbon Brotherhood. Vivian had arranged the wine tasting as an answer to the men's bourbon get-together.

"You could at least act like you'll try to enjoy it. You're always saying you want to go out."

"I don't like to drink, and an evening out with a bunch of nouveau riche social climbers that I don't even know isn't my idea of a nice evening out," Charlotte said.

145

.

The wine tasting was held at the Arts Center and served as a fundraiser for the Opera. At least these women had some taste. One other thing they had in common was their poor taste in men, a mistake Charlotte would soon remedy in our own life. Vivian waved from a table in the back of the room. She was one of those perky women who liked to manage everything. The two other women at the table looked mousy enough to be willing to let her do it, too. Charlotte weaved her way to their table.

"Oh, I'm so glad you could make it, Charlotte, I knew it was you. You're just how my Harvey described you. This is Suzy and Bonnie," Vivian gushed.

The two women nodded in unison like a pair of bobble-headed dogs. Charlotte took a seat trying to think of some air-headed conversation, as the waiter poured the first glass of wine. She wasn't a drinker, but drinking was probably the only way she was going to get through the evening.

"Harvey was right about us getting together. This is wonderful," said Vivian.

Charlotte took a big gulp of wine.

"Sweetie, it's a tasting. You better pace yourself."

"I couldn't help myself, it's very good wine," she replied, and thought that a refill couldn't come fast enough.

I've been dying to meet you," said Suzy with a big grin, which quickly faded, when she caught a glimpse of Vivian, whose eyes shot daggers at her.

"We've heard so much about your parties; that they are not to be missed if you want to see and be seen in higher social circles," said Bonnie.

"Yes, but what a shame you haven't had so many this year. Harvey has told me all about you and Parker traveling to so many Bourbon distilleries. Maybe I could help you out and take up the slack for you," said Vivian with a smug look on her face.

"It's so wonderful that our husbands share a hobby. I'm sure it's a mid-life crisis thing. It could be worse; they could be having affairs."

"And they're not drinking at a bar," Suzie chimed in.

"Oh yes dear," said Vivian "You're such a gem to let Parker use your home to host their bourbon tasting. I mean I couldn't bear them spilling bourbon on my carpet or breaking my good crystal."

"And don't forget the cigar smoke. I'm sure it makes the house reek." Bonnie managed to slip in. Charlotte cringed at the thought.

"Harvey did tell me you're particular about your home," Vivian said as she leaned closer. "Is it true what he said, that Parker has to ask permission to sit on the furniture?"

Charlotte saw a smile come across Vivian's face as her barb hit its mark.

"Parker did tell Harvey that he was proud of the care you take of your home and how he likes to show it off," Vivian added.

Charlotte had had enough of Vivian's little game. "I think I'm done for one evening," she said as she planted her glass firmly on the table.

"Oh, so early?" said Vivian. "We were just getting to know each other".

"I've learned more than enough for one evening," Charlotte replied as she rose to leave. "Oh, well, until next time," Vivian said with a forced smile.

Charlotte realized that Vivian had concocted this whole get together not only to put her in her place, but to make sure everyone else knew her place too. She was sure Vivian had invited Bonnie and Suzy, both known gossips, to make sure the word spread.

Charlotte sat in the car, gripping her steering wheel in the parking lot, trying to sort out her life. She had tried to be the first lady in the social circuit. Who was she trying to impress with her perfect home? The likes of women like Vivian, or worse, gossiping bubble brains like Bonnie and Suzy? Maybe her marriage trouble was partly her fault. She had been a shrew of a wife to Parker; no wonder he had turned to his Bourbon Brotherhood for companionship. She was totally absorbed by her family's house and moving up the social ladder, like her mother.

It suddenly struck her what she had set in motion. She frantically looked at her watch. Ten thirty.

Has it already happened? she thought. Maybe it wasn't too late. She dialed the number she had used to hire the hit man, but only got his voice mail.

She thought of calling Parker, but what would she say? *Sorry, dear, I hired someone to kill you, but I changed my mind.* Her only chance was to get there before the hit man.

Her mind raced along with her Mercedes as she sped through her upscale neighborhood and thought about how she had gotten herself into this situation. She couldn't have asked Parker for a divorce. Dividing their assets would have meant selling her beloved home and she would do anything to avoid that, including murder. Now she wished she had never seen that ad on Greggslist.

She ran up onto the curb as she careened around the corner onto her street. The short burst of a siren caused Charlotte to look and see the red lights in her rearview mirror. Panic gripped her, and she stopped so quick that the police car almost rear-ended her.

The officer stepped out of his patrol car, slamming the door. He approached the side of her car.

Stay calm, don't panic, she told herself as the officer leaned down, looked through her car window and sized her up.

"I'm so sorry, officer, I didn't realize I was driving so fast," she stammered, and prayed he would hurry and let her go.

"Ma'am, you were not only speeding, you ran up that curb back there. I smell alcohol on your breath; have you been drinking?"

"Just a glass of wine. I'm not drunk, if that is what you're insinuating,"

"Ma'am, get out of the car, please," he ordered

"Oh officer," she pleaded. "I live in that house right over there." She pointed two houses down the street. The policeman glanced over at the darkened house, "That house over there, ma'am?"

"Yes, please don't do this to me in front of my neighbors."

He straightened up. "If you don't get out of the car, I'll be forced to arrest you in front of your neighbors."

Reluctantly, Charlotte got out, held her head down, and hoped that none of her neighbors would recognize her. She performed the sobriety test for the officer in the middle of her street. She managed to control her nerves, got through it, and passed. Quickly she signed the speeding ticket, with one eye on her darkened house.

After she pulled into her driveway, it felt like an eternity as she waited for the policeman to drive off. As soon as he passed out of sight, she fumbled the keys, yanking them out of the ignition. Was it too late? She ran to unlock the front door and stepped inside the foyer. She paused to let her eyes adjust to the dark, afraid to turn on the lights.

"Parker, Parker are you in bed?" she called out, but there was no answer. *He must have done it. I am too late*, she said to herself.

Maybe it was for the best, she tried to convince herself. What would she have done if they couldn't make their marriage work? Would she have been able to go through this again? The hit man had not told her any details of how he would do it, so she wouldn't slip up and tell the police something she shouldn't have known about the murder. The only thing she needed to remember to tell the police was that the money from her recipe box was missing, so that it would look like a robbery. She had to call them soon to keep her alibi of the wine tasting plausible, especially after her traffic ticket.

She made her way in the darkness to the living room, where Parker probably would have had one last glass of bourbon after the guys had left. That's where it must have happened. Was that him in front of the fireplace? She saw something lying on the floor. She froze for a moment, but then forced herself to take a couple of tentative steps closer.

What she saw made her angry, her mother's wing back chair knocked over. "That pig!" she blurted.

The light snapped on. Charlotte spun around to see a very alive Parker and a man she had never seen before. Was this the hit man? Had she walked in before he had a chance to finish his job? Her mind was numb with shock.

"Who are you?" she asked, not sure she wanted to hear his answer.

"I believe you know me, Mrs. Brandenburg," he replied.

My God, it's the voice on the telephone. The hit man was right here in the living room.

"This is Detective David Mathers. He's the newest member of our Bourbon Brotherhood," said Parker.

Charlotte stood speechless.

"You look surprised, Charlotte."

"I just thought everyone must have gone home," she stammered, trying to quickly think of something to say. Maybe she was wrong, she thought as she struggled to remain composed.

"I met David on the bourbon forum on the internet. He's part of a special internet crime task force. They've been running a murder-for-hire sting on Greggslist. You know the ad service on the Internet. I'm sure you've heard of it."

"It's nice to finally get to meet you, Mrs. Brandenburg," Detective Mathers said.

It is *the voice!* she thought, panicking.

"Their ad on Gregglist's web site has an interesting name: Marriage Mercenaries for Hire," Parker said.

Charlotte gasped. It was the ad where she had found her hit man. Two police officers came into the room. One was the officer who had stopped her for speeding.

"Glad to see you made it home, Mrs. Brandenburg."

"What's going on here" Charlotte demanded, as one of the officers put handcuffs on her wrists.

"Stopping a murder, madam," said Detective Mathers.

Parker and Mathers walked out onto the veranda and watched the police officers put Charlotte in the squad car. "Let's open a bottle of that small batch bourbon that I had distilled," said Parker.

"What did you decide to name it?"

"Sweet Revenge," Parker answered with a smile.

JIM BEAM INC.
BY CHERYL STUCK

For Frederick Booker Noe III, being Jim Beam's great-grandson and Booker Noe's son had its perks. As a child, little Fred's playground was a bourbon distillery. Fred was born in 1957 and as soon as he was able to stand up in the seat of the truck, he rode next to his dad to the Jim Beam distillery. On weekends, four-year-old Fred hung out with his "Pop" at the distillery while his mother worked as a medical technologist in a nearby hospital. Fred described the distillery as a "comfort zone," full of "little boy stuff" like real trucks and trains. "If the engineer would see me, he'd stop and I'd ride in the engine with him."

Fred's earliest memory of the distillery is of the playful nature of the employees—all men back then. Some of the guys would be hauling barrels or trash and enjoyed playing pranks on little Fred. "They would set stuff up so it would fall, and I'd look around to figure out what the hell I did," Fred said with a laugh. But he always felt safe because he knew all the guys watched out for him. "There was somebody everywhere and I couldn't get in any trouble, so I would roam around and go to the shop where the Coke machine and vending machine was, and get a soft drink and watch them weld stuff," Fred said.

"On the grounds, there were a lot of open areas and lakes. That's where I learned to hunt rabbits and we fished. Nowadays we have no hunting allowed, but back then, there was a hill there and we would go and poke around and a rabbit would run out and my dad would say, 'Okay, shoot at it, shoot at it!'"

When Fred got a little older, around age ten, his dad taught him to check the temperatures of the fermenting mash. Fred said, "It's critical that the temperature of the mash never gets to 93 degrees because if it gets that high, the yeast starts getting killed due to the heat. We would go there with a thermometer tied to a string so we didn't lose it. We'd drop it in there and shake it around. Dad's eyes weren't that good, so he'd say, 'What's that say?' That was his way of teaching me about the distillery. We'd take samples of the pH back to the lab and see how much acid was in it, because on weekends they didn't run."

Fred said his dad (Booker Noe) was proud of every drop of bourbon he made. Booker taught his son well, even allowing Fred to help choose the small batch bourbons in the same kitchen where his grandfather used to mix the family strain of yeast.

But Booker Noe didn't take the distillery for granted and frequently warned young Fred that it might not always be there for him. "He tempered my enthusiasm, saying, 'It can go away at any time.'"

Noe's cautions were based on past experiences. Shortly after Prohibition, it became illegal to make, sell or transport alcohol in the United States, whether it was beer, wine, gin, vodka, or whiskey. But many of the distilleries affected had farms attached to them because they also sold a by-product after distilling, called stillage (also called slop). The stillage is very high in protein, so they could feed it to the pigs and cattle and sell them off as means of income.

In 1920, during Prohibition, Jim Beam sold his farm and threw the distillery in with it as part of the deal to get it out of his hands. Fred Noe said that Jim Beam didn't trust the American public to stop drinking just because a law told them to. He didn't want to be involved in any illegal activities that might result from that.

Through the years, Fred heard a lot of stories about his family's business. Regarding Prohibition, he said, "There was no cool down period. Today you're making, aging and selling bourbon and the law passes—tomorrow it's illegal. No time to get rid of inventory or anything."

During Prohibition, Jim Beam tried his hand at coal mining, citrus farming, and a rock quarry business. Through those efforts, Jim lost almost all his money, according to Fred. Making bourbon was what he was good at.

The day Prohibition was repealed, in 1933, at age 70, Jim Beam applied for a license and bought the old Murphy Barber Distillery in Clermont, Kentucky, where Jim Beam Distillery is now located. He partnered with a couple of friends in Chicago and accumulated enough credit to crank up the still again.

Fred said, "My dad always said the guys in Chicago thought Jim Beam had the money, and Jim Beam thought they did, but between the three of them, they found bankers to give them enough money. It was the 1930s and it was pretty tough, but somehow they got enough and the thing took off and as they say, the rest is history."

Jim and his son, Jeremiah (Jere), set up the new distillery in Clermont in only 120 days. Even after Jim Beam's death in 1947, Jeremiah continued to grow the business, opening a second distillery in 1954 near Boston, KY. Both distilleries continue to produce bourbon.

Over the years, the company suffered disasters, like the tornado that hit the Booker Noe plant. It destroyed several warehouses and ripped the tin off the buildings and cost the company several thousand barrels of bourbon. More recently, lightning struck one of the warehouses and destroyed 20,000 barrels.

The Family History

The company has changed hands and names several times, but a member of the Beam family has always been involved. Jacob Beam originally founded the company and sold his first barrel of whiskey in 1795. He had experimented with corn and grains that grew on his farm in Kentucky, blending them with spring water. He ran the blend through a still, then aged it in barrels.

Jacob Beam's son, David, took over his father's responsibilities in 1820 when he was only 18. He utilized new technology, including the telegraph, steam-powered ships, and railroads to expand the company's distribution. Then David's son, David M. Beam, took over in 1850 and moved the distillery to Nelson County, Kentucky, to be near Kentucky's first railroad. In 1880, Beam bourbon was bottled and called Old Tub. Thanks to the telegraph and railroad expansion, the Beam family persevered and made it a national brand.

When the Civil War broke out in 1861, Kentucky was right in the middle of it, with both Confederate and Union soldiers passing through Beam land. This was a stroke of luck for the Beams, because bourbon was used to barter and was often considered more valuable than money.

David M.'s son, James B. Beam (later, Colonel James B. Beam), insisted on being called Jim. When he took over the business from his father, it thrived until Prohibition. After Jim re-opened the distillery years later, the bourbon became known as Jim Beam Bourbon.

T. Jeremiah (Jere) Beam (Jim's son) took over the business and made it global when he shipped cases of bourbon to U.S. servicemen stationed overseas. Soon after, European pubs and restaurants began serving Jim Beam bourbon.

Booker Noe was the grandson of James B. Beam. In 1988, he introduced the world's first, small batch, uncut, straight-from-the-barrel bourbon and called it "Booker's."

In 1984, at age 27, Fred went to work for the company after trying his hand in the entertainment business. In 2007, he became a master distiller in the company his family created.

In the 1960s the company was sold to the American Tobacco Company and the name changed to American Brands, then later Fortune Brands (a sister company to Titleist, Master Lock, and Owen). But in 2011, the company officially returned to its roots and changed the name to Beam, Inc., concentrating solely on spirits after selling off its golf and home security issues.

In 2012, more than 60 other whiskey brands could be tied to a member of the extended Beam family. Jim Beam, Inc. had produced more than 12 million barrels and was considered the largest and best-selling bourbon producer in the world.

Although the family no longer owns the business, Fred Noe is the seventh generation of the Beam family to distill Jim Beam Bourbon and is still involved in the company. As of this writing, Fred still lives in Bardstown, Kentucky, in a house next door to the Beam family home. He and his wife, Sandy, have a son, Frederick Booker Noe IV. Fred III oversees production of the spirits and goes on the road doing seminars and educating people on bourbon in the U.S. and overseas. People's eyes light up when they are introduced to Jim Beam's great grandson. When asked what the best way was to drink bourbon, Fred Noe said, "Any damn way you please."

Three things Fred Noe wants the world to know about Jim Beam Bourbon:

"A Beam family member has been involved in making this bourbon since 1795 and it's a heritage. I think it's pretty neat because nobody else can say that. I'm working here as an employee and while we don't own it, I'm still very proud that my family has been making this bourbon since 1795.

"The ingredients we put in our bourbon is the best we can find. It's my responsibility to make sure that every drop of bourbon produced here is the best bourbon the Beam family can make.

"We love for people to come down and see how it's made. It's amazing when I'm on the road how many people have no clue what goes into making a bottle of bourbon. The aging takes time. Our Jim Beam White Label for example: It takes four years from the time it's made to the time it's bottled. I venture to say a lot of people can't tell you what they were doing four years ago. Our premium bourbons, like Knob Creek, is aged nine years. We put a lot of heart and soul in every bottle that goes out of here. People don't realize what it takes to put the juice in that bottle."

Jim Beam Decanters

Jim Beam bourbon decanters have been around since the 1950s. When they started filling decanters with bourbon, they were made by Regal China, which was a sister company to Jim Beam. The first decanter was shaped like a bowling pin. After that, many shapes and configurations were designed, from animals to cars and famous people.

The initial plan was to make a little more money on the bourbon by putting it in a pretty bottle, but it became a great marketing tool when people began collecting the decanters and buying Jim Beam bourbon just to enhance their collection of Beam bottles.

In the 1970s, the fad took off and other companies jumped on board.

Jim Beam stopped producing the decanters in the late 1980s due to economics.

SPECIAL LABEL
BY GWEN MAYO

Doc Haydon drove like a madman. He careened around the corner onto Short Street with only the two right wheels of the piano box buggy touching the ground. I had never seen Sam, his old horse, move so fast nor look so frightened. Sam strained against the harness, steam coming from both nostrils, large eyes bulging, his dark mane flying in the wind.

"Donnelly," he shouted. "Hold up."

It was unusual for the medical examiner to drive recklessly. Not that Doc Haydon looked much like his usual self. His round red face was contorted into an expression of pure rage. Tufts of ginger and white hair stuck out from the sides of his head in a manner that was more reminiscent of an ancient Celtic warrior than a modern medical doctor.

Doc prided himself on his appearance, but today he wore neither hat nor topcoat. His collarless shirt gaped open at the neck in defiance of the snow. His sleeves were rolled up to his elbows, exposing a shocking portion of his winter undergarments.

It was fortunate that the cold had already reddened my face. I would have been mortified to reveal my female sensibilities in front of him. I'd worked very hard to conceal my gender. I hoped he would not discover the truth until I was on his autopsy table and beyond blushing.

"Get in," Haydon ordered, as he pulled to an abrupt stop.

"Not if you're driving."

"Donnelly, it's an emergency," he said. "I need your help."

Curiosity overrode my common sense and I climbed in beside him.

Off we went. Haydon didn't take his eyes off Sam's steaming hindquarters.

"What sort of emergency are we in such an all fired hurry about?" I asked.

"I've been robbed."

He took the sharp corner of North Upper Street entirely too fast, and again almost turned the buggy over.

"Either slow down or give me the reins," I said. "No theft is worth dying over."

"A lot you know."

"Money isn't as valuable as your life."

"I don't give a fig about money. The scoundrels absconded with my bourbon."

"Bourbon? You fool. You're risking my neck over a bottle of bourbon?"

"A barrel," he snapped, slowing down a little.

I wasn't sure if we were slowing because I asked, or because we were nearly to his house. At least I could hope to survive the ride.

"Doc, leave it to the police. A whole wagonload of liquor is probably less expensive than hiring me. It's just bourbon."

Dr. Haydon pulled to a halt near his back door and stared at me like I was an escapee from the lunatic asylum.

"This is not 'just' bourbon. It's one of the barrels from Oscar Pepper's estate. Bought it at auction back in '67. Been aging it ever since."

"Pepper? Isn't that the new distiller over on Manchester Street?"

A look of exasperation told me I was wrong.

"How can you live in Kentucky for fourteen years and know nothing about bourbon? That new distiller is his grandson, Colonel James Pepper," he said as he climbed down from the buggy. "He claims that he is using the old family recipe, but it'll be years before we know if he inherited skill to be worthy of the Pepper name."

The doctor waited for me to catch up with him before going into the house.

"I can't believe you don't know about the old Pepper distillery. They made the best bourbon this country has ever known. The family sold the distillery and moved off to New York after old man Pepper died. When his estate was settled, they auctioned off his private stock. You should 'a been there. About a hundred barrels were sold for ten to fifteen dollars apiece, depending on the age."

"You paid $15 for a barrel of bourbon?"

His head dropped and his ears turned a deeper shade of red.

"No. I bought one of the cheaper ones."

"So, you want me to find a barrel of cheap whiskey?"

"It is not 'cheap whiskey'," he growled. "Just wasn't as old as some. In case you don't remember, hard coin was hard to come by after the war. I couldn't afford one of the aged barrels. Shoot fire, Donnelly! Most of my patients were paying with farm goods. I was lucky to scrape up enough cash for one of the younger barrels. Then I had to barter services to get it freighted here."

I grinned.

"Worth it, though," he boasted. "I've been aging it in the cellar, as close as I could to the way Old Man Pepper would have done it. That barrel holds some of the finest sipping bourbon ever made."

His clear blue eyes darkened with anger as he looked toward the broken cellar door.

"You gotta find it, Ness. Today."

"I know I'll regret asking, but why the urgency? You said you bought it back in 1867. That barrel has been sitting in your cellar nigh on fourteen years. Will the quality suddenly diminish if it isn't found today?"

"Exactly," he yelled. "That barrel is aged to perfection. Whoever took it knows that. That's why they took the whole danged thing. It would have been a lot easier to break the bung and drain the bourbon into jugs."

He had my curiosity piqued.

"So, the barrel is the valuable part?"

"Not without the bourbon."

Dr. Haydon grabbed me by the lapels of my coat and pulled me inches from his face. His eyes held the sort of horror that I sometimes saw in the faces of the dead. The intensity frightened me.

"I can't wait for the police. It won't exist if it isn't found today! One of the distillers I contacted about bottling my bourbon has to have stolen it. Nobody else knew or would care about the barrel. They want it whole, intact, with the Pepper stamp to prove its worth. The lout will mix it with some lesser quality distilling and make a small fortune from the result."

"The Pepper stamp?"

"Every legal barrel is stamped by the distiller and numbered by the Revenue Cabinet the day it is made. That stamp proves the age and quality of the bourbon. Some detective you are, not even knowing that."

159

He made a visible effort to control himself then, dropping his eyes to the toes of his shoes. He must have remembered that he wanted my help.

"I was a fool to want to have it properly bottled instead of tapping the barrel," he finally said. "I wanted to treat it with the respect it deserves. Good bourbon needs to be properly filtered and bottled. I was going to have a special label made. Maybe give a few bottles to my friends for Christmas."

He eyed me meaningfully. "The kind of friends who would appreciate having a pint of fine sippin' whiskey."

"Ah. But if you can prove the barrel is yours, wouldn't selling it show the distiller was a thief?"

"Donnelly, you still don't understand. He wouldn't have to sell it here. He could ship it to New York or Boston. Dang it, with the transcontinental railroad they could be selling my bourbon in a San Francisco saloon this time next week!"

"Calm down, Doc," I said. "I'll find your bourbon. Are the distillers the only people you told about the barrel?"

"Yes."

"Do you know when the barrel was taken?"

"It couldn't have been long; the tracks were still fresh when I arrived. I was up all night with the Jenkins' baby."

"Let me have a look around the cellar, then. Maybe your thief left some evidence behind."

"There's nothing there," he said miserably, "just an empty rack and puddles of melting snow."

"Footprints?" I asked hopefully.

His face brightened.

"Yes. In the snow outside the cellar."

"Good," I said. "We'll start there. There's not much traffic out in this weather. If we're lucky, I may be able to follow your thieves all the way to Manchester Street."

In truth, there wasn't much chance I would be able to follow the tracks that far. The wagon tracks were deep and wider than those left by Dr. Haydon's buggy. That was in our favor. But the city was waking up and would soon turn its snowy blanket into a patchwork quilt of shoveled walkways and rutted streets. Doc had already run over this set of tracks twice. Now the omnibuses were making their rounds in the city's fashionable neighborhoods, ready to carry whatever customers they could entice into downtown shops. Unless the wagon had stuck to the back alleys all the way to its destination, I would lose it in the jumble of tracks downtown.

Once outside, I brushed the thin layer of new fallen snow from the wheel marks. The tracks did tell a story. Broad hoofprints of a pair of well-shod draft horses and the distinct indentation of iron-plated wagon wheels told me the thief was driving a sturdy work wagon or dray. It was unlikely that an average city thief would own such an expensive rig. The distillers would need this kind of wagon to transport their spirits to the freight depot.

I turned my attention from the wagon marks to those left by its occupants. Dr. Haydon had trampled some of the prints, but the story remained.

Two men, one heavier than the other, had broken into Dr. Haydon's cellar. There was no sign that they had tried to enter the main house, so they had known what they were looking for and where to look. The scene certainly indicated that Doc was right about who was behind the theft.

The long stride and the way the heels of the larger man's brogans sank into the soft earth told me he was responsible for smashing the cellar door. I wasn't surprised that the thief had an accomplice. It would take a couple of hefty men to roll the heavy barrel up Dr. Haydon's cellar steps and load it into the back of the wagon. The brogans told me, though, that the unscrupulous distiller had not personally set foot on the property. A businessman wouldn't wear the straight-laced work shoes sold in general mercantile stores. The distinctive square toes of the brogans said our thief was a day worker, maybe one of the teamsters working at the distilleries.

I measured the footprints before looking downstairs.

The warm sweet aroma of bourbon greeted me when I approached the cellar. Dr. Haydon had obviously greatly prized his purchase. He had devised a block and tackle system that allowed him to easily turn the aging barrel. The empty rack made me angry on his behalf.

"I want it back, Ness," he said.

I hadn't heard the doctor approach. The sound of his voice made me jump.

"Didn't mean to startle you."

"No harm done," I said. "You'd better get Old Sam in a warm blanket before he catches pneumonia."

He took a yellowed paper from his pocket.

"The auction receipt," he said, handing it to me. "It has the lot and barrel numbers you need to prove it is mine."

I nodded, put the document in my vest pocket, and turned to go.

The only tracks on Third Street were those made by Dr. Haydon's buggy and those belonging to the thieves. It was easy enough to decipher which belonged to the heavy wagon. Instead of heading downtown, where I would have quickly lost the trail in the heavy traffic, the wagon turned west and wandered past the neat little row houses lining College Park.

I was able to follow the trail for about a mile before encountering difficulty. The main road leading into town was a jumble of tracks. The intersection was far too busy to study any one set closely. Even crossing the street without getting run over by one of the teamsters was a challenge. These men were intent upon making good time and paid little heed to pedestrians crossing the thoroughfare. I bolted across the street at the first opportunity and examined all the tracks that continued down Third Street toward the wire factory.

Only three wagons had passed this way, but all of them were of a similar type. The snow was obscuring them more with each passing moment. I couldn't be sure the one I wanted had even come this way, let alone which set of tracks belonged to it.

I looked at the whitened lawns of the new suburban neighborhood as I tried to decide whether I should visit the distilleries or start knocking on doors. I had little hope that anyone had seen Dr. Haydon's precious barrel pass this way, but the prospect of a two-mile hike through a snowstorm to reach the distillery district made me opt for door knocking.

Six doors later, I had been yelled at, slathered in peach preserves by an overly friendly toddler, and snapped at by a monster masquerading as a dog. The latter I managed to escape by leaving one pocket of my peach-flavored coat dangling from his fangs.

Sodden, disheveled, and utterly discouraged, I fled the house with what little was left of my dignity and crashed headlong into a young woman walking along the edge of the road.

"I beg your pardon," I said, retrieving my hat from the gutter.

She laughed.

"You're not going to put that back on your head," she said, pointing to my derby. "It's filthy."

"I suppose not," I said, looking at the disreputable hat sagging in my gloved hand. "At least not before it is cleaned and blocked."

"I'm sorry," she said, between giggles.

She hid her rosy cheeks behind her muff, but couldn't hide the laughter.

"Thanks," I said, angrily. "It's good to know someone finds my misery such a source of amusement. Perhaps you would be more delighted to know I'm traipsing the streets on a fool's errand, looking for a barrel of stolen bourbon."

"I truly am sorry, "she said more soberly. "I couldn't resist watching you try to get away from that dog. I—I guess I needed to see that someone was having a worse day than me."

Unlike me, she didn't look any the worse for wear. I was not particularly inclined to forgive her impertinent laughter.

After an awkward pause, she started to leave, then stopped and looked back at me.

"I don't know if it helps, but I saw a wagon go by about a half an hour ago. I thought it odd that there was only one barrel in the back."

"One barrel?"

Questions rolled out one after another.

"Was it an old barrel? Dark stains at the seams? What about the occupants? Did you get a good look at the driver? Maybe two men? One bigger and heavier than the other? Were they headed west?"

She laughed again. "I guess what they say about Irishmen and whiskey is right. You want your barrel back awfully bad."

"It isn't my bourbon. The barrel of bourbon belongs to Dr. Haydon, the County Medical Examiner. Someone stole it from his house this morning."

I took a card out of my pocket and handed it to her. My cards were the very best offered by Republic Printing, but she handled it as though it were diseased.

"Ness Donnelly, private investigator," I said, by way of introduction.

She eyed me critically for a long moment before saying anything.

"Mrs. Ryder," she said stiffly. "But you are not Ness Donnelly. I knew him when I was a little girl. There is a resemblance though. Kin?"

I shifted uneasily under her gaze. Had she known my brother? All traces of humor vanished from her dark eyes as she waited for me to reply.

"Yes," I said.

I didn't want to elaborate. She had already caught me in one lie. More dishonesty would only complicate the situation.

Some years ago, a shrewd woman had seen through my disguise. Though I had immersed myself entirely into the male identity, I never felt entirely safe from prying female eyes. Women noticed small details that often entirely escaped the male gaze. Much of my success as an investigator was built upon my own skill at observation.

There was a long awkward pause while I wondered whether the beast I had barely escaped was less dangerous than the petite young woman in front of me.

"There were two men," she said, at last. "They were headed toward Georgetown Pike. That's all I know—Mr. Donnelly."

She dropped the card into my gloved hand and walked away.

I watched her for a few seconds, trying to understand the encounter. After she'd gone, I realized that she had so unnerved me that she hadn't answered all my questions about the men. I hoped she was right in her observations and I was still on their trail.

My pace picked up once I got past the wire factory and the Scott Brothers warehouses. Beyond the warehouses, the street became little more than a dirt trail winding through farmland. It was impossible to distinguish between new wagon tracks and old under the growing blanket of snow. I stopped at the corner of Jefferson Street for a moment to examine the long double rows of board fences lining the road beyond the intersection. Here and there a gate had been placed leading to a barn, but an undisturbed layer of snow topped the fences. Satisfied that they could not have turned onto one of the farm roads, I decided not to trudge on. The thieves were moving slowly, probably trying not to attract attention, and the road took a circuitous route. Since only the stockyards and the lunatic asylum lay north on Georgetown, I could close much of the distance between us by heading south and cutting through back yards and alleyways.

If Mrs. Ryder was right about them being only a half an hour ahead of me, I might be able to spot them before they turned off the long open stretch of West Main Street. After that, they could easily vanish into the rolling hills of Irishtown.

By the time I reached West Main, my sides ached from running and the melting snow dripped from my close-cropped curls, running in cold rivulets down the back of my neck. I stopped to catch my breath and look for the wagon. One old farm wagon and a couple of buggies were heading into town, but nothing resembling the rig I sought moved on the slushy street.

For a moment I thought I had lost them, when out of the corner of my eye I caught sight of the wagon headed out of town. I stood panting as the slow-moving wagon continued west across the rail tussle and turned into—the cemetery? It made no sense.

Absently, I ran a gloved hand through my wet hair, as I stood there puzzling over the strange turn of events. With a shrug, I started walking toward the graveyard. There was no need to hurry now. There was only one entrance to the City of the Dead. The thieves would have to leave the way they entered.

Slowing down was not the best idea I had ever had. The wind found every thin spot in my damp clothing, and it took all my energy to trudge through what was now several inches of snow. I plunged my hands deep into the pockets of my wool topcoat, but could do nothing to stop my teeth from chattering. If I were smart, I'd turn around and go home. Then again, if I were smart I wouldn't have been tromping through the snow looking for a barrel of bourbon in the first place.

I tried to remind myself that Doc Haydon was my closest friend. When that didn't help, I started calculating the expenses for ruined clothing and fever medicines that I was going to need after getting soaked to the skin. I was contemplating whether I should make him pay for the new boots I had been admiring at Watkins & Spencer, when I spotted a pair of draft horses exiting the cemetery gate.

There was barely time to duck behind the nearest bush before the wagon pulled into view. Huddling in my hiding place, I watched it pass and saw that the bed was empty. The driver was tall and broad-chested, with a wide nose that had been broken and badly set. I was sure I would recognize him again easily. His companion was almost entirely concealed by the driver's large frame, and I couldn't get a look at his face.

"So, they stashed the barrel in the cemetery," I muttered, as a plan began forming in the back of my mind. The thieves could wait. Dr. Haydon's concern was for his bourbon.

It didn't take me long to find where they'd hidden the stolen goods. On a morning like this, nobody was inclined to pay a visit to the grave of a deceased loved one. All I had to do was follow the lone set of wagon tracks to their destination.

On my way into the cemetery, I noticed the padlock used to secure the gates at night had been left unlatched when the chain was removed. I liberated it from its chain as I passed.

The wagon tracks stopped only a short distance from the gates. Footprints and the marks of the barrel being rolled made a path down the hill to one of the family mausoleums dug out of the hillside. Along one edge of the barrel track something black had stained the snow in several places. I noted the Shepherd name above the door and began to question Dr. Haydon's assumption that only the distillers could have taken his bourbon.

Inside the tomb, Dr. Haydon's precious barrel rested peacefully atop the crypt of a long-dead Union officer. Melting snow still dripped from the side of the barrel, spreading a black stain onto the stone floor.

I slipped the lock through the latch above the one already there and fastened it with a satisfying click, then set off to find the watchman.

The elderly watchman was huddled over a brazier of coals when I entered the stone gatehouse. He seemed reluctant to leave the little warmth they offered.

"Somethin' I can do for ya?"

"I need to go fetch the police," I said. "If anyone comes through the gate, would you keep an eye on them and make sure they don't go near the mausoleums down the hill?"

"Can't imagine why anybody would be visitin' on a day like this, but the graveyard is open and somebody came by while I was on rounds."

"They were up to no good. There is stolen property stashed here, and I need to get the police and a wagon to recover it."

Indignation flashed through the watchman's eyes.

"You'd best be right about that, young feller," he said. "I don't cotton to tomfoolery on my watch."

He reached into the wooden box in the corner of the guardhouse and pulled out an old Remington revolver that looked too heavy for him to lift.

"I don't think that will be necessary," I said.

"You go fetch the police," he replied. "Won't nobody be disturbin' the final rest of those in my charge."

I bit back the retort on the tip of my tongue and prayed he didn't accidentally cause his behemoth pistol to discharge in my absence. Fortunately, I spotted Officer Watts making a return trip from dropping off prisoners at the city jail. I flagged him down not far from the gates.

"You're looking a bit worse for wear, Mr. Donnelly," he said with a grin.

"Doc Haydon has me out on a fool's errand," I groused. "A couple of hooligans stole a barrel of bourbon from his house this morning."

He laughed.

"Fine job for an Irishman," he said.

I scowled at him. I didn't see tramping all over town in the worst weather we had seen in years to be a fit job for anyone.

"Don't get your temper up," he said. "I was simply having a bit of fun."

"You could have a bit more fun helping me get the stolen property back to the Doc and arresting the culprits."

"Climb up," he said, motioning to the seat beside him. "So, where's the doc's whiskey?"

"City of the Dead."

He blinked. "Who the blazes would do a thing like that?"

"Someone who didn't think we would look for it there. Right now, though, I want to get back to the cemetery before the thieves' return. I'm afraid the watchman may try to use that pistol of his."

Officer Watts' eyes shot open.

"God Almighty. Has he still got that old Remington he used in the Home Guard?"

A shot rang out in answer to his question.

I grabbed the railing as Watts urged the horses into a trot. Neither of us dared give voice to our fear. We rounded the corner into the cemetery without slowing. As soon as we made the turn, I grabbed the shotgun Watts kept in the box and held it ready to fire.

167

"I see you found the law," the watchman shouted when we neared the mausoleums.

"We heard shooting." I said, lowering the shotgun.

"Oh that weren't nothin' to worry about," he replied, flashing a toothless grin. "I did a little lock removal. You didn't say what was stole."

I buried my head in my hand at the sight of the cemetery lock busted open by the pistol ball.

"Got to hand it to you, Donnelly," Officer Watts said. "You sure got a way of livening up a morning."

"Just give me a hand with this barrel," I said, as I climbed down from the wagon.

The rusty iron hinges creaked as we opened the door, adding to my uneasiness at entering the mausoleum. It seemed somehow wrong to take the barrel from the crypt where it rested. I had to remind myself it didn't belong to the occupants of the room. I took out the yellowed receipt Doc Haydon had given me and compared the lot and barrel numbers listed to those stamped on the barrel.

"This is it," I said, showing the document to Officer Watts.

I noticed, when I handed the receipt to Watts, that my gloves left black smudges on the back of the page. The aging bourbon had left large dark blotches of sticky candy on the barrel, but my gloves did not smell of bourbon or feel sticky. It was the same black stain I had spotted on the granite slab covering the crypt.

The stains hadn't been there before we entered. I looked more closely at the door and saw a dark handprint on the wrought iron bars.

Maybe, when we reached Dr. Haydon's house, I could examine the stain more closely. Right now, it was all I could do to handle my share of the load.

Twenty minutes later, I was knocking on Haydon's door.

"I have your bourbon," I said, when he answered.

His face lit up.

"You caught them!"

"No," I said, "but I think I know who is responsible. I only need for you to answer one question."

"What?"

"The special label you were having printed for the bourbon ... did you engage the Republic Printing House for the job?"

A look of confusion crossed his face. "Yes. How did you know that?"

"I think this is printer's ink," I said, showing him the dark stains on my right glove.

"Ink?"

"I followed the thieves to the City of the Dead, and found your bourbon locked in one of the private mausoleums. The one owned by the Shepherd family. Your thieves got the barrel wet while they were rolling it around. Wet enough to pick up ink stains from the wagon they were using. I didn't make the connection until I opened the door and got the same black stains all over my glove."

Haydon looked confused.

"That's when it dawned on me that the wagon I was following was pulled by a pair of draft horses," I said. "Two horses, not the four that a distillery wagon would need to haul heavy barrels. Then I remembered your label and realized you had told someone else about the bourbon: the printer. Republic Printing was founded by the Shepherds."

"That lowdown scoundrel," Haydon exclaimed, "they should throw him under the jail. Guess he valued my bourbon more than my business."

I pulled off the stained glove and handed it to him.

"I'm not even sure you can get him arrested. There's not much evidence," I said, unless you can match the ink to his press. You and Officer Watts can figure out what to do now."

"Prosecute vigorously, of course," the doc said. "So, Donnelly, I guess you'll be expecting a couple bottles as payment."

He patted the side of the barrel and smiled.

"A couple bottles?" I sputtered. "After what you put me through today?"

"You didn't even work an entire morning."

"I thought you were going to be giving out bottles to your friends for Christmas," I said.

He shook his head. "A real friend, Donnelly, buys boots for a friend who needs them," he replied, looking pointedly at my battered work boots. "You wouldn't expect me to have any cash left after that, would you?"

I grinned. "A couple of bottles of your special label will do just fine."

169

MAKER'S MARK
BY SUSAN BELL

In 1867, Louis Simonin, a French geologist, travelled to America to tour the gold and silver mines of Colorado. He reported on his travels through letters to a friend in Paris, later published in book form (*The Rocky Mountain West in 1867*). He describes the hospitality of the American soldiers thus:

The glass of whiskey has its numerous devotees here, for what can one who does not drink do in the desert? Each officer is the owner of a little chest with compartments which he carries with him on his travels. In it glasses and flasks are skillfully arranged. "Will you take a drink?" is the first word uttered, as soon as you enter the tent. It would be tactless to refuse. You say yes, and the "Old Bourbon Whiskey" of Kentucky is forthwith poured in your honor. The glasses go the rounds. What a bouquet, my friend, and what a treacherous liquor is this "old Kentuck!" Our old cognac is nothing in comparison.

Though it was tactless to refuse a glass of that "treacherous liquor" of "old Kentuck" in that time, it's downright foolish to refuse a glass today, especially if that glass is filled with the bouquet of Maker's Mark. And there's no better place to find that bouquet than in the heart of the Bluegrass.

Driving down a shaded lane leading to Star Hill Farm in Loretto, Kentucky, you feel not only that you are leaving the modern world, but that you are entering the rarefied reality of "old Kentuck." Star Hill Farm is home to the Maker's Mark distillery, where the traditions of distilling bourbon have been handed down from one generation to the next.

On Star Hill Farm, the visitor is greeted by color: immaculate green lawns, stately brown barns and windows shuttered in bright red. As the visitor strolls across an iron bridge spanning a sparkling stream, the aroma of mash wafts from the distillery building. Well-groomed, elegant and sensuous, the *place* re-enforces the experience of the bourbon itself.

T. W. Samuels (Bill Samuels, Sr.), the founder of the Maker's Mark distillery, inherited a love of distilling from his father, Leslie B. Samuels and previous generations of Samuels who had been distilling bourbon in Kentucky since 1783. However, the Depression and the outbreak of World War II put the family distillery through such hard times that it was sold in 1943. Bill Samuels, Sr. joined the Navy and then retired to the family farm in Bardstown upon his discharge in 1945.

In 1953, Bill Sr. bought Burk's Spring Distillery in Happy Hollow, Kentucky. Though the fourth-generation Samuels kept many of the traditional methods he had learned from his father, he decided to burn his father's recipe and start from scratch. Instead of the typical rye used in most bourbon, Samuels substituted red winter wheat to create a bitter-free taste. In 1959, the first batch was sold to Keeneland Racetrack in Lexington, Kentucky.

Red winter wheat is only one of the distinguishing characteristics about Maker's Mark. Others include the use of a roller mill to grind the grains, rather than the more typical hammer mill, because the Maker's Mark distillery believes the quality of the grain trumps efficiency. And instead of pressure-cooking the mash, the distillery allows it to stew for several days in huge crockpots, which allows the various grain flavors to meld into the final product. Again, quality trumps speed. Maker's Mark also double distills their whiskey to remove impurities and improve taste, because, according to their philosophy, "… we've never been in a rush to do anything, especially when crafting our bourbon …"

Maker's Mark ages their barrels in the brown-painted barns located on and around the farm. The dark-painted wood helps with temperature regulation, which is important to the aging process. The barrels are rotated over the duration of the maturation process to ensure consistency. In keeping with taking their time in the pursuit of quality, a barrel is deemed ready for bottling when the Tasting panel says it's ready, not according to the calendar.

The impeccable styling of the bottle—the red wax, the blob seal, and the type font on the label—was the particular genius of Marjorie Samuels, Bill, Sr.'s wife. The blob seal serves as a maker's mark, which pewter craftsmen have used since an act of the British Parliament in

1503. Mrs. Samuels was a collector of pewter, and took the notion of a maker's mark and turned it into the brand name.

The bottle, also designed by Marjorie Samuels, is inspired. It has a squat, paneled body, increasing in width from heel to shoulder where it tapers into a long neck, topped off with the *pièce de résistance*—an explosion of hand-dipped wax in signature red, covering the top of the bottle. The wax tendrils envelop the shoulder and drift towards the blob seal: the letters SIV (Samuels, fourth generation) are encased within a starred circle, denoting the Star Hill Farm. This is unmistakably Maker's Mark, as the sepia-colored label states in its hand-lettered font.

Home-grown ingredients (including the limestone-filtered water, courtesy of the lake on Star Hill Farm), time-honored processes, and tradition-steeped setting: all contribute to the maker's mark of excellence. Maker's Mark is always elegant, always in style, and suitable for every occasion.

On April 15, 2011, Maker's Mark CEO Bill Samuels Jr. retired from the distillery which he had run since 1975 when he took over for Bill Samuels Sr. His long career was capped off with an award of "lifetime honorary member" of The Kentucky Distillers' Association board of directors. Rob Samuels succeeded his father to carry on the family tradition—he's in charge of not "screwing up the whisky", which was the advice Bill Sr. gave to Bill Jr. during that transfer of responsibility.

Though the company has been run by family members since its inception, actual ownership has changed several times, starting in 1981 when it was purchased by Hiram Walker & Sons, which was then acquired by Allied Domecq in 1987. More ownership changes ensued: in 2005, Maker's Mark was sold to Fortune Brands, which split off its alcoholic beverage business as Beam Inc., which included the Jim Beam Distillery. Finally, in 2014, Beam Inc. was acquired by Japanese beverage company Suntory Holdings Ltd.

SUMMER'S END
BY SUSAN BELL

Hannah grabbed the rusted metal seat of the Farmall, put her foot on the wheel axle, and in one swoop pulled herself up onto the tractor. From this perch she could survey the tobacco barn, and that would make it easier to direct her sister Sarah in their hunt for mice. Hannah had already chased away two mice, so she felt justified in taking a break. She had squealed and jumped at that first mouse, but was sure her sister would out-and-out faint if she found one. Sarah was girly like that. At 14, Sarah was four years older, but she lacked Hannah's fearlessness.

White streaks of afternoon light streamed through the cracks in the side of the barn. The yellowing tobacco, cut the week before, hung above her head, drying in the wind. Her sister was a shadow at the far end of the barn, stepping gingerly, searching for the right board to turn over with the tobacco stick she wielded like a spear.

Hannah pulled the transistor radio from her shirt pocket, turned it on, and patiently rotated the dial back and forth, looking for a station that was more than hissing and static. She kept tuning until she heard her favorite band, The Dave Clark Five, belting out "Bits and Pieces." She settled into the seat and propped her legs over the steering wheel. She loved her radio, especially because it had been a birthday present from her brother Clark. "You'll need something to entertain yourself this summer, since Grandpa doesn't have a TV," he had told her.

Hannah squinted toward the far end of the barn to get a better look. Sarah was now prying away loose boards in the one section of the barn that had a floor. Most of the barn 'floor' consisted of packed, uneven dirt, strewn with loose hay and stray kernels of corn the mice had dropped on the way to wherever it was they were hiding.

Suddenly, Sarah gasped and dropped the stick, letting it thud to the ground. Hannah jumped off the tractor and headed toward her sister. "Did ya find a mouse?"

175

Sarah's face was white, and her mouth formed a round O like a cartoon character who had seen a ghost. Tears streamed down her face. Hannah took a step closer and followed Sarah's gaze to an opening in the floor.

She saw the dress first. The pretty dress that Laura, Clark's girlfriend, had worn the day before at Green River. Now it was smudged with dried mud and clumps of straw. Then she saw the black hair, the twisted arm, the legs, and what looked liked a wax impression of Laura's face, because it couldn't really be Laura, because what would Laura be doing in the barn?

"Is she dead?" Hannah whispered.

Sarah bent down and tried to lift Laura's wrist. It was stiff.

"She's dead." There was a catch in Sarah's voice.

Hannah kneeled and stared at Laura's body in disbelief. She could still hear Laura laughing as she splashed in the water yesterday with Clark, under the shade of the sycamore trees at Green River.

"We've gotta get Grandpa," Sarah said.

"You go get him; I'll stay here."

"I can't leave you here. Come on." Sarah was always annoying when she tried to play adult.

"I'm staying here," Hannah said firmly.

Sarah kicked one of the boards in frustration and stomped toward the wide barn door. Out in the stark daylight, she broke into a full run for the house. Hannah could see the dust kick up under Sarah's heels as she ran. Sarah was the logical one to go. She didn't enjoy unpleasant things, messy things.

Hannah turned back to the crumpled body lying beneath the boards. A splash of red caught her eye, almost hidden in Laura's clenched fist. She touched what she thought was blood and it felt soft, but solid, too. Curious, she tried to get a grip on the red object and flinched when she made contact with Laura's cold hand. She steadied her nerves and, using both hands this time, worked the object out of Laura's stiff fist.

She held up the red strand to get a better look at it, but still could not figure out what it was. It was a curved, ribbon-ish material, about six inches long, with a waxy surface on the outside and sticky on the inside, as if it had been wrapped around something. Both edges were ragged, torn. The outside was the same shade of red as Laura's lipstick.

176

"Clark likes it when I wear this lipstick," Laura had told her yesterday, as they lay on the bank of the river in the afternoon sun.

Hannah started to rise when a glint caught her eye. She glanced down again, reluctantly, and saw a knife protruding from underneath Laura's body. Clark's knife. She would recognize it anywhere. It had a sterling silver handle with turquoise stones embedded on either side. She remembered that Clark had the knife yesterday at the river. He had set it down on his clothes before diving into the water.

Hannah sat down on the dirt floor of the barn to review the events of yesterday in her mind.

Clark had borrowed Grandpa's car after church to drive Hannah and Sarah into town to get ice cream. Hannah knew that Clark wanted to go to the ice cream store to see Laura, but that was okay, because ice cream was ice cream, and anyway, she liked Laura.

Laura was at the ice cream store. They all knew she would be, but they'd all acted surprised to see each other. Laura was dressed up from church in a form-fitting white linen dress that looked all the more white against her tanned skin. Her only makeup was the red lipstick she put on after she left church but before she got to the ice cream shop. "You look like Ann-Margaret," Clark always told her. Laura would laugh and shake her thick black hair so that it fell over one eye and she'd say "Thank you, Elvis" in a huskier voice than she usually used when she was talking.

Hannah strongly disagreed; anybody who had seen *Viva Las Vegas* at the drive-in not more than a month ago would know that Ann-Margaret had *red* hair. On the other hand, Clark had dark features and wore his thick hair up high on his head and slicked back, so he resembled Elvis a little.

They had been playing this game of accidental meetings all summer, and they always accidentally had their bathing suits with them, or were wearing them under their clothes. So as they left town in Grandpa's station wagon, Laura in the front seat next to Clark, Hannah and Sarah in the back seat eating their melting ice cream cones, there was no question they were heading to Green River to swim in its cooling waters. It would be a welcome relief from the hot August air that enveloped them. And when Elvis came over the radio, they all joined him in the chorus to "Viva Las Vegas".

177

The girls undressed behind the station wagon, and Clark went behind the trees to remove his clothes. He always wore his trunks under his jeans. Hannah watched as Sarah unzipped Laura's dress for her, and then Laura let the dress drop from her shoulders to reveal a thin white slip. Hannah turned away in modesty to remove her clothes, even though her suit was under her dress.

Laura was not tall, but she had an athletic way of moving, sure of herself, and when she dove into the water she looked like a mermaid. Hannah waded into the water and Sarah sat on a blanket on the bank applying suntan lotion.

Clark came out from behind the trees in his black trunks, carrying his clothes in one hand and his belt in the other. His knife was still hanging in its sheath from the belt. He placed it carefully on the pile of clothes near the car under one of the many sycamore trees that lined the riverbank.

Clark dived into the water and swam toward Laura, who laughed and splashed water at him as he got close. They swam together in the direction of the small waterfall in the distance, and Hannah knew better than to follow them. The last time she'd followed them, she found them smooching on the limestone rocks along the river. Clark had yelled at her and Laura laughed, but in a way that didn't make Hannah feel laughed at.

An hour later, she and Laura lay on the shore on the towels they put down on the grass. Clark was trying to teach Sarah how to dive off the rocks.

"Will you come visit us when we go home?" Hannah sat up to adjust her towel and to see if Laura was even awake.

Laura turned to her and smiled.

"I won't have to visit. I'll be there, too. I've decided to go to the University of Louisville."

And with that good news Laura got up, tussled Hannah's short hair, and after a few quick steps reached the water and dived in.

Hannah was thrilled with the news that their good times with Laura and Clark would continue. She started to lie back down when she heard a motor revving in the distance and branches swooshing in the wake of a passing vehicle. She wondered who else had discovered this oasis off the main road. Hannah looked up the hill to see Buck Satterwhite easing his brand-new red Mustang to the edge of the embankment.

178

Buck was Laura's boyfriend before Clark and Laura met at the ice cream store. Hannah used to see Buck and Laura together all the time around town, holding hands and laughing and driving around in that pretty red Mustang. One time, Buck and Laura took her and Sarah on a ride in the Mustang with the top down. Hannah remembered the feel of that vinyl seat on her skin, and how the wind blew her hair around her face like she was in a tornado. And she remembered how Sarah had goo-goo eyes for Buck. Hannah had to admit, Buck was very handsome. Not in an Elvis Presley sort of way, more in a Paul Newman sort of way.

That was in the early days of summer. That was before Clark fell for Laura in the ice cream shop. And before Laura fell for him.

Buck stepped out of the car and Hannah saw he was still in his navy suit and tie from church.

"Laura!" Buck yelled.

Buck stood next to his car, hands on his hips, sunglasses hiding his eyes but not the lips that curled downward. Hannah hadn't seen Buck smile since those early days of summer, but the handsome man who had seemed so happy then was threatening now. Hannah watched as Buck bent down between the cars, then re-appeared. Just as mean-looking as before.

Laura waded back to shore, stopping to whisper something to Clark, who tried to stop her. Her luminous smile had disappeared as she stepped out of the water and walked up the hill to where Buck was waiting. They spoke in quiet voices, but Hannah could still make out some of Buck's words: "… moving to Louisville … your father told me." She heard Laura say something like, "I was going to tell you," before Buck interrupted her. "When?"

Clark had moved closer to shore but was pretending to not pay attention to what was going on, until he heard Buck yell. He stood even straighter than usual and called out, "You okay, Laura?"

"Stay out of this, Clark!" Buck sounded like a growling dog.

Clark ignored Buck's command and waded to shore. He climbed up the bank of the river and looked at Hannah as he passed, indicating with a nod of his head that she should get in the car. He called behind him, "Sarah, we're leaving!" With a few more long strides, Clark stood between Buck and Laura. "Get in the car," he said.

Laura didn't hesitate, and by the time she was seated in the front, Hannah and Sarah were approaching the car. Clark stood his ground, glaring at Buck. Buck glared back at Clark.

Once Clark heard Hannah slam the door shut, he turned around and walked back to the car. With quick, sure movements he was inside with the door closed and the motor started. He drove off fast, leaving Buck standing in a cloud of dust.

"What about our clothes?" Hannah asked.

"I'll come back later for them." Clark's tone of voice suggested to Hannah that she should shut up for the drive home.

They drove in silence, Clark focused on the road in front of him, and Laura staring out her open window. When they reached Laura's house, she got out of the car without a word, but Clark told her he would call her later. He sounded a little angry.

They ate dinner with Grandpa, and no one mentioned the events at the river. Grandpa did most of the talking, with accounts of his day harvesting the tobacco, the price he expected to get at market, the weather. Clark answered with a few mumbles here and there. Hannah and Sarah ate in silence.

At the first opportunity to leave the dinner table, Clark excused himself and went to phone Laura. Hannah strained to hear the conversation going on in the next room, but Clark was speaking too softly. Then suddenly she heard him shout, "I don't care if his parents are home, I don't want you to go over there!"

Grandpa looked up from his peach cobbler and opened his mouth to speak, but it was Clark's voice they heard. "I'm coming over, don't go anywhere!" They heard the phone slam down and the screen door slam shut, then the sound of Grandpa's station wagon revving up and tearing out down the road.

Grandpa took another bite of his peach cobbler and, to no one in particular, said, "Clark should stick to girls he can afford."

Hannah sat on the dirt floor of the barn and listened to swallows flying around the rafters. She felt a knot twisting in the pit of her stomach. Clark had been so angry last night. He had come home late and left again in the morning before Hannah and Sarah woke up.

Hannah looked again at the red strand she had taken from Laura's hand, then glanced at Clark's knife. She could just take the knife, right now, before anybody knew anything. She thought Sarah hadn't seen it.

As she reached for the knife, Hannah heard the crunching gravel of an approaching car and, without thinking, shoved the red strand in her jeans pocket. Hannah got to her feet as her Grandpa stopped in the barn doorway, leaning on his cane.

"Come on away from there, Hanny." He only had to say it once.

By the time the police arrived, the sun was low in the sky, casting an orange flush over the barn and making the corn fields seem to glow as if the light were emanating from each stalk. The road leading up to and around the tobacco barn was clogged with vehicles. Two sheriff's deputies leaned against their sedan drinking coffee. Hannah recognized one of them, Jimmy Richards, as a friend of Buck's. The other was an older man. Hannah saw his gray hair under the cap he kept taking off to wipe his brow.

One state trooper stood watch over the entrance to the barn door and another trooper talked on the radio in his car. The car had a light on the roof that resembled a cherry on top of a chocolate sundae.

She sat in Grandpa's station wagon, wondering when they would bring out Laura's body from the barn. The lights on the ambulance were still flashing, as if they had to be in a hurry *now*. Sarah was in the house phoning their parents in Louisville. No one had seen Clark all day. But Grandpa had told the police the knife belonged to Clark. If only she had grabbed it when she had the chance!

The familiar red Mustang pulled up next to Grandpa's car. The convertible, with its white vinyl seats and gleaming chrome bumpers, made Grandpa's old station wagon look meek and unworthy of being on the same road.

Buck jumped out of his car and ran toward the ambulance, but Deputy Richards stopped him. From where she was sitting, Hannah couldn't make out what they were saying, but she heard Laura's name, and heard Buck yell, "No, no!"

The older deputy came up to Buck and put an arm around him and both deputies walked him to a squad car. Deputy Richards reached into the vehicle and pulled out a thermos and cup. He handed the cup to Buck, who was so agitated that he dropped it right on the ground. As he stooped to pick it up, Hannah jolted upright in her seat, remembering a similar scene the day before at the river when Buck had stooped to the ground momentarily, right beside the area where Clark had put his clothes. Had Buck picked up Clark's knife?

Hannah stepped out of the station wagon, then hesitated. She didn't know what to do. She had not seen Buck with the knife, but it was easier to believe that Buck was responsible for killing Laura than believing her brother had done it.

Squawking came from the squad car radio and Deputy Richards shouted, "They just picked him up at Green River!"

The two deputies said something to Buck, patted him on the back, and then jumped into their car. Buck moved aside as the car backed up, then headed down Grandpa's road to the main highway, siren blaring. Hannah figured it was Clark who had been picked up at Green River.

She turned around and searched for her grandfather among the small group of troopers and men in suits who were still hanging around the barn and ambulance. Grandpa was sitting by himself under an old oak tree on a lawn chair. He grasped his cane with both hands, leaning on it even though he was seated, his head down and his face covered by the old straw hat he always wore.

Hannah started in his direction but caught movement in her side vision. It was Buck, walking back to his car. Hannah sat down and pretended to tie her shoe, so she could watch him. It was almost dark now, and the still-flashing lights of the ambulance cast an eerie, alternating red glow over the landscape.

Buck set his coffee cup on the trunk of his car and reached into the back seat. He pulled out a bottle and removed the cap, then poured the liquid into his cup. He looked around to make sure no one was watching, and Hannah jerked her head to look down at her feet. She hoped he hadn't seen her.

After a second, Hannah looked up slowly in Buck's direction and could see him leaning into the back seat again. Then he straightened up and walked off toward the barn with only the cup in his hand. He joined two state troopers who were standing there, their gray uniforms and Dudley Do-Right hats reminding her of cartoon characters.

Hannah waited until she was satisfied that Buck was engaged in conversation with the troopers, then slowly moved toward the Mustang, walking backward so she could keep an eye on Buck. She held her breath for what felt like a long time as she took step after step, until she saw the hood of the car. She took a few more steps backward, then tripped and fell. She lay still, in spite of the sharp pain in her back. All she heard was the low murmuring of the men talking.

Hannah turned over and picked herself up off the ground. She was alongside the back seat of the Mustang and she peeked into the car to get a better look. Though daylight was quickly fading, she could see the bottle, filled with liquid, though it was partially covered with a jacket. She guessed it was probably alcohol, but the bottle was different from the ones she was used to seeing in her parents' liquor cabinet at home.

Hannah looked back toward the barn once more and was relieved to see the troopers and Buck moving into the barn. It was dark now, but she remembered the flashlight in her Grandpa's station wagon. She ran to the wagon, opened the passenger door, removed the flashlight, then quietly closed the door and ran back to the Mustang. She climbed over the side and pointed the flashlight into the back seat. She pulled the bottle out from the jacket and held it up in the light to get a better look. On the label was written *Maker's Mark, Kentucky Straight Bourbon Whiskey*. The bottle had a somewhat squarish shape, with a long neck, but what caught Hannah's attention was the red wax covering the cap and neck. In fact, the wax ran halfway down the bottle.

Hannah reached in her pocket for the strand of wax and held it against the bottle. It was the same shade of red and the same texture as the wax on the bottle. She saw that the edges on the strand fit the edges of the cap like pieces of a jigsaw puzzle. The strand had come from this bottle. Hannah knew this tied Buck to Laura's murder somehow, but exactly how did the strand get in Laura's hand? As she tried to work out this puzzle in her head, she felt a hand around her mouth and a strong arm around her waist, pulling her out of the car.

"What are you up to?" Buck said in the same growling voice he had used yesterday at the river.

Hannah kicked her feet against Buck's body while hanging onto his arm with her left hand. Her right hand gripped the wax strand, but she quickly shoved it back in her pocket. With her now free hand she grabbed a chunk of Buck's hair and yanked as hard as she could. Buck cursed in pain, and as he moved his right arm to block her hair-pulling, she mustered all her strength and wriggled loose, falling with a thud to the ground.

"Grandpa!" Hannah called out.

"Hannah, where are you?"

She was never so glad to hear her Grandpa's voice. Buck was now pretending to help her up, but she broke away from him and ran to her Grandpa, who had been inside the barn. She could see his silhouette in the open barn door, as well as those of the two state troopers.

Gasping for air as she reached the barn, Hannah almost choked on her words. "Buck did it, Buck killed Laura, look!" She held up the wax strand to confused stares from the troopers.

"Got yourself a clue there, Missy?"

Hannah peered up at the trooper and saw his name on the shiny badge over his pocket. Anderson. Trooper Anderson. He was laughing at her. The other trooper started laughing, too.

Her Grandpa turned to them and said, "That's enough, boys."

"Yes sir, Mr. Rankin."

Grandpa turned back to Hannah.

"What are you talking about, Hanny?"

"Yeah, what are you talking about?" Buck had walked up to the barn door and was now glaring at Hannah.

Hannah looked up at her Grandpa and, holding up the wax strand again, said, "I found this in Laura's hand. I didn't mean to take it, and then I was too scared to say anything about it, until I figured out what it was."

"What is it, Hannah?" Her grandfather bent down to listen.

"It came from the liquor bottle in Buck's car," Hannah said, turning to accuse Buck. But he wasn't there. He was walking back to his car.

"Where 'ya going, Buck?" Trooper Anderson called out.

Buck didn't even turn around; he kept walking to his car, but he called out, "I don't need to be hanging around a cornfield listening to some kid tell lies to protect her brother!"

"Hold up there, Buck!" The second trooper took a step forward, pulled out his flashlight and shone it in Buck's direction.

Buck swirled around and stood in the light beam with his hands on his hips. "Do you know who my Daddy is?"

"Yeah, he's the guy who foreclosed on my father's farm last year. Now stay put!"

Buck jerked around and started running for his car. Both troopers jumped like bobcats to run after him, the one with the flashlight jerking it up and down with his movements so that Buck running in the distance looked like something out of a silent movie.

Trooper Anderson ran to his squad car parked near the ambulance, but Buck jumped over the door of his Mustang and had the engine started before the trooper had opened his own car door. But the trooper on foot must have been a high school track star, because he caught up to Buck and grabbed the passenger door and jumped in alongside Buck, as the Mustang slid back and forth in the dirt trying to get traction. Soon, all Hannah could see were the headlights sweeping right and left as Buck made for the highway, until the car made a screeching turn to the left and came to a standstill in the middle of Grandpa's corn.

The squad car pulled up next to the Mustang and Hannah could hear yelling. She started running in that direction when she heard Grandpa's stern voice. "Hannah, get back here!" And for the first time in her life, she disobeyed a direct order from her Grandpa and kept running.

Breathless when she reached the two cars, she could hear Buck sobbing, "I didn't mean to kill her, I swear I didn't mean to kill her!"

"We know you didn't mean to hurt her, Buck, just tell us what happened," said Trooper Anderson.

"I only wanted to talk to her, to convince her to stay," Buck said through his tears. "She was making us a drink, and was opening the bottle, and then she said she loved him, she loved that good for nothing piece of poor white trash Clark Rankin!"

Hannah bristled at his words but kept quiet.

"I flew into a rage when I heard her say it," Buck continued, his voice rising as if he were reliving the moment, "and I grabbed her and I shook her. I was so mad, and then she picked up the knife I'd left on the table and she tried to stab me with it. I wrestled it out of her hand, and she kept struggling and hitting me and then she was lying on the floor, bleeding."

"How'd you come to have Clark's knife?" the other trooper asked. Both officers were calm, as if they were asking Buck about the weather.

"I found it by the riverbank and was going to have Laura return it for me."

"He's lying!" Hannah shouted. "He deliberately picked it up yesterday at the river, I saw him!"

Buck lunged at Hannah, but the two troopers grabbed him and handcuffed him.

"You better get back to your Grandpa, Missy. We'll handle the questioning."

Trooper Anderson got on the radio and announced that they had a suspect in custody, and that Clark should be let go. With that, Hannah headed back to find her Grandpa.

After Laura's service, Hannah's grandfather pulled the station wagon behind the last car in the funeral procession. They followed the long line of vehicles moving slowly through town, Grandpa driving, with Hannah and Sarah in the back seat. Clark was driving with their parents, toward the front of the procession.

People on the sidewalk stopped to watch as they drove by, and some of the men removed their hats. They drove past the Woolworth's on the corner, then the bank that Buck's daddy owned, then entered the town square where the courthouse loomed. On the other side of the square stood the old county jail, where Buck sat alone in a cell, waiting for his trial. They made another left turn and the ice cream parlor came into view. Hannah glanced over at Sarah, who was crying softly. Hannah reached over and took her hand, and Sarah took Hannah's hand in hers and squeezed firmly.

"Do you think Clark's going to be okay?" Hannah asked.

"It's going to take time," Sarah said, "but we're going to help him through it. You and me."

For the first time, Hannah was glad that Sarah was acting like an adult, because she was going to need help getting over Laura, too.

PAST MEETS PRESENT AT WOODFORD RESERVE
BY GWEN MAYO

If you're going to visit the oldest working bourbon distillery in Kentucky, prepare to feel as though you're stepping into history long before you reach your destination. You drive through country lanes marked with wooden signs. In the morning, you'll often see ghostly tendrils of mist floating over rolling meadows and bluegrass pastures where horses have grazed for hundreds of years. When you come upon your destination, it'll seem as if it's materialized from another time.

Perhaps it has. Woodford Reserve's Versailles property is the oldest distillery in the state and was granted National Historic Landmark status in 2000. Bourbon distilling started on this spot in 1780. Elijah Pepper chose this land in 1812 for its water, specifically naturally filtered limestone creek water that's perfect to produce great whiskey. The limestone buildings we see today were built in 1838.

Due to Prohibition, the distillery wasn't in continuous operation all that time, and has changed hands on multiple occasions. The small-batch bourbon we've come to know and love as Woodford Reserve first appeared in 1996. But the distillery stays true to its history.

A huge visitors' center offers breathtaking views of the verdant Kentucky countryside. The building's long wraparound porch offers cooling shade on a sultry summer day. Inside, there are plenty of modern amenities, including a gas fireplace, comfortable couches, leather chairs, and a tasting room, gift shop, and dining area. But the space maintains a rustic, old Kentucky atmosphere, with exposed beams and rafters, tables built with reclaimed wood from a barn on the property, and a collection of faded pictures of the distillery through the years.

This is where daily distillery tours begin. Visitors board a bus for a short ride down to a stone building that houses fermenters and stills. The rich, sweet aroma of fermenting whiskey greets you as soon as you step inside the warm distillation room. The 7,500-gallon fermenters, which look enormous but are among the smallest in the industry, hold a bubbling yellow liquid that at this point in the process doesn't look or smell particularly appealing.

But the journey for that yellow mash has only begun. The fermented mash gets transferred to the first of three massive copper stills, acquired from Scotland. Woodford Reserve is the only distillery to triple-distill its bourbon in copper pot stills the way Dr. James Crow intended.

After a trip through the stills, the whiskey gets barreled. This is where the process gets serious, because there are strict guidelines that must be adhered to if a whiskey is to be called bourbon. Bourbon must be aged for at least two years in new white oak barrels that are toasted and charred. Woodford Reserve ages its bourbon for an average of seven years, during which time the whiskey takes on its distinct color and flavor by expanding into the wood during warmer temperatures and contracting during cooler ones.

The barrels weigh 100 pounds when they're empty and 500 pounds when full, which would seem to make moving them something of a challenge. But distillery staff make use of an antiquated yet effective solution—the barrel run. This set of tracks, installed in 1934, is used to transport bourbon barrels among various buildings on the distillery grounds. No trucks or fuel needed—just gravity.

After a visit to the bottling room, the tour returns to the visitors' center for a tasting. The Distiller's Select, which is the company's flagship bourbon, has been lavished with numerous quality awards and is even the official bourbon of the Kentucky Derby.

Tasting bourbon takes time. At first sip, it's a smooth, complex bourbon with a rich aroma and notes of oak, vanilla, toffee, and a variety of spices. Add a chip of ice and taste the difference. After a bite of chocolate, the bourbon takes on a hotter, spicier flavor. I recommend trying it with a little peach tea; there's a dispenser by the door. While you're sampling, have one of Woodford Reserve's famous bourbon balls. The blend of chocolate, bourbon, pecans, and creamy nougat is delightful.

FOUR EYES IN THE SHADOWS
BY DEBBY SCHENK

"Destiny, this is Maxx. I want you to teach him how things are around here," Alice said.

Destiny awoke from her usual late afternoon nap on Alice's desk to look at the new cat while she licked her paw to smooth out her disheveled whiskers. *He's kinda cute*, she thought, but she wasn't sure he had what it took to make it at the distillery.

"I found him by my back door lost, hungry, and very scared. I can't keep him where I live but I thought he would be good company for you. He has a very expensive collar with his name and a phone number but, when I called, no one answered."

Maxx wasn't sure he was going to like this place but, when Destiny motioned for him to follow, he jumped down from the desk after her.

"This is a handy invention," he said, as Destiny led the way through a door that was their size.

"Haven't you ever seen a cat door before? They have them in all the buildings so we can get in and out."

"I have never been out in the wild; evidently this is an everyday occurrence for you. Where am I? There are so many buildings around here. I miss the security of my own home." He looked around with a frightened gaze.

"I understand that, Maxx, but you live here now, at the Green River Distillery. It's great to have company. Although Alice lets me sleep on her desk and most people have been good to me, I've been lonely since they brought me from the shelter. There is Pete. He's the cat that has been here the longest, but he isn't very friendly and sometimes he's kinda scary looking. He's old and sleeps mostly. Our main job is to catch mice."

"Do you mean mice as in *rodents*? They are disgusting, disease-ridden vermin and what do you propose we do with them after we catch them?" He wrinkled his nose as if a foul odor had passed under it.

"Oh, Maxx, it's not so bad after you get used to it. How did you get lost?"

"I was traveling with my family, and it was storming dreadfully. The car veered off the road and hit a fence. The next thing I knew, I was outside in the dark. Suddenly there were all these cars with lights flashing and sirens blaring. I got scared and ran. Somehow I ended up behind Alice's house."

"This is a great place to live once you learn your way around. Stick with me, and I'll teach you. I've been here long enough to learn who likes us and who doesn't. Some people will give us special treats and others don't want us around. Let's go over to the bottling building. That's where they keep our food."

"Oh, we get real food, not just mice?"

"Gosh, Maxx, they don't expect us to eat them, only kill them! Come on; let's get a snack, and I'll show you around."

As they started into the building where the bourbon was bottled by hand, they heard voices. Two men were in there arguing.

"Shhh, that's George and Andrew. We'd better hide. George threw a paperweight at me once."

The cats with their sleek brown bodies and dark chocolate faces slipped into the corner of the building where they couldn't be seen under a large vat used for filling the bottles with bourbon.

"Andrew, what do you mean you're going to the boss with what *I've* been doing? You're as guilty as I am. Don't you realize you'll go to jail with me?" George asked. "I may have pocketed some of the profit, but you're the accountant who covered it up."

"Only because you threatened my family if I didn't go along. Now that I know my family is safe, I'm done covering up for you." Andrew replied, and turned to leave.

George looked down and saw an open box of bourbon bottles. He grabbed a bottle and hit Andrew over the head. George needed a way to get out of this. He would promise he would quit skimming money from the accounts.

George shook Andrew, then saw the blood running from the back of his head. He knew Andrew wasn't going to wake up. He never saw the four dark blue eyes watching him from the shadows. George pulled a rag from his pocket and began wiping his fingerprints from everything he thought he'd touched, and hurried out the door.

Maxx was frantic. "Destiny, did you see that? What are we going to do? Someone has to call 911. What are you going to do?"

"Calm down, Maxx, I have to think. First of all, we are cats. We can't call 911. Something fell from George's pocket; maybe we can find it after he leaves. We need to figure out how to tell someone what we saw. Since Alice lets me lie on her desk and I've seen how she uses her computer, maybe I can leave her a message," Destiny continued as she tried to soothe Maxx. "We need to go find Pete. He's been here forever, and he may have some ideas for us."

While Maxx and Destiny went to find Pete, George was in his car trying to get away without anyone seeing him. The guard would leave the gate soon to make his rounds; he would sneak out then.

He reached in his pocket for a cigarette to settle his nerves. *I didn't mean to kill Andrew*, he thought. *I just wanted to stop him until he realized confessing wasn't the smart thing to do. Here are my cigarettes but where is my lighter? When was the last time I used it? There are very few places on the property I can smoke. It should be easy to trace my steps.* Abruptly, he turned his car around because he realized exactly where he lost it. He was going to have to take his chances and go back to the body.

George rushed back to the bottling building. In a panic, he searched around the body. He grabbed a flashlight from a nearby desk and shone it along the floor. *Where is that damn lighter, anyway?* Then he saw a reflection of light from between the floorboards. It was about six inches down, and no way to get it without tearing up the floor. *I hate to leave it, but I'm sure no one will notice it down there. I'll come back later after they find Andrew's body. I need to get back to my car before I'm seen and figure out how I'll get myself out of this mess.*

"Pete, oh, Pete, where are you?" Destiny called out as she and Maxx ran into the building where the bourbon barrels were stored.

"I'm over here, little girl. What's all the yelling about?" Pete asked. "Who's this you have here?"

"Pete, this is Maxx. Alice found him and brought him here."

Pete gave Maxx a good look over. "Kid, how did you end up here? You look like a fancy cat to me with that collar and all. Cats like you don't live in places like this. I bet you are a pedigree."

"Why yes, I am a pedigree. My full name is Kentucky Siamese Maximilian Von Shyler, and I have papers," Maxx said proudly.

"Well, the dogs at the shelter I came from had papers, but no one was impressed with them!" Destiny snapped.

"Destiny, did you ever see yourself in a mirror? We are the same color. Maybe you got lost also and you were too young to remember it. You could be pedigree too!"

"Nah, I'm an ordinary cat."

"Hey you two, remember me? Why did you trespass on my peaceful existence? Little girl, you know I don't want my naps interrupted."

"We saw George kill Andrew," Destiny answered bluntly. "He grabbed a bottle with the brown water in it, knocked Andrew in the head, and he fell down dead."

"Just because he was hit on the head and fell down doesn't mean he's dead," Pete said.

"There was blood running from his head, and he didn't move anymore," Maxx added.

"I guess I had better check this out. I don't want you two causing a panic around here. I'll never get my nap then!"

Pete dragged his stubby, smoky gray body from his comfortable spot, and they set out for the bottling building.

When they got there, George was coming out of the building. He got in his car and took off.

"I thought you told me he already left."

"He did! I guess he came back after we got out of the building. Maybe he was looking for whatever it was that fell from his pocket," Maxx said excitedly.

"Kid, you didn't tell me he lost something. That's evidence. Did you see what it was?"

"No, we got out of there as fast as we could. Do we need to find it before we try to tell anyone who did this?" Destiny asked.

"It could be handy when you try to show someone what you know."

"Are you telling me we have to go back in there with the dead body?" Maxx asked with his tail jerking wildly and the hair on it standing on end. "I don't do well around dead bodies; it creeps me out!"

"Well, Mr. Expert, how many dead bodies have you found lately?" Destiny asked.

"Just this one, but that is enough to know I don't enjoy it."

"Let's get in there and see if George found what he dropped," Pete said. "I want to get back to my nap."

They padded single file through the cat door and into the building. Maxx finally got a chance to look around. It wasn't a big building, but there were several pieces of equipment that he wondered about. "Destiny, what do they do here?"

"This is where they put that nasty brown water in the bottles."

"What do you mean nasty?"

"Listen to me, kid. Don't drink it. It smells bad, tastes even worse, makes you walk funny, and burns your throat as it goes down. You'll have a horrible headache after your nap."

They walked over to the body, and as Pete sniffed it, his whiskers twitched wildly. He could tell Andrew was dead. He circled the body, but didn't see anything that George could have dropped from his pocket. Then he noticed the spaces between the boards in the floor.

"Little girl, get over here. I think I see something down there in the dirt under the floor. These old eyes of mine don't see as well as they used to."

"I see it! I think it's the gold lighter I've seen George use. I don't know how we can get it out of there, though; it's too far for us to reach. Pete, we are going over to Alice's office to try to leave a message on her computer," Destiny said.

"Be careful. You know George doesn't like us," Pete reminded her and turned to go back to his nap.

"Destiny," Maxx asked, "do you really think you can leave Alice a message?"

"Yeah, I'm sure I can. I'm a fast learner. Let's get over there before people start coming in. It won't be long until everyone comes to work."

They trotted toward the main building. In the meantime, George came in through the back and was in his office.

"This will be a piece of cake, Maxx. All I have to do is push this button and a blank screen comes up. Then I push these letters to spell out George did it." Destiny hesitated, "How do you spell George?"

"I thought you were so smart, Destiny. It is spelled G E O R G E."

"OK, got it. 'George did it.' I think that will work. Let's get out of here before someone sees us. Where did you learn how to spell?"

"In my home, I used to stretch out on the bed to bathe myself and listen to the kids practice their spelling words. Get under the desk, Destiny, I hear someone coming."

As George headed to the kitchen area to make coffee, he noticed Alice's computer was on. He was confused, because she was always so careful about turning it off every night. When he touched the mouse, a screen popped up. Someone had typed "George did it". *Who in the hell did this?* Did someone see him during the night? He was sure no one was around. Could it be one of those nosy security guards? Was someone going to try to blackmail him? He hit the Delete key and got out quickly.

"Maxx, George did something to the computer, and I might have to do it again."

"But we need to get out of here. What if he comes back?"

"I need to go back and make sure the message is still there. It's clear; I'm going. Let me know if you see anyone."

"Hurry. I want to get out of here. I think I hear someone coming."

Destiny got back under the desk but all she had time to write was "George did," hoping that was enough for someone to understand what she was trying to tell them.

At the bottling building, the security guard found Andrew during one of his building inspections. The police had been called, and the cars with their lights flashing and sirens blaring were coming across the property. Maxx heard the sounds and saw the lights and it brought back memories of the night before, when his life changed. Destiny put a paw on his shoulder to comfort him and told him they needed to get back in the building to see what was going on.

They sneaked back through the cat door and again hid in the corner to watch what was happening. After a while, they saw Andrew being taken away. There were people everywhere. One man was taking pictures of everything and other technicians had little plastic bags, flashlights, and tweezers collecting evidence.

"Destiny, what if they don't find the lighter? What will we do?"

"We just have to make sure they find it. We need to go out there and get someone's attention. Follow me to the spot in the floor and start digging at the wood. Meow and yell all you can. We have to get them to look at that spot."

"I'll be right behind you. I hope you know what you are doing," he said.

Both cats ran from their hiding place and started scratching at the floor as hard as they could. One of the investigators tried to push them away, but they both howled and kept digging at the spot.

Another crime scene technician saw how intent the cats were and became interested in what they were doing. "I have cats, and they usually have a reason for doing the odd things they do. Maybe we should look a little more at that spot they," he said to the other tech. He took his flashlight and got down on the floor with the cats.

As he pointed the light at where they were digging, both cats watched every move he made. When he looked closer, he realized there were open spaces between the boards. With a little more inspection, he spotted a reflection under them and called for a pry bar.

He pulled the gold lighter out of the dirt, and noticed some drops of blood under it. At the same time, Alice came through the door asking for a policeman to come with her, mumbling about some strange message on her computer. She and Detective Robinson were about to leave when the technician asked if she knew George Allen. His name was engraved on the lighter "For 20 years of service." Alice told the detective what she had found typed on her computer.

When Detective Robinson returned from checking Alice's computer, he asked the technician if there were any prints from the lighter and the rest of the room. When the technician described what they'd found, Detective Robinson told him to replace the lighter and put the floor back where it was. He explained that he'd told the employees they couldn't retrieve the lighter without someone from the Historical Society to supervise the pulling up of the plank, since the building was listed as an historical landmark. As the technician started to question this, the detective held up his hand in a stop motion.

"Yes, I know we can do whatever we need at a crime scene, but I'm betting the murderer doesn't."

The cats slipped back into their hiding place to watch what would happen next. The technicians packed up their equipment and headed back to the lab to process the evidence. Detective Robinson determined there would be no bottling that day. Everyone left, and the detective looked around the room for a good place to hide.

It didn't take long after everyone was gone for George to sneak into the building with a tire iron. He'd brought his flashlight, and could see his lighter was still down there. He thought he could pry up the board, grab it, and he would be home free. He noticed some marks, as if a cat had been scratching the wood, but since the lighter was still there, he dismissed the idea that it had been seen. Up came the board with one quick pull of the tire iron. When George lifted the lighter, Detective Robinson stepped out of his hiding place. George was startled and dropped the tire iron with a thud.

"I didn't know anyone was here."

"That's obvious, considering you are pulling up a floorboard to get the lighter with your name on it. The same lighter that happens to be the key piece of evidence in this murder investigation. I bet, when we compare your fingerprints to the unknown partial print we found on this bourbon bottle, we'll have a match. George Allen, you are under arrest for the murder of Andrew Jenkins."

Detective Robinson called outside to the officers he had hiding behind the building. They came in to handcuff George and take him to the station for more questioning. As they started out of the building with George, he kept mumbling he didn't mean to kill Andrew.

When Destiny saw George couldn't hurt them, she led Maxx out from their hiding place with their tails high in the air. She strutted past George with an air of superiority. George looked down and kicked at her as the officers jerked him towards the door.

"Damn cats!" George said.

Destiny and Maxx stood in the door and watched as he was put in the police car.

"Well, Maxx, we had a pretty busy night. We need to go tell Pete we helped solve the murder."

"I thought Pete got upset when we wake him from his nap."

"Don't you realize Pete's not as mean as he pretends to be? He's just a pussycat."

"Destiny," Maxx said with a puzzled look on his face, "aren't we all pussycats?"

"Oh, Maxx!" she said as she shook her head, wondering if that cat would survive in the outside world.

WILD TURKEY DISTILLERY
BY DEBI HUFF

In 1869, J.P. Stevens first founded the predecessor to the Wild Turkey distillery, built on what is now known as Wild Turkey Hill in Lawrenceburg, Kentucky. At the time, it was actually located in Tyrone, Kentucky, but over the years the village of Tyrone disappeared. When J.P. Ripy bought the plant in 1888, it was renamed the Old Hickory Springs Distillery. In 1863, the Ripy Brothers bourbon was chosen from among 400 to represent Kentucky at the Chicago World's Fair. The Ripys owned several distilleries.

Closed during prohibition from 1920 to 1933, the buildings were torn down and totally rebuilt as the Ripy Brothers Distillery in 1935. Austin Nichols & Company, a grocery and liquor distributor from New York which had been around since the 1900s, was hard hit by Prohibition. When it was over, they saw an increase in their distribution of liquor and by 1938 had sold off most of their other product lines to concentrate on the lucrative fine wines and liquors.

In 1940, Thomas McKay, an officer of Austin Nichols, brought some of a private collection of bourbon obtained from the Boulevard Distillery in Tyrone, Kentucky, to a hunt for wild turkeys on Long Island with some fellow hunter enthusiasts. The following year, they asked him to bring the "Wild Turkey" along again and the brand name was born. In 1942, the first bourbon named Wild Turkey was bottled and distributed by Austin Nichols. Prior to 1942, it was not from any one particular distillery. Austin Nichols contracted with numerous distilleries and used their bourbon in the bottles. As time passed, they became quite fond of the bourbon they obtained from the Boulevard Distillery and it became the Wild Turkey bourbon that was distributed. While known more popularly today by the name Wild Turkey Distillery, the actual name is the Boulevard Distillery.

Austin Nichols purchased the Boulevard Distillery in 1971 and began to produce the bourbon as well as distribute it under the Wild Turkey name.

The production of Wild Turkey bourbon has not changed much over the years. Mention the name Jimmy Russell in the bourbon world, and you will get immediate recognition. What else would you expect when you are talking about someone who has been a master distiller for over 5 decades? Jimmy wasn't around at the founding in 1869, although if you hear stories of his legend you might think otherwise. Since Jimmy Russell first began working there in 1954 and progressed to Master Distiller, he has continued to see to it that the recipe has remained consistent. Even with the brand-new buildings and equipment in 2010, the processes and recipes have remained the same. It's a little more expensive to make bourbon the way Jimmy does, and takes a little longer, but he considers the price worth it. Their bourbons are based on the ingredients of corn, which comes mainly from Kentucky, rye from North Dakota, and barley malt from Montana. The exact proportions are a trade secret. The differences come from the time the bourbon ages in the barrels. Very little distilled water is added to the mixture as it comes out of the warehouse, making it similar to the full-bodied flavor one gets from bourbon straight from the barrel. It is aged in heavily charred, new white barrels, which lends Wild Turkey its signature flavor and deep mahogany color. By law, it is illegal to add any coloring to bourbon. Bourbon can be made anywhere in the United States; all but a few brands are made in Kentucky and Kentucky is the only state allowed to put its name on the bottle. And, as Kentucky distillers are quick to point out, bourbon is not *bourbon* unless the label says so.

Bourbon takes its name from Bourbon County, located in the central Bluegrass region of Kentucky. It was formed from Fayette County in 1785 while still a part of Virginia, and named to honor the French Royal Family. It was once the major transshipment site for distilled spirits heading down the Ohio and Mississippi rivers to New Orleans. Barrels shipped from its ports were stamped with the county's name, and Bourbon and whiskey soon became synonymous.

In 2006, a liqueur was added to the Wild Turkey family of bourbons. It is called Wild Turkey American Honey, 71 proof, and made of a combination of Wild Turkey bourbon and pure American Honey. In addition to the usual 81, 86.8 and three different 101 proofs (depending on the aging time in the barrels), Wild Turkey came out with a small batch of Russell's Reserve Rye. This rye was first produced as a collaboration between Jimmy Russell and his son, Eddie, in his capacity as Manager of Barrel Maturation and Warehousing. The 10-year old small batch bourbon draws on over 80 years of experience in its creation. While no one is saying that Jimmy will retire any time soon, it is more likely than not that Eddie will carry on the four-generation Russell family tradition in the production of bourbon.

THE MOONSHINE MURDER
BY DIN OBRECHT DULWORTH

Eastern Kentucky—1928

Young Jake Morgan looked up as the first rays of the morning sun came over the mountain. He'd been awake all night working at his moonshine still, located deep in the woods by a limestone stream and far from prying eyes. He sat down to await his partner Clay Hawkins, who would help him bottle the batch. Jake took a test swig from a Ball jar and smacked his lips. *Best hooch in the region, maybe the state*, he thought.

He was about to take another drink when he heard twigs snapping and someone running up the weedy path to the still. He rose quickly, grabbed his rifle, and turned in time to see his partner stumbling around the bend.

"Jake! It's me. Don't shoot," he said. "I ran to warn ye. Somebody's coming."

"Who?"

"Dunno. Ain't seen him afore. Looks to be right young, though. He's on a horse and by hisself … suppose he's a revenuer?"

Jake stroked his chin. "Alone, you say? Yeah … could be one of them government agents who take money to keep their mouths shut." Jake growled and shook his rifle. "Well, he ain't getting my money and he ain't gonna smash my stash, neither."

He pushed Clay roughly aside, ran down the path and hid in the tall grasses alongside. He soon heard the clip clop of a horse's hooves and raised his rifle as the roan horse and its rider came into view.

The horse, startled by the movement in the grass, shied, causing the rider to pull up and look around. His eyes met Jake's and he reached back to his hip pocket.

Jake, assuming he was going for a gun, aimed and fired. The horse reared and dumped its rider before turning in panic and galloping away.

Clay came running down the path. "What've you *done?*" he screamed, as he turned the stranger over. "You killed him, Jake."

Jake rose and walked to the body. "Well, it was him or me. He was reaching for his gun. I had to shoot him."

Clay was on his knees, rocking back and forth and moaning.

"Stop your blubbering," said Jake. "I ain't going to prison for no government man."

Clay felt the man's pockets. "Jake," he said, his voice quaking, "this feller ain't got no gun." He pulled a leaflet from the dead man's hip pocket and held it up. "This is probably what he was reaching for, Jake. Says he's a doctor. Name's John Stoddard … says he's opened a clinic in the county."

Jake threw his rifle down. "Well, what in tarnation made him come up here for?"

"Maybe he was trying to get the word out to folks in these parts that need doctoring," said Clay.

"The durn do-gooder oughta stayed where he came from," said Jake. "Put that paper back in his pocket. We'll move his body away from here, bottle the booze, load it on the truck and get out of Kentucky till things cool off. We'll destroy the still before we go."

"Jake, you ain't got no heart," said Clay.

"Maybe not. But I got plans and I means to see them through. You with me or not?" he asked, picking up the rifle and staring at his partner.

Clay eyed the rifle and swallowed hard. "Guess I'm with ye. Just take it easy. I won't tell nobody what you done. I'll help you hide the body and get outta Kentucky. We can set up a new still somewheres else. Heck, Jake! You make the best 'shine I ever drunk. You're good enough to own a big distillery, yourself, some day."

Louisville, Kentucky—1987

Stoddard Delaney and her classmates stood at attention as their teacher, Chef Luca Lorenzo, strode into the spotless kitchen of the Institute of Culinary Arts. "At ease," he said, as he turned to address them.

202

Stoddard leaned toward her classmate Cassie and whispered, "Hope he's in a better mood than he was yesterday."

"I have an exciting announcement," said Lorenzo. "A wonderful opportunity is being offered our school and five outstanding students in this class by a benefactor from the bourbon industry. How many of you have heard of the Morgan Distillery?"

A few raised their hands.

Lorenzo continued. "The distillery's founder and longtime owner, Jacob Morgan, is planning a party at his estate in Glen Grove. He's introducing his new 'Morgan Reserve' label to a select group of guests, and has asked our Institute to prepare a five-course dinner."

There was a burst of applause. "Mr. Morgan is giving our school a fantastic opportunity to shine," he said. "Each course is to have a subtle taste of his new premium bourbon in it. At the end of the evening, his guests will choose their favorite of the five courses. The student who prepared it will be awarded a year of study at the Cordon Bleu in Paris, France."

The classroom erupted with cheers. Stoddard remained silent.

Cassie raised her hand excitedly. "Chef Lorenzo, who are the five lucky students?'

"You're one of them, Cassie. You'll do appetizers. And your friend, the talented Miss Stoddard Delaney, is another. I'm assigning you the dessert course, Stoddard. You should do well there."

Stoddard felt her face heat up. She turned to Cassie, who looked as though she had swallowed a barrel of carpenter nails.

Stoddard didn't hear the names of the next three participants Lorenzo had chosen. She was in a daze, preoccupied with the name of the distillery owner.

The name "Jake" Morgan had long festered in her family's ears and minds as the possible murderer of her namesake and grandfather, Dr. John Stoddard. Could he be the same *Jacob* Morgan she was expected to cook for?

That evening, Stoddard and Cassie were preparing dinner for the Hillenmeyer family. The nightly dinners allowed them to live rent-free above the carriage house on the Hillenmeyer property.

"I wish I'd worked harder to get a scholarship to Med School," said Cassie, sighing as she cut up an apple. "I'd rather be in an operating room than a kitchen. I loved studying anatomy and the circulatory system when I was in high school. And I was good at dissecting frogs."

"I hope it was dead," said Stoddard.

"It was," replied Cassie, laughing.

Stoddard dropped her salad tongs.

Cassie shook her head. "What's wrong with you, tonight, anyway? Is teacher's pet turning into Miss Butterfingers?"

"I've lots on my mind," said Stoddard.

"That's obvious. So, what's eating you?"

"The competition."

"Why worry?" said Cassie with sarcasm dripping from her voice, "According to Lorenzo, you've already won it."

"Cassie, quit! It's the sponsor I'm thinking about."

"Jacob Morgan? What about him?"

Stoddard stopped slicing the pineapple. "Well, I never told you, but my Grandpa Stoddard was murdered."

"Murdered? When?"

"In 1928, about five miles from where he was setting up a clinic. Never did find out who did it. It was during Prohibition, and people in that part of Kentucky were close-mouthed and protective of each other. Grandma said that getting them to talk about the murder was like pulling hen's teeth."

"How did he get killed?"

"Grandpa had gone out on horseback to tell folks about his clinic. It was thought he might have been mistaken for a revenuer and shot for that reason. A destroyed still was discovered not far from Grandpa's body."

Cassie shrugged her shoulders. "What does Jacob Morgan have to do with all that?"

Stoddard put down her paring knife and looked straight at Cassie. "Here's what I know. Grandma found out, later, that a moonshiner named Jake Morgan had disappeared from the area with his partner about the same time Grandpa was murdered. If he did it and he's still living, he'd be in his eighties, now."

Now it was Cassie's turn to drop salad tongs. "Are you saying that rich old coot Jacob Morgan might be the *Jake* Morgan you think killed your Grandpa?"

"I don't know. Morgan's a fairly common name. Doesn't seem possible that a mountain moonshiner would become a major distiller."

"Well," mused Cassie, "Seems I heard somewhere that a couple of smart moonshiners did become legitimate distillers."

Stoddard sank down on a stool. "I don't know what to do."

"I do," said Cassie. "You ought to drop out of the competition. We can't have you poisoning the man."

Stoddard knew that withdrawing from the competition would 'up' Cassie's chances of winning it. "Sure," she said. "I want to get even if he murdered my Grandpa. But it happened so long ago. All I can hope to do is get him alone, introduce myself, and see his expression when I tell him who I am."

"I see," cooed Cassie, passing Stoddard some kiwis. "So now you're planning to blackmail the man. Well, that's one sure way to win the trip to France."

"Cassie, will you stop? I hope to appeal to the man's conscience. If he has any compassion at all, he should want to make amends. Mom was only three when it happened. Grandpa was just beginning his practice."

Cassie handed a crystal cruet to Stoddard. "What did your Grandma do after that?"

"Grandma had to close the clinic, move back to Louisville and get a secretarial job. Now she's old and stuck in a second-rate nursing home. But it's the best Mom and I can afford at the moment."

Stoddard looked at the clock. "Oh, it's time to take the salad in to the table."

She picked up the fruit bowl and turned to Cassie. "You know what bothers
   me?"

"No," said Cassie. "What?"

"My wanting to win a scholarship from the man who might have murdered my Grandpa."

The Dinner Party at the Morgan Mansion

"Have you seen who's out there?" Cassie asked, as she burst through the kitchen door, showing off her empty silver tray. "Those guests in the parlor are really hungry. They loved my appetizers, particularly my Soused Sesame Shrimp."

Stoddard could barely believe her ears. She had originated that version of the sesame shrimp appetizer at the Institute, and there was

205

Cassie, taking credit for it, accepting compliments and passing it off as her brainchild to the guests in the parlor. Stoddard began to wonder what kind of 'friend' Cassie was.

"I'd like to feast on their money," said Jeremy, tasting the bisque he was preparing for the soup course.

"Me, too," said Tyler. "I wonder what a million dollars tastes like?"

Stoddard liked and admired Tyler. He excelled in the preparation of meats and seafood, and was creating a remarkable pork roast with a honey-bourbon glaze for the Morgan dinner party.

"Who else is out there?" he asked.

Chef Lorenzo spoke up. "Jack Ruberosa, the distinguished food critic of the *Suburban Voice*," he said. "And Lucie Burdine, the Society Editor. She writes up everybody who is anybody."

Marcus was arranging his salad entry on plates. "Who's the doll in the low-cut dress slit up to her waist?"

Mabel Grimes, the Morgan resident cook, stepped forward. "Oh, that's Savannah Semples," she said, laughing. Mabel knew all the guests and had stayed around to watch and help the students. "Miss Semples," she said, "is Buck Griffin's girlfriend. He owns the Bison Run Distillery."

Stoddard was pureeing the raspberries she would spoon atop her servings of Swedish cream. "That pretty woman we saw in the long blue dress … who is she, Mabel? Her diamond and sapphire necklace nearly blinded me."

"That's Mr. Morgan's daughter, Jeannie Foster," said Mabel. "That necklace, I'm sorry to say, is the only piece of jewelry she has left that her husband Freddie hasn't pawned to spend on the ponies. Mr. Morgan can't stand him."

"Where's Mrs. Morgan?" asked Stoddard.

"She's dead, poor thing," said Mabel. "Some say she died of a broken heart. Jeannie blames her father's unfaithfulness for her mother's early death."

"I see," said Stoddard, now thinking Morgan had more than one dead body to account for. She walked over to the door that led to the dining room and looked through the glassed panel.

Mabel joined her. "See the gray-haired woman standing by the column out there, Stoddard? Now, that's a real lady. That's Louella Whitaker. She inherited the Old Kentucky Distillery. Mr. Morgan wants to buy her out, but Louella doesn't want to sell. She's the guest of honor, so he'll try to sweet talk her out of it tonight."

"Can he do that?'" asked Stoddard.

"Oh, yes, my dear. He's a smooth talker. I've worked twenty years for the Morgans," said Mabel. "I was told there was a time when Jacob Morgan had rough manners and talked like a Kentucky mountain man. But you have to give him credit. When he made enough money, he hired a titled but down on his luck Englishman to tutor him in good manners and proper English. It paid off. Today, he's quite the gentleman."

And murderer, too, thought Stoddard.

Chef Lorenzo, who had been hobnobbing with the dinner guests, returned to the kitchen.

"Everyone look smart, now," he announced. "The guests want to meet you. Straighten your uniforms, put on your white gloves and walk in there with confidence. I'm proud of you."

The young chefs entered the parlor and were greeted with enthusiastic applause. Mr. Morgan turned toward them. Stoddard was stunned by his dapper appearance. She did not think the bourbon magnate looked like a murderer, or at least not how she had imagined him. Morgan stood tall and straight, belying his eighty years, and his white hair was drawn back in a short ponytail tied with a thin black ribbon. His eyes were green and piercing, and his face, though lined, was darkly handsome.

He turned from the students to his guests. "Chef Lorenzo says these five are the Institute's cream of the crop. So, I invite them to introduce themselves to you before we adjourn to the dining room."

The students circled the room exchanging pleasantries with the notables. Stoddard's eyes kept shifting to Jacob Morgan's face as she moved from one guest to another. When she finally stood before him, she said, in a lowered voice: "I can't believe I'm finally getting to meet the man who killed my grandfather."

Morgan stared at her in disbelief. "What ... what did you say? Killed your grandfather? Oh, ho! That's quite a greeting, young lady. If you're joking, you have a lot of faith in my sense of humor."

He moved closer to Stoddard and studied her face. "Still, you do appear to be quite serious," he said. "So, let me say this: I don't know what your little game is, Missy, but I'm not playing. I do extend my condolences to you for the loss of your grandfather. And I can but hope your culinary skills make me forget this unpleasant encounter. Now, I have guests to return to and I'm sure you are needed in the kitchen."

As Morgan turned to go back to the party, Stoddard knew she had only seconds left to make her case. She quickly got close to Morgan's back.

"Does the year 1928 and the name Dr. John Stoddard jog your memory, Mr. Morgan? My name is Stoddard Delaney. John Stoddard was my grandfather ... and you murdered him."

Morgan stopped short. He turned slowly, his green eyes piercing Stoddard's face. "I warn you," he said. "If you repeat that accusation to anyone else, I will see that you regret it ... permanently." Then he moved away from her as though nothing of importance had transpired between them.

When Stoddard returned to the kitchen, she felt like a walking time bomb. She was appalled by the cold-bloodedness of the man who had, she was sure, murdered her grandfather. *He's the one who needs to be gotten rid of,* she thought.

But she had to put that idea and their encounter out of her mind and concentrate on the dessert she would serve at the end of the meal. She began spooning her Swedish cream into champagne glasses.

The thunderstorm that had been forecast for the evening finally became a reality. Rain was falling hard outside.

Cassie was leaning against the kitchen wall, still glowing and bragging to Mabel about the compliments she had received on her appetizers.

Then Chef Lorenzo asked Cassie to act as sommelier for the rest of the evening. He instructed her to keep the wine and water glasses filled. Jeremy and Marcus were told to clear the plates.

Stoddard heard the guests raving about Jeremy's lobster bisque and extolling the virtues of Marcus's beautifully presented salad. It was almost time for Tyler's pork roast.

Stoddard watched Tyler pipe smoothly whipped, bourbon-laced sweet potatoes into orange rind shells, then top them with meringue which he would brown and place around the roast on a large platter.

He was shoving them into the oven when Cassie breezed back into the kitchen, flushed and excited.

"You are not going to believe what just happened," she said, giggling.

"What? Tell us," said Mabel.

"Well," she replied, importantly, "I was at the other end of the table pouring wine, when all of a sudden Freddie Foster jumped up and yelled, 'I'm sick of you trying to run my life, old man. Don't tell me how to spend my money.'"

"And that," she said, "is when Mr. Morgan looked at his son-in-law and said: '*Your* money? You mean your wife's money, don't you?' Boy! You could have heard a pin drop. Then Freddie slapped his napkin on the table and shouted: 'You've insulted me for the last time, Morgan,' and stormed out of the room."

"Oh, my!" said Mabel.

"Darn!" said Tyler, "I hope that didn't ruin everybody's appetites for my roast."

"No. I think most of the guests thought the whole thing rather comical," said Cassie. "I heard one lady say, 'I don't believe they like each other, do you?' and everybody, except Freddie's wife, burst into laughter. I bet Lucie Burdine won't put *that* little episode in her society column."

Tyler was arranging the stuffed orange shells around the roast, when lightning flashed outside and lights in the kitchen flickered. "That was close," he said.

"I'll hold the door for you," said Stoddard.

Tyler picked up the platter and moved carefully through the swinging door and into the dining room. The guests applauded at the sight of his appetizing entree. Stoddard returned to her station and noticed that Tyler had left his carving knife on the counter. She knew he would need the knife for carving the roast. She grabbed it and headed into the dining room to take it to him as surreptitiously as possible.

Cassie was carrying a silver tray with a water pitcher upon it and was about to replenish Jeannie Foster's glass. Cassie looked up with surprise as Stoddard entered with the knife in her hand. Jacob Morgan was sitting at the head of the table, his back to the kitchen door. Mrs. Whitaker, the guest of honor, sat to Morgan's right. Freddie Foster was coming back into the dining room, and Tyler was about to set the platter down on the far end of the table.

Suddenly, lightning struck close to the house. A loud crackling sound was followed by a roll of thunder that caused the house to shake violently. Lights flickered, then went out, plunging the dining room into total darkness. There were gasps among the guests. Tyler's voice was heard above it all, crying, "Oh, no! My roast! My beautiful roast!"

Stoddard had drawn even with Morgan's chair when the lights went out. She stopped to await their coming back on. Then someone bumped her forcibly, knocking the knife from her hand and causing her to stumble. She dropped down on her knees to feel for the knife on the floor and someone tripped over her legs.

When the room lit up again, all eyes turned toward Tyler at the far end of the table. He stood there, distraught, with the platter atilt in his hands. The roast had slipped off with some of its stuffed orange shells and had landed in Buck Griffin's lap.

Griffin's tuxedo was covered with meringue, sweet potatoes, and honey-bourbon sauce. Griffin quickly lifted the hot roast from his lap, dropped it onto the lace tablecloth, and made a futile attempt to clean himself up with his napkin.

Tyler was in tears. Savannah rose to comfort him just as Cassie, standing behind Jeannie Foster's chair, dropped the pitcher, pressed the tray to her chest and screamed: "Stoddard! Good Lord! What have you done?"

All eyes shifted to Stoddard, who stood beside Jacob Morgan, slumped over his plate with the carving knife stuck in the back of his neck.

Stoddard stared at the knife and began backing away.

Chairs scraped the hardwood floor as the guests scrambled to escape the disturbing scene.

Freddie Foster rushed to feel Morgan's pulse, then turned, held Stoddard against the wall and yelled for someone to call the police.

Cassie shouted, "I'll do it," and raced into the kitchen.

Mabel burst into the dining room, took one look at Morgan, and fainted.

The phone call to 911 started a rapid chain of events. Two police cars, cruising in the area, responded to the prominent address in minutes. They in turn notified the coroner, Bob Briggs, and the Homicide Unit.

Homicide Detective Drew Perkins and his partner Sergeant Anderson arrived and herded the dinner guests, Lorenzo, the student chefs, the Morgan staff, and the family members into the drawing room, took their names and learned about the student competition.

When Coroner Briggs arrived, Perkins escorted him into the dining room to see the victim.

The coroner eyed Morgan's neck. "Looks like a cut-and-dried case," he quipped.

"The crime scene unit should be pulling up any moment now," said Perkins. "In the meantime, I need to question the people in the drawing room."

Perkins stepped into the hallway just as the butler opened the door to the crime scene investigators. Perkins pointed to the dining room. "In there," he said.

The mood in the drawing room was somber. The guests were restless, and the students were bemoaning the loss of their dream trip to Paris. Jeremy, Marcus and Cassie were glaring at Stoddard, who sat alone in a far corner. Her head was down, and her arms were wrapped around herself as though she were having a chill. Tyler rose to cross the room and sit beside her.

Lucie Burdine was deep in hushed conversation with Jack Ruberosa and jotting copious notes for her column.

Perkins ran a hand through his sandy colored hair and asked for attention. "Ladies and gentlemen," he began, "I know you want to get home, but I need to ask some questions."

Buck Griffin, who had gone upstairs to clean up, returned to the drawing room and joined Savannah Semples on the sofa.

"Officer Perkins," he said, "Savannah and I are just dinner guests, as are most of the people here. You might as well let us go. Everybody knows who murdered Jacob Morgan. That young lady, there," he said, pointing to Stoddard.

"He's right," said Cassie, taking center stage. "Stoddard Delaney had *reason* to kill Mr. Morgan. He murdered her grandfather."

Jeannie Foster rose angrily from her chair. "What do you mean? My father never murdered anybody."

"Stoddard said he did," said Cassie. "Your dad was a Kentucky moonshiner in 1928, and Stoddard's grandfather was just a young doctor getting started when he made the mistake of riding up to your father's still, unannounced."

There were shocked expressions on the faces of the dinner guests. Jeannie Foster blushed and sat down.

"I'm curious, young lady," said Perkins, frowning. "Why would Miss Delaney confide all that to you?"

"Be-because we're friends," Cassie stammered.

"Friends?" he replied. "Well, for a friend, you seem rather anxious to prove her guilty. Where were you when the lights went out?"

"I can answer that," said Jeannie Foster. "She was just about to fill my water glass."

Perkins turned to Mrs. Foster. "And where were you seated?"

"To my father's left," she replied. "Why are you asking *me*?"

Perkins smiled amicably. "Everyone's a suspect, Ma'am, until proven otherwise."

"Don't you dare accuse my wife," exclaimed Freddie Foster, charging across the room.

Savannah stretched out a long, shapely leg and tripped him before he got to the detective. "Oh, be quiet, Freddie," she said, as he fell to the floor. "You're a good one to criticize anybody. You've squandered most of Jeannie's money on your stupid gambling."

Leona Whitaker threw her head back, laughed, and motioned Perkins to her side. "Freddie has good reason to want his father-in-law dead," she confided. "Jeannie will inherit her father's estate. Then Freddie will have all the money he needs to gamble with."

Tears began flowing down Jeannie Foster's face in earnest as she cradled Freddie in her arms. "Leona, don't you dare criticize my husband. Your family's fine old distillery is failing. You're mad because Father offered to buy you out. You just don't want us to have it. That's what's bothering you."

"Where were you sitting, Mrs. Whitaker?" asked Perkins.

"To Mr. Morgan's right," she replied.

"Close enough to kill him herself," said Freddie, rubbing his knee.

"Ah! And where were you, Mr. Foster?" asked Perkins.

"I had just returned to the table," he said.

Leona Whitaker whooped. "Yes, very conveniently … during the blackout," she said. "Detective Perkins, I think you ought to know that Mr. Morgan and Freddie argued at the table and Freddie threatened his father in law. He said, 'that's the last time you'll insult me, Morgan' before he stormed out of the room."

She turned to Freddie. "And it *was* the last time, wasn't it, Freddie?"

"I hate that woman," said Freddie, under his breath.

Suddenly, Stoddard came out of her stupor. She lifted her head, unfolded her arms and raised herself from her chair. "I remember, now," she said, to no one in particular.

Perkins approached her. "Go on," he said.

"I … I was taking the carving knife to Tyler for the roast," she began. "And when the lights went out, somebody bumped me … hard. The knife was knocked from my hand. I knelt down to feel for it on the floor, and … and then someone tripped over my legs."

Cassie stepped forward again. "Well, we know what you did after that," she said. "You found the knife and murdered Mr. Morgan with it."

Tyler rose and put an arm around Stoddard. "Listen," he said. "Stoddard isn't capable of killing anybody. Cassie, you're just jealous because Stoddard's three times more talented than you."

"I didn't kill him, Tyler," said Stoddard. "When the lights came back on, the knife was nowhere on the floor. When I got up, everyone was looking at you and the roast. Then Cassie screamed and pointed at me. That's when I saw the knife sticking out of Mr. Morgan's neck. I swear to God … I did not put it there."

Perkins nodded. "No, Miss Delaney. You did not murder Mr. Morgan. But I believe I know who did."

He turned toward Cassie. "I note, young lady," he said, "that you've put a clean white jacket on over your uniform. I believe that if you open the jacket, we'll see blood spots on your shirt that splattered there when you stabbed Morgan. And you're no longer wearing a white glove on your right hand."

Cassie pulled the jacket tighter around her.

Stoddard was shocked. "Why would Cassie want to kill Mr. Morgan?" she asked.

"You're the reason, Stoddard. She's jealous of you," said Perkins. "When you came into the dining room with the knife, and the lights went out, she saw her chance to kill Morgan and put the blame on you. She knew you had good reason to want Morgan dead, and she wanted you out of the competition as well. So, she knocked the knife from your hand, picked it up, and stabbed Morgan while you were trying to find it, in the dark, on the floor."

"By the time the lights came back on," he continued, "Cassie had moved back to the other side of Morgan and picked up her tray.

Then she screamed and pointed at you. You looked guilty, Stoddard, standing by Morgan with that knife in his neck."

"Of course!" said Tyler. "None of us were looking at Cassie. Our eyes were on Stoddard. When Mr. Foster yelled for someone to call the police, Cassie flew into the kitchen, like she was going to make the call. That's probably when she removed her bloody glove and put the jacket on."

Cassie stepped forward. "Oh, shut up! I didn't mean to kill Morgan," she sobbed. "I only meant to wound him in the shoulder. I figured Stoddard would get blamed for it. But I tripped over Stoddard's legs and the knife went into the back of his neck instead. I knew where to injure him and not kill him," she said haughtily. "I'm smart. I could have gone to med school. I could have been a surgeon."

"Yeah," said Perkins, sarcastically. "You could have been a contender. Okay, Anderson, cuff 'Doctor' Cassie, read her her rights and get her out of here. Everyone else can go, too."

Jeremy and Marcus approached Stoddard and apologized for doubting her innocence. Savannah and Buck joined them.

"Tyler," said Buck, grinning, "I scooped some of your sweet potatoes and bourbon sauce off my tux for a taste. It was delicious. I want you four to create a dinner for me and my guests next month. Fix the pork roast again, Tyler. Just don't serve it on my lap, this time."

Everyone laughed.

Stoddard smiled broadly. "Detective Perkins," she said, "let's all go in the kitchen. I made a great dessert tonight. Might as well sit down and enjoy it."

THE SPIRITS OF BUFFALO TRACE
BY LORENA R. PETER

I've seen 'em. Yes, indeed I have. Sometimes just a wispy, cloud-like thing. Other times, their features are visible, as clear to me as yours are right now. Some people don't actually see them, only feel 'em like a cool breeze blowing across the face or a vibration that makes the skin tingle. Doesn't matter how you sense them, there are definitely ghosts roaming the grounds here at Buffalo Trace.

Oh, I forgot to tell you who I am. My name is Adam and I'm from Frankfort, Kentucky. Born here and lived all my life in this area. In fact, I've only lived in two houses my entire life. Once I traveled to San Francisco and loved it, but this is my home.

Why do I know so much about the ghosts around here? My parents had a cleaning business and they cleaned the distillery three or four times a week. Since I was a baby, I came with them. You might say I've grown up at the distillery. I grew up seeing things that other people don't. I don't hear them talking or anything, but I do see plenty. Maybe that's why I see spirits. I mean, you might say they were my first playmates.

Not too long ago a television show was filmed here; one that looks for ghosts. They interviewed me on it. Lots of fun, but in the end they didn't include many of the stories I told them. My parents told me stories of foremen in the warehouse saving the lives of their crews. One man said that he heard a voice warning him to have his crew take their break outside the building rather than in their usual place. Minutes later the brick wall collapsed just where they would have been sitting. Man, was he glad he listened! On second thought maybe they didn't include that one because I wasn't there … didn't see it myself.

Bourbon is addictive, gets in your blood. Not just the drinking of the rich brown liquid, but the making of it. It takes time and attention to coax the flavors out of just the right mix of grains, aging it in just the right barrels, and selling it in just the right bottles. I once heard about a tasting to select the perfect bourbon for distribution under a new label at Buffalo Trace. The men helping make that decision were octogenarians with decades in the business. Their credentials read like a history of bourbon. Creating the perfect bourbon is not just a job, it's a passion.

I know you've heard about Colonel Albert B. Blanton. You haven't? Well, that was one dedicated bourbon man. (Not a real military colonel, but a Kentucky Colonel.) He steered the Buffalo Trace Distillery through tough times as president/ master distiller from 1921 to 1952. By the '20s, he'd already spent decades of his life working here. His first job was as a clerk in the office in 1897. He was sixteen. Through the years he did most of the different jobs here. Even before being promoted to master distiller, he was respected by his employees for his knowledge. He loved making bourbon, and it showed.

See that mansion on top of the hill overlooking the distillery grounds? That was his house. We have more than three hundred acres of land here on the Kentucky River. He had that house built in the Thirties so he could keep an eye on the distillery, warehouses, and the outbuildings below. It's known as the Stony Point Mansion now and used as offices, but he lived there until he died on the sun porch in 1959. There's a hut behind the Clubhouse with a cast iron kettle where the Colonel cooked burgoo, our style of stew. He cured country hams and raised fighting hens. All the stories about him paint him as an imposing figure, bigger than life. And the only one honored with a marble statue on the grounds. Blanton loved the distillery and had strong ideas about every aspect of its running. That he cooked Kentucky burgoo for the employees says a lot about his devotion to the people who worked with him.

Blanton was an important part of the history of this place. The mansion no longer serves as a residence, but the change doesn't deter Albert Blanton from roaming its corridors and climbing its stairs. Anyone who works in the building these days makes friends with the Colonel. He can be heard rocking in a chair or walking across the floor in the rooms upstairs. Some office workers have even seen him there and talk about him like an old friend.

Mom and Dad cleaned the place for years, and often met the Colonel in Stony Point Mansion. They never got used to seeing him like I did. One night they entered the building together, parting in the foyer.

Dad went to start in an office on the first floor while Mom went to the second. Soon Mom heard noises, a commotion in the next room, and called out to see if Dad had come upstairs. No answer. She moved toward the sounds and suddenly saw the dark menacing shadow of a man looming in the doorway, filling the entire space. He was wearing a trench coat and fedora. She screamed as she practically flew down the stairs, frightened by the "intruder". It wasn't until weeks later that they saw a photo of Blanton taken in front of the house. He was wearing a trench coat and fedora. Eerie.

Another time, Dad was working alone and went to finish for the night on the third floor. With the first swipe of his dusting cloth, he heard people on the second floor. Sounded like a party. He thought someone was working late, so he went to tell them he was there—as a courtesy, you know. No one was there. He found only dark and silence when he searched the second floor. Satisfied that he was alone, he returned to the third floor and the party continued on the floor below him for as long as he worked. Told me he never saw them, and hearing them all the time weirded him out.

The Colonel isn't the only one I see, but he's the one most other people know. The distillery is named for the land it's built on: a trace the buffalos followed across the Kentucky River. The animals drank here on their way to western grazing grounds. The Indians hunted here, too. They must have thought this land was special. Maybe they asked their spirits to protect it because it was important for the survival of the tribe. I don't know about that, but I do know that the pollution of this part of the river upsets someone because I feel it when I walk the grounds. Someone out there's mighty angry. Maybe they're the ones who tried to kill the crew in the warehouse. Could be the spirits of men who died during the hunt or the nature spirits put in place to protect this area. Whatever. I love this land. It's special. I do what I can to keep it clean. Wish more would pitch in. I'm sure the spirits of Buffalo Trace would be happy.

A Toast for Toofa
By Lorena Reith, Jr.

The bed dipped as Alice slipped out quietly. That means I have another ten minutes to snooze. Or to daydream. We've been married for over twenty years and I love her more every day. She is my rock. She is my helpmate in all parts of life, especially during this recent chaos at work. The smell of coffee brought me to my feet, and I shuffled toward the kitchen and the comfortable routine that starts my every day.

"Good morning, Alice. Have I told you lately how much I love you?" Oh man, am I stuck in a romantic comedy here?

Alice rolled her eyes, but a smile lit up her face. "Yes, silly, every day."

"Oh. Just wanted to make certain you knew."

Her smile dimmed. "I never get tired of hearing it. Really, Ted."

"You talked in your sleep last night. Have another dream?" Her dreams were a constant. Sometimes they entertain but lately others warn of the future. Which kind is this?

She shrugged. "I didn't understand it. I was in a crowd but moving toward some individuals who were a bit removed. They raised something glittering and I felt fear or … or … might have been guns or something else. I heard something about Toofa but got no sense of what it meant, except it didn't feel good."

Alice is a therapist and her descriptions are usually filled with evocative emotion-words. This didn't fit the norm. In my job as the president of Dan Boone Distillery, I don't deal with much in the way of emotions. Nope, we're more about the physical—the tastes and smells of fine bourbon. A marketing department supplies the visuals to sell our finest, but I don't have to come up with convincing words or images.

She broke into my thoughts. "Have you heard anything that sounds like Toofa?"

I shook my head as I cradled the mug from which wake-up smells were rising. "No. Doesn't sound familiar, but I'm not included in every meeting since the distillery was bought by that foreign conglomerate." Another sip, and the cells in my brain started firing. "You remember that we have a 'party' to introduce the new owners to department heads and their wives? I would love to have you there. In fact, it is very important."

Alice turned from the toaster to bring me an English muffin. "Saturday night. It's on my calendar. I'm glad it's being held here in Louisville. I hate driving all the way out to the distillery for these events, especially at night alone."

"I'll come home so we can drive together."

She smiled her pleasure and then moved toward the shower and the start of her workday.

As for me, I looked forward to another day of my routine inspection of areas of the facility made more complicated by having to fit in meetings with a transition team. These were not only foreigners, but they didn't understand the first thing about the art or science of distilling fine bourbon. At Dan Boone, we take pride in being the best and I wondered if any of our new staff members even drank the rich amber liquid we produce. In China, businessmen get drunk together to prove their integrity. Will they expect the same of us?

Alice stopped in the middle of putting on jewelry. "How's the transition going? Any big changes?"

"Lots of cuts. Want their own people in key positions. Haven't said who yet."

Alice frowned. "Is your job in danger?"

"Hard to tell. Everyone's worried."

"You're the best in the business."

"There's a lot of maneuvering going on."

"Be careful. You love this job. And I like you employed." She blew me a kiss.

The new owners planned the party in Louisville so they could see their newest employees in more relaxed conditions. Made sense, I guessed. I introduced Alice to my boss and his wife, Mr. and Mrs. Yuan, who were greeting guests as they walked in the door. Then she drifted off to introduce Mrs. Yuan to other wives.

Later, I joined Alice as she listened intently to Margery and George Degulasse. George is head chemist in Quality Control. He was whispering hotly, "Told me not to test every batch. Says it costs too much. Takes too much time. 'We're cutting your budget.' That's what he said."

Margery asked blandly, "What's the difference, if you still have your job?"

George almost spat his answer. "Quality goes down. Market share goes down. Then, they'll fire more people. Short-sighted, if you ask me."

Margery shrugged.

I understand George and count him as a friend. He has the passion of a true believer, currently bolstered by quantities of bourbon. "Ours is the best and we need to keep it that way." He turned to Alice. "Right?"

"We're the tops," she answered smoothly.

George went on passionately in a cloud of bourbon fumes, "Before you know it, we'll be distilling rot-gut. Been the best for so long. What a crime."

Our hosts proposed toast after toast. I made some of my own. To the new ownership. To the best bourbon in the world. To increased international market share. To the alliance between the two companies, American and Chinese.

Representatives of the parent company moved around the room, drinking with employees and meeting spouses. Their eyes scanned the room, always watching, evaluating. Alice started, "Have you noticed …" but I stopped her with a slight shake of my head. We could talk later.

Alice talked with everyone. That was her job as the president's wife. At the end of the evening, we joined the Yuans. I saw her jerk; it must have reminded her of her dream. I became as alert as I was able, given the amount of bourbon pumping through my veins.

Yuan raised his glass solemnly for the last toast. "A toast to Toofa. Toofa live. You are part."

One glance at my wife and I could see her shiver. Was it with fear, or had she remembered more of the dream? She mouthed "Toofa??" to me, but I shook my head in warning.

I put on my party face and raised my glass higher and cheered louder, playing the game.

We were the last to leave. I was so plastered, I stumbled to the rear window of the car and wrote "Toofa lives" in the dew shrouding the window. I raised my hand as if to toast, but lost my balance. I caught myself on the edge of the window. "Glad you're driving. I'm drunk."

Alice laughed. "I can see that."

I rested against the seat back with my eyes closed and head swimming, listening. I heard Alice put the key in the ignition, and then a moment of silence. Her shocked gasp brought me upright. I followed her gaze to the rear window. "Evil afoot" was scrawled across the glass.

I blinked a couple of times to clear my vision, but the words were still there regardless of the number of blinks. "What the ...? Who wrote that?"

Alice answered smoothly, "You did, dear. Remember, 'Toofa lives'?"

Suddenly sober, dread filled my very bones. *Evil afoot!* "Alice, your dream must have been a warning!"

The next morning, I sat at the kitchen table, head in hands. Alice handed me a couple of pain killers and a cup of coffee. Whatever would I do without her? "Why did I drink so much?"

Alice hugged me. "This is not the first. Probably won't be the last. You'll survive."

My brain fog cleared enough for me to remember, "I remember seeing a file labeled TOOFA LIVE in Yuan's office. He covered it with papers when he saw me looking. Mumbled something about a special project, a pet of his bosses in Shanghai. Said it'd be out in the open soon."

Alice leaned against the counter watching me. "You think Toofa's dangerous?"

"Don't know what it is … yet." She refilled my cup.

"Would they move the operation to China?"

"Wouldn't be bourbon. To be called 'bourbon', it has to be made in the US."

"Does it matter what it's called if it's made by the same recipe? If your product isn't as good as it was, won't your customers learn to drink Hung So Booze instead?"

"Our customers drink Dan Boone Bourbon." I was firm. "They're loyal."

"George was told to cut corners on testing. Remember?"

On Monday, I talked with every department head. They were all being asked to do things that could endanger the quality of our product. Each one repeated the mantra that premium bourbon is made with careful attention to detail.

In Quality Control, George was even more adamant. "Bourbon is king here in Kentucky. Making bourbon is a holy practice. Each distillery is its own temple where rituals are closely followed, and secrets guarded."

I couldn't help myself; I patted him on the back. "Amen, brother."

The Chief Financial Officer spoke in conspiratorial tones. "Our new owner is known for buying and dismantling companies. Looked 'em up. They sell the pieces and keep the secrets, the intellectual properties."

I tried to reassure him even as my own alarms were blaring. "They might try to duplicate our product, but it's not science, it's an art." I crossed fingers behind my back and wondered if Alice was right about a Chinese bourbon.

Sam Kindley, head of maintenance, started a tirade as soon as I got within earshot. "Delay repairs till they become a crisis! We had a world of trouble when a vat broke and dumped everything into the river behind the distillery!" He slammed his fist on the workbench for emphasis. "Mash traveled down the Kentucky River into the Ohio. It was a disaster; a large fish kill forced the county to call off a bass fishing tournament. Loss of television coverage for the area. A lot of trouble."

I remembered. "Yep. Lots of unhappy fishermen. Merchants complaining of lost revenues. It was a public relations nightmare."

Sam chuckled. "We joked about fishermen out for drunken bass instead of drunken fishermen out for bass."

I shook my head. "The fine was no joke."

Sam was on a roll. "Should've charged people downriver for the bourbon they got from their water tap."

"The communities downriver get drinking water from the Ohio River. EPA was not amused. And the bad press for polluting … Skimping on maintenance could cost a lot more in the long run. I'll see what I can do."

I talked with our Chinese overlords, but they responded by smiling and nodding with no light behind the eyes indicating understanding. My alarm grew, but not about my job—only about the bourbon.

Budget cuts. To underscore his point, Yuan dumped a new delivery of vat cleaning supplies in the middle of my office. He didn't want to hear how the contents of the sturdy wooden box were needed. Cut costs.

Personnel cuts. I was given a long list of employees to fire without regard to their worth to the company. It included George and half the staff in Quality Control. Yuan wouldn't budge. He put his hand out straight, palm out whenever I tried to argue. I understood the Great Wall of China! A Middle Eastern man took George's position, at lower pay. In fact, lots of foreigners replaced my people, all working for less. Profit margins were up, but at what cost? Quality remained fair, but the physical plant looked ragged.

Every time I talked with Alice, she remained adamant. "These dreams mean something. Something's going to happen … something bad."

"Everything they're doing is legal. They own the distillery." But I remained vigilant for any hints about Toofa. And then I got exciting news to share with Alice. "You know Queen Elizabeth keeps her horses in the area."

"In the Bluegrass region around Lexington, isn't it? She comes to see them often from what I hear. Why?"

"She wants a tour of the distillery. Impressed? Soon I'll be her friend in the bourbon business."

"You're everyone's bourbon buddy! You going to spruce up the plant for her visit?"

"We only got the call today. No change in direction so far. Yuan's door was closed all afternoon. Probably talking long distance."

"Say anything to you about maintenance?"

"Not to me. We had a long conference, but he didn't mention it. He made the rounds and talked to people all over. The guys reported back to me."

"Maybe he checked things out today, so he can approve the work tomorrow."

"Doubt it. He seems to be on a mission. Now, we're getting deliveries from different vendors, too, probably cheaper ones."

"You haven't been told about it? You're still president, aren't you?"

I considered the implications of her question. "Yuan left work early. I'll ask tomorrow."

"Why wait? Let's check it out tonight." Alice jumped to her feet, ready to go.

I could see danger signs all over, and shook my head to discourage her.

"As president, shouldn't you find out? What if it's something illegal?" Alice's voice rose an octave.

"Even more reason to stay away. If it is illegal, they might go to extremes to hide it."

She rolled her eyes. "What would they do? Kill us?"

"Too much TV, Alice. For now, they need me to run the business, but if I become a liability, they could replace me."

"*I'm* going to investigate. Are you coming?" Alice is stubborn. When she gets an idea, she holds onto it with all fingers, toes, and teeth. No caution here.

No options. "If it's that important… Besides, I have the keys and codes." And I hoped to keep her out of trouble.

I drove into the distillery employee parking lot. "This is the fastest route into the plant."

Alice grinned. "And no indication of who you are."

Oh, man. I could see the intrigue she was imagining.

It was change of shift and people were moving in and out. We slipped in behind workers going through the side entrance and were nodded through by a new security guard who was more intent on watching his monitors than on checking ID cards. There was probably a television somewhere nearby, too. Against the rules.

I held my wife's hand to lead her through a warehouse filled with barrels of aging bourbon and out a side door. I motioned toward the wall. "We have cameras everywhere. You can see the red light indicating they're on. We'll take a shortcut through the vat building."

The air around the vats was thick with the heady smell of fermenting grains. Each was in a different stage of the process and yielded a different aroma. "I love these smells. Ever since Dad brought me here as a kid. You get to know how each stage smells …"

Alice sniffed, but only shrugged.

225

I grinned at her confusion. "Takes an educated nose."

Suddenly a door opened, and the sound of male voices approached.

I pulled my wife behind the nearest vat and whispered, "No one should be in here at this hour."

A door slammed, and the clomp and rattle of people came closer. In the novels on Alice's nightstand, we might have reached the door in time but instead, we watched from our hiding place as a group of men appeared from behind a vat. Each man carried two five-gallon buckets. We watched as liquid from the buckets was dumped into the vat. The sound of empty buckets hitting the floor filled the air. I motioned to Alice that the cameras were off. There was no way to prove who or what, and they were too far away to read labels.

A sudden loud bang caused men to brandish guns, shouting in foreign accents. Alice gasped, but the sound was covered by the commotion in front of us. A voice in the distance, reassuring. Calm returned as well as a business-like attention to the task at hand. They moved faster. Once all the buckets were empty, a package of powder was added. One man supervised, shouting and gesturing. Empty containers were carried away. At last, a lone man waited by the "supervisor" until the far door slammed shut, and they were alone in a quiet that was eerie after the noise.

A Chinese accent asked in broken English, "How long before it ready?"

The response was in a Middle Eastern accent. "Couple days. One day to mix in and another to get strong."

"Two days, you say? Then ready?"

"About."

"How keep people away for two days? Will it look different?"

"Not look. Taste. Drink and death," replied the Middle Eastern accent. "I think death look like heart attack. Maybe not so bad."

"Death. Not good. Two days ..." the Asian said slowly.

"You keep people out?"

"Must do."

The answer was a nod as the two voices moved away. If they had turned at just that moment, they would have seen two people poised to exit the nearest door.

Outside, we pressed against the wall, breathless. I was perspiring even in the cool night air.

She whispered, "What …"

I interrupted. "I'm thinking." I squeezed her hand. "Try to look like you belong here. Everything we do now can be watched." Moving quickly, I led her around the end of the building. There were so many people, I decided it was safer to move along the dark side of the next building to follow the line of warehouses. I pointed at the nothingness from time to time to look as though this was really a tour. Finally, we rounded the end of the last structure onto an empty courtyard. The next time we saw anyone, it was the security guard engrossed in his television show. Now I was glad the guard didn't follow rules.

We threaded through cars in the lot and finally came to our own. Safe behind closed doors, we heaved relieved sighs.

Alice was breathless with excitement, "Was it poison?"

"You can bet it wasn't a different variety of barley. We have to get the police."

"But all the bottles would be recalled at the first death. Death by bourbon just doesn't make sense."

Starting the car gave me time to put my thoughts together. "They didn't know of the Queen's visit until today. Gotta be something else." I drove slowly toward the gate and grew calmer as we neared the gate.

Alice was thoughtful. "They were in a hurry."

"Yes?"

"Because of the Queen's visit?"

"She'll have lots of security following her."

Alice giggled, "And media. That's it! What we know so far is that a Chinese company bought the distillery and have replaced American personnel with foreigners."

"Middle Eastern mostly, but also French and Russian. And?'

"Terrorism."

"The Chinese have never taken credit for bombings, or any other terrorist acts."

"Maybe they're a front for people who couldn't buy it legally."

My heart sank. "Death by bourbon?" I drove slowly toward the gate. "Another creation of your vivid imagination."

Alice sounded weary. "Home, Jeeves. This was …" She swallowed her words when she saw the threatening black SUV blocking the gate. Men were standing all around. I felt the guns more than saw them and knew I had to get away.

A French accent yelled, "Stop. We want to talk to you."

"Right," My mind was already busy concocting potential futures. "Alice, call the police. Cell phone."

She moaned, "Damned thing's at home."

I dug into my pocket for mine. "Must've dropped mine."

I turned the car down another aisle only to see car lights ahead. Another right turn, more lights. I was forced to stop when we were surrounded. The doors were locked, but several men pointed guns at Alice through the window.

She whispered, "Oh, my God."

"Open the door or we shoot." On all sides men were smirking … brandishing guns.

"Let my wife go. I go with you and you let her drive away." I shouted through the closed window. That was the only option I could see.

"She dies now, or maybe you see her later. Your choice." No more laughter or conversation, only grim determination.

Alice whispered, "Not looking good."

A tap of metal on the window. "Choose."

I tried for calm confidence but didn't feel it. "Shall we?"

"I don't see any other options?"

I unlocked the doors. "Nope."

Strong hands yanked us from the car.

I yelled, "What the hell are you doing? I have every right to be here, I work here. Don't hurt her!"

I was answered by taunting voices speaking foreign languages.

Somewhere, Alice screamed, "Don't you touch me!"

I was pushed into the back seat of a car and didn't see what happened to my wife. My mind raced through ways I could rescue her, but for now I was captive.

I was surrounded by obvious disagreement. Guns waved in my face. Angry voices. I was dragged into a building and locked in a closet. And soon there was silence outside the door. My brain was stuck in a panicky loop, grinding over and over the question of where Alice was and how I could find her.

Hours later, the door opened. Yuan stood with several hostile strong men. No guns. He said in an oily tone, "I am so sorry that our new employees did not recognize you and your lovely wife, Ted."

Gentler hands pulled me from the floor.

Yuan continued smoothly, "You have been treated unkindly because our new friends saw you on security monitors. You looked like an intruder, an industrial spy. They were protecting our secrets."

What secrets? I wondered. "I was showing Alice around at night because she works during the day. Your party reminded her that we are a family, a bourbon family."

"Yes, of course. But so secretive? It is late. Go home, Ted. Tomorrow is almost here, and you don't want to be tired for work." He moved toward the door.

"And Alice? Where is Alice?" My voice sounded urgent, lacking the confidence I hoped to project.

Yuan's annoying, even tone stoked my fear. "Your wife is missing? Perhaps she spends a couple of days with her sister. She will turn up." The door closed behind him.

One of the strongmen walked me to the exit. "Where's my wife?" I repeated. Silence. My car waited just outside.

During the drive home, my mind traveled faster than the car— *Alice is a hostage.* I drove directly to George's house and banged on the door. "George, you've got to help. I know it's late, but they've got Alice."

I sat on the edge of a chair in George's den and described the events of the night. I was rattled.

George asked, "What do you want from me?"

"I can't go to the police. Those men wouldn't hesitate to hurt Alice. We have to do this on our own."

"We? What can I do?"

"You're a chemist. If I bring you a sample, can you analyze it? I want to find out what they're cooking."

George smirked. "Sure, I have a complete lab in my basement."

I considered the question. "Could you use the lab at the university?"

George nodded. "Yep, but I need time."

"That, I can't get you; it'll be full strength in two days."

At work the next day, I slipped an empty vial into my pocket as I started my normal rounds. When I neared the vat warehouse, a man appeared out of nowhere. His grimace screamed a warning: the building was off-limits. He flashed a photo of Alice to underscore the point.

I made my way back to my office to find a plan of the facility. There must be a way in. There had to be. The roof was out of the question. Both doors into the building were probably guarded. Then I saw it: a pipe carried overflow from the vat to a waste tank buried outside. My heart raced with excitement.

Why didn't I think of this? The system was designed to remove overflow in case the vat got too full. With so much added last night, there must be overflow. Since it drains from the top, it should be concentrated. Again, I turned toward the vats. I forced myself to move slowly, speaking with each person along the way. I worked to act calm even though my heart beat like a drum. As I neared the building, I heard dripping. I dipped the vial into the drain, hoping to look as though I was making a routine inspection.

I left for lunch at the regular time. As planned, George sat at the second table in my favorite restaurant. We shook hands and I passed the vial to him. Was anyone watching? We couldn't risk looking. George soon left. I lingered over lunch, greeting all the regulars, and hoped they didn't notice my shaking hands.

That night I paced instead of sleeping. George called at three. "Finished."

"Analysis and antidote?"

"Yeah. Will fill you in with the details."

"Small packages?"

"Ready for you to pick up."

"In the morning?"

"Yeah."

On my way to work, I stopped at George's. He motioned me into the garage and closed the door.

George gestured with the package in his hand. "In the trunk under the spare … in case you're searched."

When I drove away, the parcels were tucked under the spare. Still, I worried. One day until the poison was full strength. One more day. This thought raced through my mind. Now, how to get the stuff into the vat?

As soon as I turned off my engine, two men roughly pulled me out of the car and searched it, passenger compartment and trunk. Nothing. I sent a thought to George: *Thanks, Buddy, I owe you one.* My office had been turned upside down. Hints that they were worried. I stormed into Yuan's office to protest, but it was empty. The secretary explained the Asians' sudden departure for China. Why hadn't I been told?

I was on my own, with no one looking over my shoulder. One by one, I brought parcels into my office and hid them in the box of cleaning supplies destined for the vat house. No one would look there.

Hope against hope, I walked past the vat house. Guards. Some other way.

That's when it happened; a government security detail arrived to secure the facility for the Queen's visit. And they were brought straight to me. The agent in charge said gruffly, "Take us on the route you'll use tomorrow. We'll have men with her, but we'll do what we can today. You understand."

My brain screeched, *This'll take too much time. Time I don't have.* I said nothing but grew more anxious as we walked the route. At the vat house, a dark-skinned guard surreptitiously flashed the photo of Alice to me as he let us pass. I shrugged to show that I was only following orders. Agents swarmed the building, inspecting every inch of it for the Queen's safety.

I wondered if Alice was safe. Then, I remembered the wooden box in my office. I took a deep breath to calm myself and explained to the agent, "If the Queen stands in the middle here, she can see the entire room from a place of safety. Once I explain the process, she can walk around as she pleases."

The agent laughed. "You're kidding right? She's shorter than I am, and I can't see from here."

I smiled. "There's a sturdy box in my office she could use as a viewing platform. She'll see everything."

Finally, the agent said, "OK. You men get the box and we'll see how it works." The agents positioned the box and left, patting themselves on the back for a job well done. I was alone in the building for a few minutes before being ousted by guards yelling in a confusion of languages.

The next day, just as the Queen's entourage entered the building, an explosion ripped a hole in the vat and the wall next to it. Chaos— screaming people were running in every direction. The Royal party was surrounded by agents and rushed away. Only the media remained. A torrent of mash spilled out through the wall and down the bank to the Kentucky River. The entire incident was filmed. Reporters were ready

231

to blame the distillery for polluting … *again.* Then they found a recording from a terrorist group taking credit for the explosion as part of a plot they called TOOFA LIVE. No mention of poison. The perpetrators probably wanted time for it to work into the water supply and into the homes of local residents. And I didn't tell anyone because they still had Alice.

It was hours before the officials released me. They asked me the same questions over and over during those hours, only to hear the same answers. I repeated over and over that terrorists had taken my wife. I pleaded with them to let me look for her, but they answered that the greater good was more important than the safety of one woman. Easy for them to say; she wasn't their family.

The house was empty when I finally got home, so I broke the land speed record to get back to the distillery. George met me with everyone he could find to help with the search.

At last we found Alice, bound and gagged, in a storage room. As soon as she was safe, I rushed to tell the police of the poison. Authorities tested water at the intakes and found it was safe to drink. The antidote had worked, and we all felt an enormous cloud of tension lift.

The search party was gathered in my office, so I broke out a bottle of the good bourbon. Pouring the stuff was more difficult with my arm around Alice, though; I wasn't ready to let her go. I made the first toast, "Here's to bourbon and the best bourbon makers in the world." Everyone raised glasses and cheered.

George raised his glass for another, "And here's to Ted and Alice!" And the response was ear-splitting yelling, followed by more drinking.

And then I wondered who would own the distillery? Surely, it would be confiscated because of the attempt to kill so many people living on the riverbanks. I searched the happy faces around me and wondered if *we* might take on the job of owning the distillery we love.

DUSTY HUNTS
BY DEBORAH ALVORD

You have heard of Easter Hunts, Fox hunts, Man hunts, Big Game hunts, Job hunts, and Treasure hunts. But have you ever heard of a "Dusty Hunt"?

The Dusty Hunter's eyes ceaselessly scan the landscape for an unsearched, by him, liquor store. This is his lucky day. He enters the store full of hope. Finally, he spots his prey, an out of production bottle of bourbon, resting forgotten under its cloak of thick dust. He places it in his hands and brushes aside the dust to admire the old bottle. What can he learn of the history of this bourbon and its glass container?

The bottle is going to give up its age. Distillers do not stock glass bottles due to their fragility and space taking. They use them as soon as possible. Most bottle manufacturers place two numerals on the bottom. If the manufacturing year was 1975, then "75" would appear.

We have another clue from the label of the age of the bottle/bourbon. Pre-1980, volume was listed using the standard terms: pint, quart, and gallon. The years between 1978 and 1980 served as a transition time with both standard/metric volumes listed. Finally, if only the metric volume is given, the label was printed from the early 1980s onward.

The label can tell even more. If there is no UPC code, that would indicate production before the late 1970s. The existence of a UPC symbol allows learning the heritage of a particular bourbon. Each change of ownership results in a change of the symbol. A search on www.upcdatabase.com will give the owner's name. Using an internet search, you can then find much information. Remembering that the recipes and grains have changed over time, you can gain an appreciation for the dusty bottle in your hands.

Much of this information was gleamed from Ms. Brbnizgud's website www.Bourbon-Central.com.

HARD FACTS
BY M. E. GASKINS

How do bartenders measure bourbon?

Methods vary according to the bartender's style. A bartender can measure accurately using a shot glass or jigger. Some bartenders prefer to "guesstimate" by pouring a serving while counting to three, or to the height of two fingers held against the outside of a glass.

How much does a shot glass, or a jigger hold?

A survey of bartending texts and websites shows amounts varying from one to two ounces. The usual measurement at most establishments in the United States is 1.5 ounces.

What does '80-proof bourbon' mean?

Bourbon is produced in batches with different amounts of alcohol. The batch's proof correlates to twice the percentage of alcohol. For example: 80-proof bourbon is 40% alcohol; 100-proof bourbon is 50% alcohol.

Does bourbon have calories?

Yes. The calories in bourbon come from alcohol (ethanol), which has 7 calories per gram. Estimate 100 calories in 1.5 ounces of 80-proof bourbon, and 125 calories in 1.5 ounces of 100-proof bourbon.

How long does it take to metabolize the alcohol in one drink?

Many factors will affect metabolism, such as height, weight, gender, and genetics. Generally, it takes a healthy adult about one hour to process the alcohol in 1.5 ounces of bourbon.

Does alcohol evaporate when bourbon is heated?

It's been estimated that igniting a flambé will cause about 25% of the alcohol to evaporate. Baking for thirty minutes will cause about half the alcohol to evaporate. Simmering for two-three hours will remove approximately 90-95% of the alcohol.

How much bourbon is usually added to a recipe for flavor?

Adding one teaspoon bourbon per serving will enhance rather than overpower the flavor of food.

How much bourbon should be added to a meat marinade?

A good rule of thumb is to add 1-2 tablespoons of 80-proof bourbon to the marinade per pound of meat. Bourbon can replace up to ¼ of the liquid in a marinade. A mixture with higher alcohol content may make the meat texture spongy. Marinating meat should be refrigerated. The marinade itself should be discarded or cooked thoroughly before eating.

GLASS CEILING
BY HEIDI WALKER

Sweat trailed down Jen Lambert's back. The musk of bourbon filled her nostrils. She shoved a loose strand of damp hair off her face. Where did her father get off making her work this job? Instead of a position at the Lambert Distillery headquarters, here she was at this blasted Fourth Street Bourbon Bar washing bottles.

"The Bourbon Bar is our largest customer in the region," her father had said. As the president of the company, he ought to know.

"But I want to work with you at headquarters," Jen had insisted.

Her father hadn't met her eyes. "This is a position of responsibility, pumpkin. Let's see how it goes."

She wrenched the spray nozzle from its holder and doused a dozen bottles. Would he ever trust her? Sure, she'd racked up some shoplifting charges, but that was in high school. She'd put in two exemplary years at junior college, but that evidently wasn't enough to convince him she'd reformed. What else could she do? College had focused her goals, and working with her dad at headquarters topped her list. This job was as low down the company hierarchy as you could get. At this rate, it would take her decades to rise through the corporate ranks.

She'd been about to ask him to reconsider when last week's truck heist put everyone on edge. The company lost two hundred cases of its premium aged bourbon. It was all her father would talk about.

"Your work at the Bourbon Bar is a critical job, Jen," he'd said. "If we don't keep track of our empties, bootleggers could pour their own rotgut brew into our labeled bottles and sell them on the black market. That, on top of the stolen cases, would be economically catastrophic."

Jen glanced at the wall clock. Time to get the empties onto the bar's loading dock for pickup. Hot spray soaked her sleeves above the rubber gloves as she hurriedly rinsed the last bottles and placed them in plastic Lambert Distillery crates. She peeled off the dripping gloves and wiped her sweaty hands on her jeans. She hoisted a case from the stack by the bar's rear entry. Using her back to push open the swinging door, she set the heavy container on the edge of the dock beside the other crates.

The distillery's truck was already backed up to the platform, its rear door raised. Rand, the driver, swaggered toward Jen, his leering grin exposing a crooked front tooth. As flirtatious as ever. She'd kept secret that she was the daughter of the distillery's owner, but she'd play that card if she had to. So far, he seemed harmless enough. His pathetic ogling didn't hurt her and making a big issue of it to management would get her a reputation as a snitch. Besides, she wanted to show her father that she could handle the job herself.

Rand still had a bandage above one eye from the hijacking last week—Jen's first week on the job. She knew that Rand had been grilled by the police about whether he'd had anything to do with the theft. He'd told the investigators that he'd been yanked out of the truck cab and knocked out by a guy in a ski mask.

As Rand approached, Jen smelled alcohol on him. Great. Company rule number one: no drinking on the job. After what'd happened to him, he must be nervous about driving alone. Still, driving drunk was inexcusable.

"You look hot when you're hot," Rand said. "Know what I mean, sugar?"

Oh, brother. He thought he was God's gift to women. Jen's resolve to overlook his drinking evaporated. She leaned in to get a good whiff of his breath. "You been drinking?"

"Just one shot, I swear," he said. "Bartender offered me a taste, is all. From a vintage bottle. Real smooth."

Only high rolling customers ordered the aged brews. Jen was surprised the bartender would waste such expensive drink on Rand. "How's your head?" Jen said, pointing to the bandaged wound.

"Could be worse." He looked at the crate Jen had carried out. "That the last one?"

"There's more inside."

"I'm on a schedule, you know." He squatted on the dock floor. "Get a move on, girl. You know how I love to watch you work."

What a jerk. As Jen turned away, Rand pulled a cell phone from his pocket, a fancy type she'd seen advertised on TV. How'd he afford that model on a truck driver's salary?

She brought out the last crate of still damp bottles and loaded it onto the truck with the others. Should she give the man a second chance for drinking on the job? She knew what it was like to make a mistake. Wasn't her father giving her a second chance with this job? Rand didn't seem tipsy, so maybe he'd told the truth about just the one shot. She'd report him if it happened again.

"It's all on board," she said.

Rand gave her a two-fingered salute and drove off.

She'd have to hurry now. Only an hour break for dinner, and she had someone she wanted to see. There was barely time to clean up, add a trace of perfume, and walk to Matt's art studio.

Matt yanked off the elbow-length insulated mitts and flung them on the bench. He'd spent the day slicing the bottoms off liquor bottles, shaping them in the kiln, and laying them in a pattern on the floor. With the sun low, the shadows in the building made continuing to work on the art piece impossible. He pulled the canvas apron over his head and tossed it at a nail on the rough concrete wall. It missed and crumpled onto the dusty floor.

He pushed his fingers through his thick hair and shook his head, releasing bits of glass and ash into the stifling air. When he tried to turn off the furnace, the switch stuck and he had to ram it with a metal rod. The iron kiln ticked loudly as it cooled in the crisp fall air blowing through the raised garage door of the old armory building. He'd been lucky to find the rundown windowless brick warehouse. It was for sale, well beyond his price range, but the owner let him rent it for almost nothing until someone bought it.

"Matt?"

Jen, slender and nearly as tall as he was, stood outlined in the doorway. Matt grinned, his frustration forgotten.

"Hey, Jen."

"Done for the night?"

Matt laughed. "It's safe to come inside, if that's what you mean." He strode toward her. He wanted to pull her into a tight hug, smooth his hand over her thick auburn hair. But they'd only met a few days ago at a neighborhood association meeting, and he wasn't sure how she felt about him. She'd recently bought the red brick tri-story that dominated the intersection at the end of the alley, and planned to renovate it. It was good to have more people his age living in Old Louisville.

"How's it going?" Jen asked.

"Awful." Matt laughed ruefully. "I don't have enough material for what I want to do."

"What do you want to do?" She moved closer, and he smelled the light scent of lavender. Nice. He was tempted to talk about his design with her, which surprised him. He made it a practice to never share his art concepts.

She spun in a slow circle and looked around the studio. The place was a mess. The floor was covered with chunks of fused glass, cut bottle bottoms welded together to form a translucent patchwork quilt which caught the last rays of the sun. Cardboard boxes littered the floor against a far wall.

"You on dinner break?" he asked.

"Yeah. Thought I'd go to Ermin's for some soup. Want to come?"

He turned away so she couldn't see his grin. He liked her being the one asking.

Jen worked hard for the rest of her shift, going over the dinner with Matt in her mind as she rinsed and stacked. He was funny, smart. Attractive. But private about his art. The little he'd let her see of his work impressed her. When she'd tried to move closer, curious whether any of the bottles in the piece were from her father's distillery, he'd intercepted her, urged her out of the studio. She dropped a cleaned bottle into its slot and straightened her sore back. Where'd he gotten so many liquor bottles? She wouldn't have thought twice about it if not for the recent heist of the truck. A thread of worry wove through her thoughts. Why was he so secretive?

Before going home after her shift ended, she returned to the cobblestone alley outside Matt's studio. A small dumpster parked under the sole streetlight was loaded with liquor bottles with their bottoms cut off, from the tiny two-sip to multi-liter size. Some of the labels read "Lambert Distillery."

Three days later, Rand paced nervously outside his boss' office. Hauling him up here again so soon after the hijacking really pissed him off. The door burst open and his manager, Joe, beckoned him inside with a burly arm.

"Sit." Joe said, going behind the dented metal desk and lowering his bulk into the chair.

Rand sat on the edge of his seat.

"The Old Man's breathing down my neck about the drop-off in empties coming in from the Fourth Street Bourbon Bar," Joe barked. "What's going on?"

Rand cringed and held up his hands as if fending off a blow. "Don't blame me, man. I just drive. That new girl on the dock's the one who loads the stuff."

"Yeah, well you're the one needs to ask her what's with the missing bottles."

"She ain't responsible for who's buying." Rand was surprised to find himself defending the girl. Maybe he owed her, after she'd kept his drinking to herself. If he played his cards right, he might have a chance with her. She acted all holier-than-thou, but look what she did for a living. He could show her a good time, take her places. She'd come around.

"That's just it," Joe spat. "Sales aren't off. The bar's ordering as much as ever. But the empties aren't making it back to the plant." Joe pointed a thick finger at Rand. "Since the hijacking, the company's not letting anything slide. You find out what's going on down there and come tell me. Hear?"

Rand nodded and hurried out. They'd grilled him about the hijacking last week. Now this. Who did they think they were? To them, he was just a lowly driver. No one realized what he was capable of, except maybe that hot chick working the loading dock downtown. He wouldn't mind sharing some good fortune with her.

"Load seems light tonight," Rand said to Jen that night. "Customers stop drinking?"

He'd snuck up from behind as she loaded the last crate. She dropped it in surprise, the clink of rattling bottles echoing inside the truck. "Watch it, Rand. Give me some space here," she said, turning to face the man.

He stood with one arm behind his back. He slowly ran his tongue across his front teeth. "I asked you about the empties, girl."

"What're you talking about?"

"Boss is mad 'cause the bottle count's short going back in."

Jen swallowed. "What, you think I stand around and count them? Why ask me?"

"Take it easy, gal. Just doing my job. Boss man's all over me about it."

"Well don't try to put it onto me, Rand." She let her breath out at his shrug.

"Okay, calm down, sugar. Look here. I got a present for you." Rand whipped his arm from behind his back and handed her a rectangular bourbon bottle sealed with blue wax.

"What's this for?" Jen asked.

"For not making a fuss the other night about my sip of bourbon on the job."

"We all deserve second chances. But that's it. No more, Rand."

"Sure, sure, sweetie. You like the gift?"

She'd initially intended to thrust it back at him. Taking the gift would just encourage him, and she didn't need that. But she wanted to examine the bottle more closely.

"You've got good taste in bourbon," Jen said. "This is expensive stuff. How'd you afford it?"

Rand tapped the side of his nose with one finger. "I've got ways. Stick with me, sugar. You could learn a lot."

Jen turned away so he wouldn't see her roll her eyes. The man had an ego the size of a brewing vat.

Matt stepped back to look at his creation. He'd worked on it non-stop the past few days, and it was so big now, he could only take it all in from the far wall. Today he'd done the wiring and positioned the bulbs so the light would pass through the prisms created by the edges of the thick glass bottle bottoms. The piece stood upright in a stand nailed together with scrap lumber. The overhead light fixtures were off, the large room in darkness except for faint light from the setting sun coming through the open garage door. He thought he'd got it right, but this was the test. The first time he'd see how close he'd come to the vision in his head. He took a deep breath and began to depress the switch to turn on the artwork's lights.

"Matt?"

He froze. In the excitement over completing the piece today, he'd lost track of time. He and Jen had gone to dinner together every night since they'd met. She stood by the door, peering into the gloom.

242

He didn't want anyone, not even her, to see his finished work. Not yet. Headlights from a passing car canted across his creation in a spray of light, illuminating the whole piece.

"I'll be right out," Matt called. "Don't come in, you might trip on something." He locked up and went to pull her into a hug.

"You seem happy today," Jen murmured in his ear.

He lifted her off the ground and twirled her around in his arms. "It's done!"

She laughed and gave him a quick kiss on his cheek.

He put her down and looked into her eyes. "You've inspired me, Jen." He bent his head to kiss her, but she stepped out of his arms. Matt chided himself for rushing things.

Charles Lambert slammed the phone down. His daughter had only been working for the company a couple of weeks, and already she'd messed up. She'd been a handful in high school after her mom died. Sneaking out at night, lying, stealing. He'd had to hire a lawyer to get the shoplifting charges off her record. A couple of years of junior college had gone well, and he thought she'd gotten the law-breaking out of her system. Maybe he'd been wrong. He'd given her a job with the company, hoping steady employment would give her some focus. At first it seemed to be working. She'd bought that historic building with the money her mother left her, had big plans to fix it up. But now the empties from the bourbon bar weren't making it back to the plant. Distillery security had been on high alert ever since the hijacking. He'd assured the investigating team that his daughter had nothing to do with the heist or the missing empties. But did he believe that himself? And now this call confirming that the missing empties weren't smashed in a bar fight, that the bar was ordering the same amount as before. The bottles had just vanished. On Jen's watch.

His gut tensed. He swept his fist in an angry arc across his desk, sending his mahogany nameplate onto the floor. Without his wife, he was an utter failure as a parent.

Steeling himself for the worst, he pressed his daughter's number. She was still at the bar.

"Jen, what's going on down there?" he said. "I sent you to that bar because it's a critical market for us, and now I hear you've let crates of empties disappear."

"Dad, I've got something to show you."

243

"Jen, this is serious. I want an answer!"

"I am answering you. I know who took those empties. And I've got a lead on the hijacking. Meet me at the corner of Sixth and St. Catherine at seven tonight."

"What the …?"

"Finding those hijacked cases is important to the company, isn't it?"

"You know it is!"

"Dad, it'll be okay. Meet me. Please?"

He sighed. What choice did he have? He'd give her another chance. And another. They'd been so close when she was a child. He wanted that again. "All right, pumpkin. I'll be there."

Matt rubbed a lint-free cloth over each contour of the massive construction of glass. Those crates of empty bourbon bottles had been a godsend. Some people might call him a thief, but the chance to complete his artistic vision had overcome his unease. With them, he'd been able to complete the full pattern he'd envisioned for the piece. He was amazed at the beauty of his creation. He'd closed the garage door this afternoon and tested the lights. It was the best thing he'd ever done. Now he had to find a buyer.

"Matt?"

His heart raced. Jen!

"There's someone I'd like you to meet."

What? She wasn't alone?

Jen walked into the building with an older man in a business suit. Matt straightened and turned to them, shoving the polishing cloth into his back pocket.

"Dad, this is Matt. Matt, this is my dad."

Her dad? They'd only known each other a couple of weeks. He wasn't ready for this. What was going on?

"Please, call me Charles." Jen's father stretched out a hand.

Matt wiped his hands on his jeans before he shook.

"I wanted Dad to see your finished work," Jen said.

Matt frowned. He hadn't shown it to anyone yet, not even Jen. He stared at the floor. "Jen, I'm sorry, but …"

"He's a potential buyer, Matt," Jen said quickly. Both men turned to stare at her. "Dad, trust me. Wait 'til you see it. You'll love it."

Matt stuffed his hands into his pockets. His face flushed red. How could she do this to him? Jen slipped her hand into the crook of his arm.

"Matt, I'm the one who left those crates of bottles in the alley for you."

Matt lifted his head and stared at her in surprise. "You?"

"I got in big trouble about it at work," Jen laughed, winking at her father. "But I knew you'd create something wonderful with them. My dad buys art. Especially art with a bourbon theme. Please, let him see it."

Matt glanced at Jen's father. He'd walked up to the wall of glass and was examining it. "Some of this glass has the distillery's imprint," Charles said.

"That's why I brought you here, Dad."

Matt sighed and shook his head. It was too late now. Jen squeezed his arm. He walked over to her father.

"It's designed to be installed on the ceiling," Matt said. "It lights up."

"Cool!" Jen said. "A literal glass ceiling."

"A what?" Charles asked.

"An invisible but impenetrable partition," Jen said, looking pointedly at her father. "That keeps women from rising to top management positions."

Her father laughed. "I'd love to see it lit, Matt. May I?"

Matt gave in and gestured for them to stand against the far wall. The sun had already dipped behind the trees, casting the interior of the warehouse in shadow. Here goes. He plugged the cord into the wall socket and the room glowed with soft, muted light interspersed with shimmering rainbows. Matt heard Jen gasp and clap her hands. Her father said, "Wow," under his breath. Matt smiled. They liked it.

Jen walked down the alley with her father. "Thanks, Dad."

"It's a spectacular piece of art, Jen. Just what we've been looking for to go in the headquarters lobby."

She glowed inside. She'd missed the closeness she'd had with her Dad before her Mom died. "One more thing, Dad." From her purse, she pulled the bourbon bottle Rand had given her and handed it to her father. "I think this came off the hijacked truck. Can you check the markings on the bottle against what was stolen?"

He pursed his lips and frowned. "How'd you get this, Jen?"

A pang of sadness shot through her. He still didn't trust her. She told him about Rand. Relief and excitement brightened her father's face.

"I always suspected Rand had a part in the hijacking. This could be our first break in the case. I'll have it checked out right away."

He smiled. Now was the time to ask him.

"Dad, I'm grateful to you for giving me a job with the company."

He frowned. "Jen, you appropriated our inventory without permission, and …"

"I did it for the company, Dad." And for Matt. Moving those crates of empties from the Bourbon Bar to Matt's alley allowed him to complete the art piece. From what she'd seen of it in his studio, she'd known it would be perfect for the lobby. He just needed a little help with materials to finish it.

"You should have asked," he berated her.

"Matt's an artist and he needed the bottles right then. If I'd gone through channels, it would've been too late to get our bottles into the piece. It's a vision thing."

He grinned. "A vision thing?"

Jen smiled back. "Dad, I want to work at headquarters." This was the last piece of her plan: the house in Old Louisville, convincing her father to trust her again, and working at headquarters. She held her breath.

Later that evening, Jen explained to the bar owner that this would be her last night because she'd been promoted. Back in the washing area, she hurried to finish rinsing the day's bottles. She jumped when Rand yanked open the door from the loading dock.

"What's the hold up?" he said. "I've got better things to do than wait for you."

She glared at him. If her hunch was right, he'd be arrested by tomorrow. Her father was on his way now to check if Rand's gift bottle was part of the heist.

"Something came up," she said. "I'll be ready to load in a sec." She grabbed the spray nozzle and an empty bourbon bottle. Then she sensed him right behind her and flinched as he rested his hands on her shoulders.

"Back off, Rand. I mean it," she said firmly, her body tense with alarm at his touch.

"Baby, baby. Relax. I'm just going to rub your shoulders for you. Been a long day." His voice dropped. "I'll do you, then you can do me."

He began kneading her neck and she swirled around, still gripping the bottle she'd been washing.

"Get away!" she shouted, brandishing the heavy glass at him.

He laughed and forced her arms against her sides. Their faces were inches apart. Jen could smell his rancid breath. He tightened his grip on her wrists and the bottle she held smashed to the floor. She felt a prickle of pain as a glass shard cut into her ankle.

"Who do you think you are?" he hissed. "You've been coming on to me ever since you started working here. And tonight, I'm collecting." He leaned in to kiss her.

She brought her knee up and Rand grunted in pain, releasing her hands. She shoved hard on his chest and he fell onto his back. She ran toward the door to the loading dock. The door opened, and she saw Matt and a police officer in the doorway. The policeman rushed past her and snapped handcuffs on Rand. The officer jerked him to his feet and, reciting his rights, led him away.

Matt rushed to Jen and they hugged until Jen stopped shuddering.

"Matt?" she breathed. "What brought you here?"

"Your father. Corporate security confirmed that the bottle you got from Rand came from the hijacked truck. Your dad asked me to come warn you, since I could get here faster than he could. The police arrived the same time I did."

Jen took Matt's warm hand in hers. "Rand never suspected I was on to him."

"You solved the hijacking case, Jen. Maybe you should consider a new career in investigation."

"I don't think I'll have time. Starting tomorrow, I'll be working with my Dad at headquarters, and I've got the house renovation, and …"

"And?"

"And you." Matt hadn't been in her original plan. But he was now.

BULLEIT FRONTIER WHISKEY EXPERIENCE
BY KAREN QUINN BLOCK

Hosted on the grounds of the Stitzel-Weller Distillery, the Bulleit Frontier Whiskey Experience is a hands-on experience and an historical glimpse into the past. From its location outside the urban corridor of Metro Louisville and only a short hop from the L&N railway tracks, the Stitzel-Weller Distillery sits at the end of a long curving drive in a grove of old trees. The red brick visitor center and corporate offices with its charming white portico conjures up an image of a gracious Southern courthouse, while a backdrop of vintage, black-sided storage warehouses and red brick factory-like buildings transport visitors back to a post-Prohibition time when boys wore knickers and bourbon was king. Although nothing is distilled on the Stitzel-Weller site anymore, it serves primarily as a storage site for up to 400,000 thousand barrels of aging spirits.

Back in 1987 Tom Bulleit (pronounced "bullet"), Louisville native, combat veteran, attorney, local businessman, and descendant of an early Kentucky pioneer family wanted to recreate his great-great-grandfather Augustus Bulleit's bourbon recipe and give modern folks a taste of that old-time religion. Augustus had disappeared while on a business trip to New Orleans in 1860, and, with his presumed death, the flavor of his high-rye bourbon whiskey also died. As the adage says, time goes by and trends change. What was a high-kicking good drink in 1860 would be considered a little raw in this day and age of designer vodkas and fou-fou cocktails. Tom Bulleit, understanding the palate of today's bourbon aficionado, jimmied with his ancestor's recipe until satisfied it both remained true to its roots but also provided a quality flavorful spirit. Consequently, Bulleit Frontier bourbon contains an unusually high quantity of rye, specifically 28%, which gives the spirit its unique spicy aroma and soft finish. And, of course, Kentucky's famous limestone-filtered spring water ensures that the flavor of the mash blend is unsullied by any earthiness.

The tour itself is an exceptionally well-done bourbon educational experience that starts in the recreated atmosphere of a frontier trading post. Stepping off the wooden porch into the heart of the site, visitors breathe in the scent of the "Angels' Share" (the evaporating portion of the aging spirit in the barrel) which permeates the air and sets the stage for the next hour. To begin, the tour guide describes the early days of the enterprise, such as information about the construction of the distillery and what products were once produced here and their current owners. Visitors learn of the partnership of two sets of siblings, the founding Stitzel brothers, German immigrants, and the Weller brothers, Louisville Whiskey Row distillers, plus other famous and colorful figures associated with the distillery, such as Pappy van Winkle.

Moving inside, visitors encounter a mini-museum of old equipment, including a hammer mill which cracks open the grain to expose its starch and jumpstarts the fermentation process. Visitors are invited to push buttons, pull levers, and turn gears to get a feel for the process. The tour moves on to a mini distillery where a master distiller is on hand to demonstrate the process and answer questions. Next on the tour is a warehouse that illustrates the technique of *ricking*, or storing the aging bourbon, purportedly invented onsite by Fred Stitzel. From there, visitors enter a cooperage where they view how to build a barrel. The tour finishes with a tour of Tom Bulleit's office and a visit to the tasting room, an elegant wood-paneled saloon.

Diageo, a global spirit company, owns the Bulleit brand along with many other famous brands. A new Bulleit distillery in Shelbyville, Kentucky, began production of its signature spirits in 2017. With this increased capacity, all of us can now enjoy a little Bulleit in our bellies.

Unlawful Taking
By Barbara Blackburn

Three grim-faced individuals gathered in the dark driveway, shivering in the cold November chill. An abundance of stars flickered in the moonless sky over their heads. Officer Gallo popped the trunk. Sullivan, ramrod straight and breathing hard, stood behind his daughter as she poked the monster flashlight inside the Cadillac DeVille. The cavern shone empty as a spent drum. Someone had stolen the eight bottles of single batch, 25-year-old bourbon worth $2,400, that Sullivan had bought that afternoon. Teresa thought she knew who.

Teresa poked an errant black curl into the loose pile on top of her head. Out of the corner of one eye, she saw her father dozing. His color worried her, as did the puffy bags under his eyes and the expanding waistline. She walked over to him and leaned down. Her crystal earrings glinted in the light from the table lamp as she listened to his breathing. She touched his forehead. Warm, not hot. Her frown melted. Reluctant to wake him, she picked up his car keys from the coffee table. She'd call from the party, tell him she borrowed his car.

The platinum Caddie zipped smoothly out of her subdivision into the darkness, onto the county road. She passed the uncultivated fields, not yet transformed into suburban housing, and woodland covering more land than the smattering of tract homes and intermittent islands of fast food and gasoline. As she slid a CD into the player, she noticed the red light on the dash. She needed to stop for gas.

The deep, liquid voice of Norah Jones poured through the speakers. Teresa raised the volume, filling every inch of the car with bluesy sound. As she sang along, she let the music fill the hungry emptiness that had plagued her lately. She knew what Cory would do as soon as he climbed in: try to replace the lady's sound with pop rock or rap from the radio. They'd argue again.

She pulled onto the state route, passing a subdivision of half-constructed houses on a graded landscape. In the darkness she couldn't see the lake the contractor had dredged out of the field, but she knew it was there. Several miles further, an identical site lay along the opposite side of the road, and beyond that was a finished subdivision similar to the one she lived in. By the time she finished college, the fields and woods would be gone and the road would be a logjam of traffic.

Nora launched a fresh number. Teresa enjoyed cruising the emptiness of the landscape. It gave her time to think about her classes and the exciting ideas she was learning. Ideas she wanted to talk about, but every time she mentioned a class or a professor, Cory pushed her away. More and more, she realized the boy she fell for at sixteen had become stuck in time. Sexy good looks could no longer carry him.

An explosion of brightness in the rear-view mirror blinded her. She cursed the inconsiderate fool behind the wheel. Slowing the car, she pushed in the emergency flasher, a trick her father taught her. The vehicle with the offending lights backed off for a moment, then charged, bumping her lightly. She pressed the gas. Her brain raced with the adrenaline rush.

The driver peeled around the Cadillac, drawing alongside. She saw the passenger's grinning face. He rolled down the window and, leaning out, shouted something she couldn't hear. When he threw an empty beer can, she flinched as it bounced off the windshield, but gripped the wheel harder. Shaking, she focused on the road ahead and pressed on the gas pedal. The 1970s vehicle, with chrome bumpers and dual exhausts, suddenly roared past and cut sharply in front of the Cadillac. She jammed on the brakes. Thoughts of crashing her father's pride and joy made the blood rush to her head. Other thoughts scared her more. The Cadillac skidded sideways and stopped dead.

The yellow car stopped, too. Doors opened and four guys in their early twenties climbed out. As they swaggered toward her, she tried to restart the engine, but it wouldn't catch. Two of them bounced her hood and the others tried the locked doors. They shouted at her to "open up, bitch." Her heart pounded. She twisted the key and pressed the gas. Nothing happened. The guys on either side rocked the car.

Despite the escalating danger, Teresa forced herself not to panic. As she reached for the mace in her purse, she remembered what her cop-father taught her. Stay calm and think. When Sullivan retired from the job, he went to work for A. J. Crump, entrepreneur, doing errands and some protection, often late at night. He kept a gun in the car, for security, and he had taught her to use it.

Lifting the cover of the center console, she eased out the .380. Flipping on the overhead light, she gripped the gun. She aimed at the guy on the driver's side door, shoving it close to the window so he'd be sure to see the barrel. Then while she had his attention, she reached for the key in the ignition and pressed the panic button.

The burst of sound from the car alarm and the sight of the gun startled the man. He retreated. She fanned the weapon slowly past the front and side windows. Angry, confused faces recoiled. She made a mental note of the driver's short, lean build, the shaved head and straggly goatee, as he rushed to his car. She prayed he didn't have a gun. The others scrambled after him.

After the danger vanished into the dark road ahead and her nerves had calmed, she searched for her phone. She pounded the seat with her fist when she remembered sticking it in the charger. Weighing the risk of carrying her father's gun against the possibility of meeting up with her attackers on the road, she shoved it into her purse.

Her mid-heeled boots gave her a wobbly footing as she walked along the gravel shoulder. Once she twisted her ankle badly enough to send a sharp pain up her leg. Cold seeped under her short fleece jacket. She wound the long, loose-weave scarf around her neck twice, grateful she'd decided to wear the blue jeans instead of the short skirt. Her purse, weighed down with the gun, bounced against her hip.

Teresa scanned the strip of roadway for dark patches where four dangerous, pissed off guys could be waiting in ambush; she noted the distant house lights that shimmered on the horizon. She considered going back home but, recalling the Thornton's at the junction ahead, guessed it was closer. Either way the distance to a phone or help was miles.

Hugging the gravel shoulder, she saw disks of light coming toward her. Instinct pushed her toward a cluster of trees. Crouching, she saw clearly the long yellow hood and wide boxy fenders. When the car slipped past, she noticed a red design like flames or waves along the sides. She pushed deeper into the tall grass and bushes around the trees, and, sucking in her breath, shivered in the cold night air. Bright headlights swept the shoulder as the car moved slowly past. Men's voices drifted through the open windows. She gripped the mace.

Teresa stood still in the dark grove of trees, waiting until the car disappeared. Cold air and fear numbed her fingers. The car moved on. She shivered, still scared but feeling safe in the darkness. As she climbed out of the copse, she remembered the abandoned Cadillac. Her attackers would revenge themselves as surely as the sun sets in the western sky.

Light from the shopping area at the juncture of highways cast an eerie glow onto the sky. Even before she could make out the neon signs of the gas station and fast food restaurants, she knew help was nearby. Still, she couldn't shake the fear of the yellow car coming up behind her. Only one other car had passed. The woods along the road gave her momentary shelter, but she knew that before she reached the safety of the gas station, she had to cross a stretch of land newly graded for construction. She'd be an open target if they returned, and there was little doubt they'd be back.

She reached the empty stretch. Finding the dry drainage ditch in deep shadow, she descended. When she heard a car pass above her, sending out a throbbing beat from its speakers, she pressed into the hard clay dirt, making herself compact. She stayed in that position, hidden in darkness, for what seemed an eternity until she could shake off the dread.

The crowd in the Thornton's reassured her. After using the washroom, she looked for the phone. Using her credit card, she dialed Cory's cell. Loud music and voices in the background surprised her.

"Cory, it's Teresa, I had trouble. I need you to come get me."

"Your dad said you had his car."

"Well, I don't know. Can you pick me up in your mom's car?"

"She's at work. Sorry."

Background music and voices threw up a red flag. "Where are you? What do I hear?"

"Just the radio," and the sound was muffled somewhat.

"Get one of your friends to drive you over here."

"I don't know. I'll try." She heard the resistance in his voice. Her anger rose.

"Are you at the party?"

"No," he said.

She hung up the phone, certain he'd lied.

At that moment she saw a police officer she knew, one that used to work with her father, enter the store. Her father walked in behind him. When she waved to get their attention, her father grinned and rushed to hug her.

"What happened?"

His face showed the strain of the last hours. On the verge of telling him about the four guys, she hesitated.

"I ran out of gas. I'm so sorry I made you worry."

As Officer Gallo drove them home, Sullivan told her about the bourbon in the trunk. He'd picked it up that afternoon for his wheeler-dealer boss. Crump planned to give out the special bottles of bourbon as gifts to a group of potential foreign investors, incentive.

"He needs it Monday morning. I was going to take it to him after dropping you and Cory off. And I was going to get gas. When I woke and saw you'd taken the car, I tried to call your cell."

"I left it at home."

"I know, I heard it ringing. I called Cory."

Gallo had found the car abandoned in a ditch. He saw the name on the registration and called Sullivan. They went looking for her, first. Another officer had the Cadillac towed to the house.

Later that night, after discovering the theft, Teresa tried to recreate the frightening incident. She strained to recall the faces of the men who beat on the car and windows. She'd be able to recognize the driver, but not the others. They were lost in a blur of terrifying movement. The emotional memory returned, and she shuddered. She focused on the car. Distinctive. Bright yellow. Vintage make, with some kind of vinyl art, red or black, on the back fenders. She'd left the Cadillac on the side of the road, but Gallo had found it in the ditch. They'd trashed the car, pushed it in, and stole the bourbon.

Saturday afternoon, Teresa drove a rental to Cory's house. Dressed in dirty jeans and a Colts sweatshirt, he climbed in, folding his long legs under the dash. "Where we going?"

Teresa examined his expression. Edgy. He avoided her eyes, squirmed as though he couldn't get comfortable. If he felt guilty for not helping her last night, it would be a breakthrough.

"Cruising. Looking for a yellow vintage car with an unusual design on the rear fender. Red flames or waves, I'm not sure. I need you to tell me the hangouts. I'm looking for the owner, mid-twenties, the arrested development kind." She tossed him a sarcastic look. "Driving around with a pack of misfits, looking to hurt innocent people."

"I don't do that," he said.

Delighted she'd managed to spark anger in Cory. "I didn't say you did, but you know the type, right?"

"I guess so."

They searched the parks along the river and a dozen fast food restaurants. At each place, they asked if anyone knew a guy who drove a yellow '70s model Chevy or Ford with vinyl art on the fenders. They studied the cars in the lots.

They had just parked outside a sports bar when she spotted the car. Excited, she inspected the yellow Chevelle with a red dragon on the back fender as it eased into an available slot. Two-door. That explained why they had fallen over each other. The driver climbed out, hitched up his jeans, then grabbed a lightweight black jacket. He wore a baseball cap. She couldn't tell if his head was shaved, but he had the goatee. The face was ordinary, older than she remembered. She couldn't swear it was the guy, but the car was unforgettable.

"Hey," she shouted as she walked up to him.

They stood face to face. He didn't recognize her. "What?" He squinted.

"I want the bourbon back." She folded her arms across her chest and planted herself between him and the front door.

"I don't know what the fuck you're talking about." Spit flew off his words and he rammed her shoulder with his, hard, pushing her aside.

She rubbed her shoulder and followed him.

The room was packed and loud. Waves of second-hand smoke washed over her from the bar. Televisions competed from each corner, two on the same channel, two on different channels. Her prey squeezed up to the bar between a pair of leather jackets. He ordered a beer, said something to the others and the three of them cast a quick glance in her direction.

She wondered if she should interrupt the party, but Cory, who'd followed her in, pulled her toward the door.

"Let's go."

"Are you crazy? He's the one we've been looking for all day." She gestured in their direction. "Do you know him? Or any of the others?"

Cory barely turned toward the bar. "No. Let's go. You don't want to mess with them now."

She thought about it and decided he might be right. A better idea would be to follow him and find out where he lived. Then she'd call Officer Gallo, tell him everything.

She took a chair at an empty table by the window. Cory didn't move, just stood over her, staring blankly like a dazed deer.

"Get me a Pepsi," she said, handing him a five-dollar bill.

He sighed, picked up the money and went to the far end of the bar to order. When he returned, he set her drink on the table. "I need to get home."

"Whatever for?" she asked.

"I don't like this."

She focused on Cory's eyes, trying to pin them down. Usually compliant or pushy, today he was wishy-washy. Resisting her but doing what she asked. Was he afraid of them? Understandable for several guys she knew, but not Cory.

"They tried to assault me. They wrecked my father's car and stole his bourbon. When they leave, I'll tail them. If you don't want to help, go. Just don't get in my face."

Cory clinched his fists. "Teresa, don't do it. You'll get hurt."

Unmoved, she said, "I have to find the bourbon, or what happened to it."

"Why? Won't insurance cover it all?"

"Evidence. I want those scumbags in jail."

"Cory." A big-haired blonde girl in skin-tight jeans, layered thin knit sweaters and two-inch silver hoops in her earlobes, approached them. She threw an exuberant embrace on him. "Man, you are The Man. You were definitely the life of the party last night."

Cory spun around in his seat like he was possessed. His face turned bright red. Rubbing his mouth with his hand, his eyes met Teresa's glare.

"Oops, did I say the wrong thing?" Blondie backed off.

Teresa relaxed her fierce look. "No, of course not. Sit down. I ran out of gas on the way to the party." She watched Cory squirm. "And what made my boy so popular?"

"He brought a really good treat to the party." Blondie giggled and rushed off, saying something about needing to get back to her friends.

"You dog, you went without me. What did you bring?"

Cory slumped over the table, muttering something.

"What did you bring?"

"Beer," he stammered, "Coors."

"I don't think so. She was way too enthusiastic."

"Who knows? She's kinda dumb, anyway."

"You are lying, Cory. What did you bring? The truth."

Pounding his head, he looked up at her, the eyes pleading like a dog that'd just peed on the carpet.

His actions the past two days flashed like a slide show on speed. He failed to pick her up. Went to the party without her. Then her mind leapt to a horrible realization. The sleaze-bag guys in the yellow car attacked her, scared her half to death, and would have done much worse if she hadn't run them off. They wrecked the car, but they didn't take her father's bourbon.

She stared out the window, feeling the momentary rage melt into cold disappointment. He'd professed to love her. She'd trusted him, and he betrayed her confidence.

"You took it, didn't you?" Her voice cracked. "How did you know it was in the trunk?"

"I didn't take it, I swear. I would never," he protested.

"My father called, didn't he? He told you about the bourbon."

She watched Cory dissolve. He stared at the table, picked at his nails. "I was worried about you," he said, "Mom had come home, so I took her car and went looking."

"Well, I was out there, walking along the highway for miles. You found the car in the ditch, right? Was the trunk open? Did you find the bourbon in the trunk or was it gone? Tell me the truth, Cory. If it was gone, I'll accuse those guys of stealing it. You'll be my witness."

When he didn't answer, hope wilted. Teresa pushed the chair back, stood and walked toward the guys at the bar. Cory jumped up and grabbed her arm. "Don't." He led her back to the table. His hand trembled. He eased her down on the chair.

They sat. He spoke softly, staring out the window. "The boxes were there. I took them to keep them safe, I swear. I was going to keep them safe till you got to the party. But you never came, and ... somebody started ragging on me, saying I never brought nothing to parties. I never contributed. I felt like such a loser. Then one thing led to another. Things got outta hand."

Leaning back, she laid her palms on the table. Her thoughts raced as the irony hit her: pig's ear drinkers guzzling silk purse liquor.

"Any left?"

"If I'd given it back then, you'd known." He reached for her hands, but she pulled them away. "Don't turn me in, Teresa, please. I'll go to jail."

She glared at him, making him wait. "That's all that matters to you, isn't it? Your own pitiful skin." Then she looked over at the men who had wrecked her father's car. "Did you see those guys at the car?"

Cory glanced over and back. "Not really," he said.

"Not really? What the hell does that mean? Did you see them or their car?"

Cory let out a sigh. "Getting in the car. Maybe it was them. I can't swear to it."

"Here's your answer. You stole over a thousand dollars' worth of bourbon. They trashed the Cadillac, worth a hell of a lot more. Now you can testify you saw them running away from the wrecked car and we'll settle with you, so you don't do jail time."

"They're dangerous, Teresa. I don't want them coming after me. Just let me pay your dad. I'll get the money from my mom."

Teresa looked at him and wondered what she'd ever seen in him. He'd contributed very little to their relationship.

"Let me make it simple. Either way you'll testify because I'll tell the police what you told me. I'll also tell them what you stole. If you deny it, I'll tell them about the party and name people who were there, who saw you passing around expensive bourbon. Those guys may not go to jail, but you surely will, Cory. Does this make your choice clearer?"

She looked up to see the driver of the yellow car take off his cap, revealing a shaved scalp. Then he slapped it on his head and stood. Glancing over at Teresa, he winked. The group headed for the doorway.

"Think about your choice, Cory, and I'll get back to you."

Outside Teresa pulled her rental out of the lot, a cautious distance behind the yellow car with the red dragon.

A History of Pepper Brand Bourbon
By Edmund August

In the annals of Bourbon whiskey production, Elijah Pepper and his descendants have been one of America's most important families. Their history began in 1776, and early bottles of Pepper whiskey proudly displayed the slogans "Old 1776," "Born with the Republic," and "The Oldest and Best Brand made in Kentucky." The influence of the Pepper family on the Bourbon industry has been felt from that time to the present.

Elijah Pepper moved from his home in Virginia proper and settled at what was to later become Old Pepper Springs in Versailles, Bourbon County, Kentucky (at that time still a county of Virginia). Farmers in the area found that rather than risk their surplus grains rotting during the slow process of transport, they could convert their crops to whiskey, a product that could easily be shipped in oak barrels down the Ohio and Mississippi Rivers to Cairo, Illinois and New Orleans. These barrels of whiskey were stamped with their point of origin, Bourbon County, Kentucky, and thus became known as Bourbon Whiskey.

Elijah established himself as a farmer-distiller, a person who raises cereal grains, vegetables, fruits, and hops to produce alcoholic beverages. He often traded his whiskey with people passing through the area and with neighbors, many of whom were also farmer-distillers.

With the advent of the 1791 excise tax imposed on whiskey by the federal government, farmer-distillers, unable to pay the tax, began attacking excise agents. These attacks, which came to be known as The Whiskey Rebellion, escalated until July of 1794 when they culminated in an attack on a federal marshal and the home, barn, and other outbuildings of a regional inspector were burned to the ground. Considering these attacks an illegal rebellion, President Washington called out a militia of 13,000 men to quash the uprising.

Because he was the only farmer-distiller in the area who had enough money to pay the excise tax, Elijah found himself in a unique position. One by one, his less fortunate neighbor farmer-distillers abandoned their stills and sold their crops to him to produce whiskey, making it possible for him to concentrate more of his efforts in distilling whiskey than farming and to help his neighbors avoid losing their farms, thus establishing a camaraderie that lasted until Elijah's death in 1831.

In 1812, Elijah moved his distillery from behind the courthouse in Versailles to Glenn's Creek. The creek itself was a seemingly inexhaustible supply of limestone water. One report claimed that the distillery pumped 700 gallons per minute without overtaxing it or interfering with the purity of the water. Limestone water is essential to the making of fine Bourbon whiskey. Limestone filters out most of the impurities, and the resulting water is a key ingredient in the unique flavor of Bourbon.

Elijah was succeeded by his son Oscar as the owner-operator of the Old Pepper Distillery which, two years later, he renamed the Old Oscar Pepper Distillery and hired James Crow as his distiller. Crow was a Scottish-born chemist and a die-hard perfectionist who had learned a great deal about whiskey making during previous work in two other Woodford County distilleries. With that experience and his knowledge of biochemistry, Crow created a new formula for making whiskey which was a huge success. Under his watchful eye, he and Oscar made and marketed Old Crow Bourbon, a roaring success in the whiskey world. Although Crow died in 1856, their Bourbon Whiskey was probably the best and most widely sold whiskey through the years of the American Civil War. Oscar's death has been variously reported as 1864, 1865, 1867, and 1869. None of these dates has been well corroborated.

In 1873, the distillery burned down. In 1879, Oscar's son, James Pepper, purchased the property and rebuilt the distillery. James played on the reputations his father and grandfather had built by placing his own signature, Jas. E. Pepper, on every barrel and bottle of his bourbon. He also placed on each bottle his grandfather's slogans, "Born with the Republic" and "Old 1776." James also made a reputation in Kentucky's elite sport—thoroughbred horse racing. The new distillery was hit hard by the depression of 1893, but in the same year his horse, The Dragon, came in fifth in the Kentucky Derby. In the previous year his horse Mirage won the Oaks. However, things continued to run downhill for the distillery, which went bankrupt in 1896.

James died in 1906, and two years later his family sold the business to a group from Chicago that, fortunately, kept the business name as the James E. Pepper Distillery Co.

During Prohibition (1920-1933), the distillery was used as a warehouse. Foreseeing Prohibition, the Pepper Co. shipped thousands of barrels and bottles of bourbon to Europe.

In 1934, the distillery was ravaged by a fire that destroyed most of the buildings and over 15,000 barrels of bourbon. The new company was quick to rebuild, mainly because Prohibition had just ended and the demand for alcoholic beverages was as great as expected. A distillery with the awesome reputation and name of Pepper was a sure bet to make a lot of money.

The Pepper brand name was discontinued in 1960 and re-established in 1994 when it continued to produce under the Pepper label, but the bourbon was (and is still) sold only outside the United States.

The Long and the Shorter of It
By Elaine Munsch

I nearly broke my arm trying to push through the door to the editor's office of *The Bugle*.

"Lois, are you in there? What's with the locked door?" I shouted.

Lois Shorter, editor-in-chief of the St. Winifred College newspaper, cracked open the door and pulled me, the crack reporter Lane Long, inside.

She stared into my eyes. "Lane, we have a problem." The statement was whispered but came across in forty-eight-point bold-faced type.

Lois is one of the calmest people I know. This could not be good. "What's wrong?"

She pointed to the oblong box on her desk.

"Please don't tell me there's a body part in there," I implored.

She let go of my arm in disgust and plopped down in her chair. "It's a bottle of bourbon, you idiot."

I started to shout "Bourbon?" but the look on her face stopped me. I walked over to the box. It was nondescript except that it was addressed to 'Lois Lane'. No postage, so hand delivered. The plot—and my thirst—thickened.

"'Lois Lane'; are you kidding me? This should have been delivered to Metropolis, not Mayland, Kentucky. And since when is bourbon a problem, other than our lack of glasses in which to pour it? Drinking President's Choice straight from the bottle would be sacrilege."

Lois picked up a slim book and slid it across the desk to me. It was the campus handbook, updated for the 1960s.

"Check out Rule V. 'No alcoholic beverages shall be consumed on campus.' Unspoken: none should even be on campus. Remember that incident our freshman year, when those juniors were expelled for having beer in their rooms? No exceptions."

My first thought was to thank her for bringing me into this debacle, but then I realized that 'Lois Lane' obviously referred to the both of us, Lois Shorter and Lane Long. We had been joined at the hip since our freshman year.

"Lois, the rules are being re-written as we speak. Maybe drinking will become a recognized sport."

"I don't care about the future of college sports. Lane, what should we do? I just know that rotten Phil Craddock is behind this. He's still seething because I was named editor and he wasn't."

"Oh, be rational, Lois. You were selected because you were the best choice. And you didn't write the rule stating a three-point-five grade point was needed to be editor. If Phil is upset, he should have studied harder."

Lois leaned back in her chair. "You're right, but that doesn't stop me from being scared and angry. If only Mr. Roberts was here. Just like a faculty advisor to be out of town when you really need advising."

"We could take this to our beloved Dean of Women, Sister Benedictus, and fall on bended knee to plead our case. Though it'd be a shame to give up the bourbon."

"Lane, please. Benedictus and I haven't been on speaking terms since I wrote that spoof about her. Some nuns have no sense of humor."

"Why are you so sure that it's Phil and not someone else?" I asked.

"I've been thinking about it all afternoon. Who else has motive and means? He has a car, so he can get to a liquor store and he has money to spend on a 'joke' like this."

She was right.

When I looked back at Lois, her demeanor had changed. "You want revenge, don't you?"

She smiled. "We could make sure this bottle winds up in Phil's hands, not ours. Put on your thinking cap, my friend."

I stood up. "I think better on the move. Don't worry. We'll come up with a plan."

That said, I left the office.

I roamed around, admiring the Indian summer foliage. The cream-colored stone buildings and the sweet smell of fall roses were juxtaposed with thoughts of revenge and bourbon. Signs announcing the mandatory "Welcome Back" meeting to be held at seven fifteen p.m. kept interrupting my thoughts. Since Phil was the chairman of the welcoming committee, he'd certainly attend. His dorm room would be empty. A plan began to form.

Three years ago, as a freshman, I had been assigned to a work/study program. It entailed working with the housekeeping staff, distributing clean sheets and towels to the dorm rooms. Okay, so it didn't have anything to do with my field of study, but it was easy work for the pay and a wonderful way to meet those 'invisible' people who make our lives more comfortable. I kept up the friendships, and not merely because the ladies were an excellent source of information for my *Rumor Has It* column.

I stopped in to chat with Marla, head of the housekeeping crew. Sweet-talking her into letting me borrow two uniforms was almost too easy. She didn't notice when I slipped a pass key from the hook in her office to one of the uniform pockets.

I headed back to get Lois and the dratted, increasingly tempting, bottle of bourbon.

When I arrived, Suzanne Green, the freshman class correspondent, was in the outer office gathering her notebook. Her first article would be coverage of the meeting this evening. She looked up and smiled. I realized she was looking past me to her new beau, Buddy Pearson, who was standing in the hall.

"Hi, Lane. Ready, Suzanne?" Buddy called.

"Any last-minute instructions?" she asked.

I shook my head. "See you at the meeting," I said. I almost asked Buddy, who had been Phil's shadow until this year, whether Phil was capable of this type of prank. But since I knew the answer, I just waved goodbye.

Lois and I waited until a few minutes past seven before we crossed campus, toting a book bag to hide the bottle of bourbon.

We made straight for the dormitory basement where we put the uniforms over our street clothes, covering our hair with scarves. After filling one of the laundry carts with clean sheets and towels, we took the elevator to the second floor.

The disguise wasn't necessary. The hall was deserted; either everyone was at the meeting or secluded in their rooms. Lois would be the lookout while I hid the bourbon in Phil's closet. He had the typical senior suite consisting of a small study area adjoining the bedroom.

Hide the bottle, skedaddle, an anonymous call to the floor monitor and Rule V would be Phil's problem, not ours.

That was the plan.

Once in the room, I headed for the closet. But, as I crossed the bedroom, my foot hit something. I looked down at another bottle of President's Choice. Then I saw Phil lying on the floor, arm outstretched. My first thought was that he'd gotten drunk, passed out, and ruined my great plan.

I leaned over to take a closer look. He was as white as a bleached sheet and one side of his head had a bloody dent in it. He didn't seem to be breathing.

Like any true friend, I called Lois so she could share in the fun.

She came into the room, ready with "What's the matter now?" on her lips, but stopped short when I pointed to Phil on the floor.

"Lois, Phil's hurt pretty bad. We have to call the nurse."

She knelt beside him, checking for a pulse. She looked at me and shook her head.

"Lane, I think he's dead. And not long; he's still warm."

My legs gave out. I sat down on the bed. "Holy Josephine."

Grabbing my shoulders, she said, "We need to do two things: call the cops and get out of here, not necessarily in that order."

We fled.

Outside, we gulped the autumn air. Shaking, we looked at each other and then at my bag containing the bourbon.

Lois shook her head, "We can't drink it. Remember the fifth rule."

"Didn't we just break a ton of rules by sneaking into the men's dorm, borrowing uniforms and pass keys, and missing a mandatory meeting? I'm too rattled to remember all of them clearly, but I'm sure the list is long."

"Still, we need to keep our wits about us. What do you think happened?" she asked.

"I think Phil sent a bottle to someone else who did not take kindly to it. He, or she, returned the bottle, an altercation took place, and Phil got whacked, maybe harder than intended, but definitely whacked. We can phone from the auditorium and then observe the meeting. See if anyone looks nervous."

Lois muttered, "You mean besides us. If we don't stop shaking, we'll be the ones being observed."

She was right, as usual.

We slipped off the uniforms, tucking them into my bag before heading to Catsby Auditorium. We discussed calling Will Snook, our friendly but incompetent campus guard, or the Mayland cops. We opted not to disturb Snook's evening nap, dropped a dime into the payphone, and dialed 0 for operator.

I relayed the basics: O'Daniel Hall, Room 24, Phil Craddock dead on the floor.

We slipped into the last row of the auditorium. I was trying to sit still; Lois was trying to breathe. The meeting was moving along despite the absence of the Committee Chair.

If anything of significance happened, we missed it.

Then we heard the sirens.

Everyone in the hall quieted. Father Ryan, Dean of Men, left the stage.

The meeting adjourned. We hung back, letting the others drift out. We exited with some of our classmates, pretending to join in the 'can you believe this is our senior year' discussions.

There was a police car in front of O'Daniel Hall. Sister Benedictus and Father Ryan were talking to a sandy-haired gentleman.

Deciding it would look odd if Lois and I weren't curious about what was happening, I pulled her towards a nice looking young uniformed officer and smiled.

"Officer Thompson, is it?" as I glanced at his name tag. "I'm with the campus newspaper. Can you tell me what is going on?"

Thompson returned my smile and said, "We received a call about a dead body, but it was a false alarm, college prank."

I blurted out "No body?" As the words exited my mouth, I saw Lois cringe. Feeling eyes boring into my back, I turned to see the sandy-haired man excuse himself from the two deans and head our way.

"Do you have reason to believe that we should have found a body?" he asked, flashing his badge which identified him as Detective John Robb.

Sister Benedictus joined our little group. As they waited, I tried to think of a suitable answer, one that wouldn't land Lois and me in jail.

Taking my arm, Robb said, "If you don't mind, Sister, I'd like a word with …"

269

"Marlaine Long, but my friends call me Lane." That much was true.

He motioned to Officer Thompson to follow. Lois followed uninvited. Robb's first mistake was not stopping her.

We were off to the dorm office.

The 'word' turned into many, mostly uttered by Robb demanding information, but quite a few uttered by Lois who was quoting all kinds of rights and amendments. She even threw in a few rules from the handbook. Neither policeman was much older than we were, so the authoritarian act didn't frighten us. They needed a page from Sister Benedictus' book on intimidation before we would cower.

Thompson sat silently, glancing my way ever so often. For once I clammed up, thinking of ways to explain to my parents that I wouldn't graduate simply because we would still be in this room arguing with the cops.

Finally, I gave up. I raised my hand in the best schoolgirl fashion. All heads turned my way.

"Do you have to use the bathroom, or do you want to add to the conversation?" Robb asked.

"Sorry, Lois, if this violates some journalistic code, but we are getting nowhere. More importantly, it's getting Phil nowhere. If he isn't dead, he is wandering the campus with one horrendous headache."

Then I told the tale.

After a moment of incredulous silence, Robb suggested returning to Phil's room to recreate our actions, but not before the darn man remembered to confiscate our bourbon.

As we walked upstairs, I turned to Lois, "See, we no longer have the bourbon. The fifth rule satisfied."

She countered, "I have a feeling Rule V won't compete with breaking and entering. Expulsion vs. prison term … great job reference."

Phil's room was empty, really empty. I mean, no body, no bottle.

One look at Robb's expression, and I was glad that I couldn't read minds. Thompson seemed more open-minded. He knelt, studying the floor. All he needed was a magnifying glass and a deerstalker hat. Finally, he pointed to some small spots, saying they could be blood. Robb realized that he had to seal the room. Police procedure, like Rule V, had to be followed: the spots must be analyzed.

270

We returned to the dorm office, where Sister Benedictus and Father Ryan were waiting. The tale was told again with the same unsatisfying ending. Both deans left to organize search parties. Phil was wanted dead or alive.

The police finally left, promising to return the next day, since Benedictus refused to allow us to leave after the ten p.m. curfew. Rule XX was alive and well.

We returned to our room and tried to make sense of the last few hours.

Lois said, "The killer had to be hiding in the closet when we were in the room. After he heard us say we were calling the police, he decided to move the body."

The shiver was uncontrollable.

"Let's hope it was an accident. Phil got hit harder than intended and the person panicked. No premeditation. Nothing to do with the bourbon or us," I said.

"But there has to be a reason," Lois replied.

I got up to retrieve my stash of old *Rumor Has It* notebooks, the ones containing all the dirt I'd uncovered over the past three years. Most of it was trivial gossip, never seeing typeface. What had I missed? Something personal, seething under the usual campus hijinks?

Just as I was about to announce that I had found nothing, Lois popped up with "Marcy Davenport! Phil stood her up at the Mayland Festival. Remember, she was the queen without a king? Then he strolled in with that floozy Barbara Whitehouse on his arm. I'm surprised Marcy didn't bash his head in that night."

"One doesn't murder over an embarrassing moment. I'm sure that's in the handbook under 'decorum'," I said. "Anyway, Noreen got a postcard from her. She's in Paris with a new love interest."

I ditched the notebooks and headed to my file of old *Bugles*. Lois and I pored over them looking for anything that would help explain tonight's incident, but found only articles about outdated rules, bad food, and campus politics and events. Phil's name appeared a number of times, but nothing stood out. Then we found the article about the car accident our sophomore year.

The freshmen had arrived for orientation. Phil and Buddy were among the student volunteers who helped them settle in. Phil and a freshman named Sam Greenwell went out joyriding in Phil's car on the country roads. The car hit a slick patch and flew off the pavement.

Greenwell was killed. Even though it was Phil's car, Sam was driving. Interesting.

We needed to read the reporter's notes, unfortunately locked up in the *Bugle* office. Nothing could be done until morning. Rule XX had its downside.

The next morning, much too early, Sister Benedictus pounded on our door.

I stumbled over, inched it open.

"Officer Thompson is here to take you to town for your statements," she informed us, making it sound like she preferred that we be taken in for incarceration.

"Has Phil been found yet?" Lois asked.

"No; do you know how upset everyone is?" Sister asked.

"We're much better, Sister. Thank you for asking," I said sweetly, only to receive an ecclesiastical glare.

Officer Thompson took one look at us and suggested we get coffee before we went into town. In our crowded cafeteria, his presence turned a few heads. I held my hands up to indicate 'no handcuffs'.

After a few sips of coffee, I turned to Thompson.

"How hard it is to move a body like Phil's? He wasn't fat or tall, but dead weight must be difficult. How did the body get moved without being seen by anyone? Obviously not everyone attended the meeting last night. Would it take one or two, do you think?"

He looked at me. "Are you asking if I think you two couldn't move the body, so someone else had to? Of course, yesterday doing the sensible thing and staying with the body ..."

"And getting our heads bashed in," Lois said. "You could be looking for three bodies instead of one."

"Where's the nearest liquor store, Thompson?" I asked, switching topics.

Both stared at me, a sign that Lois needed more coffee.

She usually is a step ahead of me.

"No, I don't want a drink. I think we should find out how many bottles of President's Choice have been sold recently. If only two, and we find that the buyer was indeed Phil, we know what happened to both bottles. But, if there were three or four or more bottles purchased by Phil, or whomever, who's got them?"

272

Lois interjected, "What if Phil wasn't the sender but a receiver? Thompson, get your minions to search Phil's room for a box that would indicate he was a recipient."

"Ma'am," Thompson said with a smile. "I am the minion. We'll stop at the liquor stores here in town, but we can't be driving all over the state asking about this bourbon. We don't have much time before Robb gets twitchy, wondering where his star witnesses are."

"As long as we're star witnesses and not star suspects," I muttered.

For a small county, there were more liquor stores than I imagined, but none of them sold the premium brand. Somehow, we skipped the station for a stop at Fred's Diner, the only place in town for burgers and cokes. Over lunch, Thompson decided we should head to the distillery that bottled President's Choice.

Hancock Distillery was right inside the next county, not too far for a student with a car. And it had a gift shop which, you guessed it, sold President's Choice. The fine folks were even able to identify Phil from a photo in *The Bugle* which Lois thoughtfully brought along. Phil had purchased three bottles.

Around this time, a second nagging question began to kick around in our heads: Was Phil the victim of a crime of passion or were we all on some 'fermented' hit list?

Hungry once again, we adjourned to Fred's, this time for his out-of-this-world homemade pie. The door to the diner flew open and Detective Robb stormed in, not twitching yet, but his neck veins were bulging.

"Since when is Fred's the *#@ station?" Robb asked. I prudently didn't point out that there were more sheriff's personnel in the diner than regular customers.

Thompson put up his hand, "Ladies present, Robb. Sorry, but we've been working on the case. We discovered that the bottles could only have been purchased at the Hancock Distillery. The clerk there recognized Phil's photo."

Robb gave him the "I'm not happy with you" look but sat down and ordered a Coke and fries. He gave us the bad news: "The body, if there is one, still hasn't been found. Students and staff have been helping us comb the campus, including those underground tunnels. Rather strange place."

Before I could defend my college, Robb continued, "Oh, those spots were blood. We checked with Craddock's doctor and the blood type matches. Maybe you ladies weren't imagining things after all."

Lois and I looked at each other. Score one for 'the ladies.'

The waitress brought the food. Robb stuffed his mouth, and then tried to tell us something.

After swallowing hard, he choked out, "By the way, a laundry cart appears to be missing. Could be the one you took."

"Of course." I smacked my head. "We left it outside the room when we scrambled. Was it there when you first arrived last night? That would be an excellent way to transport the body out of the building. You could keep it in there until everyone was asleep, and move it in the dead of night via those tunnels. Would it take two guys if you had the cart?"

"No. If we find the cart, we'll check for blood stains. Are you sure you left it in the hall?"

I was about to spit out a rude reply when Thompson caught my eye. Shaking his head slightly, he said, "Any idea about motive, putting aside for the moment that it was an argument gone wrong?"

"Other than he was a real SOB, you mean," Lois replied.

Stuffing another fry into his mouth, Robb said, "Explain."

"Well, for starters, he was self-important and didn't mind hurting people to get his way. His family has money, so when words didn't get him out of a jam, Daddy Craddock would pay Phil's way out. Scuttlebutt had it that he was heading into state politics after graduation, which is why he wanted to be editor. You know, looks good on the resume," Lois said.

Robb asked, "Why do you think he sent you the bourbon? What did he have against you?"

"We were always calling his bluff," I said, "asking him the tough questions about his views. He blamed us when he lost the election for Student Government President."

Lois added, "There was talk a few years ago that Phil got one of the day students pregnant. She dropped out while the rumor was still young. Maybe Daddy Craddock paid her off. And there was a car accident a couple of years ago."

Thompson asked if we had the girl's name. We didn't, but would try to remember it. Maybe her daddy was itching for a different kind of payoff.

Robb checked his watch. "Ladies, it's time for your official statement. Then Thompson will drive you back to the dorm, where I suggest you spend the rest of the day in your room since we still don't know if someone has you in his sights or not."

With those comforting thoughts, we headed downtown, gave our statements, and returned to campus.

We waved as Thompson drove off. Ignoring Robb's suggestion to stay in our room, we headed to the *Bugle* office. On the way, I asked Lois why she didn't stress the car accident to Robb. After all, someone did die.

"It doesn't feel right, and I don't want to say anything until we know more. After we check in with the staff and pull the file on the accident, we'll find Buddy. Maybe he can shed some light on this whole mess."

The office was empty except for Suzanne, who told us she had started on an obituary for Phil, 'just in case his body is found.'

Lois unlocked her office, but stopped short in the doorway and let loose a stream of profanity that had Suzanne and me gasping. We crowded in behind her.

Phil Craddock was sitting in her chair. His head was cocked to one side, showing a lot of dried blood. His mouth and eyes were open, almost a look of surprise to be finally in the editor's chair. It would have been perfect if he had been holding the dreaded bourbon bottle.

"Well, Robb can stop harping about 'no body,'" I said 'I vote that one of us stays with Phil this time. Flip you for it."

Lois marched to the telephone and dialed. She barked into the receiver, "Tell Detective Robb to get his …"

I waved off the word.

"Tell him Lois Shorter called. I've found Phil. Come to the *Bugle* office, Fields Hall."

Suzanne had collapsed into a chair, wrapping her arms around herself, shivering.

I went to her, asking if she needed some water. She shook her head. I went to the cabinet and pulled the file about the car accident, then stuffed it into my bag.

Lois raised her eyebrows.

"Once Robb gets here, we won't be able to touch anything. What he doesn't know can't hurt us."

Robb and Thompson showed up in ten minutes, a new world's record from downtown to campus.

"We kept the door open so Phil wouldn't wander again. And before you start, we did not put him there, not last night, not this morning, not ever. And we accept your apology for not believing us," Lois said.

Robb started to answer her but instead marshaled the forces, phoning for the coroner, screaming at Thompson to find out who searched this building. Then he informed us that the office would be sealed, adding, "Don't even think about it".

As if we would.

I turned to Thompson. "If we must make another statement, I may have to walk to town. I can't believe it, but I'm hungry again. If we don't solve this soon, I'll weigh 200 pounds."

Thompson quickly turned his laugh into a cough when he saw Robb's expression.

Lois, Suzanne, and I went into the hall towards the staircase.

"Suzanne, where's Buddy?" I asked. "We'd like to ask him a few questions about a car wreck a few years ago."

She moved closer to the stairs, biting her thumbnail, eyes downcast. I glanced at Lois, thinking she would prod Suzanne, but she was absorbed in the photos from the Sam Greenwell file.

Lois shifted through the photos, frowned, and then stared at Suzanne.

She handed me the photo of the Greenwell family at the campus memorial service. She said, "You see it, don't you, Lane? She's Sam's sister."

Suzanne made a grab for the photo, but Lois held it out of reach.

"Suzanne," I said in my best imitation of Sister Benedictus, the Grand Inquisitor. "What's going on? Green or Greenwell? Sister or relative?"

Tears welled up in her eyes as she slumped down on the stairs. "Sam was the best brother ever. After he died, the good sisters offered me a free ride here at St. Winifred's. Changed my name so I wouldn't be 'poor Suzanne'; no crime in that. What I didn't realize was how hard it would be to see Phil every day, merrily going his way. I wanted to kill him."

"Did you?" Lois asked softly.

276

Before she could answer, Buddy stumbled around the corner, clutching a half empty bottle of President's Choice. The missing bottle of bourbon, I presumed.

"Leave her alone, you snooping bitches. Phil got what he deserved, and I gave it to him. Good old Phil held onto the wheel while Sam was thrown from the car."

"Held onto the wheel? The reports had Sam driving," Lois said.

I noticed a black shadow on the steps but held my tongue.

Buddy waved the bottle, "I went looking for them when they were late. I found Phil in the driver's seat. He was my best pal; he begged me to lie for him. Sam was dead. Nothing would change that, but Phil had plans, great plans. So I went along with him until I couldn't take back the story without getting myself into trouble. Then I met Suzanne. She's my world now. I needed to stop the hurting."

I had to ask. "Did you intend to kill him last night, or was it an argument gone wrong?"

He pulled himself up as straight as a weak-legged drunk could.

"The bastard wouldn't come clean. We've been arguing about this for months, but last night he told me he wasn't going to jail over some soppy girl. He shouldn't have said that. I lost it; the bottle was handy, that's all. He dropped like a rock."

He laughed loudly, falling back against the wall. "I rolled him through the underground tunnels in a laundry cart. Very fitting, since Phil was just another piece of dirty laundry. Papa Craddock will turn forty shades of purple when he hears about that. Then I had the brilliant idea to put Phil where he always wanted to be: the editor's chair. That's all he talked about since he lost the job. That son of …"

Before he could finish, Sister Benedictus' booming voice said, "Leroy Robert Pearson. I have heard enough profanity for one day."

She flew down the stairs, veil and habit streaming behind her. Lois and I flattened ourselves against the wall. Suzanne grabbed onto the stair post. Buddy's eyes bulged out of his head.

Sister reached for the bottle when another disembodied voice was heard.

"Don't touch that bottle, Sister. It's evidence."

We all turned to see Robb and Thompson trotting down the hall.

"How much did you hear?" I asked.

"More than enough," Robb said, ripping the folder from Lois' hands. "You two …"

"Watch your language, Detective Robb," Sister Benedictus cautioned.

"Thompson, take Suzanne and Buddy back to the office." Robb glared at us. "Don't move. Thank you, Sister, we'll take it from here."

Sister put her arms around Suzanne. "Come, dear. I'll stay with you."

Robb sputtered, but Thompson raised his hand.

"Language, sir." Holding Buddy firmly by the arm, Thompson guided him back to the office.

Suddenly the hall was quiet. Lois rubbed her nose.

"You moved," I said.

She glared at me. "The newspaper needs to be put to bed and we can't do that standing here. We'll do it from our room. You up for some coffee?"

Coffee wasn't the drink that I wanted.

WHISKEY ROW
BY SUSAN BELL

Whiskey Row has risen from the ashes. Over the course of the past 150 years, this historic distillery district in downtown Louisville, Kentucky has experienced everything from economic depressions, multiple Ohio River floods, an F4 tornado (the Louisville Cyclone in 1890), to fires, Prohibition, and World War II. Whiskey Row went from being the center of the bourbon universe in the late 19th Century to a symbol of urban blight, such that by the 1970s the once proud buildings of this district were abandoned and almost beyond repair. Almost.

With the vision of city leaders, developers, preservationists, community commitment, and lots and lots of money, Whiskey Row is experiencing what can only be described as a breathtaking rebirth. The surging popularity of all things bourbon has added fuel to this renaissance: there are now a barrelful of bourbon distilleries in and around the original Whiskey Row. Evan Williams Bourbon Experience was the first to open in 2013, across from the Yum Center. Then came Kentucky Peerless Distillery on North 10th Street in 2015, followed by Angel's Envy on East Main in 2016, and 2018 saw the opening of Old Forester and Rabbit Hole. 2019 saw the opening of Michter's Distillery on West Main, across from the Louisville Slugger museum. You can also find the Kentucky Bourbon Trail Welcome Center at the Frazier History Museum on Main Street.

Louisville has been the center of the distilling industry since the confluence of river transportation (steamboats), railroads, and bridges across the Ohio River acted to turn the city into a hub of making, selling, and shipping of distilled spirits, particularly bourbon.

As noted in Caron's 1885 *Louisville City Directory*:

> The steamboat business ... is still greatly contributory to the City's prosperity, but the great stimulus to her business expansion and connections was through the building of railroads, which naturally

placed her in convenient propinquity to a wide area of Southern trade, and brought hitherto inaccessible portions of Kentucky into trade relations with her merchants ... There are about seventy-five houses in the wholesale whisky trade, and the various distilleries in the district produced, in 1881, 15,571,000 gallons of fine whisky.

Today's investments in Whiskey Row—the new distilleries, hotels, living spaces, museums, eateries, bars, and sports centers—are a testament to the enthusiasm expressed by the city at the end of the 19th century.

Some of the new distilleries have renovated existing historic structures. Michter's was the first distillery to commit to moving to Whiskey Row in 2011. They selected as their site a historic cast iron and stone building on Main, near the old Fort Nelson site, and planned a two-year renovation with an opening date of 2013. However, the renovations of this unique building proved very challenging, and required more time and money, plus 400,000 pounds of structural steel, delaying the opening of their facility to February 2019. But the renovated building is beautiful, and it is now open for business: you can observe the distilling process and participate in tastings of the product on their guided tour, drink at the second-floor bar, or just browse the first-floor gift shop and soak up the history.

Angel's Envy renovated a warehouse that was built in 1902 and was originally the home of the American Elevator & Machine Company. In the mid-20th century, ownership changed hands to the American Saw & Tool Company.

Rabbit Hole built an ultra-modern, 55,000 square-foot facility on Jefferson Street. According to *Architect Magazine*, October 23, 2018:

The extensive use of metal wall panels lended itself to the modern design both outside and inside. Located in the trendsetting NuLu neighborhood of Louisville, this new open floor plan distillery lets guests see all aspects of the bourbon making process.

Kentucky Peerless restored a 1912 tobacco warehouse for their distillery, located on North 10th Street. Designed by architectural firm Joseph & Joseph, they say:

> *In this artisan distillery located in a restored 1912 tobacco warehouse, visitors can see where corn, barley and rye are delivered, milled, fermented and then processed through the custom-designed 26-ft. column still. Fourth- and fifth-generation descendants of Peerless' founder Henry Kraver, combine history and technology to bring back this esteemed brand.*

Bravura's renovation for Old Forester's distillery at 117 and 119 West Main Street won an AIA Merit Award for Excellence in Architectural Design.

One recent weekend, I decided to do a tasting of tours at three of these Whiskey Row distilleries: Kentucky Peerless Distilling, Old Forester and Rabbit Hole. Just like each distillery offers a variety of *expressions* (or flavors) for their bourbon, each distillery tour has its unique expression, reflecting their history, their style, their vision.

Each of these distilleries are operational, and each allow you to observe most of the distilling process (except for the growing of the grains, which happens offsite, out in a field somewhere). In each you see where the grains get milled, the cooking of those grains, you watch (and taste) the mash in huge fermentation vats as the yeast does its job, then you get blown away by the massive copper column still (all three distilleries use stills manufactured by Louisville's own Vendome Copper & Brass). Here, the mash becomes alcohol. That final product of the distilling process is known as either "New Make" or "White Dog." *White*, because at this stage it is clear, and *Dog* because, well, it has a *bite*. The White Dog is then transferred to charred oak barrels. Old Forester makes their own barrels and demonstrate that process on the tour. Peerless and Rabbit Hole both get their barrels from Kelvin Cooperage, here in Louisville.

The barrels are aged on site at Old Forester and Peerless. Rabbit Hole transports their barrels to another distillery near Frankfort, where they are leasing space until their own facility is built. All three distilleries bottle on site.

You might ask: "Since the processes are basically the same, aren't these tours all the same? Isn't the experience the same?" No.

Just as each charred barrel imparts to its aging bourbon a unique flavor based on the oak used, where that tree came from, what level of char is applied, and where the barrel lives in the rick house, each distillery tour is imbued with the history, personality, and lore of that distiller.

The Old Forester Distillery is elegant, chic, luxe, designed to be seen and admired. The Kentucky Peerless Distillery embraces its generations of family history, and though it is perhaps the most automated of the distilleries in operation today, the feeling is one of a family operation, a labor of love. Rabbit Hole, the new guy on the block, is bold and modern and hip. All the tours are entertaining and informative, and each tour ends in a generous tasting of the product.

Take a stroll through history on Whiskey Row and visit the distilleries, where you will meet a mash of old and new expressions, observe a distillation of 19th century processes and 21st century technology, and inhale an angel's share of bourbon ambience and Kentucky soul.

GLOSSARY

aging – A process of using time to change raw alcohol into refined drinkable bourbon. Raw distilled bourbon is put into new white oak barrels after the inside has been charred to caramelize the sap of the wood. As the temperature changes, the bourbon inside the barrel is pushed into and out of the wood, giving the liquor its amber color and smooth caramel flavor. Most bourbon is aged for at least four years.

alligator char number 4 – All bourbon is aged in new oak barrels. The inside of the barrel is heated until charcoal (char) forms. This char ranges in depth from an eighth to a quarter inch. Number 4, favored by most bourbon distillers, is the thickest. 'Alligator' comes from the blistered surface which looks like the hide of an alligator.

Angels' Share – The amount of liquid evaporated during aging in oak barrels. If distilling is done in a low humidity area, the share consists mainly of water. Aging with a higher humidity causes more alcohol to be included in the share and thereby reduces the alcohol content. Without this reduction, the alcohol content is so high that the beverage is non-potable.

barrel houses (also known as **rick houses**) – Structures storing bourbon-filled oak barrels during the aging process.

Baudoinia compniacensis – A black fungus, fed by the ethanol vapor of the Angels' Share. The airborne spores cover objects around the distillery. Many distilleries paint their buildings black to hide the fungus, which does not harm trees and other plants.

Bottled in Bond – The Bottled in Bond regulations require that one distiller at one distillery creates the bourbon in one calendar year. They were developed in 1897 in response to the questionable ingredients included in distilled spirits. Bourbon which has been produced in compliance with the United States government's Standards of Identity for Distilled Spirits may be identified with the *BIB* on their label. Many distillers no longer choose to include the BIB on their labels or follow the processing requirements. Others are still proudly advertising their compliance. Until the 1980s, federal agents controlled access to a compliant distillery.

bourbon – A type of American whiskey, defined by the Federal Standards of Identity for Distilled Spirits (27 C.F.R) made of at least

51% corn which is put in new barrels of charred oak at a maximum of 125 proof (62.5% alcohol by volume). The mixture is distilled to not higher than 160 proof and 80% by volume and finally bottled at 80 proof and 40% by volume.

bung – A tapered wooden stopper inserted into a hole in the side of a barrel.

congeners – Chemicals, other than alcohol, resulting from the fermentation process. All distilled liquors produce their signature combination of congeners, resulting in unique aromas and tastes. The number of congeners in darker liquors, for example in bourbon and red wine, is greater than the number in lighter products, such as in gin and white wine. While alcohol is the prime cause of the dreaded hangover, congeners increase the severity of the drinker's distress. There is some truth to the saying that the darker the liquor, the bigger the hangover.

cooperage – A facility in which barrels are manufactured.

copper kettle – Historically, large copper cauldrons are used for distillation because copper is an excellent conductor of heat. Today, huge stainless-steel stills are more frequently used to process the quantities of liquid needed to make bourbon for commercial sale.

Devil's Cut – The amount of liquid absorbed by the oak wood used in the barrels. For many years, bourbon barrels have been reused by other spirit distillers for scotch, rum, and brandy.

jug – Ceramic jugs, large deep containers with narrow necks, were some of the first vessels to contain distilled spirits. The maker stenciled his name on the jug so the buyer would know its origin. Jugs were eventually phased out and glass bottles became the standard vessel, with printed labels identifying the brand and proof.

Kentucky Bourbon Trail – The Kentucky Distillers Association established a tour of various distilleries in the Commonwealth. Each has its own interesting history and unique methods. For more information, visit the website: www.kybourbontrail.com.

mash – Crushed grain or malt steeped in hot water to make a wort. Unlike Scotch whiskey, which comes from wort, bourbon comes from mash, either sweet or sour. The mash leaves behind grain during fermentation, which should be cleaned out between distillations. Today, bourbon is made with a continuous still and the solids settle in the bottom in the spent beer.

A **sour mash** uses some of the liquid from previous distillation, which ensures consistency to balance flavor. The sour mash is also more acidic, preventing the growth of bacteria.

mashing – Brewer's term for the hot water steeping process which puts moisture into the barley, activates the malt enzymes, and converts the grain starches into sugars. Several key enzyme groups take part in the conversion of the grain starches to sugars. Brewer can alter mash temperatures to favor an individual enzyme's function and to change the wort.

moonshine – Illegally made and distributed corn whiskey, usually associated with the Appalachian Mountains of Kentucky and Tennessee. It is also known as white lightning, Appalachian white, hooch, mountain dew, and many other names. The name *moonshine* probably came from the idea that it was usually made and distributed at night. During the Prohibition years, its distribution expanded far beyond the mountains of Appalachia. Moonshine is still made today, but mostly as a novelty.

Prohibition (also known as the **Volstead Act**) – Ratified on January 16, 1919, becoming the 18th Amendment to the US Constitution, which made it illegal to sell, transport, import, export, or make potable drinks containing more than 2.75% alcohol, anywhere in the USA. Going strictly by letter of the law, it did not specifically prohibit owning or drinking alcohol, and medical doctors could write prescriptions for alcohol to their ailing patients. Supporters of Prohibition believed that the absence of alcohol would dramatically reduce crime; however, the crime rate soared. Making and marketing illegal alcohol created a whole new world of criminals, from the local bootlegger to Al Capone. It also reduced tax revenues. In 1933, relief came with the ratification of the 21st Amendment, which repealed the 18th Amendment and legalized alcohol again.

proof – A measure of ABV (alcohol by volume) as opposed to ABW (alcohol by weight). ABW is a comparison of the weight of the alcohol in a particular drink compared to the weight of all other elements of the drink; ABV is a comparison of the volume of alcohol in a particular drink compared to the volume of all other elements of the drink. Alcohol is lighter than water. Bourbon is distilled to no more than 160 (U.S.) proof (80% alcohol by volume), put into the barrel for aging at no more than 125 proof (62.5% alcohol by volume), and bottled at 80 proof or more (40% alcohol by volume).

racks – Structures used for storing barrels of bourbon. There is no one-of-a-kind design blueprint. They can be built of wood, metal, plastic, or any combination of the three, and built to hold different numbers of barrels.

rick houses (also called **barrel houses**) – Buildings where barrels of bourbon are stored and allowed to age until time for the bourbon to be bottled.

sour mash – A step in the whiskey making process where up to one-third of the liquid from an older batch of mash is used to start fermentation in the new batch. The liquid ensures a consistent pH and helps prevent the growth of bacteria. The process is used to produce nearly all bourbon and is a legal requirement for Tennessee whiskey.

still – A stainless steel container lined with copper used in distillation. Continuous column and copper pot stills are both used in distilling bourbon. The alcohol from the fermentation process is heated in the bottom of the still to the point where it turns into a vapor, which evaporates at a lower temperature than water. The alcohol vapor rises to the top of the still through a coil of metal and glass tubing where it cools and condenses, then is siphoned off into another container. The result is a purer and higher proof alcohol.

tail – Final drops of concentrated congeners removed from a still. The tail is not tasty, and it has no productive use.

tail house – Location where the tails are stored prior to disposal.

Urban Bourbon Trail – More than 50 Louisville establishments celebrate the local beverage. All offer special bourbon cocktails and 50 different bourbon labels on the bar with trained staff that can explain the subtleties of each offering. Establishments vary from historic hotels to modern trend setters. Find more information at this web site: https://www.bourboncountry.com/things-to-do/urban-bourbon-trail/.

whiskey – According to the Federal Standards of Identity for Distilled Spirits (27 C.F.R), whiskey is "an alcoholic distillate from a fermented mash of grain produced at less than 190° proof in such manner that the distillate possesses the taste, aroma, and characteristics generally attributed to whisky, stored in oak containers (except that corn whisky need not be so stored), and bottled at not less than 80° proof, and also includes mixtures of such distillates for which no specific standards of identity are prescribed." Bourbon is a type of whiskey, composed of fifty-one percent corn mash. All bourbon is whiskey, but not all whiskey is bourbon.

Whiskey Rebellion – In January 1791, George Washington's Secretary of the Treasury, Alexander Hamilton, proposed an excise tax on spirits distilled in the United States because of the burden of the federal debt from the Revolutionary War. Congress passed the tax. Residents on the frontier in Western Pennsylvania were opposed and refused to pay the tax. Within 3 years, the Whiskey Rebellion threatened the stability of the country when the protests became violent. 400 whiskey rebels near Pittsburgh set fire to the home of John Neville, the regional tax collection supervisor. Washington organized a militia force of 12,950 men and personally led them towards Western Pennsylvania, which effectively ended the Whiskey Rebellion. When the militia reached Pittsburgh, the rebels had dispersed and could not be found. This was the first challenge to federal authority. In 1802, then-President Thomas Jefferson repealed the excise tax on whiskey.

Whiskey Row – Located on West Main Street, downtown Louisville, KY, this stretch of property was once the unofficial home to the bourbon industry in Louisville. The buildings, constructed from 1850 until early 1900, were in the Revivalist or Chicago style, with cast iron store fronts. With the resurgence of interest in bourbon over the past decade, several of the buildings have undergone extensive, and expensive, refurbishing to open again as home to several distilleries. Additionally, the area of Whiskey Row has expanded to include other parts of Main Street, as well as other venues nearby. Distilleries now calling Whiskey Row home include Evan Williams, Old Forester, Kentucky Peerless, Angel's Envy, and Rabbit Hole. These distilleries offer a glimpse into the history of their company, its distilling process and, finally, a taste of the product.

Whiskey Tax – In 1790, the federal government, having recently assumed states' debts, passed an excise whiskey tax on both domestic and imported alcohol to help offset this new expense. The tax was met with protest, culminating in what history called the Whiskey Rebellion. President Washington dispatched troops to deal with this uprising. Today, alcohol sales are taxed by almost all levels of government.

worm – A long copper tube immersed in a coiled fashion (like a worm) in a large-capacity wooden vat filled with water. The vat is known as a worm tub. The alcohol vapor from the bourbon distillation process flows through the worm, and the cooling waters condense the vapor to a strong spirit, which is then deposited into barrels for aging. Distilleries used this method of condensing alcohol vapor for many years, until modern distilleries switched to shell and tube condensers as a cost-savings measure. Some distilleries continue to use the worm tub method because they believe it enhances the bourbon flavor.

wort – A sugary liquid created during the mashing process. Brewer's yeast is added to cause it to ferment, producing alcohol.

yeast – A single-celled fungus that feeds on simple sugars. To ensure absolute purity, distillers save and protect small amounts of their yeast and use it to grow more of the same yeast. Older distilleries have used the same yeast since Prohibition was repealed. But what is the role of yeast in making bourbon? Mash, a ground-up combination of grains (usually corn, rye, and barley), is cooked, then poured into a fermenter and allowed to cool until it's ready for the yeast to be added. Yeast devours the sugar in the mash and converts it to carbon dioxide and alcohol. The distillers keep their yeast recipe secret, so no other distillers can produce bourbon that tastes exactly like theirs.

BIOGRAPHIES

Deborah Alvord is celebrating the 20th anniversary of her family's move to the Bluegrass State and has finally managed the correct pronunciation of *Louisville*. But being from Marblehead, Massachusetts, she still returns there annually for baked haddock and the smell of the sea.

Besides reading mysteries, Deborah still enjoys helping clients with tax returns and dreaming of writing a mystery with an accountant as the sleuth!

Edmund August has had two books published: *Moon Dogs*, a collection of his poems, and *Tobacco: A Literary Anthology*. His poems have appeared in *Poetry Magazine*, *The Louisville Review, Greensboro Review* and many other literary magazines and journals. He holds an MA from the University of Louisville and an MFA from Vermont College. Born in Typo, KY, he has lived his entire life in Kentucky.

Susan Bell was born in coastal California, then proceeded to travel the country in her role as daughter of a Naval officer. She learned to walk in the Mojave Desert, to swim in Virginia Beach, and to read in Washington State. She fell in love with Dr. Seuss and hasn't stopped reading since. She combined her love of reading, writing and arithmetic and became a technical writer, working in the defense, aviation, and telecommunications industries. "Summer's End" is her first published fiction.

Barbara Blackburn was born in Joliet, Illinois, but spent most of her life in Louisville, Kentucky. She graduated from the University of Louisville and taught writing at five different universities. She was a talented artist, poet, and writer. One of her passions was *Who Dunnit Mysteries*, an interactive audience theatre production. Sadly, Barbara passed away in 2017.

Karen Quinn Block loves reading and writing about character flaws and the foibles of everyday life. An expat Canadian, Karen writes from her home in the mountains of North Carolina.

Mike Bradford is a retired healthcare executive and pastor with the Christian Church. He is a native of Johnson City, Tennessee, and long-term resident of Kentucky. Bradford is a hobby novelist with three books in print and one short story in a murder mystery anthology. Mike and his wife, Julie (Garrett), currently reside in Bardstown, Kentucky, where he serves as pastor for Boston Christian Church. The Bradfords have two children, five grandchildren and four great-grandchildren.

Virginia 'Din' Dulworth has written in many genres, her favorite being children's literature. She is a member of the Society of Children's Book Writers and Illustrators. She was previously published in the anthology *Low Down and Derby*, a collection of mystery stories centered around the Kentucky Derby. She and her family are long-time horse people. Din, a former resident of Louisville, now resides in Lexington.

M. E. Gaskins is a registered dietitian/nutritionist and diabetes educator. Her mother made the best donuts on the planet, and introduced her to the heady smell of yeast, which she remembers every time she drives past a brewery. She enjoys writing poems, songs, short stories, and articles. "Hard Facts" was a fun research project for the foodie detective in her.

Sarah E. Glenn has a B.S. in Journalism, which is redundant in her case. Later, she did a stint as a graduate student in classical languages. While she didn't get the degree, she's great with crosswords. So far, her most interesting job was working the reports desk for the police department in Lexington, Kentucky, where she learned that criminals really are dumb.

Sarah's great-great aunt served as a nurse in WWI. A hundred years later, this would inspire Sarah and her partner in crime, Gwen Mayo, to write the *Three Snowbirds* series, featuring two retired WWI nurses and an inventor slightly younger than Moses. Learn more about Sarah and the *Snowbirds* series at http://www.sarahglenn.com/.

Debi Huff was born and spent her formative years in South Bend, Indiana. The first song she ever learned was the Notre Dame Victory March. Debi has always been interested in writing and spent much of her school time as a journalist for her high school paper and as a student writer for the local newspaper. She is trying to merge her interests in writing and mysteries by writing her first political thriller. She is a member of Sisters in Crime and attends many of the yearly international Bouchercon conferences.

Shirley Jump is a New York Times and USA Today bestselling author who writes romance and women's fiction that has been called "brilliant" and "spellbinding" by reviewers and authors like Kristin Higgins. She's published more than 60 books in 24 countries and lives in Florida, where the beaches provide the perfect retreat and inspiration (and procrastination excuse). You can visit Shirley's website at www.ShirleyJump.com for author news and a booklist and follow her on Facebook at www.Facebook.com/shirleyjump.author for giveaways and at www.Facebook.com/EatingMyWords for deep discussions about important things like the best way to make a French *omelette*.

Sandra Cerow Leonard. After many years of writing legal and bureaucratic documents, Sandra Leonard has considerable respect for creative authors who construct plots and characters in fiction. She served as president of the local mystery reading and writing group for more than 12 years.

Gwen Mayo is a native of Eastern Kentucky, transplanted to the Sunshine State. Her home state's colorful past forms the backdrop for her Nessa Donnelly mysteries and informs the Three Snowbirds series she co-writes with Sarah E. Glenn. She is a graduate of the University of Kentucky, a member of the Short Mystery Fiction Society, and Sisters in Crime, including local chapters in her home state, online, and Florida. Her short stories have appeared in anthologies, webzines, and microfiction collections. Her novels can be purchased wherever books are sold. To learn more, visit her online at gwenmayo.com.

Elaine Munsch grew up on the shores of Lake Erie, but has made Louisville, KY her home for several decades. An avid reader, bookselling seemed to be the ideal profession, which she has practiced for over forty years. She is the author of the Dash Hammond series: *The Price of Being Neighborly, The Cost of Kindness* and *The Expense of Family.* She can be reached at authormunsch@gmail.com

Lorena R. Peter (**Lorena Reith, Jr.**) writes novels and short stories with paranormal elements, under the name Lorena Reith, Jr. Her book, *Gaff—Wisdom from the Sea*, is an inspirational fiction. Thirty short stories involving Gaff and his friends were published in a regional newsletter. The *Sylvia Series* starts with a suspense, *Searching for Sylvia*, and includes several novels describing cases Sylvia solves with her new-found psychic abilities. Books are available through Amazon. Dr. Peter has a medical counseling practice in Louisville, KY. In other words, she is a psychologist who has developed her psychic connections! They do say to write what you know.

Debby Schenk was the first female to attend Ivy Tech. Her passion was radio where she worked as an engineer at the start of her career. She was very proud of *The Delilah Show*, which she produced. She loved her cats, her husband, children, and her grandson (not necessarily in that order). Unfortunately, Debby lost her battle with cancer in 2015.

Tamera Shaw is a reporter and photographer based in Louisville, Kentucky. She works for the *Henry County Local*, a weekly newspaper in Northeast Kentucky. She happily shares her life with her husband, daughter, and sage cat Sophie, who grudgingly shares her home with the newest member of the family—Nieko, a strange and wonderful rescue kitten.

Sheila Shumate, though born in Louisville, Kentucky, is a Hoosier who calls Clarksville, Indiana home. When not being a mom, she likes to read mystery thrillers, the more twists and turns the better. Her short story, "The Bourbon Brotherhood", is her first venture into fiction writing.

Cheryl Stuck is a freelance writer with nonfiction articles in several regional publications. She writes copy, edits, and critiques work for individuals and businesses for web pages and autobiographies as well as fiction. Cheryl is a Louisville native, currently working on a novel, screenplay, and a play.

Milton C. Toby is an attorney and award-winning author of nonfiction books and articles about horse racing. He won the $10,000 Dr. Tony Ryan Book Award for the best book about Thoroughbred racing and an American Horse Publications editorial award with *Dancer's Image: The Forgotten Story of the 1968 Kentucky Derby* and a second American Horse Publications award with *Noor: A Champion Thoroughbred's Unlikely Journey from California to Kentucky*. His most recent book, *Taking Shergar: Thoroughbred Racing's Most Famous Cold Case*, recounts the true story of an Epsom Derby winner stolen by the Irish Republican Army and held for ransom at the height of the Troubles. Toby is President of the American Society of Journalists and Authors.

Jo Tucker is a licensed civil engineer, consulting and teaching in the fields of geotechnical and environmental engineering. She is a long-time Kentucky resident, and now lives with her husband in Wisconsin. She is the author of several published technical papers, an unpublished mystery novel, and short stories.

Heidi Walker writes published short stories and award-winning plays from her farm in Kentucky. She polished her work as a two-year playwright-in-residence in the New York Public Library's Wertheim Scholars program.

CPSIA information can be obtained
at www.ICGtesting.com
Printed in the USA
JSHW021552310522
26390JS00001B/3

9 781949 281125